ARIEL TACHNA
Historical Romance at its Finest

A Summer Place

"…a captivating and exciting read." —Coffee Time Romance

Checkmate

"…an exciting and well-written novel that I found difficult to put down." —Romance Junkies

All For One

"I've always loved a good swashbuckling story involving swords, danger and conspiracy. And these authors delivered all three with deeply seated passion and a desperate need to find that one person to cherish." —Two Lips Reviews

"With well-drawn characters who all ring true, the erotic scenes have that vital emotive quality, from playful pop and sizzle to beautifully tender." —Whipped Cream Eroric Reviews

Rose Among the Ruins

"Ariel Tachna's setting, plot, and characters are brilliantly written, drawing me into the era and holding my senses captive until the very end. I couldn't help but enjoy this tale." —Fallen Angel Reviews

"…a poignant love story, rich in language and details, and beautiful in its entirety." —Literary Nymphs

Novels by Ariel Tachna

All For One (with Nicki Bennett)
Checkmate (with Nicki Bennett)
Her Two Dads
Hot Cargo (with Nicki Bennett)
The Matelot
Out of the Fire
Seducing C.C.
A Summer Place
Sutcliffe Cove (with Madeleine Urban)

The Partnership in Blood Series
Alliance in Blood
Covenant in Blood
Conflict in Blood
Reparation in Blood

Perilous Partnership

Novellas by Ariel Tachna

Healing in His Wings
Rose Among the Ruins
Why Nileas Loved the Sea

The Exploring Limits Series (with Nicki Bennett)
Book 1: Exploring Limits
Book 2: Stretching Limits
Book 3: Refining Limits
Book 4: Breaking Limits
Book 5: Transcending Limits
Book 6: No Limits

the Matelot

Ariel Tachna

Dreamspinner Press

Published by
Dreamspinner Press
4760 Preston Road
Suite 244-149
Frisco, TX 75034
http://www.dreamspinnerpress.com/

This is a work of fiction. Names, characters, places, and incidents either are the product of the author's imagination or are used fictitiously, and any resemblance to actual persons, living or dead, business establishments, events, or locales is entirely coincidental.

The Matelot
Copyright © 2010 by Ariel Tachna

Cover Art by Analise Dubner   http:// www.dubnerdesign.com

ISBN: 978-1-61581-583-8

Printed in the United States of America
First Edition
December, 2010

eBook edition available
eBook ISBN: 978-1-61581-584-5

To John Simpson, who put pirates in my head.

Prologue

The West Indies, 1641

The *Dark Dream* was barely afloat, taking on water from so many leaks that the carpenter couldn't keep up. The crew bailed manfully to keep her from foundering, but everyone knew they had only a small chance of reaching Tortuga alive.

"Bail faster, lads, or we'll all be sleeping in the deep tonight!" Quinn Davies, quartermaster of the foundering vessel, exhorted, moving through the hold and the knee-deep water with all the confidence of his position as the keeper of order on the pirate ship. Her captain, Amery White, might choose the heading, but Quinn made sure the orders were carried out. When he was sure the crew was working their hardest, he returned to the main deck. Amery stood on the quarterdeck, steering rod in hand as he fought the wind and the drag of the ailing ship. Determination showed in every line of his face and body as the setting sun limned his golden head in a reddish glow. Automatically, Quinn sought out Gavin, the third of their merry band, the ship's surgeon in time of need and an able seaman in his own right. His heart leapt as he caught sight of his friend high in the rigging. He didn't bother to shout at him to be careful, but he wanted to. He glanced back at Amery, wondering how the captain felt about having his lover aloft in the precariously swinging ropes.

"Land ho!" Gavin shouted over the roar of the wind, for while the storm that had scuppered them had passed, the near-gale winds remained.

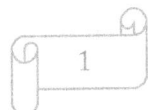

"Quinn," Amery called, the familiarity unusual on the deck of the ship. However comfortable they were with each other in private—a level that had varied drastically in the twenty years of their friendship—Amery never used Quinn's or Gavin's first names in front of the crew. That he used it now told more clearly than words could ever say how desperate the situation truly was. "Take the spyglass up to Gavin. We need to know where we're heading."

"Aye, Captain," Quinn replied, trying subtly to remind Amery of their audience, but the captain didn't seem to notice or care. His eyes were fixed firmly on the horizon as if he could bring the land Gavin had spotted closer by will alone. Quinn fetched the spyglass and scrambled up the rigging with the ease of nearly twenty years at sea.

Gavin took the glass in silence, peering through it in the direction of their destination.

"Can you make anything out?" Quinn asked, studying Gavin's face.

"Not enough," Gavin replied. "I don't have Amery's memory for landmarks. There's a reason he's captain and I'm the ship's surgeon."

Quinn laughed. "Because he fainted when he had to watch you amputate that boy's leg."

"Don't say that where the crew can hear you," Gavin laughed. "They'll vote him out and try to make one of us take his place."

"And that would be the death of us all," Quinn agreed, sobering. "Let me see if I can make anything out."

Gavin handed Quinn back the spyglass, moving over to make room for Quinn in the crow's nest. Scanning the horizon, Quinn located the shadow of land Gavin had sighted, running its length with his eyes, searching for any recognizable features. He could not find the distinctive headland that marked Tortuga, but it was only visible from the south, and as buffeted as they'd been by the storm, they were not coming toward the island from that direction. The island was lush with greenery despite the mountainous terrain, though, suggesting they could at least find fresh water and game, as well as plenty of wood, while they tried to repair the ship.

"I can't tell either, but it's land. I don't think we have any choice but to make landfall. The *Dream* isn't going to hold together much longer than that."

Gavin looked down at the listing deck. "Unfortunately, I think you're right."

"Let me go tell Amery," Quinn said, throwing a leg back over the wall of the crow's nest and descending to the deck again.

"Well?" Amery demanded.

"It's a port in a storm," Quinn said with a shrug. "The *Dream* has held together better than we could have hoped after the beating we took, but she isn't going to hold much longer."

"Assemble the crew," Amery ordered. "We'll take a vote to see if we beach here or try to make it to Tortuga."

Quinn nodded. They weren't in battle now. A decision of this magnitude belonged to the whole crew, not merely to Amery and himself.

"All hands on deck," he cried, even knowing the risk they were taking abandoning the pumps.

When everyone had gathered, Amery strode to the railing on the quarterdeck. "We've sighted land," he told them, "but we aren't close enough to tell if it's Tortuga, some other colony, or an uninhabited island. We can put ashore and take our chances, or we can keep going in the hopes of making it to a friendly harbor. I know what my preference would be, but this isn't my decision. What says the crew?"

The thirty men muttered and argued for a few minutes, but finally Cullen, the boatswain and unofficial spokesman of the crew, stepped forward. "We'll heed your judgment and the quartermaster's. If you think we can make it to Tortuga, we'll give it our best to hold her together. If you think we should go ashore here, we'll do our best to get the *Dark Dream* back in shape as quickly as possible."

"Let's see what a closer look reveals," Amery proposed. "We can decide once we know where we are. For all we know, we could be on the north side of Tortuga."

"Back to your stations, men," Quinn ordered. "We've come too far to sink within sight of land!"

The men scrambled to return to their posts, throwing themselves into their work with even more energy than before, the sight of land enough to give them the hope of survival. Whatever Amery ended up deciding, the crew would respect that decision more for having been given a say.

An hour later, the island having come into full view, Amery made his decision. "We've found Tortuga. We need only circle the island until we reach the harbor."

The men gave it their best effort, but the ship simply had no more to give, and before they could reach the port, they had no choice but to beach the ship's remains.

Quinn, as quartermaster, saw to the division of the resources left on the ship, promising to seek out the crew when they had a ship again, but releasing them in the interim from the Articles of Agreement that had held them together these past months. If they so chose, they could find a new ship without repercussions.

They were a ragtag bunch as they straggled into Tortuga, carrying only the clothes on their backs and the few belongings they could salvage from the beached vessel.

The officers' quarters had been particularly hard-hit, leaving Quinn with the bit of change in his pocket but not even a change of clothes. Amery and Gavin had fared only little better, able to salvage a few of their belongings from the captain's cabin. The rest had washed away when the glass windows shattered in the storm.

Quinn regretted very little of what he'd lost except in terms of the cost of replacing them, but he knew Amery would miss his charts. Quinn wondered what a new set would cost.

When they reached Tortuga, the crew scattered, carrying the news of the *Dark Dream*'s demise to every corner of town. If there were captains in port in search of a crew, they would know by morning that sailors were available. Quinn didn't know what would happen to Amery, Gavin, and himself—he couldn't imagine returning to the status of grunt after having been quartermaster. Gavin would always be in demand as a surgeon with some actual skill, having apprenticed with a ship's doctor on the first pirate ship the three of them had sailed on at seventeen, when they'd escaped the merchant ship they'd worked on. But while Quinn and Amery had twenty years of sailing experience and five years as captain and quartermaster, many of their crew had as much experience or more, and no captain would hire on someone who might displace him in the esteem of the crew. Quinn rather feared they were stuck until Amery could beg, borrow, or steal another ship.

"We need a place to sleep," Gavin declared. "We've been fighting the storm and the sea for too many hours to think clearly now. We can decide in the morning what we want to do next."

They inquired in four seedy taverns, the smoke in the air so thick they could barely breathe before they found one with rooms to rent. The proprietor looked askance when they insisted they would share a room, but ultimately the sight of their gold was enough to persuade the man to turn a blind eye and provide a trundle bed for Quinn.

After Gavin's comment about sleeping, Quinn fully expected to fall into bed and not move for the next twenty-four hours, but Amery obviously had other intentions, drawing Gavin into a torrid kiss as soon as the door shut behind them. Quinn suppressed a sigh, putting out the stub of the candle the innkeeper had provided. He couldn't blame Amery for wanting to spit in the eye of fate and celebrate their survival. He could have wished, however, that he had a room of his own while his two best friends were tupping like rams.

"I'm going to see if they serve food as well as ale in the tavern," he said abruptly, not sure he could stay and listen to the sounds of their lovemaking, knowing they would never invite him to join them.

A muffled grunt was their only reply.

Quinn closed the door behind him, a husky moan he recognized as Gavin's following him down the hall.

With a soft snort, he set out to find his own bedmate for the night, or at least the next few hours.

Chapter 1

THE *Dark Dream* was gone.

Amery might deny it still despite the hours they had spent cataloging the damage that afternoon, but Quinn knew better. So, Quinn suspected, did Gavin. Gavin was usually more than a little reluctant to let Amery have as much drink as they'd had tonight. Despite all the generalizations about pirates and their rum, Captain White had never been one to indulge heavily. Gavin had suffered too much at the hands of a drunken captain, back on the *Lady Grace*, their first ship, for Amery to do anything to remind his matelot of those days. Quinn might not have the bond with Gavin that Amery did, to his everlasting regret, but he knew both men well enough to recognize the stress they were suffering. Now he just had to figure out where they were going to get another ship, because he knew something else: Amery would go mad confined to land for more than a few weeks.

"Captain White?"

All three men turned to look at the new arrival, his evening dress out of place in the cantina where the most one could usually hope for was to have all body parts decently covered.

"Who wants to know?" Gavin asked, drawing the gentleman's attention away from Amery's golden head to his own chiseled face.

"It's come to the attention of the Crown that Captain White might be lacking a ship at the moment," the dandy explained. "And if that were to be the case, an interested party might have a new one for him."

"The *Dark Dream* isn't lost," Amery insisted, "merely damaged. Thank you for your—"

"And what would said interested party's offer be?" Quinn interrupted before Amery could dismiss the man entirely. Amery looked like he was about to protest, but Gavin silenced him.

"A letter of marque, a fully equipped English galleon, and a generous percentage of whatever treasure you capture," the elegantly dressed man replied, "but only if Captain White can be persuaded to actually identify himself."

"I'm White," Amery said finally after Gavin nudged him a couple of times. "Why me?"

"Because rumor has it that you're the finest captain in the West Indies and that you aren't given to drinking, despite what I've seen tonight," the noble replied, reaching in his pocket and pulling out an envelope with the captain's name inscribed on it in a bold hand. "Sober up and meet me at the wharf at noon tomorrow. If you're late or drunk, I'll consider it a refusal of my offer."

The gentleman had left their table and the tavern before they had time to do more than blink. All three men stared in silence at the envelope sitting on the scarred wood between them. Finally, Gavin picked it up and handed it to Amery. "It's got your name on it. Open it and put us all out of our misery."

Amery glared, but that had been his typical expression since they'd limped the *Dark Dream* into port and let the crew go a week ago with the promise to hire them on again if they could get the ship seaworthy. Amery hadn't given up hope, but Quinn didn't see it happening. She had holes in her hull the size of a house and the masts and yardarms were shredded. They had outfought and outrun many foes, but the maelstrom that caught them in its teeth and then spit them out again had been too much for their valiant lady.

"Give it to me," Quinn said impatiently. "I'll open it if he won't."

Nobody else would dare to speak to Amery that way, with the possible exception of Gavin, but they weren't on a ship at the moment and in private, Quinn treated the other two men as equals. Honestly, he treated them that way most of the time aboard ship as well, except

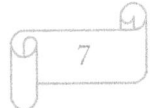

when they were preparing for battle. They only had two secrets between them, as far as Quinn knew, and neither of them was Amery's.

Amery's glare turned on Quinn at the comment as he snatched the envelope from Gavin's hand. "That won't be necessary, Mr. Davies," he slurred. "I might be drunk, but I can still read m'own post."

Inwardly, Quinn flinched a little, but he didn't back down. Amery only called him Mr. Davies when they were in front of the men or when he was extremely put out with Quinn. Like the one time he'd caught Quinn and Gavin together, back when they were all mere sailors before Amery and Gavin formalized their matelotage. It was the one time he'd actually feared his friend.

Now he saw it for the sign of more general annoyance that it was. He'd chosen Quinn to bear the brunt of it, because being angry with Gavin was like being angry with the other half of his soul.

"So what does it say then?" Gavin asked as Amery opened the letter.

"I didn't believe him," Amery murmured, not answering Gavin's question directly. "A new ship, freshly outfitted, a crew of more than twice what we've commanded before, and a commission to take any Spanish or pirate ship that comes within view of our crow's nest. If the ship is all the gentleman says it is, we may have a new berth, mates."

"And what do we do with them once we've taken them?" Gavin inquired.

"We'll have to ask our mysterious guest tomorrow," Amery replied. "The letter doesn't say. Either way, I think we can have one more drink to celebrate"

Quinn wasn't sure that was a good idea, but even Gavin knew better than to counter Amery in certain moods, and this was one of them, that dangerous line between joviality and fury that always accompanied Amery's drinking binges. It was one of the reasons Gavin rarely let it go this far. Amery had already swaggered toward the bar.

"After this drink, get him out of here," Quinn hissed at Gavin, "even if you have to start stripping to get him to take you back to our rooms."

"He's as likely to fuck me over the table as take me somewhere private when he's like this," Gavin reminded Quinn. "And here in Tortuga, no one would think twice about it, except perhaps to egg him on."

Quinn had to admit the truth of both those statements. As it turned out, he needn't have worried. Amery brought back another round of drinks and then insisted they finish them quickly so they would be sharp for the meeting with their benefactor at noon. "It wouldn't do to miss out on an opportunity because we were too drunk to arrive on time."

Quinn quaffed his rum quickly and followed Amery and Gavin back to the rooms they'd taken while they were in port, his hand on the hilt of his sword as he glared left and right at any who thought they might take advantage of a man in his cups. That Amery was nearly as dangerous with his sword when he was drunk as he was when he was sober didn't mean Quinn had to give any of the thugs lying about the chance to get themselves killed.

Particularly since Amery seemed to have decided he was more interested in Gavin than in his own safety. Then again, Amery was always more interested in Gavin than in just about anything except his ship. Since they were between ships at the moment, Gavin was the sole focus of Amery's attentions, a fact Gavin relished, even if he didn't flaunt their relationship the way Amery sometimes did.

Arriving back where they had taken lodging, Quinn pulled the covers over his head and turned his back on his friends as soon as he could get settled, because Amery hadn't even waited for him to put out the lamp before grabbing Gavin and manhandling him onto the bed, his intentions clear as daylight. There was little privacy aboard a sailing ship unless you were the captain or one of the officers, and Quinn had more than his share of experience at ignoring the nighttime activities of the men in the bunks around him. He'd gotten used to being quartermaster, though, and having at least the screen of walls between himself and Gavin and Amery. Not that the walls on the *Dark Dream* had been particularly thick, but they had allowed Quinn to see to his own needs when the sounds of his friends' passions roused his own. If he imagined it was Gavin's hands on his body instead of his own, no one else would ever be the wiser.

"Amery," Quinn heard Gavin protest, "Quinn is—"

"I've got my fingers up your arse and you're worried about Quinn?" Amery growled in reply. "He's a grown man. He knows what we're about and can leave if he wants."

They all knew he wouldn't, that he'd stay and savor his own little corner of their intimacy. They just weren't quite as blunt about it most nights. Only when they'd all had too much to drink did they silently acknowledge that, but for a twist of fate, the bond that had forged between Gavin and Amery could have formed instead between Gavin and Quinn or indeed between Amery and Quinn. On nights like this, Quinn wondered what would happen if he left his lonely bunk and joined them like he had when they were all little more than boys and had nothing but bravado to show for themselves. He never took the chance because he knew that, regardless of the vagaries of fate leading to the promises between the two men in the next bed, Amery and Gavin loved each other, and he would rather suffer the tortures of the damned than do anything that might upset the balance of their lives. He had nearly driven them all apart once before when Gavin had come to his bed in a fit of pique. He would not risk doing it again.

It didn't take long for the sounds from the next bed to take on a desperate tinge and then cease altogether. When Amery was drunk, his usual self-control deserted him. A few moments later, he heard muffled snoring and let out a quiet sigh.

"I'm sorry, Quinn," Gavin whispered into the darkness. "He isn't usually quite so—"

"Yes, he is," Quinn interrupted. "Not usually with me, maybe, but he doesn't have to be drunk to stake his claim on you, and who'd blame him? Go to sleep, Gavin."

Gavin didn't reply, leaving Quinn to sigh again and try to find a comfortable position in an uncomfortable bed with an erection that showed no signs of abating. He ought to get up and leave, go down to the street and find a two-bit whore to suck him off. They'd flip up their skirts or fold down their blouses and offer him whatever he wanted for the right price. Even their pert—or not so pert—behinds. One arse was as good as another in the dark, he reminded himself, but he didn't rise, didn't seek congenial company of either gender. He told himself he needed the sleep so he'd be sharp tomorrow when they went to check out the ship they'd been offered, to make sure they weren't buying a pig in a poke.

He figured the only person who would buy that tale was lying in the next bed. Amery was about the least gullible man Quinn knew, but he had a very large, very determined blind spot where Quinn was concerned, a condition which let them all bump along together without ever having to address the rest of the reason Quinn had stayed with them instead of finding another ship. He'd never have made officer, much less quartermaster, if it weren't for Amery's blind spot. The scraps of affection the two men threw him because of their long-standing friendship, being able to see them, talk to them, occasionally even touch them, were what kept Quinn going, the reason he woke up each morning and the hope that carried him through each day.

Whatever might have been if circumstances had been different, if the Spanish slavers had turned left instead of right, had captured Amery instead of Quinn when they took Gavin, leaving Amery to rescue them both from a fate far worse than death, Amery was the conquering hero, the one who saved them and won Gavin's undying gratitude, respect, and love as his prize. Amery had gotten them back aboard the *Dark Dream* and gotten them the hell away from the burning slave ship, and then he'd disappeared into his cabin with Gavin. When they finally came out, three days later, they looked exhausted, but they both wore smiles and they carried a signed matelotage. The crew witnessed it, and that was the end of that. Quinn's parents, God rest their souls, had imbued him with too great a respect for the institution of marriage for him to do anything that might upset the pirate version of that estate.

Quinn seriously considered leaving after that, but Gavin had asked him to stay, saying that while he loved Amery and wanted to be with him and him alone as lovers, only Quinn truly understood the nightmare he'd gone through, the rapes they had suffered at the hands of the slavers who wanted to make sure their captives were completely broken before they sold them in the slave markets of the Barbary Coast. Quinn had tried to convince Gavin that Amery wouldn't want him around, particularly not when it hadn't been all that long since Gavin had sought comfort in Quinn's arms during one of the times when he and Amery were fighting.

Gavin disagreed, assuring Quinn that everything was forgotten now, that Amery was perfectly happy to let bygones be bygones. When it came down to it, neither Quinn nor Amery could say no to Gavin, and so Quinn stayed. Most days, most nights, Quinn was even glad of it. He couldn't ask for better friends than Amery and Gavin nor for a better position. Amery was an uncanny sailor, seeming to pull the best prizes out of thin air, navigating even the most treacherous waters with ease and prevailing far more often than he failed in battle. On any other ship, Quinn would never have made it to quartermaster at barely thirty, his ability to read Amery, even when he couldn't figure out anything else, making him invaluable to the captain. Quinn might not be able to come up with the strategies to find their quarries and take their booty, but he could read Amery's intentions like an open book once the captain had made up his mind, saving Amery from having to explain everything. He had an idea; Quinn made sure it got done.

Ultimately, Quinn had come to two conclusions. First, he needed Amery and Gavin too much to leave and start over. Second, even if Amery hadn't wanted Gavin, Gavin wouldn't have ever turned to Quinn, because Quinn had been with him on the slave ship. Quinn was the only person who understood, which was comforting outside of the bedroom, but Quinn *knew*, and that would have kept Gavin from ever totally relaxing in any sort of intimate interaction. At least on the ship with Amery and Gavin, Quinn could be with his friends, could know the companionship of over half their lifetimes spent serving together. He had a position, an income, a livelihood and a life, more than he would have if he'd left five years ago when Amery and Gavin formed their matelotage in the wake of the rescue from the Spanish slave ship. If, occasionally, in the dark watches of the night, he dreamed of something more, he kept those thoughts entirely to himself.

Chapter 2

LONG before noon, Amery rousted them from their beds, insisting Quinn and Gavin accompany him to the wharf to see if they could spot the mysterious ship the gentleman had mentioned the night before. Sure enough, a galleon bobbed in the waves a few hundred yards offshore. Amery pulled out his spyglass, one of the few things he had salvaged from the *Dark Dream*, and studied every inch of the hull visible from land.

"She looks clean," he told Quinn and Gavin. "So why is he giving her to us?"

"I don't know," Quinn replied, "but if there's a fault on her, we'll find it. We won't agree to anything until we've checked every inch of her over."

Gavin grinned. "No woman will have ever been examined the way we examine her."

"Not by you, that's for sure," Amery retorted.

Quinn laughed, the tension from the night before chased away by the morning light. He'd known Gavin and Amery since they were all unblooded boys. They'd served together as apprentices from the time they were ten, working their way up through the ranks, first on a merchant vessel, then on pirate ships. They'd tended each other's hurts, dried each other's tears, and watched each other's backs for nigh on twenty years. If anyone knew how little experience Gavin had with women, it was Quinn and Amery.

Of course, Gavin could make the same accusation about them.

"We've two hours still until we're supposed to meet the gentleman," Amery said after a moment's more staring through his spyglass. "We won't learn anything standing here. Let's find something to eat and see if anyone's heard anything about the ship or our sponsor or anything else we'd find worthwhile."

"So we'd be hunting pirates and the Spanish?" Gavin verified as they settled at a table in the tavern closest to the wharf. Quinn already knew Amery had picked it so it would be in sight of the ship. Easier to ask people what they knew about the vessel if it was right in front of them.

"That's what the letter said," Amery replied. "It's not the official letter of marque—and I'd want that in my hands, too, before we set sail—but it's the offer of one."

"I'm not sure I much like the idea of hunting the brethren," Quinn admitted. "We've been on that side of the law for too long ourselves."

"Honor among thieves, Quinn?" Amery laughed. "Unless our benefactor has more detailed orders for us than what was in the letter he gave me last night, it isn't an order to hunt pirates so much as permission. And if that's the case, there's nothing to stop us from only hunting the Spanish."

"I'll not say no to that," Gavin muttered. "I've a bone to pick with the scurvy bastards."

Quinn's eyebrows rose in surprise as Amery's face hardened. Rarely did Gavin make any reference to the Spanish slavers who'd made his and Quinn's lives hell for a week before Amery had managed to catch up with them and rescue them. Maybe the morning light hadn't chased away as many of the shadows as Quinn had thought. They needed to settle their affairs and get back out on the open sea where they didn't have time for such tangles. He glanced toward the galleon in the harbor. If all went well, they might be sleeping in her arms tonight.

An hour of asking questions left them no wiser as to the ship's origin or its current owner than they were when they'd woken up that morning, a fact that currently had Amery pacing the docks. If there was one thing the former captain of the *Dark Dream* hated, it was not knowing who held the cards. He didn't have to know what all the cards were, but he had to know where they were, or he drove everyone around him a little insane until he did. Usually Gavin could calm him down, but the ship's surgeon was even more on edge than the captain. Quinn didn't blame him. The harsh sounds of Spanish had assailed their ears all morning, a pirate ship full of Spaniards having anchored in the bay as they were having breakfast. Any other day, he'd have insisted Amery take Gavin back to their room and find a way to take his mind off the Spaniards' presence in the port, but today they didn't have the luxury of pretending. They had to meet their sponsor in half an hour, and that didn't leave time for the kind of extended distraction Gavin needed. Quinn only hoped going out to see the galleon would take his friend's mind off the other ship and its crew. The last thing they needed was to lose the potential patronage of the unknown man because of Gavin's distraction.

"You're early, Captain White." All three pirates spun at the sound of Amery's name, hands on the hilts of their swords in automatic defense. "I like that in a man."

Amery inclined his head but otherwise held his silence.

"Have you considered my offer?"

"Considered it," Amery allowed slowly, "but I'll be needing a bit more information and a closer look at that beauty out there."

"Easily enough arranged," the gentleman agreed. "I imagine you'd prefer if your friends accompany us out to the ship."

"I'll have yer name as well before we'll be going anywhere with Yer Excellency," Amery insisted.

Quinn frowned. The request was a reasonable one, but the sudden reemergence of Amery's accent was troubling. He hated to sound less than well-educated. They had spent hours as boys imitating the speech of their first captain, the first gentleman any of them had met. Between that and the illicit hours poring over the few pieces of parchment they could find as Gavin shared his knowledge of letters, they had managed to become literate men.

"Captain William Jackson," the gentleman said with a sketched bow, "in the service of the Earl of Warwick and the Providence Island Company. And your friends are?"

"Quinn Davies, my quartermaster, and Gavin Watson, ship's surgeon," Amery said, pausing a moment before adding, "and my matelot. That won't be a problem for his lordship, will it?"

Quinn braced automatically for a fight. If Jackson was one of the brethren like them, it would be fine, but if he was a Navy man, they could well have a fight on their hands.

"What you do in your cabin is your business," Jackson replied smoothly. "I only care what you do on deck."

Quinn smothered a chuckle. Amery had never been quite bold enough to bugger Gavin in the open that way. Or more likely he wasn't willing to share the sight of his lover lost in passion. It might have been five years since Quinn had seen it, but he had not forgotten how the flush of arousal highlighted Gavin's dark beauty.

"Then we have an accord," Amery declared. "Tell me about the ship."

"She's a good English galleon," Jackson assured them, gesturing toward a dinghy with two sailors manning the oars. "We took her back from a group of pirates and refitted her for the company. She's as fine as any ship in the West Indies."

"We'll be the judge of that," Amery declared as they climbed into the dinghy. The sailors cast off, rowing out toward the galleon. "Tell us more about the terms. The letter yesterday mentioned a generous percentage without specifying what that might be."

"Thirty percent of any treasure plus the same for the sale of the vessel, if it's sold rather than outfitted for another crew, until the cost of setting up this ship is paid back, and then fifty percent of the same," Jackson explained. "You won't get better from any other company or even from the King himself."

"We got one hundred percent of the take on the *Dark Dream*," Amery reminded him.

"Yes, but you bought your own supplies and powder and shot and took your chances with the weather," Jackson countered. "All you risk now is your lives."

Quinn thought it sounded like a fair deal, but he kept his opinion to himself for the moment. As far as Jackson was concerned, this was Amery's decision. He didn't need to know how much Amery relied on Quinn's and Gavin's opinions.

"Have them circle the ship," Amery directed when the sailors headed straight for the rope onto the deck. "I want to see her lines."

"Do as he says," Captain Jackson ordered.

Quinn studied the way the vessel sat in the water and the planks themselves with careful eyes, looking for any flaws. As far as he could see, she was in remarkable condition, even the tar seeming fresh. When they reached the stern, Amery ordered the dinghy to stop. Without waiting to be told, Quinn started stripping down.

"What are you doing?" Jackson demanded.

"I've only the one set of clothes at the moment," Quinn explained, "and I just paid good coin to have them washed last week. I'd rather that not go to waste if it's all the same to you, sir." He didn't bother to recount how the storm that had scuppered the *Dark Dream* had laid waste to the officers' quarters, washing away nearly all of Quinn's possessions except those he'd had on his person. It was a risk sailors took when they went to sea. The deep gave and she took away.

Without waiting for a reply, he dove nude into the turquoise water, eyes open despite the sting of the salt as he examined the rudder. Coming up for a breath of air, he dove again, legs kicking hard to take him all the way down to the keel. His lungs burned as he swam along its length as far as he could. Finally, gasping for breath, he broke the surface, pulling himself up onto the side of the dinghy so he could speak to Amery more easily. "I can't find a thing wrong with her beneath the water, Captain."

"Then we'll go aboard, Captain Jackson," Amery declared. Quinn doubted the agent of the Crown could discern it, but Quinn could practically see Amery rubbing his hands in glee.

Rather than trying to climb back in the dinghy, an undertaking sure to shred his dignity if not his knees, Quinn swam to the hanging lines, climbing them with the ease of a man at home in the rigging. The rope was thick and fresh, not yet dirtied by saltwater and time. Someone who knew ships had spent a lot of time making sure this one was in prime condition. Amery and Gavin clambered aboard moments before Quinn did, their gaits adjusting instinctively to the gentle roll of the ship in even the quiet waters of the harbor.

"Mr. Watson, check the stores, if you please," Amery ordered, voice taking on the familiar cadence of command. "Mr. Davies, the riggings are all yours."

Quinn didn't hesitate, scrambling up through the shrouds off the mainmast all the way to the crow's nest. Not finding anything to question, he slid down and repeated the process on the foremast and the mizzenmast, but he couldn't find a problem anywhere. "Everything seems to be in order, Captain," he reported, returning to the deck.

"Good," Amery declared. "I think you've dried off enough for these." He offered Quinn his clothes back. Unselfconsciously, Quinn dressed again, not at all bothered by his nudity. No one had secrets on a ship this size.

"The lower decks are well-stocked and in good condition," Gavin reported, climbing back up through the hatch. "She even has a separate surgery."

"And the quarters for the officers and crew?" Amery inquired.

"Basic but adequate," Gavin replied. "Enough for half a dozen officers and a hundred sailors."

"Quite a generous crew for a vessel of this size," Amery observed, turning to Captain Jackson. "Is there a reason for such a large berth space?"

"If you capture an enemy ship, you'll need sailors to bring it into port on Providence Island or, barring that, to Barbados," Jackson explained. "You won't be able to trust the captured crew, so you'll need enough men to crew your ship and a prize. And a first mate who's competent enough to get her to port."

"I have one of those already," Amery replied coolly, clearly not amused by the slight slur against Quinn. "Two, indeed, for Mr. Watson could captain a ship as well were Mr. Davies unable to take the helm. If you'll take us back to shore, I'll give you my decision by sundown."

Captain Jackson seemed to want to press for a decision right away, but he backed down when Amery's expression turned mulish as he vaulted down to the main deck from the aftcastle. The others followed at a more sedate pace, Quinn trailing last to watch Amery's back. It had become such a habit that he didn't even think about it anymore. Amery led; Quinn followed.

Captain Jackson left them on shore with the promise of meeting them at the same tavern as he'd found them in the night before. Only when he was out of sight did Amery begin the trek back to their rooms.

In silent accord, they waited until the door shut behind them to discuss all they'd seen and heard.

"I fear it's almost too good to be true," Gavin admitted when Amery asked their opinions. "I can't figure why anyone would give us a ship like that for no reason other than to have us plunder where we please."

"The Providence Island Company was founded by Puritans, wasn't it?" Amery asked. "It seems odd to me that the good captain was so willing to turn a blind eye to our ways if that's the case."

"Unless the lure of the gold we can bring them outweighs everything else," Quinn suggested. "Jackson had heard of you, enough to ask for you by name and to know something of your reputation, if the conversation last night was anything to judge by. If that's the case, he'd know your only real vice in the eyes of God and man is sitting in this room with you, since they're offering you a letter of marque to take you away from your godless pirating."

Amery and Gavin chuckled. "As long as they don't try to take me away from Gavin, I'm amenable to listening to the rest."

"God Himself couldn't take you away from Gavin," Quinn reminded them with a grin. "The Providence Island Company hasn't a chance. So are we going to do this?"

"I don't see any reason why we shouldn't," Gavin replied.

"And a fine many reasons why we should," Amery concluded, "not the least of which is that I'm getting antsy confined to land."

"I'm all but out of gold," Quinn agreed. "Whatever we do, we'll have to do it soon or I won't have the funds to keep a roof over my head or food in my belly."

"I don't understand how you let gold slip through your fingers the way you do," Amery scolded. "We took equal shares of the last bit of treasure, and yet you're the one short on funds."

Quinn shrugged, not willing to admit he'd slipped from the room during more than one night to seek relief from the needs he couldn't sate with them sleeping in the next bed. They wouldn't ridicule him for it—what pirate hadn't occasionally paid for company?—but they'd pity him, and that would be even worse. "It must be the laundry I had done."

Amery and Gavin looked skeptical, but they left Quinn his fiction, and ultimately, that was all Quinn could ask.

Amery flipped a crown in Quinn's direction. "Get yourself a second set of clothes at least. As soon as Captain Jackson delivers the letter of marque and we can gather a crew, you'll have to look respectable again."

The coin in Quinn's hand would buy far more than a second set of clothes. It would buy him a night with the finest companionship money could provide. Had it been his coin, he wouldn't have hesitated. As it was, he'd spend another restless night listening to Amery and Gavin in the next bed.

Chapter 3

AT SUNSET, they met Captain Jackson in the same tavern as the night before and delivered their decision. He didn't seem at all surprised, taking the rolled letter of marque from a satchel and offering it to Amery with a flourish. "We'll look for you on Providence Island when you've taken a prize," he said by way of farewell.

"A drink to celebrate," Amery declared. "And then tonight we sleep aboard our new lady, boys!"

Quinn's cheer was easily as loud as Gavin's, and Quinn wondered if he would do better to sleep in the crew's quarters tonight to spare his ears the sound of his friends' passion. Tomorrow they would start recruiting their crew, and he would sleep in the quartermaster's cabin, but tonight he could have any bunk on the ship with the exception of the captain's, the one bed other than his own where he had any interest in sleeping.

Amery returned with three mugs of ale, distracting Quinn from his dour thoughts. They toasted their new ship and new commission.

"She needs a name," Gavin observed.

"We could name her after the *Dark Dream,*" Quinn proposed.

Amery shook his head. "The *Dream* was a different life than the one we'll be leading now. We need a new name for a new chapter in our lives."

"*Dark Queen,*" Gavin suggested.

Amery shook his head. "The *Silver Queen,* for she'll bring us enough silver to live out our days in luxury."

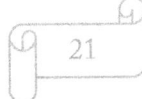

"And those seeing the name won't immediately know she's a privateer's ship instead of a merchant vessel," Quinn agreed. "What are you thinking about for a crew?"

"Experienced sailors all," Amery replied immediately. "We'll be fighting for our treasure. There's no place for inexperience. Beyond that, no one in trouble with the authorities. I don't want to spend my days flogging a bunch of rowdies into submission. Any who come in pairs are doubly welcome."

Quinn knew that already, familiar with Amery's contention that no one would fight as hard as a man defending his lover. Quinn was pretty sure that was why Amery had made captain before he turned twenty-five.

"I'll put the word out tonight," Quinn declared. "We'll see how many of our old crew are still at loose ends."

"They're all welcome back, the officers most of all," Amery said. "It'll be easier breaking in a new crew if I don't have to train new officers as well. We'll have a cooper aboard as well this time. We don't want to lose our supplies to rot or our powder to damp."

"A boatswain, a gunner, a cook, a carpenter, and a cooper then?" Quinn verified.

"With a crew of a hundred, we'll want a mate or three to help you keep discipline, Quinn. We're privateers now, not pirates, and we'll act accordingly," Amery insisted.

"You may have some who will protest," Gavin warned. "They won't like not being able to elect the officers."

"Then they'll sail on another ship," Amery growled. "The letter of marque has my name on it, and that makes the ship ours. Make that clear as well when you put out word we're seeking a crew."

"Aye, Captain," Quinn said with a smile. Their ship. Their own ship with none of the tension and constant worry that the crew might vote one of them out of office for whatever reason. It hadn't happened, but that didn't mean it couldn't.

"Give me an hour, and I'll be ready to go out to the ship," Quinn requested. "I want to make the rounds now before the men get too drunk to remember our offer come morning."

"We'll wait for you," Amery promised. "This is our future, yours as well as Gavin's and mine. We won't leave you out of it."

If only that were true, Quinn thought with a sigh as he left the tavern and began his rounds of the public houses in Tortuga. They varied little one from another, low structures of wood and stone, windows thrown wide to catch any breeze, raucous laughter spilling into the streets. At each place he stopped, he approached the tavern keeper first.

"Captain White wants it known he's seeking a crew," he told each man. "A privateer mission with plenty of share for all. Anyone interested should report to the wharf at dawn. Captain White has no patience for tardiness or drunkenness."

When he'd fulfilled his duty to the owner of the establishment, he sought familiar faces among the patrons, hoping to find as many of the crew of the *Dark Dream* as he could. They knew Amery, knew Quinn himself, and could speak to their fairness before the others. That would be doubly important when they asked the crew to accept a military rather than a pirate command. Amery's word, and by extension Quinn's, would be law.

At his third stop, Quinn found word had preceded him. The former boatswain of the *Dark Dream* approached Quinn even before he made it up to the bar. "Is it true the Cap'n has a new ship, Mr. Davies?"

"God's own," Quinn promised. "I saw her myself this afternoon. She's a beauty, she is, and Captain White said he'd welcome back any of our old crew. We'll be privateering for an English company with a portion of the profits for our own."

"Privateers, you say," Cullen hesitated. "Military rule?"

"Only in that once the rules are set, the Captain will enforce them rather than a jury," Quinn explained, "and that the crew won't be able to vote us out. The letter of marque is in the Captain's name. Without him in command, we'd lose our legitimacy."

"So he wouldna be worried about the grog or a little slap and tickle on the side?" Cullen verified.

"Mr. Watson has signed on as the ship's surgeon," Quinn said mildly. "You know the captain won't be bothered by anyone else's preferences."

"I suppose not," Cullen allowed. "We'll see the ship's code afore we sail?"

"Do you really think the Captain would play you false after all the years you sailed with him?" Quinn challenged.

"It's not that I doan trust Captain White," Cullen backpedaled, "but on a pirate ship, we all 'ave a say, and the captain 'as to listen t'us just as we listen to 'im—and to you as quartermaster. I'm leery of giving up that protection."

"I might share your concern if we were sailing with a different captain," Quinn admitted, "but you've known Captain White since you started on the *Dark Dream*. Have you ever disagreed with a decision he made or felt he did anything to abuse his position?"

"No," Cullen replied. "It isna Captain White I doan trust. It's the ones givin' 'im 'is orders."

"I've seen the orders, if it makes you feel any better," Quinn offered. "They say simply to take any Spanish vessel that crosses our path and to bring the ships and the plunder to Providence Island to be sold. Everything else is up to Captain White and the crew."

"And when would he want us t'gather again?" Cullen asked.

"At dawn. He hopes to sail with the afternoon tide," Quinn replied.

"I'll keep it in mind, and I'll pass the word t'any o' the others I see."

"You won't find a better man or a better captain than Amery White," Quinn reminded him in parting, turning his attentions to the tavern keeper and the other patrons. Cullen would show up or not; Quinn had done what he could.

Another sailor, one he did not know, approached him as he was leaving the same tavern. "Beggin' yer pardon, sir. What manner of a crew be ye seeking?"

"A crew willing to hunt the Spanish," Quinn replied easily. "Captain White of the *Silver Queen* has a letter of marque to harass the Spanish treasure ships."

"A privateer, then, not a pirate," the sailor hesitated. "What manner of man is the captain? If I'm to serve at his mercy, I want to know I'll not find myself flogged for nothing."

"You sound as if you speak from experience," Quinn observed. "Captain White is the best of men and as fair as the day is long. He's been a pirate for enough years to believe in the code. There won't be any talk of voting him out, but beyond that—and not challenging his matelotage—serving on the *Silver Queen* will be like serving on any pirate ship."

"Perhaps my partner and I will see you in the morning then," the sailor said with a smile.

"A man with a partner is doubly valued in the Captain's eyes," Quinn assured him. "Come hear what he has to say. You can always change your mind before you sign the Articles of Agreement."

An hour after he left Amery and Gavin, Quinn returned to the tavern where they'd met Captain Jackson. As they walked toward the wharf again, Quinn brought up his conversation with Cullen.

"I think we'll have some men concerned about the Articles of Agreement," Quinn warned Amery. "If you intend to have anything out of the ordinary in them, we should be prepared for a fight. Even Cullen, who knows you, is worried about signing on with you if you have the authority of a military captain rather than a pirate captain."

Amery shrugged. "Nothing out of the ordinary, but I can't spend my time worrying about my crew changing their minds about my position. We'll write up the official Articles when we get out to the *Silver Queen* so we can present them to the crew in the morning before they even come aboard."

They rowed out to the galleon and retired to the captain's quarters in the stern of the ship. The room stretched across the full width of the vessel, wide windows giving a view of the waters behind them. The bed, while built into the wall, was a true bed, not simply a bunk or a hammock like most of the crew would have. Quinn watched in half-repressed jealousy as Gavin tested the mattress with his hand before sinking onto the feather expanse as if he had every right to be there. He would be assigned quarters, Quinn knew, off the surgery, but he doubted Gavin would ever use them for anything other than for storing the contents of his medicine chest.

Amery drew a sheet of paper from the supply allotted by the company for the captain's log and took up a quill. They spent the next two hours in discussion of the perfect wording for the Articles of Agreement, the law by which they would all be governed during Amery's tenancy in these quarters. Finally, the candle guttered low in its lantern, and none of them could stifle their yawns any longer.

"I'll take myself off then," Quinn proposed, "and see you both at first light. Sleep well."

"G'night, Quinn," Amery said, rising from his seat and stretching broadly. Gavin rose as well, stepping behind Amery and beginning to massage the knots from the muscles of his back. Quinn paused on the threshold of the cabin to take in the sight of them together, but he had no real excuse to linger. They were already lost in their own world, oblivious to his presence, and if he stayed much longer, he would be trespassing on their privacy. With a sigh, he stepped into the corridor, shutting the door behind him as he went to his own quarters, not far away, wishing he'd found an excuse to sleep on shore one last night.

Chapter 4

AT DAWN the next day, Quinn and Gavin rowed the dinghy back to shore and took up position on either side of Amery. The captain had taken extra pains with his appearance that morning, polishing his boots and making sure his doublet was brushed. Quinn would have been amused by the way Gavin fussed around him were it not for the importance of the morning's endeavor. Their success depended on Amery's ability to persuade the sailors to accept his command.

To their delight, a large crowd had gathered on the docks. Amery stepped lightly from the boat onto the wharf. He made a show of turning back to help Gavin out of the dinghy as well. Quinn knew not to expect the same treatment. He might be Amery's best friend and quartermaster in his own right, but Gavin was Amery's matelot, and now everyone knew it.

"Gentlemen," Amery began, his voice ringing out in the still morning air, "behind me you see the newly christened, newly commissioned *Silver Queen* in the service of the Providence Island Company. Since she's a commissioned vessel, we'll be sailing her under slightly modified Articles of Agreement."

A murmur ran through the crowd. Quinn braced automatically, ready to draw his sword in defense of his friends and himself, but Amery simply let the murmurs run their course. When silence fell again, he drew out the paper he and Quinn and Gavin had compiled the night before.

"Even before the Articles of Agreement, the most basic tenets of our voyage are these: I am the undisputed captain by virtue of the letter of marque issued in my name, and Mr. Davies and Mr. Watson speak with my authority. If at any time they issue an order, it carries the same weight as if I had spoken. I have been a pirate long enough to value the opinion of my crew, but ultimately all decisions will be mine."

"And if you abuse that power?" a sailor Quinn did not know demanded.

"Then you're welcome to leave the next time we make port," Amery replied coldly. "I want no man on my ship who questions my judgment. If you've heard enough already, feel free to leave now."

He paused for a few moments to see if anyone would leave. A few men did, but most stayed where they were.

"For those who want to hear more, these are the Articles of Agreement we will all be bound by, myself included." Amery unfolded the parchment and began to read.

"1. Every man shall obey civil command; the Captain shall have one full share and a half in all prizes; the Quartermaster, Surgeon, Carpenter, Boatswain, Cooper and Gunner shall have one share and quarter.

2. If any man shall keep any secret from the company, he shall be marooned with one bottle of powder, one bottle of water, one small arm and shot.

3. If any man shall steal anything in the company, or game, to the value of a piece of eight, he shall be marooned or shot.

4. That man that shall strike another whilst these Articles are in force, shall receive Mose's Law (that is 40 stripes lacking one) on the bare back.

5. That man that shall snap his arms, or smoke tobacco in the hold, without a cap to his pipe, or carry a candle lighted without a lantern, shall suffer the same punishment as in the former Article.

*6. That man that shall not keep his arms clean, fit
for an engagement, or neglect his business, shall be
cut off from his share, and suffer such other
punishment as the Captain and the company shall
think fit.*

*7. If any man shall lose a joint in time of an
engagement he shall have 400 pieces of eight; if a
limb 800.*

*8. If at any time you meet with a prudent woman,
that man that offers to meddle with her, without her
consent, shall suffer present death. The same shall
be true of any man who meddles with another man
without his consent."*

"And if the attention should be welcome?" another sailor inquired. "I'd rather not hang for sleeping with my matelot."

"Then it's no business of mine," Amery said simply. "I'll have no rape aboard my ship, but as long as both parties are in agreement, matelots or merely passing the time, they have my blessing and support."

Quinn hid a smile at the murmur of surprise and approval that went through the crowd. Gavin took a step closer to Amery, subtly reinforcing his position.

"As you can see, Mr. Davies, the quartermaster, Mr. Watson, the ship surgeon, and I have already signed. We sail on the afternoon tide with the first hundred sailors to add their signature or make their mark. There's place as well for some officers if any have served in the past. Mr. Davies will take names. The best bunks will surely be claimed by the first aboard."

Quinn took the parchment from Amery and stepped forward to begin accepting pledges from interested sailors. Not everyone who had come to listen stayed, but Quinn was pleased to see a large number of men milling around still.

Cullen was among the first to approach. "I shouldna doubted ye, Mr. Davies," he said, taking the quill and making his mark beneath Gavin's name. "The Articles are nearly the same as they always were aboard the *Dream*. I'll sail with the Cap'n again gladly."

"Welcome aboard," Quinn smiled. "See the Captain about your quarters."

Cullen nodded and moved toward Amery and Gavin. Quinn could hear them greeting Cullen warmly, but he focused on the men in front of him instead, taking names and asking about experience.

"I heard the ship needs a cooper," an older man said.

"The Captain wants someone who can maintain the stores," Quinn agreed. "Are you interested?"

"I am. My wife died over the winter, and I've no reason now to stay ashore," the man explained.

"You'll need your own tools," Quinn told him. "The company will provide your supplies. Your name, sir?"

"Farnham," the cooper replied. "Peter Farnham."

"Have you sailed before, Mr. Farnham?" Quinn inquired.

"Only to get to the islands," Farnham replied, "but I never had no problems with seasickness or nothing. Healthy as a horse."

"Can you handle a sword or a gun in a fight? You won't be part of the boarding party, but if the fight comes to us, can you defend yourself?" Quinn asked.

"I can handle a pistol," Farnham affirmed. "Never been much for a sword."

"Very well, Mr. Farnham," Quinn declared. "You have a job if you want one. Make sure you have two pistols. If you don't use a sword, you'll want a second one in case you miss with the first. We sail with the tide. Make sure you're back in time to get your tools aboard. We don't wait for anyone."

By the time the last sailor in line made his mark, they'd signed the full complement of crew. "We'll have to keep a close eye on supplies,"

Quinn observed as they went to a nearby tavern for lunch. "Even here in the islands, we don't want to run short."

"Definitely not," Amery agreed. He knew the West Indies well enough to have found hidden coves in several places where they could take on supplies in an emergency, but with the company agreeing to stock the ship, they could spend more time hunting if they kept the hold full.

After lunch, they returned to the wharf to find the boatswain already supervising the ferrying of men out to the ship. "Nicely done, Cullen," Amery praised. "The quartermaster, Mr. Watson, and myself will go aboard on the next boat to make sure everything is in order."

"Aye, Cap'n," Cullen said with a sharp nod. "Nisbett, from the *Dark Dream*, came aboard and I asked 'im t'make sure the bunks was divided fair-like, sir. I thought you wouldna mind 'im keepin' order in yer absence."

"I see you've lost none of your initiative," Amery praised the boatswain. "Keep up the good work, and you'll have earned your share and more of the treasure. Oh, and inform Nisbett he's been promoted to second mate. Mr. Davies will need someone to see to discipline when he's off shift."

"Aye, sir," Cullen said with something akin to a salute. Quinn approved the thought behind the gesture even if the movement itself was somewhat awkward. He'd been worried about the change in discipline on the new ship, but perhaps his concerns would amount to naught. He certainly hoped so. It would make life aboard the *Silver Queen* much easier.

"We can take ye out to the ship, sirs," two of the sailors called as they brought the dinghy up against the pier.

"Thank you, gentlemen," Amery replied with a nod.

"Seaton and Clay," Quinn supplied. "Partners, I understand."

"Yes, sir," Clay agreed. "For fourteen years now. We was very glad t'hear ye say ye'd support our union."

"It would be churlish of me not to, when I've been with Mr. Watson for five years myself," Amery said with a smile. "You'll always have my support if you need it. I won't have my matelot hassled, nor anyone else for choosing that path."

"That's a real relief. Even on pirate ships, not everyone feels that way," Seaton replied. "Cap'n on deck!"

The hands snapped to attention as Amery boarded the ship, Quinn and Gavin right behind him.

Quinn waited for Amery to order the men to return to their tasks before beginning his own round of inspections. He started toward the bow of the ship, ducking to avoid hitting his head on the low entrance to the forecastle. All along the walls, sea chests claimed a portion of the open space for their owners. A few of the crew were still in their quarters, arranging their possessions. He spoke to them all before climbing down the ladder onto the gun deck. Gallagher, the gunner from the *Dark Dream*, had already taken charge there, checking stores of powder and shot and inspecting the cannons. "This is one fine ship we're to be sailing, Mr. Davies," he said when he saw Quinn.

"Indeed it is, Gallagher," Quinn agreed. "Is everything to your satisfaction?"

"Oh, aye, sir," Gallagher replied immediately. "The powder is right and tight in its barrels, and the guns are in excellent condition. We'll be ready when we sight our prize, I promise ye."

"The captain will be glad to hear it," Quinn commended. "I imagine you'll want to fire a few practice rounds once we get out to sea, to test the range and accuracy of the guns."

"'Twouldn't go amiss," Gallagher allowed. "These are demi-culverns, not minions and falcons like we had on the *Dark Dream*. They work the same, but I'm not as familiar with their power."

"I'll speak to the captain about it as soon as we sail," Quinn offered. "He'll want us to be ready for battle as quickly as possible."

"Aye, sir, we'll be ready," Gallagher promised. "An hour to give them all a good firing, and we'll take on any vessel the watch finds for us. There won't be many who'll stand against this beauty."

"The captain named her well," Quinn agreed. "The queen of all she surveys. She'll make us rich men."

"Your words in God's ear," Gallagher replied piously as Quinn continued his rounds. The lower holds contained ballast, supplies and stores, all lashed down against the possibility of stormy seas. Quinn had seen men maimed or killed by poorly stowed barrels, and he refused to have that happen on his watch. He checked every rope on every barrel as he made his way through the currently dry hold. He doubted it would stay this dry once they set sail, the wind and waves tossing water aboard at random, but for now, the wood was dry and clean. He'd talk to the carpenter about keeping it that way as much as possible. The last thing they needed was to spend longer paying back the initial cost of their charter because neglect ruined their supplies.

He found Farnham, the cooper, in the lowest hold, examining the barrels there. "Is everything in order, Farnham?" he inquired.

"It appears to be, sir," the cooper assured him. "I've been inspectin' the barrels t'make sure nothing needed my attention right away like, and I haven't found a thing out of place."

"That seems to be the report from everyone I've asked," Quinn commented. "The company obviously intends for us to have a successful voyage."

"I find that a most reassuring thought," Farnham said.

"So do I, Mr. Farnham. So do I. Carry on and report anything amiss to me or to the Captain at once," Quinn directed. "We want to keep everything in top shape for as long as we can."

"I'll do just that," Farnham promised. "It's easier to replace a plank than to make a whole new barrel. Before you go, sir, I have a question. I hope you won't think I'm overstepping my bounds, but the captain and Mr. Watson...." Farnham trailed off, clearly not sure exactly what he wanted to ask.

"They're matelots," Quinn said.

"I've heard the word, but I don't know what it means," Farnham admitted.

"Matelotage is a contract," Quinn explained. "It's like getting married, only with two men and no priest."

"Oh, I see," Farnham said, an odd tone in his voice.

"Captain White and Mr. Watson aren't the only matelots on the ship either," Quinn warned the cooper. "You'll find it's rather common among pirates. It's not an institution you'll want to question."

Farnham nodded, turning back to his barrels, and Quinn left him to it.

Reaching the stern, the quartermaster climbed up toward the officers' quarters, passing the pens where the chickens were kept so they'd have fresh meat and eggs during the voyage. The cook, Mr. Peele, was checking his stores as well. "Is everything in order?" Quinn verified, though he suspected the answer would be no different here than anywhere else.

"Aye, 'tis, laddie," the older man replied, his brogue thick as he peered into a barrel of flour. "An' enough o' it t'last a good two months or more. We'll nae be needin' t'do more than watch the water barrels."

"Keep an eye on those and on everything else," Quinn directed. "We're not a poor pirate vessel anymore. If we need something, we have but to sail to Providence Island to restock. The captain doesn't intend for anyone to go hungry aboard his ship."

"Aye, sir," the cook agreed. "I'll make sure t'keep ye or Captain White aware o' the situation."

Satisfied with his inspection, Quinn made his way to the quarterdeck where Amery surveyed the hive of activity on the main deck as hands scurried about readying lines and checking sails.

"Well, Mr. Davies?" the captain asked as Quinn took his place at Amery's side.

"You have a beautiful ship and a crew who recognizes that fact," Quinn reported. "We'll be ready to sail with the tide."

"Very good," Amery said. "Set a course for Puerto Rico. We'll find our prize from there."

Chapter 5

"GOOD evening, gentlemen," Amery said as he came into the officers' dining room. "I see Mr. Peele has prepared another fine meal for us."

"It were my pleasure, Cap'n. I doan usually 'ave such a bountiful larder at me disposal."

"We're a proper ship now, with a company supplying us and everything," Amery declared. "We'll replenish our stocks at need."

"Sorry to disturb yer dinner, Cap'n, Quartermaster, sirs," Cullen said, his expression conveying his urgency, "but the lookout's spotted a sail."

"Could he see the colors?" Amery asked, his voice calm despite the sudden tension investing his frame. Quinn could tell the others didn't see it, but to his eyes, Amery was suddenly a line pulled taut, a bird dog ready to be released after his prey.

"No, Cap'n," Cullen reported. "If'n we could borrow yer spyglass?"

"No need," Amery said. "I'll come up to the quarterdeck myself. As much as I hate to waste Mr. Peele's wonderful meal, we mustn't miss our chance to take our first prize."

"I'll just put th'plates back on the stove, shall I?" Peele asked. "They'll be ready for ye when ye've made yer decision about the ship."

"Thank you, Mr. Peele," Amery said. "We'll be back to enjoy the meal before long, I'd wager. Even if she's a prize, we can follow her from a distance long enough for us to eat. Going into battle on an empty stomach is a recipe for disaster."

"Aye, Cap'n," Peele agreed.

Amery led the rest of the officers up to the main deck, drawing his spyglass and peering in the direction the lookout indicated. "Aye, there she is," he murmured after a moment. "A galleon from the look of her sails, but no colors I can see yet to tell if she's friend or foe." Looking around and not seeing the man he sought, he called for the second mate. "Nisbett!"

"Aye, Cap'n?" the man asked, heeding the summons.

"Keep her in sight, Nisbett," Amery directed, handing the spyglass to the second mate. "If you can make out her colors and she's a friend, let her go. If you see her flying the flag of Spain, run up the Spanish colors and start to close with her so we can engage her before nightfall. I'll be back after I finish my dinner."

"As ye say, Cap'n," Nisbett promised. "I'll alert ye if aught changes."

"We'll have our dinner now, Mr. Peele," Amery called when they returned to the officers' dining room. "The ship's too far away to tell yet whether she's the prize we seek, and Nisbett is perfectly capable of manning the helm until we close the distance. There's no reason to deny ourselves your delicious fare."

Peele served the plates again immediately, hovering in the background as the officers ate.

"The guns are ready," Gallagher assured Amery. "We tested them and good the first few days out to sea, and my boys know how to use them. When we're in range, our quarry will feel our presence, that's for sure."

"Wonderful," Amery praised. "We'll have to be careful to leave her in sailing condition if we don't want to tow her all the way back to Providence Island or sink her where she sits, but I'd rather not risk the men with a boarding party until we're sure the enemy is ready to surrender."

"The men'll fight for ye, Cap'n," Cullen interrupted. "Ye need not worry about that."

"I mean no insult to the crew, Bosun," Amery assured him, "but we have the firepower to take the ship without the risk of boarding straight away. There's no reason to throw lives away needlessly."

"Aye, that be the truth," Cullen agreed after a moment's consideration.

"There will be plenty of fighting for the men who want to see that action," Quinn promised. "Even after we've shown the strength of our guns, I suspect there will be some on our quarry who won't give up easily. If not this time, then other times. The Spanish don't give up their treasure lightly."

"Indeed they don't," Gavin and Amery muttered at the same time, though the difference in their tones was marked. Quinn hid a frown, remembering the helplessness he had suffered on the slave ship, trying always to convince Gavin that Amery would come after them while fearing in his own heart that all Amery's efforts would be in vain. When Amery had finally caught up with the Spaniards, they'd preferred to see their ship burned and sunk than to surrender to the "English bastards" who pursued them. Quinn still wasn't sure how Amery had managed to rescue Gavin and him from the slave hold as the flames licked the walls around them.

"They're no match for English tenacity," Amery added to the cheers of the officers. Quinn met Gavin's eyes across the table, heart clenching at the pain in the hazel eyes. Quinn wondered if they were making a mistake going after Spanish ships this way. Gavin wouldn't be any good in a fight if fear paralyzed him every time a Spanish vessel hove into view. They didn't particularly need him on deck, and in fact having him in the surgery to deal with any injuries would almost be a necessity, but neither Amery nor Quinn would go comfortably into battle if they feared for Gavin's ability to defend himself should the battle come to him. As Quinn watched, Gavin's face cleared and hardened, reminding Quinn that while Gavin had suffered, in many ways worse than Quinn himself, the surgeon had more than earned his place on this crew and, having known Spanish cruelty, would fight all the harder to make sure he never experienced it again. "We'll lure them in with the Spanish colors and then take them for every ounce of gold they have."

"Where would I be the least trouble durin' a battle, Cap'n?" Farnham asked. "I done figured out what t'do and where t'go during the sailing times, but I ain't been in a battle at sea before."

"Belowdecks with Mr. Jennings," Amery replied. "I doubt our prey will outgun us, but that doesn't mean she'll be helpless either. If you'd be so kind as to help out with any repairs to keep us seaworthy until the battle is over and we can refit properly, the entire crew would be grateful."

"I can swing a hammer," Farnham acknowledged. "And I'll keep my pistols handy, just in case."

"Mr. Peele," Amery called, his summons bringing the cook from his alcove, "would you assist Mr. Watson in the surgery? I don't expect the crew to get off any more lightly than the ship, and Mr. Watson will need someone not bothered by the sight of blood."

"I doan know how much help I'll be, Cap'n," Peele replied, "but I want t'do m'part."

"Most of the time, simply having another pair of hands is all I need," Gavin interjected. "With a crew this size, I hope to find a real apprentice, but until I do, an extra pair of hands will be welcome, whether it's to fetch and carry or hold a thread as I tie it off or staunch the bleeding on one man while I tend to another."

Quinn hid a grin behind his cup as Amery blanched at the sudden gory turn to the conversation. The sight of blood never slowed him down in battle, but the captain absolutely could not deal with it otherwise. Quinn supposed battle fever and the desire for survival provided the motivation Amery needed to overlook it during a fight.

The meal finished, the junior officers returned to their stations to prepare the crew for battle. "How you can be married to a ship's surgeon and captain your own vessel and still be so squeamish is beyond me," Quinn teased Amery as the three of them lingered for a moment after the meal.

Amery shrugged in reply. "Is the crew ready for this engagement?" he asked, his voice grave as he considered the risk of the upcoming battle.

"Every crew has to have a first battle," Quinn reminded the captain, "and the longer we wait, the harder it will be, I think. They want the gold to be had. We may not work like a well-greased machine yet, but only time and battles will breed that kind of familiarity among the men. That's why Gavin and I can read you so much better than everyone else, even the men who were on the *Dark Dream* with us. We know you as well as we know ourselves."

"Better," Gavin quipped with a smile.

Amery nodded. "You're right, of course. Let's ready the men. We have a prize to take."

Quinn started toward the door, realizing as he reached for the handle that he hadn't heard footsteps behind him. He glanced back to see Amery pull Gavin into a tight embrace. Feeling like a voyeur, he slipped outside, leaving them alone.

"Are you ready for this engagement?" Amery asked Gavin when the door shut behind Quinn. He appreciated his friend's discretion in providing them with the moment of privacy. They so rarely found any during the day.

Gavin glanced away, increasing Amery's concern. "Gavin, talk to me," Amery cajoled, giving his lover a slight shake. "I can't help you if I don't know what you're thinking."

Gavin's eyes closed in momentary distress, the realization that Amery could still not read him the way Quinn could a spike to his heart. "I'll be fine," he promised his matelot. "Once the battle starts, I fear I'll be too busy to fret about anything but whether you'll be the next man carried through my door."

"I won't let anything separate us again," Amery swore.

Gavin wished he believed that, but he knew the secret still weighing on his heart. Amery would never accept how differently Gavin and Quinn had suffered at the hands of their Spanish captors. Deciding more words would prove fruitless, he framed Amery's tanned face with tender hands, drawing his lover's mouth to his in a needy kiss designed to erase all thought of anything but him from Amery's mind. It worked, if Amery's reaction was any indication. The blond returned the kiss with all the desperate passion inspired by the looming battle, the very real chance that one or both of them would not survive. They faced it every time they attacked a ship, every time they faced a tempest, but nothing ever eased the fear in the lull before the storm.

"We don't have time," Amery groaned against Gavin's lips.

"They haven't sent for you," Gavin countered, bumping his groin against Amery's. "I want to go into battle with the feeling of you still inside me." He reached for the ties on Amery's breeches, slipping them down over the narrow hips and sliding his hands beneath, over the smooth skin of Amery's arse. "Push me up against the wall or turn me over the table and fuck me hard, Amery." *Give me something to remember you by if the Spanish dogs take you from me tonight.*

Amery had no hope of resisting such an impassioned plea, spinning Gavin in his arms and pressing him face first into the wall of the dining room. Gavin grunted as his chest hit wood. He pushed his own breeches down, not waiting for Amery to do it, pressing his buttocks back against Amery's erection. He heard Amery spit in his hand a moment before the blunt head nudged his backside. "Do it," he hissed, knowing it would hurt at first, but they'd made slow, lingering love that morning. He would still be open somewhat from that, and his body knew the routine. The pleasure would outweigh the pain long before he climaxed.

Amery obeyed, to Gavin's moderate surprise, since his matelot usually made him wait even when they were in a hurry, plunging inside Gavin's body with his full strength. Gavin groaned despite himself as the thick shaft pierced him, forcing his muscles to loosen. "Harder," he insisted.

"Demanding bastard," Amery hissed as he reared back and plunged again, feeling the rough pull of flesh against flesh. He thrust a few times, but the angle was awkward. Drawing back, he spun Gavin again, pushing him toward the table, uncaring of the cutlery that went flying as Gavin's hands hit the wooden planks, his body bending forward automatically, presenting his perfect arse for Amery to plow.

Gavin cried out in frustration when Amery pulled back, only to have the cry transform to one of delight as his lover crowded up against him, filling him again, more fully this time. "Yes," he moaned. "Like that."

Amery grabbed the strong hips, thrusting with all his might as the thought that this might be the last time they were together drove all other concerns from his mind. If he had to die, if he had to lose Gavin, he wanted this to be their last memory of each other, their dying thought. He could tell from the tenor of Gavin's cries that he wouldn't last much longer, but suddenly even this wasn't enough. He needed to see Gavin's face.

Gavin's release built inside him with ever-increasing urgency, the pounding rhythm of Amery's cock driving him hard. His shout of dismay echoed off the walls when Amery withdrew. "No," Gavin begged, starting to rise. Before he had fully straightened, Amery flipped him, Gavin's back hitting the table hard as Amery lifted his knees, catching them with his elbows and stepping back between Gavin's legs.

"I'm not done with you yet," Amery promised, returning his cock to its berth with practiced ease. "Not until you come for me, lover."

"Soon," Gavin gasped, knowing it wouldn't take much, not now that Amery had bent him double. He loved sex with Amery in every configuration, but the inherent vulnerability in his current position always added an extra bite to their interaction. He would never trust anyone else to make love to him this way.

"Now," Amery countered, releasing one of Gavin's legs to reach for the brunet's leaking erection. "With me now."

Gavin arched up off the table, his cock disgorging spurt after spurt onto his shirt and vest as Amery thrust deep and stayed there, twitching hard as he filled Gavin with the proof of his desire and devotion.

"Thank you," Gavin murmured as Amery released his other leg and drew him up to sitting. Amery didn't reply, sealing their lips together in a tender kiss.

"Captain, we've raised the Spanish colors. The ship's within sight."

Quinn's voice intruded, though Amery and Gavin parted reluctantly. "Go," Gavin whispered. "Take our prize and prove yourself to the men who don't know you. I'll be waiting for you in our cabin when all is said and done."

Chapter 6

AMERY strode out of the dining room into the corridor, fastening his breeches as he went. Quinn stood alone in the narrow passageway. Amery felt the weight of his friend's gaze, but he refused to apologize for making love with his matelot, even now with battle looming. "Tell me about the ship."

"She's a Spanish galleon," Quinn replied, "riding low in the water and unwieldy from what we've been able to see. We'll sail circles around her easily."

"Good," Amery said with a decisive nod. "Let's use that to our advantage. I want her under our colors by nightfall."

Quinn refrained from commenting that the likelihood of that would have been greater if Amery had followed him onto deck as soon as dinner finished. He already knew his friend would tell him to mind his own business.

On deck, Amery took his place at the helm, though he left Nisbett holding the steering rod. He needed to be free to move about the quarterdeck and down to the main deck if necessary. Nisbett was a capable sailor. He would get the ship where Amery wanted it to be. "Trim the sails," he called down to Quinn. "I want her running as tight before the wind as we can make her. Our speed will be our greatest advantage. We don't want to be where the enemy thinks we'll be."

Quinn shouted orders to the sailors in the rigging on the foremast and mainmast, though he had already checked the sails once. If Amery wanted them trimmed more, Quinn would see it done.

"Mr. Gallagher!"

"Aye, Cap'n?" the gunner replied, his head appearing through the hatch down to the gun deck.

"Are the guns primed?"

"Aye, sir, they are," Gallagher assured Amery. "They're all ready to fire and a second round ready to load as soon as you give the order to fire."

"We want to take her, not sink her, so aim above the waterline," Amery reminded the gunner. "She's no good to us on the bottom of the sea."

"Aye, sir, those were the orders I gave m'boys."

"Nisbett, close with our quarry," Amery ordered.

Nisbett shouted an acknowledgement of the order, changing the ship's tack so it aimed to intercept the other galleon rather than keeping a parallel course.

"All hands to stations!" Quinn ordered as soon as he felt the change in course. Amery was going in for the kill. Many of the crew, aware from those on watch that a battle was approaching, had already prepared, manning their stations, but those who had not yet left their quarters swarmed onto the gun deck and the main deck, ready to fight. The men not assigned to the gun decks were armed with a motley collection of arquebus and muskets, whatever they had with them when they signed on with the *Silver Queen*. Between the ship's guns and the sailors' weapons, Quinn hoped the Spanish ship would surrender without much difficulty.

Before long, they approached the other ship, close enough that Quinn could see the other crew going about their tasks with lackadaisical ease. Yes, they would be an easy target indeed for a crew as hungry for gold as the men on board the *Silver Queen*. "Steady, men," he warned softly, not wanting his voice to carry across the water. "Wait for the captain's orders."

Amery waited until they were fully broadside. "Fire!"

The gun ports dropped, the culverns pushed into range, and the powder boxes lit. Seconds later, the ship's port guns belched smoke and flame, the balls crossing the water to tear into the other ship's masts and rigging.

"Take us closer, Nisbett," Amery directed, moving to the quarterdeck railing. "Fire at will!"

The sailors braced their arquebus and muskets on the railing of the deck, firing and then stepping back to let another group fire as they reloaded, a move they had practiced repeatedly.

A second round of cannon fire struck the Spanish ship.

"Raise the skull and crossbones," Amery shouted.

Quinn struck the Spanish colors and sent the pirate flag aloft, seeing an almost immediate change in the manner of the enemy crew. They had been confused when the *Silver Queen* first attacked. Now they were scared. He glanced at Amery and waited for his nod. When it came, Quinn shouted across the intervening waves, "Surrender if you value your lives."

A volley of cannon fire was the other ship's answer, but Amery's tactic of trimming the sails paid off, the *Silver Queen* moving past the Spanish galleon and coming about to rake her again from starboard with both cannons and musket fire. "Grappling hooks," Quinn ordered. "If they won't give us what we want, we'll take it!"

The ropes went flying toward the other ship, catching on the railing and pulling taut. The Spanish crew scrambled to cut the ropes or release the hooks, but to no avail. The pirates were faster and more experienced, drawing the two ships inexorably closer together.

"Surrender or die!" Quinn shouted to the Spaniards one last time as the crew of the *Silver Queen* made ready to board the other ship.

The Spanish captain's reply was lost in the wind, but one of the crew lowered the Spanish flag.

"Secure the ship," Amery ordered his crew as he saw the sign of surrender. "We'll honor their surrender. Seaton," he added, calling the seaman over, "fetch Mr. Watson. The Spanish crew suffered more than we did. They may need his services."

"Aye, Cap'n," Seaton replied, hurrying belowdecks to the surgery where Gavin waited on tenterhooks for news of the battle.

"Is it over?" he asked as soon as Seaton walked in.

"Aye, sir," Seaton assured the doctor. "The Spaniards surrendered afore we even boarded them, so there's nobody as needs yer help on our ship, sir, but the cap'n, being the gentlemanly sort, said ye'd want t'check with the scurvy dogs and see if any o' them was hurt bad enough to need ye."

Gavin wanted no such thing, but he saw no point in berating the sailor for something Amery had said. He would have words with his lover later, but for now he needed to see for himself that Amery was alive and well. He led Seaton back onto the main deck, his eyes drinking in the sight of Amery in all his glory directing the securing of the Spanish ship from his place atop the quarterdeck. When Cullen reported that all was secure, Amery descended to Gavin's side. "Shall we go inspect our prize?"

Gavin nodded. "Where's Quinn?"

"Already aboard," Amery replied. "He insisted on going over with the first wave of crew to keep order if necessary."

"Let's go see what we've captured," Gavin agreed, "but don't expect me to do anything but put a sword through any of the bastards if they make so much as one false move. I have no compassion for any of them."

Amery didn't point out that the men who'd captured and abused Gavin and Quinn were all sleeping in watery graves. Gavin knew it was well as Amery did, but that didn't seem to matter to the surgeon. Anyone from Spain was Gavin's enemy.

They leapt from the *Silver Queen* onto the deck of the Spanish vessel, welcomed with a rousing shout by the crew of the *Silver Queen*. Quinn met them a moment later, the crew parting to let the quartermaster pass. "The crew is secured in their quarters until you decide where you want them, and the ship is ready for your inspection," he reported with a smile.

Amery returned it, clapping a companionable arm around Quinn's shoulders. "Let's see what treasures she has in her hold."

Together, the three of them descended past the gun decks to the cargo holds, their eyes growing wide as they opened chests and barrels to find every one full of gold and jewels. "Even with the cut the company takes, we're about to be rich men," Gavin commented softly.

Amery nodded his agreement. "We'll transfer half the treasure to the *Silver Queen* because her holds aren't as heavily laden. Have Gallagher and Peele take anything they need from the ship's supplies as well, although we'll have to leave enough for the men who stay aboard to sail her into port."

"I'll see to it immediately," Quinn replied. "The sooner we're under way, the happier I'll be."

"We can also restock on Providence Island," Gavin reminded them. "All we really need to do is make sure she's seaworthy."

"Cullen already has Jennings repairing the hull and others aloft checking the riggings," Quinn reported. "The cover of night will protect us somewhat from anyone else who might be seeking treasure, and we'll be under sail before morning."

"Pick the men you want as your crew," Amery directed. "She's a bigger ship, a heavier one."

"I was thinking about making Nisbett acting quartermaster," Quinn commented. "He's done well as second mate and this will give him some more experience."

"Good idea," Amery agreed. "Keep Jennings and Farnham aboard as well in case you need more repairs."

"Thank you," Quinn said. "We have no real idea what this ship's capable of when she isn't so low in the water she can barely maneuver. It will be an interesting voyage to Providence Island."

"You're up for it," Amery assured his friend. "You may even find you like the feel of command."

Quinn shook his head emphatically. "Not me! I can get her to port, not to worry, but I've no interest in captaining a vessel permanently. I don't have the head for strategy."

Amery thought Quinn was selling himself short, but he had yet to win that argument with the other man, and truth be told, he had no interest in losing Quinn as his quartermaster, so he never argued too hard. Only once had he considered sending Quinn away, when he caught Quinn and Gavin together during a time when he and Gavin were estranged, but the familiarity of years had outweighed his anger since he was as much to blame for their argument as Gavin was. Quinn had taken advantage of the situation, but he had not created it. "Let's start the transfer," he said instead.

Quinn barked out orders for the crew to report to the hold, and he and Amery selected barrels and chests to be moved, taking care to keep the remaining cargo balanced in the hold.

"Check all the remaining chests," Amery told Seaton and Clay. "Make sure none of them contain anything that could be used as a weapon. We'll lock the Spanish crew down here and be done with them."

"And if they try t'take some o' the gold?" Clay worried aloud.

Amery, Quinn, and Gavin all laughed. "It's a little hard to hide treasure on your person when you're wearing naught but your skin," Amery replied. "It's warm enough and the hold's dry enough that they can survive a few days down here without their clothes. We'll let them dress again before we bring them up on deck in Providence Island, supervised of course. The treasure is all ours."

"It should be more than enough to pay off the initial cost of outfitting the ship as well," Quinn pointed out, "which means the ships we take from now on will be even more profit for us."

"Indeed," Amery agreed. "Let's see what we can do about getting this lady ready to sail."

Three days later, they sailed victorious into the harbor on Providence Island, the English flag flying proudly on the masts of both ships.

Amery and Quinn went ashore, leaving Gavin and Cullen in charge of the *Silver Queen* and Nisbett of the captured ship while they searched for the offices of the Providence Island Company.

"It's a nice little town they have here," Quinn observed as they passed the log cabins and buildings.

"No more women than anywhere else in the West Indies though," Amery commented as they passed the townspeople on the street.

"As if you cared," Quinn laughed. "You wouldn't want a wife even if one was available."

"True," Amery had to agree. "It's one of the reasons to stay here rather than going back to England where I'd have no choice."

Privately, Quinn prayed Amery would be able to stand by that decision, that the Puritan founders of the company would not force him into making a choice, because losing Amery to the pressures of society would kill Gavin. He hated to think it would come to that. Indeed, he would never voice such doubts because the mere thought seemed disloyal to his friends, but he had seen the security of a place in society lure men into situations they would not have chosen on their own.

They found the company office a few minutes later and met Mr. Thorn, agent of the Earl of Warwick in the West Indies.

"Captain White, it's a pleasure to meet you," the agent said when Amery introduced himself. "Captain Jackson assured me you were a worthy addition to our fleet, but I didn't expect to have the honor quite so soon. What can I do for you?"

"We've brought a galleon into port," Amery replied. "We captured it three days ago, laden with gold and jewels."

"I see Captain Jackson was right," the agent declared. "Let's go out to the ship and tally up your earnings. I imagine your sailors would like to see their share."

"I'm sure they would," Amery agreed. "Will the good people of the town mind them coming ashore to spend some of their gain? My previous ship met with misfortune and some of my men need clothes and other necessities, but they're a rough pirate crew, not the kind decent folk are always comfortable having around."

"They're employees of the Providence Island Company," the agent insisted. "As long as they behave within the bounds of the law, they're welcome on the island. The shopkeepers will care only about the quality of their coin, not of their persons. Your crew will hardly be the first privateers to dock here."

Amery guided the agent back to the *Silver Queen*, tied up at the wharf. The agent walked up the gangplank onto the deck. "You've kept everything in good shape, I see. Do you need supplies?"

"We replenished our stores from the foodstuffs and powder aboard the Spanish galleon," Amery replied. "We're ready to sail again as soon as we unload the gold and give the crew a day's shore leave."

"Well done," the agent praised. "Let's see what we have then."

They went down into the hold and examined the cargo, the agent exclaiming more with every chest and barrel they opened for him.

"And there's this much again, perhaps even a little more, aboard the other ship," Amery said when they'd finished taking an inventory of the treasure. "You'll need to decide what you want us to do with the crew of the captured ship as well."

"We'll release them, of course," the agent assured Amery. "Their only crime is the land of their birth. They can take a ship to a neutral port if they choose or sign on with a good English vessel. Perhaps you might even take a few?"

Amery shook his head. "My matelot has a dislike for Spaniards, and I won't make him suffer the presence of one on our ship."

The agent's eyes widened. "I've heard tales of the pirate contracts, but you're the first I've met who has one."

"Captain Jackson said it wouldn't be a problem," Amery said, drawing himself up to his full height. At his side, Quinn reached reflexively for his sword, not pulling it from its sheath yet, but ready for whatever came.

"It was an observation, not a criticism," the agent insisted, obviously aware of the sudden tension in the hold. "My only interest is in the plunder you bring me."

Quinn didn't know how true that was, but he accepted it because Amery did.

They took Thorn across to the other ship, arranged for the Spanish crew to be sent ashore, and began unloading the chests onto the carts the agent supplied. When everything was arranged to the agent's satisfaction, he returned to the *Silver Queen* with several of the chests full of pieces of eight. "I've brought the crew's portion in gold," Thorn said. "I thought the men would prefer that to English coin, since I know you put in at a variety of ports."

"We've learned to make do with whatever we have over the years," Amery replied, "but they won't say no to gold."

"Very good," the agent said. "Here's an accounting of what you brought to the company and what we've brought back for the crew. I'll leave you to divide the spoils as you see fit. I look forward to seeing you again soon, Captain White."

To Quinn's surprise, the company agent offered his hand, shaking Amery's firmly when Amery offered his in return.

"Let's get the gold into the hands of the men," Amery said to Quinn. "The sooner it's distributed, the sooner we can all replace what we lost on the *Dark Dream*."

Quinn nodded and set about dividing their payment between the men. Even divided by as large a crew as they now had, they each received a generous portion, more than some of them had ever had at any one time in their lives. When Quinn announced the sum each man would receive, a cacophonous cheer went up from the crew.

Cullen and Nisbett organized the men into a file to keep order as Quinn began distributing each man's pay. Amery kept them all on board until everyone had been paid, not wanting anyone to be able to say someone else had received more or less than his fair share.

"Mr. Thorn has said we're welcome in town as long as we conduct ourselves with decorum," Amery announced when Quinn had finished dividing the gold. "We sail on the morning tide. If you aren't on board, you'll be left behind to fend for yourself. Have a good evening, gentlemen."

The privateers let up a raucous shout as they streamed down the gangplank and into the town. Quinn wondered how many of them would end up in the local jail before morning. When the crew was all ashore, Amery turned to the officers. "Cullen, you outrank Nisbett so you'll go ashore first, but make sure you're back in time for Nisbett to have some shore leave as well."

"Aye, sir," both men replied.

"Mr. Davies, Mr. Watson, shall we go ashore?"

Quinn laughed as he put his own share of the gold in his pouch. He had some shopping to do.

Chapter 7

A WEEK later, Quinn had not entirely gotten over the novelty of having money in his new sea chest, even after having replaced everything he lost aboard the *Dark Dream* and more. He wasn't sure he'd ever owned a different shirt for each day of the week before or more than one pair of boots. He certainly had never had a brush and comb set of the same quality as the set that now graced the drawer beneath his bunk. He had a new oilskin and three coats—two for wearing on the ship and one for when he went ashore as well as several new pairs of hose and some linen drawers, a luxury he'd never allowed himself before.

The rest of the crew seemed to be feeling the same euphoria. Most of them had made it back aboard at nightfall, Providence Island not boasting the number of taverns and whorehouses available in Tortuga. A few of them had straggled back just before dawn, having obviously found rum or ale somewhere to judge by their inebriation. A few had not returned at all, for reasons Quinn could only guess at. Perhaps they'd decided the gold they'd earned was enough for them. Perhaps they'd gotten so drunk they didn't wake up in time. Perhaps they'd run afoul of the local law and ended up in jail. The reasons ultimately didn't matter. They weren't aboard when Amery ordered the crew to set sail, and so their names were struck from the Articles of Agreement.

Amery had ordered them to head once again toward Puerto Rico, since their first prize along those shipping lanes had proven so lucrative. Flush with success, the crew was raring to take a second prize. Quinn almost felt sorry for whatever ship crossed their bow next.

Almost.

"Sail ho! Bearing Spanish colors!"

"All hands to stations!" Quinn shouted, the cry from the crow's nest bringing him out of his thoughts. "Seaton, fetch the captain!"

"Aye, sir," Seaton replied, running toward the stern and the captain's quarters.

"Where's the sail?" Quinn called up to the lookout.

"Four points to starboard," Clay called back down. "She's not as heavy as the last one, but she's a cargo vessel for sure, sir."

Quinn peered through the spyglass in the indicated direction, finding the ship. She wasn't a galleon, but a barca longa, a ship far too often used by slavers for Quinn's peace of mind. Whether this one was simply a cargo vessel or a slaver, he couldn't tell, but he had no intention of letting them get away without finding out.

"What do we have?" Amery asked, joining Quinn on the quarterdeck.

"A barca longa flying Spanish colors," Quinn replied, his voice tight. "She isn't heavy like the galleon was."

Amery's face reflected Quinn's determination. "We can still outsail her, but I suspect we'll have a true fight on our hands this time."

"I suspect you're right," Quinn agreed, concerned about what they would find when they captured the vessel. A cargo ship full of gold or supplies for a colony would be sitting lower in the water. Human cargo didn't weigh as much. The thought turned his stomach.

"I'll take the helm," Amery decided. "Get the gunners ready. I doubt she'll be as ill-prepared to counter us as the last ship was. And send Jennings and Farnham into the hold."

"What about Gavin?"

"I think the less Gavin knows right now, the better," Amery said softly. Quinn winced, but Amery was the one who would have to live with the consequences of that decision so Quinn let it go.

The crew scrambled into action, taking their stations, manning the cannons, and loading their muskets for battle. They strapped on swords and knives and any other manner of weapon they could find. Amery's position at the helm proclaimed the probable challenge of the battle to come to the men as clearly as if they had overheard his conversation with Quinn.

It didn't take long before Gavin appeared on deck. "What are we facing?" he asked Quinn.

"A Spanish barca longa," Quinn replied honestly, not about to lie to Gavin even if Amery would have preferred the surgeon remain in the dark. "Amery's at the helm."

Gavin's face tightened. "I'll speak to the captain then," he said, understanding Quinn's silent message. Quinn winced as Gavin marched toward the quarterdeck and the man who could infuriate him faster than anyone else on earth.

"Were you planning on warning me we were about to fight?" Gavin demanded when he reached Amery's side.

"Of course," Amery replied calmly, his eyes never leaving the point on the horizon where they'd spotted the barca longa, "but we aren't facing them yet. I intended to come tell you before we engaged them."

"Damn it, Amery," Gavin muttered. "You can't keep protecting me from things. It doesn't help me, and it doesn't change the outcome."

Amery knew that, but he couldn't seem to help himself. He hated the tension he could see now in Gavin's shoulders, not merely the tension of going into battle but of facing his past. He wanted to spirit his lover below, into their cabin and their bed to distract him from the upcoming battle as they'd done before the previous one, but they were already closing on the barca longa, and he was at the helm. He could not leave his post now, even for Gavin.

"You can take it out of my hide once the battle's over," Amery offered.

"Don't think I won't, Amery White!" Gavin muttered, stalking back toward the surgery.

He wouldn't. He never did if a battle interrupted their argument because he was too relieved to see Amery unscathed at the end of it to remember what they'd been arguing about before. Amery smiled fondly at Gavin's retreating back before turning his attention back to the ship in front of them. Through the spyglass, he could see the crew of the barca longa already on deck, armed as heavily as he and his crew. They hadn't opened the gun ports yet, but he could see them the length of the ship and the activity on deck left with him no illusions about the activity below deck.

"Mr. Davies, Cullen! Tell the men to be prepared to board. This one's going to fight."

Amery's mind raced as he considered the possible turns the upcoming battle could take. Barca longas were nearly as agile as the *Silver Queen*, so they wouldn't necessarily have the tactical advantage they'd had with their first prize, but they didn't require as large a crew—an advantage when it came to carrying fewer supplies and more cargo on a long voyage, and that gave Amery hope that with twice the usual number of sailors on his own vessel, they could overwhelm the other ship's crew once they could get close enough to board. A heavier vessel, the *Silver Queen* also carried bigger guns than most of the lighter ships.

The helmsman of the Spanish ship seemed to have no intention of letting them get that close, though, sailing with a skill that matched Amery's own, making Amery even more determined to take the prize. He refused to let a Spaniard outsail him. "More speed," he shouted down to Quinn who passed the appropriate orders on to the men in the riggings. They adjusted the sails, catching the wind with greater efficiency.

Amery studied the fleeing ship, trying to learn and predict the helmsman's pattern. Every helmsman, captain and sailor alike, had one, the set of tricks he relied on to outwit his enemies. If Amery could discern his adversary's methods, he would know how best to counter them and close the distance enough for the *Silver Queen*'s cannons to come into play. Eventually, he found the pattern—and the weakness—and they approached the other ship. "Prepare to fire!"

Quinn and Cullen echoed his shout, with Gallagher repeating it on the gun deck below. The gun ports lifted, the culverns slid into place, and every man on the ship braced for action.

Gavin heard the orders and met Peele's eyes, the cook having once again agreed to serve as his assistant. He hadn't needed any help during their first battle, but he didn't dare believe they'd be as lucky a second time.

The guns roared to life, the deafening detonations echoing through the entire ship. Gavin winced slightly, finding it all too easy to visualize the scene abovedeck. He might spend battles in the surgery now, but he'd fought in his share before the surgeon on their first pirate ship had taken him on as an apprentice. He heard a volley of cannon fire from the Spanish ship and braced for impact. Amery, he knew, would shoot at the riggings and above the waterline so they could capture the ship, but their intended prize wouldn't have the same concerns, as content to sink them as to fight them off. The roar grew constant, each group of gunners reloading and firing at different speeds. The cabin rolled as Amery turned aggressively, hopefully taking the ship out of broadside range, but Gavin couldn't tell for sure. He cursed under his breath, wondering as he always did if it would be easier on deck where he could at least see what was happening. The stern chasers roared to life then, giving him an idea where the barca longa was. "If you ruin our new cabin, Amery White, so help me God...." Gavin muttered. The *Silver Queen* turned again, nearly knocking Peele off his feet, and then he had a different reason to curse because the door opened and two sailors carried in a third man, bleeding profusely.

Gavin fell into a routine, bandaging, suturing, cleaning wounds and covering them in plasters. He helped those he could and murmured prayers for those he couldn't, cursing regularly the limits of his abilities. When the noise above his head finally ceased and the flow of bodies in need of his assistance slowed, he looked around the surgery in dismay. Ten dead, another ten who wouldn't survive despite his best efforts, and half the crew, it seemed, with injuries of some kind. Those he could help, if he could keep the gangrene from setting in. He thanked God he hadn't needed to amputate any limbs this time. He could do it, indeed had on many occasions, but it was the one part of his job he hated most of all.

Wiping the blood from his hands as best he could, Gavin gave Peele directions for the care of those still suffering—grog for those in mild pain, some of their precious opiates for those whose injuries were more serious—and went onto deck to seek out his lover. Amery and Quinn hadn't made it into the surgery during the battle, but that didn't mean they were unscathed. He wouldn't be able to relax until he'd seen for himself that they were unharmed.

Amery stood exactly where Gavin had last seen him, his hand on the steering rod, his face grim as he surveyed the damage to the *Silver Queen* and to the vessel they'd captured. "Is it over?" Gavin asked, joining him.

"All but the mopping up," Amery replied. "Quinn is securing the other ship now. How many did we lose?"

"Ten for certain," Gavin mourned, "and another ten I've tried to help, but I don't expect any of them to pull through."

Amery nodded. "We'll lay them to rest when everything is settled on the Spanish vessel."

"Four of them were from the *Dark Dream*," Gavin confided softly.

"Who?" Amery's voice revealed the depth of his pain, though his face did not change expression.

"Abney, Dalton, Watkins, and Kincade."

"Did any of them have family?"

"Not that I was ever aware of," Gavin replied, trying to remember every scrap of conversation he'd overheard during the past five years. "I can ask around."

"Ask around for all the deceased. If we can find a family, they'll get the men's portion of this treasure and whatever the men had left from the first prize," Amery declared.

It was exactly the kind of generosity Amery was known for, one of the myriad reasons Gavin loved him to distraction, even when he was annoyed at him. "I'll see what I can learn," Gavin promised. "How bad is the damage?"

"Worse than the last time, but nothing we can't fix," Amery assured Gavin. "The shots we took were all well above the water line. They were flying the Spanish flag, but they fought like pirates who wanted to capture a prize."

Chapter 8

"MR. DAVIES, come quickly!"

Quinn looked up from where he was supervising the disarming of the Spanish crew. "Finish up here," he told Cullen. "I'll see what Nisbett needs."

"Aye, sir," Cullen said, his eyes alight with an unholy glee as he manhandled the enemy crew roughly into position.

"What is it, Nisbett?" Quinn asked, crossing to where the second mate stood at the entrance to the hold.

"There are… there are people down there, sir," Nisbett whispered.

"I feared as much," Quinn replied in comparable tone. "We won't be getting any prize but the ship from this one, but we'll have the pleasure of setting them free. Let's see if we can find the keys. If not, we'll have to see if Farnham has anything among his tools that will break the manacles."

"You!" Quinn said, pointing to the Spaniard who had marshaled the crew after the captain had fallen. "Where are the keys to free the slaves?"

"*No comprende ingles,*" the man replied, shaking his head.

"In drawer in captain's *cabana,*" a heavily accented voice replied.

Quinn didn't wait for more detail than that, heading toward the stern and the cabin in question. He dug through the chest until he found the key, returning to the main deck and gesturing for Nisbett to open the hold. "Let's get these people out."

They went carefully down into the stinking hold, even more shocked when they realized the slaves were Europeans. "What the hell is this?" Quinn muttered as he approached the first group. "We're the crew of the *Silver Queen*. We're going to get you out of here."

"Start behind the ladder," the man closest to Quinn told him. "That's where they keep the women."

Quinn's face hardened even more. "God's mercy!" he cursed under his breath, rounding the steps to see a small group of women huddled together. Their tattered dresses barely covered their skin, and he recognized all too easily the haunted look in their eyes. They were afraid, not in the abstract, but because they had been hurt and badly. "Somebody get Mr. Watson and the captain!" he shouted up to the crew. "And bring me some blankets. Clean ones!"

Turning back to the women, he approached them slowly. "Do any of you speak English?" he asked.

"A few of us do," one woman replied.

"If I undo your manacles, will you release the others?" Quinn asked. "I promise you're safe now. No one will hurt you again."

The woman nodded, tears beginning to fill her eyes as she held out her hands for Quinn to release her.

"What is it, Mr. Davies?" Amery asked, coming down into the hold.

"Not slaves, but Europeans and women," Quinn reported, handing the woman the key and backing away slightly. "None of them look in good health."

Amery frowned, mind racing as he worked out the logistics of this unexpected development. "All right. Release them all and send the men up first. Let us get things set to rights on both ships, and then I'll talk to the men about the women. We'll put them in the officers' quarters on the *Silver Queen* until we can get back to Providence Island. They'll probably feel safer there than in the officers' quarters here."

"Probably," Quinn agreed with a shudder, remembering all too well what it felt like to be dragged down the passage to the captain's quarters, knowing what lay in wait at his destination.

"Lock the Spanish crew down here," Amery added as he started back up to the main deck. "Let them see what it feels like to be in chains for a few days."

"The women are all free."

Quinn turned to see the woman he'd spoken to before offering him the key back.

"What will happen to us?" she asked.

"We'll take you to Providence Island," Quinn assured her. "It's an English colony. From there, it's up to each of you."

"Will we be safe until then?"

"Captain White won't let anything happen to any of you," Quinn promised. "He'll hang any of his crew who touch you without your consent."

"Will he hang the bastards on this crew?" another woman asked, joining the first.

"He doesn't have that authority," Quinn apologized. "Our crew signed Articles of Agreement pledging to abide by certain rules, but they apply only to us. We can't impose them on another crew. I'm sorry. Why don't you all wait where you are until we can get you some blankets to preserve your modesty? I'm going to release the men now."

"The Lord bless you all," the first woman said. "They were going to sell us as slaves."

Quinn already knew that, but hearing it confirmed only increased his anger. He couldn't kill the slavers outright, but he could make their lives hell for the time it took to get back to Providence Island. Returning to where the men were chained, he began releasing them as well. "How did you come to be here?" he asked as he unlocked their manacles.

"They might have flown a Spanish flag, but they weren't engaged in honest commerce," one of the men replied. "They captured us a few at a time from ships they attacked. They'd keep the sailors they thought they could sell as slaves and kill the rest before they sank the ship. I speak a little Spanish, and I overheard them saying they had their full capacity and were heading back to Spain, and from there on to the Barbary Coast where they could sell us to the Moors."

"And the women?" Quinn asked. "They certainly aren't sailors."

"They were indentured servants for the most part," the man replied, "passengers on the ships that were captured."

Quinn frowned. "All right. Everyone go up on deck. Captain White will see to your berths until we can get back to Providence Island."

The men trooped up the ladder, leaving only Quinn and the women in the hold. A moment later, Clay came scurrying down, arms laden with blankets. "Cap'n White said there were women down here," he said, sounding horrified.

"Back there." Quinn indicated with a wave of his hand.

"Oh, the poor things!"

Quinn let Clay go back to them and work his charm on them. For all that Quinn had seen him in battle, once the fight was over, Clay was probably the gentlest man on the crew, and the women seemed to sense that in his respectful demeanor as he distributed the blankets to them. Quinn made a mental note to suggest that Amery let Clay deal with the women as much as possible until they could put them ashore. Seeing everything under control there, he went back onto deck.

Amery had divided the freed slaves into two groups, half to move onto the *Silver Queen*, the other half to stay on the slave ship in the crew's quarters so no one would have to return to the hold for the duration of the voyage. Given the number of men they'd lost during battle, they could use the extra hands on both ships. That taken care of, he had Cullen summon the crew of the *Silver Queen*.

"It's bad enough, them taking honest sailors as slaves," Amery said to his men, "but they took women as well. Not many, but even one is too many. I'd kill them all if I could, but they'll face the Lord's judgment in their own time."

Quinn watched the reactions among the crew, the fury on the men's faces as they listened to what Amery had to say. He wondered for a moment if they would direct that wrath at the Spanish sailors still tied behind them, but Amery didn't give them the chance, going on with his instructions.

"Our job is to make sure the poor lasses aren't bothered again before we get to Providence Island. They'll be sharing the officers' quarters among themselves, so the officers who stay on the *Silver Queen* rather than coming onto this ship with Mr. Davies will have to move to the crew quarters for a few days, and no man but Mr. Watson and myself are to come into the aftcastle while they're aboard. Mr. Peele, you'll have to cook as usual, but Mr. Watson and myself will bring the food for the ladies up to the officers' quarters. I won't have them frightened that someone will abuse them while they're aboard my ship."

"Clay, you can bring them up now," Quinn called down into the hold. "We'll get them settled in their temporary homes."

"Aye, sir," Clay called back up. Quinn knelt and stretched his hand down to help the women up onto deck one at a time. When the last one had exited, he turned and had to smile as the other officers stood guard at the rails of each ship, helping the women to cross from one vessel to the other. Gavin waited on the other deck to escort them all to their new quarters. Women were a rarity in the West Indies, and every man on the ship remembered his own mother or sisters as he looked at the poor women. They would be treated as well as any queen while they were aboard the *Silver Queen*.

With a nod, he turned his attention back to the Spanish sailors. "Get them below decks," he ordered his men, "and into irons. I don't want to look at their filthy faces again."

"*Signore*," the same sailor who'd told Quinn where to find the key cried as Quinn's men moved to follow his orders. "They force me on boat also, only they no sell me."

"Bring that one here," Quinn said. "Take the others below."

Nisbett separated the young man from the rest of the crew, though he did not undo the ropes that bound his hands.

"Where are you from?" Quinn asked.

"Venezia," the young man replied. "I sail with Portuguese crew. They take our ship. They kill or sell others, but they make me stay 'ere."

Quinn suspected the young man was not telling him the whole story, but he nodded and untied his wrists. "The captain needs a cabin boy," he declared. "You can start there and work your way up."

"I no be any man 'ore," the sailor spat.

Quinn threw his head back and laughed. "You have spirit. That's good. You don't have to worry about Captain White bothering you. He has a lover already, and Mr. Watson doesn't share." *Even with me.* "What's your name, boy?"

"Eliodoro, and I no boy. I *diciannove.*"

"Nineteen?" Quinn guessed. "You're practically an old man. You'll have to stay on this ship until we reach Providence Island since Captain White won't allow any men into the aftcastle while the women are on the *Silver Queen.* You can tend my cabin until then."

"*Bastardo,*" Eliodoro muttered as Quinn's attention shifted back to the Spaniards and the rest of his crew. The young Venetian wanted to stomp away in disgust, but he had learned the lessons of his captors well. He absolutely did not want to end up in the hold with the others, and he'd heard the other captain, the golden blond one, give the orders to release the captives and to respect and protect the women. He hoped that meant the one on this ship, the one with the dirty blond hair and eyes the color of the sky, would abide by the same policy in his respect. If not, he could always leave the ship with the rest of the released captives. He would not be abused again.

The days it took the two ships to reach Providence Island were an education for Eliodoro. The crew from the *Silver Queen* worked hard but seemed to have no fear of the acting captain, *Signor* Davies. They called him "sir," but they didn't act cowed. From the oldest to the youngest, a twelve-year old boy, they spoke their minds freely and expected their word to carry weight. Even more interesting, *Signor* Davies listened. Eliodoro tried to imagine the unlamented *Capitano* Gomez giving any credence to the opinion of his crew and failed utterly.

When they reached Providence Island, and the freed captives and Spanish crew were sent ashore, Eliodoro watched the looks his former crewmates gave him and made his decision.

The *Silver Queen* was now his home.

Chapter 9

"SAIL ho!"

Quinn grabbed the spyglass and glanced up at the lookout to see the indicated direction. He peered that way, praying that this time, it would be a ship they could take. In the month since they rescued the captive sailors from the slavers, they hadn't sighted a single ship they could attack under their letter of marque or without violating the tenets of their conscience. They had seen other English ships, French ships, pirate vessels, and even one Portuguese flag, but no Spanish ones, and the men were growing restless. They received some prize money for the barca longa itself, but nothing compared to their first take. If this ship turned out to be another untouchable one, Quinn would recommend they make for Tortuga. The men would be more focused after a few days' shore leave.

Finding the ship, Quinn kept it in sight until he could make out the flag. Another pirate ship.

"She's not for us, lads," Quinn announced to the men who had gathered at the lookout's shout, including the Venetian. Eliodoro had proven his abilities as a cabin boy, keeping Amery's quarters spotless, and as a sailor, volunteering for even the most menial tasks and performing them with experienced ease, making Quinn wonder how long the young man had sailed with the Portuguese ship before being captured by the Spaniards. For no reason he could name, he had assumed the young man was new to the profession, but Eliodoro had more than proven him wrong. Quinn tried to ignore his awareness of the younger man, but everything about him seemed to demand Quinn's attention, from his darkly tanned, nearly hairless skin to his dark hair and exotic eyes and his sensual voice, his thick accent making it impossible for Quinn to confuse the sound with any other sailor. He'd watched Eliodoro over the past month, though, becoming familiar with the nuances of his body language. Eliodoro only relaxed with the youngest members of the crew, the ones who couldn't possibly hurt him. It saddened Quinn to recognize those signs so easily. He hoped Eliodoro would find a friend or several among the crew. It had made all the difference in his own youth. "She's flying the skull and crossbones."

Disappointment showed on the men's faces along with a fair degree of disgruntlement. It was definitely time to head for Tortuga. He'd talk to Amery when he finished his watch.

ELIODORO loitered in the passageway leading to the officers' quarters, hoping the quartermaster would return to his cabin soon. He had gotten complacent, believing *Signor* Davies when he said no one would abuse him aboard the *Silver Queen*. No one had approached him yet, but he knew one of the younger lads hadn't been so lucky. Despite all the insistence on everyone signing the Articles of Agreement, including Eliodoro and all the freed sailors who had chosen to stay, Dickerson had been hurt. Eliodoro didn't know who his assailant was, but he recognized the signs, the odd way the boy walked, the way his eyes darted right and left constantly. Someone had hurt him, and he hadn't gone running to the captain. That was his choice, but Eliodoro wasn't going to let it happen to him, even if he had to seduce the quartermaster to ensure his own protection. He'd rather be one man's whore willingly than be raped by God knew how many sailors.

"'Ello, *signore*," he purred when the quartermaster entered the passageway. He pushed away from the wall and approached *Signor* Davies, standing far closer to the man than he usually did. At least he could give himself to an attractive man this time, perhaps even a kind one if the interactions he had seen on the ship were any indication.

"Eliodoro," Quinn said with a nod, not sure what to make of the look on the lad's face or the way he was standing. If they'd been on the streets of Tortuga, he would have said the boy was about to proposition him, but Eliodoro had barely spoken two words to him that didn't involve ship's business.

"You 'ave difficult day," Eliodoro continued, sliding his hand down the quartermaster's arm. He had learned aboard the slaver the niceties that soothed the savage beast, sometimes anyway.

Eyes widening, Quinn stiffened, trying to ignore the spark that raised goose flesh on his skin. "No different than any other day," he demurred, pulling away gently.

"I 'elp you," Eliodoro offered, "relax."

The images that assailed Quinn were vivid and arousing and entirely inappropriate given their relative positions on the ship. He had promised Eliodoro that no one would make him a whore aboard the *Silver Queen*. Quinn had no intention of being the one to break that promise. "That isn't necessary. I'll be fine."

"'Is no good be alone," Eliodoro countered, surprised to meet such resistance. He had grown used to men desiring his beauty, however much he had hated the results of such desire. To be rejected now, when he offered himself, was an unexpected blow to his pride.

"You told me you'd be no man's whore," Quinn reminded him, "so why are you approaching me now?"

"You tell me no one abuse me either," Eliodoro retorted.

"Who abused you?" Quinn demanded immediately.

"No one yet," Eliodoro admitted, "but someone 'urt Dickerson, and no one dare 'urt me if I with you."

Quinn's face tightened. "Find Dickerson and take him to the surgery," the quartermaster ordered. "I will find Mr. Watson and meet you there."

Ten minutes later, Quinn walked with Gavin into the surgery. Dickerson sat on the table, shoulders hunched, Eliodoro standing next to him, his own posture proclaiming his defensiveness. "I'll leave you to check Dickerson," Quinn told Gavin softly. "I want to talk to Eliodoro. We'll be in my cabin if you need me."

Eliodoro's eyes widened. Surely the quartermaster wouldn't make such an offer to the surgeon if he intended anything other than talking with Eliodoro. Then again, that had never stopped the officers on the slaver.

Taking Eliodoro's arm firmly, Quinn propelled him down the passageway and into his own quarters. "Now, tell me everything Dickerson said about what happened."

"'E said *niente, euh*, nothing," Eliodoro insisted, "but 'e walk like 'e 'urt. Is no first time I see."

"From captives on the slaver?" Quinn postulated, remembering all too well that awkward gait that resulted from being raped.

"They use women and sometimes men," Eliodoro agreed, relieved to have an explanation that was both true and misleading.

"Did you see anyone sniffing around him?" Quinn questioned. "Or anyone he particularly avoided?"

Eliodoro shook his head. "*Spiacente*," he apologized. "I no know."

"We'll find out who it was," Quinn assured him, "and he'll pay the price. Captain White won't tolerate that kind of behavior on his ship. Dickerson will be safe, and so will you."

FOR the first time since his rescue from the slavers five years ago, Gavin dreaded walking into the cabin he shared with Amery, not because of what lay behind the door but because of what he brought with him and all the memories it evoked. He needed to be strong, to defend the young man Quinn had brought to him rather than give into the dark morass of his own pain and shame. Taking a deep breath, Gavin walked into the cabin and into Amery's arms. He simply stood there for a few moments, drawing strength from the strong arms and solid body. Having Amery close settled his fears.

"We have a problem," he mumbled against Amery's neck.

"One that will be solved by us getting naked, I hope?" Amery quipped.

"I wish," Gavin sighed, "but I'm afraid it's the kind that will keep us from bed for some time."

Amery groaned. "Do I need to get Quinn?"

Quinn would understand both what the boy felt and why Gavin was so shaken up, but Gavin would feel self-conscious about leaning on Amery with Quinn there, and he needed that support for a little while longer. It wasn't as if Quinn didn't already know anyway.

"Not yet."

When Gavin did not continue, Amery frowned and tipped his lover's chin up so their eyes met. "What is it, Gavin?" Amery prompted. "Whatever it is, you know you can tell me."

I can never tell you I was a whore, Gavin thought, heart clenching at the bone-deep shame and overwhelming helplessness that had driven him to offer sexual favors to the slavers who had taken him and Quinn rather than suffering another rape. Quinn insisted Gavin had been forced by the circumstances even if he hadn't fought the intrusive hands and demanding cocks, but Gavin knew Amery wouldn't see it that way.

"Someone raped young Dickerson," Gavin said when he could work up the courage to speak. "He wouldn't tell me if it was once or multiple times, nor would he give me a name, but he was torn and bleeding badly when I saw him."

Amery's entire body tensed beneath Gavin's hands. "He'll tell me, and I'll see the whoreson hang."

"Please, Amery," Gavin begged. "Tread lightly with him. Remember what it was like when we were boys and at the mercy of the older sailors."

"He shouldn't have to be at anyone's mercy," Amery insisted.

"No, he shouldn't, and he isn't because you will make an example of the blackguard," Gavin reminded Amery, "but it doesn't make the boy less scared now. He's young, he's new to our crew, and I suspect he became a pirate to escape an abusive master. Hang the man who raped him, but go gently with the boy."

"I won't yell at him," Amery conceded, the best he could promise with anger bubbling inside him. He had sworn something like this would never happen on his ship. To be foresworn now, a mere two months after he'd taken command of his new ship, galled him. A boy had suffered, and he hadn't been able to stop it. "Fetch the lad and Quinn. We'll have the truth out of him and deal with his aggressor."

Gavin nodded and left Amery alone with his dark thoughts.

"I haven't forgotten everything about our younger days," Amery murmured to the empty room. He hadn't been raped as Gavin was before they deserted and joined their first pirate crew, but he remembered living in fear that he would be next. One of the men had caught him in the hold as he went about his tasks, cornering him and grabbing his cock as he whispered obscenities in Amery's ear. Another sailor had interrupted them before Amery's attacker could make good on his lewd promises, and they had put into port the next day. Quinn, Gavin, and he had swum ashore and never looked back.

He couldn't change the past for himself, for Quinn and Gavin, or for the boy, but he could make sure the lad and the crew realized how serious he was about this never happening again. Quinn's entrance into the cabin disrupted his black thoughts.

"We may have to hang a man tonight," Amery told Quinn. "Gavin's gone to fetch Dickerson to see if he'll name his attacker."

"I don't know who did it, but Eliodoro told me what happened," Quinn recounted. "He hasn't noticed anyone sniffing around Dickerson, but that only means the whoreson's smart enough to protect himself. He must have some hold over Dickerson to think the boy wouldn't simply tell us."

"Gavin never told anyone but us."

"Gavin didn't serve on a ship where anyone cared," Quinn reminded Amery starkly. "You remember as well as I do what happened when we tried to complain in his defense."

"It ends tonight," Amery declared, shuddering at the memory of the vicious caning he and Quinn had received for insubordination when they had tried to protect Gavin. "I won't have a rapist on my ship. I won't have Gavin living in fear."

A knock on the door interrupted them before Amery could say more.

"Come," Amery barked, unable to the anger out of his voice.

As Gavin opened the door, Amery and Quinn heard the boy pipe up. "Really, Mr. Watson, there's no reason to trouble the cap'n when he's already in a bad mood."

"I'm in a bad mood because someone dared to hurt one of my crew," Amery replied, gentling his voice through force of will alone. "I'm sorry you didn't feel you could come tell me yourself."

"I'm just a nobody," Dickerson demurred. "Why would anyone care what happens to me?"

"This is your first time with a pirate crew, isn't it?" Quinn asked before Amery could reply. Amery's voice was too hard, too angry to cajole the information they needed out of the lad. If he could temper that with a little kindness, he hoped Dickerson would finally talk to them.

"Yes, sir."

"Let me tell you something about pirates. Every man on this ship is running from some bad experience. A cruel master on land. A cruel captain at sea. No one becomes a pirate without a reason, and no pirate ever forgets his, no matter what he says. We're all nobodies, Dickerson, even Captain White and Mr. Watson and me," Quinn assured the boy. "Every man on the *Silver Queen* agreed to abide by the Articles of the ship. Every one. And it's the responsibility of the three of us in this room to enforce those Articles. Do you remember the last one?"

Dickerson shook his head.

"In prettier words, it said I'd hang any man guilty of rape aboard this ship," Amery declared. "Mr. Watson tells me you were abused. Name the man, and he'll never trouble another soul."

"But that would make me a murderer!" Dickerson protested.

Gavin shook his head. "You didn't ask him to hurt you. Telling us who did doesn't make you anything but avenged. And it keeps him from hurting anyone else the way you were hurt."

"Lewes," Dickerson said, his voice so soft the others could barely hear him.

"Clap him in irons, Mr. Davies, and summon the crew. I'll see justice done, but I want no question later about why or how," Amery ordered.

"With pleasure," Quinn growled, stalking out of the cabin and into the hold where they kept manacles they could use to subdue unruly sailors from captured vessels. Quinn had never expected to use them on his own crew, but Lewes had given them no choice. He didn't know the man well, Lewes having signed on when they docked in Providence Island to release the crew of the slaver and the rescued sailors. Since then, the demands of overseeing such a large crew had kept him from getting to know all the new sailors as well as he knew those who had sailed on the *Dark Dream*. Perhaps if he had, this situation could have been avoided.

The off-duty crew looked up in surprise when he marched into their quarters, every one of them snapping to attention when he shouted Lewes's name.

"Is there a problem, Quartermaster?" Lewes asked, rolling indolently from his hammock and coming to stand before Quinn.

"There is indeed," Quinn replied, slapping the irons on the man before he could protest. He fought the moment they closed around his wrists, though. "All hands on deck," Quinn ordered as he forcibly marched Lewes up the stairs.

Amery stood there already, Gavin at his side. Usually the surgeon stayed one step behind Amery, choosing not to take advantage of his position as Amery's matelot, but now they stood shoulder to shoulder, a protective wall between Dickerson and his abuser.

"What's all this about?" Lewes shouted when Quinn threw him to his knees and strode to Amery's other side, an unbreakable triumvirate of authority.

Amery waited until he was sure every crew member was accounted for before producing the Articles of Agreement. He read them aloud from the beginning, pausing after each clause. When he was finished, he addressed the crew. "Were those in truth what you signed before joining the *Silver Queen?*"

The crew replied with a resounding "Aye, Cap'n."

"Lewes, is this your signature on the Articles?" Amery continued.

"Ye know it is," Lewes huffed.

"Then perhaps you'd like to explain to me and to the crew why you didn't abide by them?" Amery demanded, grabbing Lewes by his hair and jerking his head back. "I know for a fact there are several men aboard who enjoy the company of other men and aren't currently spoken for, so why in God's name would you force yourself on Dickerson?"

"Is that the story he's tellin'?" Lewes demanded. "The little sneak. He were willin', no matter what he says now."

Gavin backhanded the man before Quinn or Amery could stop him. "If he was so willing, why was he still bleeding hours later?"

"I weren't willing," Dickerson piped up from behind Quinn and Amery. "Not the first time and not this morning either. And I told you I weren't willing. You didn't listen."

The roar of outrage from the crew gave their opinion of the situation so clearly Amery did not even bother to ask what they thought the man's sentence should be. He suspected they wouldn't stop at hanging him.

"*If at any time you meet with a prudent woman, that man that offers to meddle with her, without her consent, shall suffer present death. The same shall be true of any man who meddles with another man without his consent,*" Amery repeated. "Make your peace with the Lord, Lewes. You'll not be making peace with us. You're sentenced to hang at sunset."

Chapter 10

"YOU'D take the word of a boy and a two-bit whore over that of a grown man and honest sailor?" Lewes protested.

"Be glad I already sentenced you," Amery said in a voice so cold it gave Quinn shivers. "If I hadn't, you'd be facing far worse than a mere hanging for insulting my matelot. Get him out of my sight, Cullen, before I do something I regret."

Cullen dragged the man to his feet and over to the hatch that led into the deepest hold on the ship. He shoved hard, unable to hide his glee when Lewes stumbled and then tumbled head over heels to the bottom of the steep stairs. "Let him rot," he spat, coming back to where Amery, Gavin, and Quinn still stood. "Don't ye listen t'him, Mr. Watson. The crew knows what kind o' doctor and o' man ye be."

"Thank you, Cullen," Gavin replied, his voice barely steady. "I appreciate the vote of support."

"Dismissed!" Quinn shouted, knowing how fragile the veneer of Gavin's control had to be. They needed to get him below and away from the crew as soon as possible. "Let's go," he murmured to Amery.

Amery nodded, returning to his quarters, Quinn ushering Gavin ahead of him as he followed. The crew would think they were going to discuss what had happened or to prepare for the hanging. They didn't need to know anything else.

"They're never guilty, are they?" Gavin asked bitterly. "The men who force themselves on helpless boys? They always believe their superior strength gives them the right to do what they please. It isn't right. It's never right!"

"Easy, Gavin," Amery soothed, drawing Gavin into his arms. "They're dead now, and he will be, too, before the sun sinks below the water."

"That doesn't change what they did to me, and it won't change anything for Dickerson. He'll live his entire life knowing he was too weak to keep from being some man's whore."

"It wasn't your fault," Amery murmured, his hold tightening as he led Gavin to their cabin. Quinn let them go, his presence another reminder for Gavin of all that had happened.

"'E 'urt too, *si*?" Eliodoro asked, stepping from the shadows.

"What are you doing back here again?" Quinn snapped, not sure his control could deal with another seduction attempt from the too tempting young man.

Eliodoro shrugged. "You no answer question."

"Yes." Quinn begrudged the youth an answer that was not his to give, but he had already learned Eliodoro was as tenacious as the barnacles that encrusted their hull. Once he latched onto something, he never let go.

Eliodoro nodded slowly. "'E is right. The memories, they no leave."

"I'll tell you the same thing I told Dickerson earlier," Quinn replied. "Every man on this ship is running from something in his past, either grief or abuse or starvation. None of us came here unscarred by life."

"What scars you 'ave?" Eliodoro dared to ask.

Quinn glared. He might hide his painful past better than Gavin did, but it didn't make having the scars picked at any easier. "What scars do you have?" he countered.

Eliodoro looked down. "I tell you. The crew decide no sell me. I too pretty. They want me for themselves."

Quinn's eyes grew wide, but before he could press for more, Eliodoro shoved past him and disappeared onto the deck. Quinn let him go, not sure what he would have said if Eliodoro had stayed. The lad was right about one thing: he was far too pretty. If he could have stopped at admiration of Eliodoro's physique, he could have let it go, but the Venetian had won his respect as a sailor and a man as well, and that was much harder to resist. He glanced toward the captain's cabin, his thoughts torn between Gavin and Eliodoro. He had yearned for Gavin for so long that it seemed strange to think of another man in that light. And yet….

On deck, Eliodoro realized quickly he would find no solitude there. Casting a glance skyward, he saw the mizzenmast crow's nest was empty. He climbed up and hunkered down in the small space, grateful for the modicum of privacy it allowed him as he tried to make sense of everything that had happened that afternoon.

It hadn't taken him many days aboard the *Silver Queen* to see that the quartermaster had told him the truth about the captain and *Signor* Watson or to decide that he'd made the right choice in joining this ship rather than taking his chances on Providence Island. This captain and his officers wouldn't abuse a boy the way Captain Gomez had abused Eliodoro, raping him at least once a day to remind him of his place and offering him as a reward to his officers whenever they pleased the captain. He had lived with the ache in his backside for so long that he'd forgotten what it felt like to be able to move without pain. They were still pirates, though, lawless men who believed might made right, or so he'd believed.

It appeared he was wrong.

He wasn't entirely sure where that left him.

He suspected he would find a sympathetic friend, perhaps even an ally, in Mr. Watson. He hadn't seen it before now, but the conversation he'd overheard a few minutes ago seemed to suggest that Mr. Watson had suffered as Eliodoro and Dickerson had suffered. Perhaps to a different degree, but the bitterness he'd heard in the surgeon's voice resided in Eliodoro's heart as well. He shivered at the memories. He'd learned ways to lessen the pain, stealing oil or grease whenever he could to keep himself slick, but nothing could lessen the humiliation of being offered as a reward, a whore for the officers to use or abuse when they pleased the captain and to humiliate whenever he was on deck, shouting foul names at him or comparing stories of how they'd fucked him and how he'd pleaded and begged like a good little whore, all loudly enough for the rest of the crew to hear. The other sailors hadn't raped him because they feared the captain too much, but they'd scorned him, and that was somehow worse. A part of him wanted to confide in *Signor* Watson, or perhaps in *Signor* Davies, but he feared their ridicule nearly as much as he feared the abuse he was beginning to believe had finally ended. A man would hang tonight for such abuse.

This ship had one other complication he hadn't known in his previous life, Eliodoro mused as the quartermaster's voice rang out on deck, ordering sails trimmed, decks swabbed and guns checked. The hanging tonight didn't change the necessity of running a tight ship. *Signor* Davies occupied far too many of Eliodoro's waking thoughts and almost all of his sleeping ones. Occasionally he would awake covered in cold sweat because he'd relived his life aboard the slaver in his dreams, but most nights, he awoke instead from dreams of *Signor* Davies touching him. He had hated every single one of his abusers, but he didn't think he'd hate *Signor* Davies's attention, a fact that made his stomach churn with dread during the day and with desire when he slept. It had been enough to lead him to offer himself in exchange for the quartermaster's protection, an offer the man had refused, much to Eliodoro's surprise. He had never met a man who would refuse an offer of sex, even if he wouldn't force his attentions on anyone.

He peeked over the edge of the crow's nest, watching the swarm of activity on the decks below. *Signor* Davies was no taller or broader than the other sailors, but even from the crow's nest, Eliodoro had no problem picking the quartermaster out of the crowd. He stood differently, his carriage more erect, his bearing proclaiming he was a man of importance even though his rank would mean nothing outside the West Indies, perhaps not even off the *Silver Queen*. The sun reflected off *Signor* Davies hair, not the same brilliant gold as the captain's, but a deeper color that reminded Eliodoro of a sandy beach. He shook his head at himself. He shouldn't have these thoughts about the quartermaster. He shouldn't have them about any man if he listened to the Church, but the Church wasn't here, and *Signor* Davies was.

Shimmying down from the crow's nest, Eliodoro told himself he had left his refuge because he didn't want to be idle any more, not because he wanted to do something to attract the quartermaster's attention for real this time.

As the sun inched toward the horizon, Quinn and Amery strung up a line to be used as a noose, affixing it to a yardarm so it would hang to a few inches above the height of a man. "Nisbett," Quinn called, seeing the second mate, "we need an empty barrel to put the condemned on before we tip him off."

"Aye, sir, I'm sure I can find something fittin'," Nisbett promised. "We been at sea long enough to have used up a portion of our supplies. I'll find something for ye."

As the two officers tied the noose, making sure the knot slid easily over the rope, Nisbett returned with Seaton and Clay, the three of them rolling a large barrel. "This should do, sir," Nisbett proposed. "Get him up high enough that the fall will kill 'im good."

"Well done, gentlemen," Amery replied. "That should suit admirably."

"Lewes weren't listenin' too well when ye brought us all aboard," Clay said as they set the barrel up beneath the noose. "Or else he didn't think ye was serious about takin' care of yer men, Cap'n. Dickerson's young still, but he's got the makin' of a fine sailor. He didn't deserve to be raped."

"No one ever deserves that," Quinn snapped.

"I didn't mean they did," Clay replied hurriedly, "only that the rest of the crew likes the lad. He works hard and folk like him. Don't know why Lewes picked on him."

"It doesn't matter why. He did it, and now he'll pay the price," Amery declared. "The sun's setting. Nisbett, if you'll gather the men. Mr. Davies and I will fetch the prisoner."

"Aye, Cap'n," Nisbett saluted. "They'll all be waitin' for ye when ye bring the bastard out."

"Let's get this over," Amery muttered to Quinn. "Gavin needs me."

Quinn had no doubt of the truth of that statement. He wondered if the surgeon would attend the hanging.

Lewes fought them when Amery and Quinn grabbed his arms to take him onto deck, but they were no mere boys, incapable of defending themselves, and they overpowered the man easily, forcing him up the stairs and onto the barrel. Quinn examined the faces of the gathered crew, nodding in approval when his eyes found Dickerson among the crowd, face pale but composed. The boy had the makings of a fine officer with a little age and experience under his belt.

He should have known he'd find Gavin standing directly behind the boy, hand on his shoulder. The entire situation had to be tearing Gavin to shreds, but he wouldn't make the boy face this alone. His compassion wouldn't let him.

When Amery was sure the entire crew had gathered, he said a short prayer for the repose of the soul of the condemned man, though everyone on deck understood the words were for form, not out of any genuine sentiment, and then he and Quinn knocked the barrel from beneath Lewes's feet.

Lewes fell sharply, his neck breaking instantly when the rope pulled taut. The body twitched a few times on the end of the rope as the bowels emptied.

"Let this be a lesson to you all," Amery said coldly. "I won't tolerate rape aboard my ship. Cullen, leave him there until dawn to make sure he's well and truly dead, then cut him down and feed him to the fish."

Without waiting for an acknowledgment, Amery turned on his heel, his hand going to Gavin's back, urging him ahead of Amery into the aftcastle. "Are you well?" Amery asked as soon as they were alone in the narrow corridor.

"Sometimes I don't think I'll ever be well again," Gavin replied with a deep sigh. "I think I've left the memories in the past where they belong, and then something like this happens, and I'm right back on that leaky ship, shivering beneath my thin blanket in the hope he won't come looking for me tonight."

Amery was relieved to hear Gavin speaking of their youth rather than the slave ship. He'd been equally helpless both times, but he didn't blame himself for the first experience the way he did for not protecting Gavin later, when his failure to fend off the Spanish slaver had led to Quinn's and Gavin's capture.

Reaching their cabin, Amery ushered Gavin inside, pulling his lover into his arms, letting Gavin lean back against him, dark head resting against Amery's shoulder. Amery kept hoping, believing, that they'd finally left the past behind them, but then something like this would happen to force it all back into the present. Amery had tried to talk to Gavin about it, but his matelot hadn't wanted to discuss it, and Amery hadn't known how to insist. He still didn't, so he did as he always ended up doing: holding Gavin in his arms and hoping his actions spoke more clearly than his words could ever do.

Gavin turned in Amery's embrace, leaning against the captain's strong chest, letting his lover's nearness steady him. He hated this feeling of weakness, but only time seemed to have any effect on it. And sometimes Amery's closeness.

"Take me to—" Gavin began.

The rest of his request was lost in Amery's mouth as his matelot took possession of it the way he had taken possession of Gavin's heart. Gavin gave in willingly, needing the passion between them to sweep away the nightmares of the day.

"Are you sure this is what you want?" Amery murmured when he felt Gavin melt in his arms.

"Yes," Gavin insisted. "I need you to hold me, to love me. To help me forget for a few hours."

Chapter 11

THE sun shining through the cabin windows woke Gavin the next morning, his awareness returning slowly. His body bore the proof of how thoroughly Amery had loved him the night before, with little bruises and bites covering his chest and thighs. It had been exactly what he needed at the time, the reminder that Amery loved and desired him and would always give him what he needed. Last night he had needed to be taken. This morning he needed to take.

With a low, rough growl, he grabbed Amery's hips, rolling him onto his stomach and startling him awake. Amery started to struggle, but Gavin pinned the captain beneath his body. "Let me have you," he demanded, his voice low and harsh with desire.

Amery subsided beneath him.

"Warn a man next time," Amery snapped back in reply. He knew this routine now, knew exactly how the next hour would go. Gavin would drive him out of his mind and then take his own release after pounding Amery's arse for all it was worth. Amery shivered despite the heat. His normally gentle matelot lost control only rarely. Amery remembered each time with great fondness.

"Where's the fun in that?" Gavin snapped, dragging on Amery's hips until he pushed up onto his hands and knees. "Head down," he ordered.

Amery complied, dropping his head onto his forearms so his arse stuck up in the air wantonly. He knew the picture he presented, but it didn't matter, not when Gavin was the one behind him, the one loving

him, the one—'Sblood!—the one jabbing his tongue up Amery's arse. He groaned loud and long, the sound praise and encouragement in one.

It was all the invitation Gavin needed to tighten his grip on Amery's hips and devour him mercilessly. All the fear and anger and pain and hopelessness churned up by the previous day's events rushed back at him, seeking release. In all his life, Gavin had only found one safe place to let those emotions go: into Amery's keeping. Smearing his thumbs through the saliva running down Amery's crease, Gavin lifted his head, the wet digits replacing his tongue as he stretched his lover's entrance.

Amery let out a hoarse shout as Gavin's thumbs speared him, pulling sharply at flesh not accustomed to such activity, but he didn't make any move to stop his matelot. The pain, little enough compared to the bumps and bruises he acquired every day aboard his ship, would fade momentarily, to be replaced by pleasure when Gavin finally consented to fill him. He didn't mind the roughness at any time, but especially not now when he knew what drove Gavin's actions. Better that Gavin snap now, with him, than later during a battle or when he was trying to save a sailor's life. Besides, he didn't want to share Gavin's passion, even his angry passion, with anyone else.

Sharp teeth attacked the curve of Amery's arse, each bite eliciting a short gasp. Amery pressed back against Gavin's mouth, silently inviting more. He might not sit comfortably for a few days, but he considered that a small price to pay for Gavin's peace of mind. Not that he'd ever admit either of those things. Gavin would feel guilty if he realized he'd hurt Amery in even the most pleasurable of ways, and he'd argue until he was blue in the face over Amery making any kind of sacrifice for his happiness. Amery had learned a long time ago how to take care of Gavin without his lover being any the wiser.

Gavin was blissfully unaware of the thoughts going through Amery's mind, his sole focus on seeing how loud he could make his lover scream. He pulled his thumbs free, replacing them with three fingers, pumping hard and deep, plundering the upturned arse as he reared up to search for the tin of salve they kept by their bed to ease their lovemaking. Finding it, he smeared some around the edges of the loosening muscle, working it inside as his fingers continued to plunge in and out of the snug hole.

Amery moaned like a two-bit whore, egging Gavin on with every trick he knew. "Swive me like you mean it," he goaded. "I can barely feel you."

Gavin growled low in his throat, the words a spark to the tinder of his emotions. Withdrawing his fingers, he seated the tip of his cock in the narrow portal and slammed home as hard as he could. Amery gasped beneath him, but he rocked back with full force, his actions making clear his willing participation. Gavin groaned as Amery's tight heat squeezed around his shaft, his movements slowing momentarily as he savored the pleasure of topping his lover. Amery's natural dominance, the very trait that made him such an efficacious captain, carried over into their cabin more nights than not. He never refused if Gavin asked to reverse their roles, but he rarely thought to ask Gavin's preference.

Today Gavin wasn't in the mood to ask for anything, needing to take instead. Fortunately, Amery was inclined to indulge him, wriggling his arse against Gavin's groin until Gavin responded, his hands falling hard and heavy on Amery's hips again, stilling them, holding them in place for the pounding he intended to deliver. Amery grunted and hissed as Gavin began to move, pummeling Amery's arse with the full force of his considerable strength.

Amery closed his eyes and let himself be ravished, secure in the knowledge of the depth of Gavin's feelings and the skill of his lover's cocksmanship. Gavin might take his release, but he'd see to Amery's before all was said and done, and that gave Amery the patience to wait as Gavin used his body. Gavin's callousness never lasted beyond his release, and his innate decency insisted he then make Amery climax spectacularly.

In a matter of moments, Gavin's thrusts grew erratic, his hips jerking desperately against Amery's buttocks as his orgasm overtook him. Amery rocked back against the stuttering thrusts, the hot rush of fluid its own aphrodisiac. Gavin's weight pressed him deeply into the mattress, compressing his cock uncomfortably between his thighs and his belly. He shifted to relieve the pressure, the movement enough to return Gavin to the present.

"Turn over," Gavin ordered, his voice softer now in the aftermath of his release.

Obediently, Amery rolled to his back, waiting to see what Gavin would request next. His matelot didn't speak, though, nudging Amery's thighs until they parted and he could kneel between them, bending to lap enthusiastically at the tip of Amery's cock. Amery opened his mouth to beg for more, but before the words could escape, Gavin's lips slid down his shaft and his fingers found Amery's entrance again, filling him almost as full as Gavin's erection had done. They sought his pleasure spot, exploiting it with careful precision.

The sudden focus of his lover's unwavering attention, Amery felt his patience and his control desert him. He'd held back his own needs in favor of Gavin's when he realized what his matelot needed, but that time had passed, and he could delay no longer. "Gavin!"

His lover's only response was to frig him harder.

Amery quivered, every muscle in his body taut with need as his climax approached. He reached for it, his body desperate for release, but it eluded him, Gavin's attentions enough to have him aching but not to make him come. He thrashed on the bed.

"Hold still," Gavin ordered, lifting his head. Amery could have wept at the loss of the heat of his lover's mouth, followed immediately by the disappearance of his fingers.

"Make me come, bastard," Amery growled.

Gavin glared down at him, straddling Amery's hips. "When I'm good and ready," Gavin snapped back. Reaching behind himself, he stroked Amery's cock with slick fingers and sank down on the long shaft. Amery wouldn't have the patience to wait until Gavin could come a second time, so Gavin concentrated on making him climax as quickly as possible, massaging his lover's cock with his internal muscles as he squeezed the heavy bollocks. He rode Amery hard, spurring him toward release. The tenor of Amery's moans changed immediately, assuring Gavin he had his lover's full attention. Amery bucked beneath him, driving his shaft deep into Gavin's willing body.

"Now," Gavin ordered, leaning back enough to drive his fingers into Amery's sheath.

That was all it took. Amery climaxed hard, spurt after spurt filling Gavin's passage. Gavin rode out the aftershocks until Amery lay still beneath him, face soft with repletion. Relaxing down onto his lover's chest, Gavin let out a long, deep breath, feeling the last of the anger and resentment fade as Amery's arms came around him.

"The men will be looking for us soon," Gavin murmured against Amery's neck.

"Let them look," Amery shrugged. "Quinn will keep them in line until we're ready to go topside."

"We have to deal with Lewes' remains."

Amery shook his head. "Cullen will have done that already. I told him to cut the bastard down at dawn. It's well past that now, thanks to your enthusiasm this morning."

"I didn't hear you complaining," Gavin retorted, trying to push up onto his elbows. Amery's arms kept him firmly in place.

"Maybe because I wasn't," Amery replied equably. "There's nowhere I'd rather be, day or night, than in bed with you. Or anywhere else with you."

"I know that," Gavin murmured. It was the one thing that kept him sane on days like yesterday. It was the one thing he didn't think he could do without, and that was the reason he kept silent.

"SOMETIMES I don't think I'll ever forget the fear," Dickerson confided. "I know he's dead. I watched him die, but I still catch myself looking over my shoulder to make sure he isn't there."

"Is only a week," Eliodoro reminded him. "It grow more easy in time."

Quinn drew back into the shadows, not wanting to draw attention to himself. He wanted to hear what advice Eliodoro would give the other youth. He suspected, indeed had suspected for some time, that Eliodoro had too much experience for a lad of his age.

"Truly?" Dickerson asked.

"It no 'appen in day or two, but *sì*, the memories fade."

"Thank you for listening," Dickerson said. "Mr. Watson said I could talk to him if I wanted, but I don't like to disturb him."

Eliodoro nodded. "'E is very busy man, but 'e is also proof I am right. 'E love captain very much, and I think 'e 'urt much more than you."

Quinn still shuddered when he thought of their last voyage across the Atlantic, five years after they signed on as sailors. The new gunner on the *Lady Grace* had taken an interest in Gavin from the first day, although it was longer before the actual abuse began. Quinn and Amery had wanted to help, but the one time they tried to interfere, they were caned for disobeying orders. Quinn still didn't know whether the captain hadn't known about or had simply turned a blind eye to what the gunner was doing to Gavin, but the rapes had gotten worse, not better after that, and Gavin made them promise not to say or do anything else. As soon as they reached a port, they jumped ship and swam to shore, the captain having granted leave only to the officers.

Quinn was so lost in his memories that he didn't hear what Dickerson might have said by way of parting, but Eliodoro was walking toward him alone, the narrow corridor giving Quinn no place to hide.

"Oh, *Signor* Davies, I no see you," Eliodoro said, face visibly flushing despite his dark skin.

"No reason why you should have," Quinn replied. "What did they do to you, Eliodoro? You've talked more than once in vague terms."

"It no matter now," Eliodoro insisted. "Is in past. I no more on their ship."

"It matters to me," Quinn retorted. "Tell me who hurt you."

Eliodoro's laughter barked out cynically. "So you feel sorry for little 'ore?"

"You aren't a whore," Quinn snapped back. "You were the one who told me that the day we met, and you've more than proven the truth of your words since then."

"'Ow?" Eliodoro asked. "By try seduce you when Dickerson was raped?"

"By not seducing anyone since you've been aboard. Who hurt you?"

"The captain, 'e use me as reward for officers. If I lucky, is only twice a day. On a bad day, is six, seven times."

"That's inhumane!" Quinn cried.

"They Spaniards," Eliodoro replied with a shrug. "What you expect?"

"We should have killed them when we had the chance," Quinn muttered, "or at least marooned them somewhere. I swear, no one will ever bother you again. I'll kill before I'll let that happen to you again."

The vehemence of Quinn's comment surprised Eliodoro. "*Grazie,* but why?"

"Because when you thought you needed protection, you came to me," Quinn replied honestly. *Because if I believed you'd tell me the truth rather than feeling coerced, I'd try to seduce you myself.* Those were words he would never say aloud. "I should check on Dickerson," he said, changing the subject. If he didn't, he wasn't sure he would be able to stop from kissing the soft smile Eliodoro gave him.

"'E is better," Eliodoro assured him. "I fight my own battles now, *Signor* Davies. You give me that. *Grazie.*"

Quinn watched Eliodoro go with mixed emotions. A part of him raged at what the young man had suffered, far worse than what Quinn had undergone. He hadn't asked Eliodoro how long he'd been on the slaver, but he was sure it had been far more than the few days Quinn and Gavin had been held captive on the Spanish slaver. While Gavin had suffered near-daily rapes the last few months on the *Lady Grace*, it had only come from one man, not all the officers, and only until they could escape. Another part of Quinn admired Eliodoro for his quiet dignity, for the courage it took to speak up and ask to join the *Silver*

Queen not knowing what manner of men crewed her. A final part desired the Venetian, the lithe body and exotic features haunting Quinn's dreams at night. He had accepted that his desire was pointless, but it did not stop the lad's face from torturing him night after night. He lay in his cabin alone, listening to the muffled sounds coming from the captain's cabin, and imagined Eliodoro there with him. The boy worked shirtless many days, even the thin cotton of his threadbare shirt too heavy in the humid air, giving Quinn plenty of opportunity to study his physique. He knew every line of Eliodoro's smooth, wiry body, far stronger than it looked at first glance. The lad had proven himself a capable sailor, and Amery had dismissed him from his position as cabin boy, promoting him to deckhand along with the others. It wasn't his skill as a sailor that interested Quinn most, but the dark, wide nipples and the pert arse that caught his eye every time he had to look up at Eliodoro in the rigging or watch him bend over to swab the deck. The Venetian's breeches were nearly as threadbare as his shirt, and Quinn kept expecting the seam to split open at any moment, giving him a view of the surely delectable body beneath.

'Sblood, they needed to make port. He didn't know how much longer he'd be able to restrain himself without some sort of release, and he intended to keep his promise to Eliodoro.

Chapter 12

QUINN wasn't sure land had ever looked so appealing. He loved sailing, loved the sea, but occasionally he needed a break from the ship. From listening to Gavin and Amery love each other. From fighting his new desire for Eliodoro.

The last time they made land in Tortuga, their fortunes had been considerably diminished, and so Quinn had settled for sharing a room with Gavin and Amery. The gold in his sea chest now allowed him the luxury of his own room. They had arranged watches so all the men would have an extended shore leave. Amery had declared his intention to spend a week in port, and Quinn planned to enjoy every minute of it, with rum and sex and more rum. And then hopefully more sex. Anything to forget about Gavin and Amery and Eliodoro for a few days. In the time it had taken him to cross town, he'd already been propositioned a dozen times, but he could afford to be particular. He reached the small tavern away from the central district, smiling as he entered the dim room. The tavern was no less seedy, no fancier than any of the others, but the proprietor was an old shipmate who'd lost an arm in battle and had used his portion to set up this establishment. Whenever Quinn had the funds, he sought his rum and his company here.

"In port for a few days, are ye?" Hodges asked when he saw Quinn.

"Aye, the captain's given us a week's shore leave," Quinn confirmed.

"Then I imagine ye'll be wanting a bottle of rum and a bit of Tom's time," Hodges observed.

"If he's available and interested still," Quinn agreed, thinking of the young man Hodges had taken on to help him with the heavy work he couldn't do on his own with only one hand. Tom wasn't averse to being paid for his company, but only if he liked the man to begin with. He wouldn't entertain anyone who hadn't bathed, anyone who showed any sign of syphilis, or anyone who otherwise disturbed his sensibilities. Hodges let him make his own decisions and keep his own earnings.

"I'll let him know ye're here," Hodges offered, drawing a bottle of rum from behind the bar. "In the meantime, here's a bit of drink to get ye started."

Quinn took the bottle, tipping it in Hodges's direction as he looked around for a table, putting his back to the wall out of habit. He hadn't shown the size of his money pouch, but the cut of his jacket and the shine of his boots would proclaim his relative wealth, even if that was only a recent development, and Quinn didn't intend to be taken off guard by anyone with dishonest intentions. Hodges discouraged—at the point of a sword if necessary—such activity, but he couldn't be everywhere at once.

A few moments later, Tom appeared behind the bar, sending Quinn a dazzling smile. As he always did, Quinn found himself seduced by the light in Tom's eyes. "Hodges said you'd come to see me," Tom teased as he joined Quinn at the table.

Quinn offered him a swig of rum, but Tom shook his head. "How long are you in port for?"

"A week," Quinn replied, "although I can't spend all of that in your bed even if I could afford it. I have to serve my watches on ship like everyone else."

"For a week of your time, we could strike a bargain, I'm sure," Tom winked. He ran curious fingers over the cut of Quinn's jacket. "I see your fortunes have improved since the last time we met."

"We took a prime galleon," Quinn admitted. "I spent a bit of my share on new clothes since the ones that weren't lost with the *Dark Dream* were more than a little threadbare."

"I heard about that," Tom sympathized. "I was disappointed you didn't come see me."

"We were only in port for a few days," Quinn demurred, "and we spent most of that trying to get a new crew for our new lady."

"I'll forgive you this time," Tom flirted, "but don't let it happen again."

Quinn knew Tom wasn't pining away for him in port because on more than one evening, he'd had to wait for Tom to finish with someone else before he entertained Quinn, but the thought that Tom wanted to see him, to be with him, was flattering after Gavin's and Amery's inability to see anything outside of each other and Eliodoro's equation of sex with protection.

"I'll make sure it doesn't," Quinn promised.

WHEN Quinn left Hodges's tavern several hours later, he was pleasantly drunk and pleasantly sated. Tom had been a most willing partner as always and had made Quinn promise to visit him again before the *Silver Queen* sailed. The sounds of swords clanging barely even registered in Quinn's mind, so normal an occurrence it was in Tortuga, but his nerves jangled suddenly when he recognized the musical lilt of one of the voices. Drawing his sword as he fought the haze of drunkenness, he detoured toward the sound. The scene could have easily come from his nightmares. Eliodoro stood at the end of a narrow alley in the center of a circle of jeering men, his sword drawn, full of bravado as he goaded them to face him like real men, one at a time, rather than in a pack like miserable dogs, but Quinn wasn't entirely sure the young sailor would be able to hold his own against even one of the slavering men, all of whom were taller and broader than he was.

"What's going on here?" he demanded, trying to keep his voice from slurring too badly.

"Ah, *Signor* Davies," Eliodoro exclaimed, "I teach *bastardi* lesson."

The pirates laughed at that, closing in on Eliodoro.

"Be on your way, *Signor* Davies," the leader mocked, "unless you want to be stuck like a pig next to your pretty companion."

"I no man's 'ore!" Eliodoro shouted, lunging for the man who'd spoken. The thug easily evaded the somewhat inept lunge, knocking Eliodoro on the back of the neck with the hilt of his sword and sending the lad tumbling to the ground.

"There's one taken care of, boys," he laughed. "Shall we see if the rescuer is any better?"

That was all it took to ignite Quinn's usually dormant temper. With a roar of displeasure, he stepped between Eliodoro and the oafs, his sword engaging the leader's with a sharp clang. If he wasn't at his finest because of the rum he'd consumed that evening, none but his own shipmates would know it as the blade flashed and parried. In a matter of moments, his opponent's sword went flying. The rest of the band attacked in defense of their leader, but Eliodoro had recovered from the blow to his head and automatically took up position at Quinn's back, so they were fighting two against three instead of one against four. A slash across one man's belly and a stab to the second's shoulder were enough to convince the thugs they'd picked the wrong victim.

When they were gone, Quinn turned on Eliodoro. "What do you think you were doing?"

"Enjoying my leave, same as others," Eliodoro retorted. "Is no my watch until tomorrow."

"That isn't what I meant," Quinn scolded. "What would you have done against four of them if I hadn't stumbled along?"

Eliodoro shrugged. "Fight."

The resignation in Eliodoro's tone snapped Quinn's restraint. Angrily, he grabbed the lad's shoulders, propelling him back against

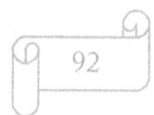

the wall of one of the buildings framing the alley where they found themselves. "How?" Quinn demanded. "Show me how you'd fight them."

Eliodoro struggled weakly in Quinn's grasp, his strength no match for Quinn's larger frame, honed by years of hard work at sea. The restless movements did nothing to dislodge Quinn's grasp, but they had the unintended effect of rousing his passions, so recently sated in Tom's willing body. Quinn had told himself a hundred times why he shouldn't have sex with Eliodoro, but he'd consumed the better part of a large bottle of rum, more than enough to silence his scruples, and Eliodoro was in his arms, smelling of soap and rainwater. The image of him bathing burst across Quinn's mind, and he lost all hope of resisting the young man's temptation. The tin of salve he'd filched from Gavin's medicine chest before leaving the ship dug into his hip as he leaned into the lithe body. Eliodoro arched up against him, rubbing their cocks together, startling a groan from Quinn's throat. He lowered his head as his hands released their grip on the Venetian's shoulders, pushing aside cloth in search of the smooth skin he'd studied obliquely for weeks.

Eliodoro's head was spinning from the lingering fear inspired by the attack, the surge of relief at *Signor* Davies's arrival, and now the morass of conflicted emotions aroused by the quartermaster's hands on his body. He'd offered himself to the quartermaster before with the idea of gaining the man's protection, but this was different. There was nothing of a transaction in this encounter. The hands that swarmed over his body demanded only his surrender. Eliodoro was frightened—he knew how much it could hurt—but he couldn't deny the arousal either as the hot hard palms worked to incite his passions. His tormenters had never done that, had never cared if he found any pleasure in their games, and in fact had often bragged about how much they had hurt him, how badly they'd made him bleed. *Signor* Davies's seduction brooked no refusal, but it demanded Eliodoro's participation in a way the rapists had never done.

Eliodoro gasped as *Signor* Davies's hand slipped beneath his breeches, encircling Eliodoro's unruly cock, the hard shaft betraying Eliodoro's interest in the proceedings. Instead of mocking him for it or squeezing until he cried out in pain, the quartermaster stroked firmly, adding layer upon layer of pleasure to the desire Eliodoro was already feeling. He bit back a sob, not wanting to do anything that might make the older man question his willingness. His body shook with rapture as he learned what it felt like to be touched with an eye to his own pleasure rather than in an effort to cow and control him. For the first time, his enjoyment mattered. He blinked hard to stop the tears he could feel welling, not wanting the quartermaster to see and misunderstand them. Then those hands left his cock and landed on his arse, caressing, squeezing with solicitous urgency before lifting him, pushing his breeches down and stepping over them into the space between his legs.

"Put your legs around my hips," Quinn ordered, wanting to feel the wiry muscles holding him even tighter than the press of cloth against the backs of his legs where Eliodoro's breeches hung from his ankles.

Eliodoro bit his lip as he raised his feet as directed, feeling intensely the vulnerability of his position. He reminded himself repeatedly that *Signor* Davies wouldn't hurt him, wouldn't force him. Even that couldn't stop him from tensing when he felt fingers probing his entrance. To his surprise, the digit penetrated his guardian muscle easily, something slippery abetting his taking. He moaned when the quartermaster's thumb massaged the skin behind his bollocks, arousing him further. He squirmed against the pleasurable sensations, his movements causing the finger inside him to go deeper, brushing over a spot inside him that made sparks dance behind his eyes. He wanted to ask what it was, but he didn't have the breath to speak, nor did he want to do anything that might cause *Signor* Davies to stop what he was doing.

Warm breath ghosted across his cheek, spooking Eliodoro enough that he turned his head away, but the quartermaster never paused, his lips moving to the line of the young man's jaw and teasing the smooth patch of skin behind his ear. Eliodoro gasped and whimpered, so swamped with pleasure that he didn't care about the stone wall cutting into his back or the fact that someone could walk by at any time and see them. In Tortuga, nobody would care. They'd see a handsome sailor with his pretty whore, and they'd go on their way, except that Eliodoro didn't want to be *Signor* Davies's pretty whore. He wanted to believe the other man felt something for him, something beyond physical gratification. Silently he scolded himself for being a fool, and then he felt the fingers inside him withdraw and the tip of a hard cock take their place. He braced for the pain to come, but *Signor* Davies didn't simply spread his cheeks and plunge inside. He teased Eliodoro with the head of his shaft until the young man relaxed. Only then did he press inside, and, to Eliodoro's surprise, his body stretched willingly to accommodate the invader instead of resisting and tearing. Suddenly the wall and the alley and what anyone else would think if they saw the two men didn't matter. Eliodoro felt like the most precious thing in the world, and as the quartermaster filled him carefully but inexorably, he sighed the man's name.

"*Signor* Davies."

"Quinn." The voice was warm and soft in Eliodoro's ear, his breath smelling faintly of rum, but not overpoweringly so, with an underlying hint of mint and with none of the rotting stench Eliodoro had so hated on the slaver.

"Quinn," Eliodoro repeated, savoring the name and the invitation to use it.

The sound of his name in Eliodoro's lilting accent classed easily as one of the most erotic things Quinn had ever heard. Lowering his head to the elegant curve of the boy's shoulder, he nipped at the smooth skin, his hips beginning to move in earnest as he felt all resistance leave his partner's body. "That's it," he urged when Eliodoro shifted to meet him. "Take me all the way inside. You feel so good, so hot and tight and sinful around my cock. Moan for me, pretty one."

Eliodoro was quite sure he should take umbrage at the endearment, but he couldn't put together a coherent protest with Quinn moving inside him, pressing against the spot his fingers had found earlier. Then one of Quinn's hands closed around Eliodoro's cock, and he couldn't think of anything but his own release, his body bouncing on the other man's hard shaft as he strove desperately for the one final touch that would send him flying. Hot lips closed over one dark nipple, licking it rather than biting cruelly, and Eliodoro was lost, his body convulsing as stream after stream of fluid left his cock to stain his shirt and Quinn's. He opened his mouth to apologize, but no sound came out as Quinn suddenly jerked against him, flooding his insides with wet heat. For the first time in his young life, Eliodoro wasn't ashamed of the stickiness between his thighs. He'd wanted this as much as Quinn had, and having gotten it, he couldn't regret it now.

Strong hands returned to Eliodoro's backside, steadying him as Quinn withdrew. "Can you walk?" he asked solicitously.

"*Sì*," Eliodoro said after taking a moment to make sure his legs would hold him.

"Go back to the ship, and don't get yourself in trouble again," Quinn directed. "I might not be around to help you the next time."

Before Eliodoro could ask what Quinn intended to do, the quartermaster had straightened his breeches and strode out of the alley, taking with him all sense of well-being. Shivering despite the heat, Eliodoro curled in on himself, feeling far more the whore now than he'd felt after all the rapes on the slave vessel. At least there, he could console himself that he hadn't been willing.

Chapter 13

QUINN met Gavin and Amery on the gangplank of the *Silver Queen* when he reported for his watch late the next afternoon. He smiled as he waited for them to join him on the wharf, but they didn't return his smile. Surprised, Quinn joined them on the deck instead. "What's going on?" he asked.

"I don't know," Amery said, "but I'd like to. My former cabin boy came back last night, tears streaming down his face but refusing to tell me what happened. And all day today, he's scowled and spat any time anyone mentions your name. I thought maybe you could tell me why."

Quinn flushed, his own dark thoughts from the past day coming back to the fore. "Because I'm a bastard who can't keep his cock in his breeches," Quinn muttered in annoyance. "I told myself I wasn't going to touch him."

Gavin and Amery exchanged sharp looks. "Maybe we should continue this conversation somewhere a little more private," Gavin suggested.

Quinn nodded and followed them into their cabin.

"Start at the beginning and don't leave anything out," Amery directed, his voice brooking no dissension.

"I went to visit Tom after I had a bath," Quinn began, knowing the other two would not be at all surprised by that admission. "I wanted to get drunk and forget about everything for a few hours."

"There's no harm in that," Amery allowed. "Tom was as obliging as always, I assume."

"He took good care of me," Quinn assured them. "I was walking back to my lodgings when I heard fighting and realized Eliodoro was one of the people involved. A closer look revealed that he was outnumbered four to one. That didn't seem fair so I ran the men off."

"That doesn't explain why he's cursing your name this morning," Gavin reminded him.

"When they were gone, he was still so insistent he could have handled them alone," Quinn continued. "I challenged him to show me how he'd have run them off. Instead of fighting me, he melted the moment I touched him. I told myself I wasn't going to have anything to do with him beyond his responsibilities on the ship. Whole lot of good that did me."

"He was willing?" Amery asked, his voice hard.

"Yes!" Quinn all but shouted. "I swear it to you. If he'd given me any indication he wasn't willing, I'd have stopped instantly!"

"Where, exactly, were you while all of this was taking place?" Gavin inquired, his voice nearly as hard as Amery's had been.

"In an alley," Quinn mumbled shamefaced.

Gavin was on his feet, towering over Quinn in a heartbeat. "Tell me why I shouldn't beat you into next week! How dare you treat that boy that way? I know you aren't blind or stupid. You know he was abused on the slave ship."

"I know," Quinn admitted. "He told me the captain passed him around as a reward for the other officers."

"And yet you saw fit to fuck him up against a wall like a cheap trull," Gavin spat. "No wonder he spits at the sound of your name."

"You can't say anything to me I haven't already said to myself," Quinn replied glumly. "I knew better, but I did it anyway. I couldn't seem to help myself."

"Find a way to fix this," Amery ordered.

Quinn hung his head. "I didn't mean to hurt him."

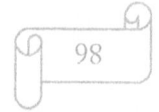

"I don't think he's hurt physically," Gavin interjected. "He isn't walking like he's in pain. I think his heart is hurting because he feels like a whore again."

"He wasn't a whore on the ship!" Quinn protested. "He was a prisoner."

Gavin's gaze met Quinn's, the hazel eyes hard. "As if that makes any difference in how he feels. Having fought them is little enough consolation as well you know."

Quinn did know, all too well. He had fought in hope of being rescued because he knew Amery would die before he'd leave Gavin in the hands of slavers. He didn't imagine Eliodoro had ever felt such confidence in being rescued. Gavin had capitulated rather than being hurt again, a lesson Quinn would not be surprised to hear Eliodoro had learned as well. "I know. That's why I went to visit Tom. I needed the release so I could resist the temptation he represents. When I went into the alley, all I wanted to do was keep the ruffians from killing him or raping him or both. I swear I didn't have any expectation beyond that."

"So what happened?" Amery insisted. "You aren't some green boy to lose control, especially after visiting Tom earlier in the evening."

Quinn laughed bitterly. "I wish I knew. I'd just rescued him. I was giving him a dressing down for getting himself in a situation four against one, and he had this mixture of resignation and bravado on his face, insisting he'd have run them off yet so clearly aware that he'd have failed. Something inside me just snapped. I don't know how else to explain it. One minute I was yelling at him; the next minute he was pushing against me, just as hard as I was. I swear to God, Amery, he was willing. I know what all this looks like, but he wanted it too."

"I believe you," Amery said. "He was the one who brought what happened to Dickerson to our attention."

"He wouldn't speak against Quinn even if he hadn't been willing," Gavin said with a shake of his head. "Against anyone else, but not against Quinn. That would be the same as accusing you in his eyes."

"It gets even more complicated," Quinn warned. "I found out about Dickerson when Eliodoro tried to seduce me to get my protection so no one would bother him the way Lewes bothered Dickerson. I refused and made him tell me why he thought he needed that kind of protection, but that history is between us as well. That was one of the many reasons I intended not to have sex with him at all. As long as I'm quartermaster and he's a simple sailor, the inequality of our stations makes a real relationship impossible. I knew that. I know that. It just didn't seem to matter last night."

"Why did he come back alone afterward?" Gavin asked.

"I couldn't face him," Quinn admitted. "I was afraid that if I stayed anywhere near him, I'd lose control again. If I'd taken him back to the room I'd rented, if I'd brought him back to the ship, I wouldn't have let him go, and that would only make matters worse."

Gavin wasn't so sure, but he knew Quinn, knew how stubborn the stupid bastard could be. The only way to change Quinn's mind once it was made up was at the point of a sword. And that assumed the person trying to change his mind was good enough to defeat him, something few of the men on the ship could do. "So how are you going to make it up to him?"

"What?" Quinn asked, startled.

"How are you going to convince him you don't see him as a toy or a whore or any of the thousand miserable things he's thinking about himself because of last night?" Gavin asked, knowing he was twisting the knife, but knowing as well that nothing else would work.

"I don't know," Quinn said miserably. "I can't even claim I was so drunk I didn't know what I was doing. Yes, I was half-drunk, but I knew exactly what I was doing the entire time. I want to regret it, but then I remembered how he melted in my arms and…."

And he was so damn in love with the boy it was obvious to everyone but Quinn. Gavin sighed. "You could tell him that."

"He wouldn't believe me," Quinn bemoaned. "He'd think I was just saying that to get him back in bed again."

"You mean you aren't?" Amery quipped.

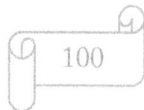

"Only if he wants it," Quinn said immediately.

Gavin shook his head at the ridiculousness of that statement. He'd watched Eliodoro watching Quinn and saw the hero worship that had developed. He found it telling as well that when Eliodoro thought he needed protection, he'd gone to Quinn, not to anyone else. Granted, Quinn as quartermaster was better protection than anyone but Amery himself, but Eliodoro could have approached any of the officers and probably found his offer accepted. Instead he'd chosen Quinn, the one available man on the ship with the conscience to resist him. "You still haven't answered my question. How are you going to make it up to him?"

"And what are we going to do about the bastards who abused him in the first place?" Amery added. "I don't like the idea that they'll escape justice."

"If we'd known when we had our hands on them still, we might've done something," Quinn agreed. "No one would have cried tears over seeing a few more of them die, but we missed our chance."

"Did we?" Gavin said slowly, a plan hatching in his head. "We have a letter of marque to hunt Spanish ships, and we have a reason to want the heads of a certain number of Spanish sailors. It seems to me we could target certain ships if we wanted. Eliodoro won't forget what happened to him, but there is a certain consolation that comes with knowing the bastards responsible are dead. If Michaels ever crosses my path, he's a dead man."

The only question, Gavin knew, was whether he'd kill the officer from the *Lady Grace* who abused him or whether Amery would beat him to it.

"So we do what?" Quinn questioned. "Ask for information on anyone who sailed with *Nuestra Señora de Madrid*?"

"If Eliodoro will give us names, we can do even better than that," Gavin replied. "We can ask for the men by name and kill the worst offenders rather than hoping to catch them randomly."

"I don't know how Eliodoro will feel about that," Quinn hesitated. "I mean, he told me what happened finally, but I don't know how he'd feel about everyone knowing."

"We don't need to tell the crew why we're hunting these particular Spaniards. We needn't even tell any but the officers what Spaniards we're hunting. As long as we continue to take prizes, the men will be happy. Even if we're seeking a particular ship, we can take other prizes as we hunt. If any of our quarry joined a ship returning to Spain, it could be months before they're back in these waters."

"Some of them may never return to the West Indies," Quinn agreed. "Eliodoro said they were based along the Barbary Coast, sailing to the islands to take slaves and then returning home."

"It isn't the success of failure of our hunt but the fact that we're trying," Gavin assured them. "And for all that Eliodoro has no desire to see Quinn right now, Quinn's the one who's going to tell him what we're planning."

"Why?" Quinn asked, desperate to avoid that confrontation.

"Because he already knows you know what happened to him," Gavin said, "and because you're the one who has to prove you deserve his trust. Even if he never returns your interest, he needs to trust you in battle and on the ship. We can't have him continuing to flush or spit every time he hears your name or your voice. We're in port for a week. We can start asking around as soon as he gives us names."

"He isn't going to talk to me," Quinn protested.

"Maybe not if you're alone, but he'll come if Amery summons him, and once he's here, he'll hear us out."

Quinn frowned again, dreading the upcoming conversation, but Gavin was right about one thing. He had to find a way to make amends. "I guess I should go find him then."

"I'll go," Gavin said. "He isn't angry at me at the moment, and we don't want him to cause a scene on deck. Stay here with Amery."

Gavin left before Quinn could reply.

"I know you," Amery said when they were alone, "so I know you're telling me the truth, but I have to have Eliodoro's confidence as well. I have to ask him what happened and I have to ask him if you forced him."

"And if he says I did?"

"Then I have to think of a way to punish you that will satisfy him and keep you alive," Amery replied, "but I'm hoping that with you here, his honesty will compel him to deny any force on your part. I don't have any desire to whip you publicly or privately, much less to hang you as we did Lewes."

Quinn nodded. "It would almost be a relief to let you cane me and be done with it, although I'd rather avoid the noose. Gavin's punishment will be far more painful."

Amery laughed. "He's a subtle one, my Gavin, that's for sure. If you're going to capture the attention of your fair friend, however, his plan will put you farther along that path than a caning. Unless you think the sight of your back and arse covered in stripes would appeal to him?"

"Only to his need for revenge," Quinn replied. "Gavin is right as usual. That doesn't make it any easier."

"Apologize and keep apologizing until he believes you," Amery advised. "And that's experience talking, let me tell you."

Quinn laughed. "Yes, I imagine so. Gavin never let either of us off lightly."

Gavin's knock interrupted them.

"Come in," Amery called.

"What 'e do 'ere?" Eliodoro demanded as soon as he saw Quinn in the captain's cabin. "I no want to talk to 'im."

"I'm sorry," Quinn broke in before Amery could reply. "I shouldn't have treated you the way I did last night."

"I no man's 'ore," Eliodoro repeated. "Even yours."

"I know that," Quinn swore. "I never meant for you to think I felt that way."

"Eliodoro," Amery interrupted. "Mr. Davies told me his version of what happened last night, enough for me to know he's an insensitive bastard who deserves a good whipping for treating you with so little consideration, but he says you were willing. Is that true?"

Eliodoro looked up at the ceiling, at the walls, at the floor, everywhere but at Quinn. "Is true." His olive skin flushed even darker.

Quinn breathed a sigh of relief at knowing he had not totally misjudged the situation. The cane would have been a small price to pay if he'd been wrong.

"He still owes you an apology for the way he acted," Gavin said firmly. "He was beyond inconsiderate to act as he did."

"Why are you so *protettivo* of me?" Eliodoro asked.

"Because I know what it feels like to be forced," Gavin said starkly.

"We both do," Quinn added, baring his painful past in hope of convincing Eliodoro to accept his olive branch. "The men who captured us are dead thanks to Amery, but the ones who took you are mostly still at large. We can hunt any Spanish or pirate ship we find. If you can tell us the names of the men who hurt you, we can go after their ships instead of just any ship."

"You tell them?" Eliodoro asked, voice tight.

"He confirmed what we'd already guessed," Gavin corrected. "I recognized the signs the moment you came aboard the *Silver Queen*. I'm a surgeon. I'm trained to observe the way people act."

"We won't say anything else to the rest of the crew," Amery promised. "It is your story to tell, not ours. If you agree to tell the other officers or to let us tell them, it will make searching for information faster."

Eliodoro shook his head. "I leave that behind. I no want anyone to know."

"Then we won't tell them," Quinn promised. "We *will* find the bastards, even if takes months, and when we do, they're dead men."

Eliodoro didn't understand the reasons for the quartermaster's vehemence, but he recognized the sincerity. Perhaps last night was one big misunderstanding.

"The men may ask why we seem to be hunting specific ships instead of taking any one we pass," Amery warned. "I don't have to answer every question, but I don't want a mutiny on my hands either."

"If that happen, tell them," Eliodoro directed after a moment's contemplation. "I no want another captain, even *Signor* Davies or *Signor* Watson. They good mates. You good captain."

Quinn flinched hearing Eliodoro reverting to calling him by his surname after moaning his given name so sweetly the night before. He could hardly take Eliodoro to task when if he had been less shocked and guilty over what had happened, he could have found a way to keep Eliodoro gracing his bed for days, perhaps forever.

Squashing that thought, he turned his attention back to Eliodoro. "The names?"

"Romero, Vasquez, Ortega, Valdez, Munoz, Medina," Eliodoro said.

"It's Mr. Davies's watch," Amery said, "so Mr. Watson and I will be heading to shore this afternoon. We'll see what we can learn, and Mr. Davies can continue the hunt when we return."

"If they can be found and brought to justice, we will see it done," Quinn seconded. "Perhaps then you will be able to live without fear."

Eliodoro squelched the thought that he had known nothing but joy in the quartermaster's arms until he had pushed Eliodoro away. He could not rely on anyone for his happiness. He had learned that long ago. "If you excuse me, Captain, *signores*, is my watch. I do my duty."

Amery nodded and Quinn watched helplessly as Eliodoro walked out of his sight again.

Chapter 14

ELIODORO left the captain's cabin completely discombobulated by the conversation. He wanted to hate the quartermaster for treating him like a lightskirt, yet he had apologized profusely. He hadn't, however, given any explanation, a fact that still rankled. If Eliodoro could understand what had happened, he could keep it from happening again. *Signor* Davies had touched him like he cared, like he wanted to be with him. He'd given Eliodoro pleasure for the first time in his life, something he didn't think men did with prostitutes. Eliodoro knew nothing of what should be where sex and its aftermath were concerned, but he didn't think the captain dismissed *Signor* Watson when he was done the way *Signor* Davies had dismissed him last night. And yes, the alley was hardly conducive to post-coital snuggling, but *Signor* Davies had not returned to the ship until morning. He had spent the night somewhere, and he hadn't taken Eliodoro with him.

He wanted to hate the quartermaster, to despise every moment of an act that had left him feeling dirty when it was over, but it hadn't felt that way until after. While *Signor* Davies had been touching him, it had felt like the best thing that had ever happened to him. For the first time since he left Venice, it had felt that someone cared about him for more than the job he could do or the release he could give. He had felt like first his safety and then his pleasure mattered to *Signor* Davies as the quartermaster caressed him eagerly but tenderly, in a way that brought him pleasure rather than reinforcing his helplessness and subordination. As he found release, the sense of well-being that radiated through him surpassed any he had known since before his mother died. At one kind word from *Signor* Davies, he would have promised the man anything. Instead, he'd gotten a pat on the head and a dismissal.

He could feel his anger growing again. He hadn't asked the infuriating man to rescue him from the ruffians who'd intended to rob him. He certainly hadn't asked to be ravished thoroughly up against the wall or anywhere else. His arse clenched as he remembered what it felt like to have *Signor* Davies inside him, pleasing him. He knew, for he needed to bathe still, that the quartermaster had found his release too, but it had felt different from his experience aboard the slaver. *Signor* Davies—Eliodoro refused to remember the sinful voice asking him to call the man Quinn—hadn't simply thrust inside him. He'd taken his time, stroking Eliodoro's body, his cock, his passage, readying him for the penetration. His body reacted to the memory, his cock filling in his breeches.

Scowling, he clambered up into the rigging, though he hardly needed to sit in the crow's nest while they were in port. No one would bother him up there. No one would see the way his traitorous body reacted to the memory of his first orgasm. No one would see if he slipped his hand beneath his smallclothes and stroked himself. And if he imagined it was *Signor* Davies's hand rather than his own that tantalized him, no one would know that either.

Eyes closing, he imagined the inside of *Signor* Davies's cabin, imagined the quartermaster laying him on the bunk with exquisite care before lying down beside him, hands moving over his body in tender apology as he whispered that he'd been drunk, afeard for Eliodoro's life, desperate to reassure himself that Eliodoro was unharmed but too timid to speak of any of his feelings. That he *did* care about Eliodoro and want only his pleasure. He moaned softly, not wanting to admit even to himself how much he wanted the hint of adoration he occasionally glimpsed on the captain's face when he looked at *Signor* Watson. If *Signor* Davies looked at him that way, even once, there was nothing he wouldn't do to see it again. His imagination conjured up that expression and his body seized, his seed coating his hand and soaking his breeches. With a muffled sob, he contemplated the deck below and wondered how much it would hurt if he threw himself over the edge of the crow's nest. Knowing he was too much of a coward to ever actually do it, he straightened his clothes as best he could and decided he'd have to find a stream to do his laundry when he went off watch. The smell of sex clung to him, evoking too many memories, good and bad. On the slaver, he'd had no choice, but he was his own master now.

"GAVIN, Amery," Hodges called when the two walked into his tavern, "or should I say Captain White and Mr. Watson?"

"Hodges, you old seadog, we'll always be Gavin and Amery to you," Amery replied with a laugh.

"It's been too long since I saw you last," Hodges chided. "What can I get you?"

"Information," Amery replied, his face growing grave. "We're looking for some former members of a ship we took. We didn't know at the time what crimes they'd committed."

Hodges was familiar enough with his former crewmates to guess the subject of the crime. "Even information comes at a price," Hodges warned.

"Grease whatever palms you need to," Gavin insisted. "We have the means to pay these days."

"So what—or who—are you looking for?"

"The former officers of the Spanish barca, *Nuestra Señora de Madrid*," Gavin said, voice low as he glanced around the tavern. "*Señores* Romero, Vasquez, Ortega, Valdez, Munoz, and Medina, by name. They'd have been separated from their ship about a month ago. We'll be in port for the rest of the week. We'll check back or send Quinn to check and settle our accounts before we sail."

"I'll see what I can learn," Hodges promised. "It might be worth asking Tom as well, but he's off for the night. And be careful. Not all of Tortuga is as fond of the English as we are here."

"It isn't the English looking," Amery explained. "It's just the *Silver Queen*."

"I see the line you're drawing, but I don't know as others would," Hodges warned.

"It's a risk we'll simply have to take. If those men can be found, we'll find them, and they'll taste justice," Gavin declared. "Thank you for any help you can give."

Hodges nodded. "Send Quinn to see me before you leave port. I'll learn what I can."

"You didn't expect it to be easy, did you?" Amery asked Gavin as they left the tavern, the look on Gavin's face such a mixture of mulish determination and forlorn misery that Amery couldn't help but feel for his lover.

Gavin shrugged. "No, I suppose not, but I hoped perhaps they'd visited Tom and left enough of an impression for Hodges to remember them since they used Eliodoro rather than the women on the ship."

"He didn't say that," Amery reminded Gavin. "Quinn said he was passed around as a reward. That doesn't mean the men preferred male company, only that the captain did."

"There were women on board. The men would have demanded them as a reward if that was their preference," Gavin countered.

"Maybe," Amery allowed, trying to get into the mind of a slaver, "but the captain wanted to sell the women, which meant not hurting them too badly. He didn't care about how badly they hurt Eliodoro because they weren't going to sell him. Either that or the captain did both. If Tom knows anything, Hodges will tell us before we sail."

QUINN didn't find a moment during his watch to approach Eliodoro. The Venetian made himself scarce or kept busy in the midst of the few other men on watch, and Quinn didn't feel right about making a scene in front of the other sailors. When the watch changed, Gavin and Amery had not yet returned, leaving Quinn stuck on the ship as Eliodoro went ashore. Scowling and squinting against the sun, Quinn took note of the lad's direction, wondering what he intended to do out in the woods that surrounded the town when he saw the young man walk down the beach instead of into the city.

Gavin and Amery still had not returned, but Nisbett arrived a few minutes later, saying the captain had asked him to take the next watch. Relieved of duty, Quinn hurried down the shore, hoping to find Eliodoro before he disappeared completely. Ten minutes later, Quinn found his quarry, and he was arrested by the sight in front of him. Stripped all the way down to his skin, Eliodoro knelt by a small stream, scrubbing his clothes against a rock. Casting back mentally, Quinn tried to remember if he had seen the young man with any other clothes. With a shake of his head, he realized Eliodoro probably did not even have the funds to buy anything new since he had not been a part of the crew when they took their big prize. Leaving as silently as he had arrived, he went back into town in search of a tailor.

When Quinn returned an hour later, Eliodoro had put his smallclothes back on, but the rest of his garments were spread out along the bank of the stream to dry.

"I hope these fit you," Quinn said softly, not wanting to startle Eliodoro.

"You no 'ave buy me things," Eliodoro scowled.

"Consider it an apology," Quinn requested.

"I no 'ore you 'ave buy," Eliodoro spat.

"It's not like that," Quinn protested. "It's a gift. Nothing more. I had no right to treat you the way I did yesterday, and I want to make amends."

Still not completely appeased, Eliodoro took the clothes Quinn offered and dressed hastily. Feeling more confident now that he was fully dressed, he addressed the question foremost in his mind. "*Perché?*"

Quinn shook his head, not understanding the question.

Eliodoro's brow furrowed as he sought the word he wanted. "Why?" he asked after a moment. "Why you treat me that way?"

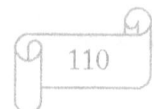

Quinn flushed, looking away and scuffing the toe of his boot in the sand. "Because I'm a stupid idiot who deserves to be shot," he answered.

"Is no answer," Eliodoro insisted.

"No, it's not," Quinn agreed. He took a deep breath and bared his soul. "I was drawn to you the moment I laid eyes on you, but I knew you'd been hurt, even if I didn't have the details, and I knew you didn't have any reason to trust me. I swore to myself I wouldn't treat you the way they did, that I wouldn't touch you unless I knew you wanted me to. Not for protection, but for the pleasure of it. I was drunk last night, and I let my cock do my thinking for me. Then, when it was over, I panicked because I'd done exactly what I'd promised myself I wouldn't do. I needed to get away, to think. I didn't mean to make you feel cheap. I know you have no reason to believe me, but I'd like the chance to show you I'm an honorable man."

"I know you 'onorable man," Eliodoro said softly, hearing now all the words he'd wanted to hear the night before. He searched the quartermaster's face, seeing only sincerity. He had learned far too young to recognize dissemblance when he saw it. "You tell me no when I offer myself to you when Lewes 'urt Dickerson. Last night, I only no like one part. I no like when you leave me alone. All the rest, I...." Eliodoro looked away, embarrassed to admit his feelings and yet sensing that his dreams might be within reach if he would only take the risk. "All the rest, I do again if you no leave me alone."

Quinn started forward without thinking, catching himself before he reached Eliodoro's side. "You don't have to say that," he assured the other sailor. "You don't have to sleep with me to have a place on the *Silver Queen*. No matter what you decide, you'll still be a part of the crew, and I won't begrudge you the right to tell me to go to hell and never touch you again."

"No!" Eliodoro insisted, his confidence growing as he listened to Quinn's assurances. "I mean what I say." He closed the remaining gap between them. "You want I show you?"

"Not here," Quinn demurred. "I don't have anything with me to ease the way, and even if I did, I made the mistake of a quick tumble last night. You deserve better than that."

"So take me somewhere better," Eliodoro proposed.

Quinn's mind raced as he weighed the possibilities. The tin of salve he'd carried the night before was in his cabin, but that would expose their liaison to the eyes of any of the crew still aboard the ship. He had gold to rent a room—lamp oil would suffice in place of the salve—but he feared that would make Eliodoro feel cheapened by the setting. After a moment, he realized he didn't have to decide. He could leave the choice up to his soon-to-be lover. "Which would you prefer? A room at a tavern where we needn't worry about the prying eyes of our shipmates or my cabin?"

"If we go your cabin, the others, they know."

Quinn shrugged. "They'll know once we leave port anyway. You can't keep secrets on a ship the size of the *Silver Queen*."

"Then take me to your cabin," Eliodoro said, the thought of being not just in bed with Quinn, but in Quinn's bed enough to have his nerves vibrating.

Chapter 15

THE sun was sinking into the ocean in a dizzying array of light and color, but neither Quinn nor Eliodoro paid any attention to Mother Nature's display. They had eyes only for each other as they stumbled up the gangplank and toward the aftcastle.

Eliodoro froze momentarily as they entered the dark corridor, the sound of the door closing behind them and the sudden darkness of the walls around him enough to bring back memories of another ship and another set of officers. Before he could change his mind, Quinn nuzzled his neck from behind, the affection implicit in the gesture enough to shatter the nightmarish flashback and return Eliodoro to his current surroundings and the very different man he had *chosen* as his lover.

Turning in Quinn's embrace, Eliodoro tipped his head back automatically as the contact between his skin and Quinn's lips continued. Hard hands gripped his hips, pulling him closer. The gesture reminded him too much of being grabbed by his captors. Suddenly skittish again, he wriggled away breathlessly, his eyes wide.

"Don't be coy," Quinn growled, eyes dark with passion, the fleeting sensation of Eliodoro's body against his enough to set his nerves aflame.

"Be gentle with me," Eliodoro requested softly.

Tamping down the urge to simply throw Eliodoro over his shoulder and carry him down the hall, Quinn held out his hands. "You have nothing to fear from me," he swore, guessing all too easily where Eliodoro's hesitations sprang from. "All you ever have to say is no. I can hardly deny I want you, but I have never—will never—take my

pleasure from another against his will. I know what it feels like to have the choice taken away from me, and I won't do that to you. If you come into my cabin with me, we will end up in bed because I can only resist temptation for so long, but the choice to cross that threshold is yours, and the choice to leave at any time is yours as well."

Eliodoro took a deep breath, steadying himself. Quinn had proven the truth of his words the night before, taking care of Eliodoro as no other had ever done. He could know that joy again, without the dismissal, if he found the courage to take the outstretched hands. "I no promise I no 'ave fear, but I want trust you."

The words humbled Quinn. "You can trust me," he promised again, squeezing Eliodoro's hands gently. "Let me prove that to you. Let me make love to you."

"You stop if I say?" Eliodoro asked again.

"Always," Quinn reaffirmed. "I want to take care of you, to show you that your pleasure matters, but if it would be easier for you to take the lead, you have but to say."

Eliodoro froze, mind racing at the images that evoked in his mind. After a moment, though, he shook his head. "I know only 'atred. I no know 'ow make you feel good."

Quinn doubted that was true, but he didn't argue. He certainly wasn't averse to stretching Eliodoro out on his bed and making slow, sweet love to him. "Then I'll have to teach you," Quinn murmured, his voice a rumbling purr in his chest as he bent his head to the curve of Eliodoro's cheek again.

Eliodoro melted into the embrace, every inch of his body flushing hot at the thought. He had learned to remain silent and endure on the slave ship, but lying with Quinn would bear no resemblance to that if their one encounter was any indication. The idea of learning to express his desires was nearly as seductive as the possibility of experiencing pleasure again at Quinn's hands. "Show me."

Cock jumping at the blatant invitation, Quinn backed Eliodoro the rest of the way down the corridor to his cabin, continuing the affectionate nuzzling the entire time. If the way the lad squirmed and sighed was any indication, those signs of caring would be what truly won him over. With a smile, Quinn pushed the door open and danced Eliodoro inside, kicking the door shut behind him. Showering Eliodoro with tenderness would be no hardship.

Lifting his head, Quinn stroked his thumb along Eliodoro's jaw until the dark eyes opened. When the heavy lids parted to reveal the Venetian's mahogany gaze, Quinn smiled tenderly and lowered his head again, intending to kiss Eliodoro. The younger man had other ideas, though, turning his head slightly so that Quinn's lips skimmed his cheek again rather than meeting his lips. The rejection stung, but Quinn reminded himself that Eliodoro had been abused repeatedly and in God only knew what ways. If a kiss, no matter Quinn's intentions in bestowing it, brought back unpleasant memories, he would respect Eliodoro's fears and try something else instead. Keeping his touch light, he threaded his fingers into the long, dark hair, angling Eliodoro's head so he could blow lightly across the whorl of one ear. That provoked a delicate shiver. Deciding he liked that reaction, Quinn did it again. And again, until Eliodoro leaned against him fully, prey to constant trembling.

"You'd be more comfortable on the bed," Quinn murmured, his lips a hair's breadth from Eliodoro's skin.

Eliodoro shook harder in Quinn's arms, but he nodded, the movement so slight that Quinn might have missed it had his lips not been pressed against Eliodoro's hair.

Quinn tightened his embrace, steadying Eliodoro as he lowered him onto the bunk, brushing his hair away from his forehead as he perched on the edge of the mattress. The trembling increased again, Eliodoro's hands clutching at Quinn's wrists.

"What do you want?" Quinn prompted.

Eliodoro shook his head in mute supplication, not sure he even knew what he needed, beyond Quinn's arms around him. The night before, Quinn had swept him up in passion before Eliodoro had a chance to react or even to think. The deliberate pace of their current encounter gave him far too much time to think of all the ways things could go wrong between them, of the countless ways he'd been hurt in the past.

Quinn wished he could draw Eliodoro into his arms and kiss the lad senseless, but he'd promised he wouldn't do anything Eliodoro didn't want, and he'd made his antipathy toward kissing quite clear. He'd have to distract Eliodoro some other way. Brushing his fingers over Eliodoro's eyelids, he encouraged them to close. "Relax," he urged. "You don't have to do anything but lie here and feel. Let me make you feel good."

Eliodoro bit back a half-sob at the words, wondering what he had done to deserve this unexpected blessing. He let his eyelids fall shut and tried not to tense in anticipation. A moment later, he felt fingers on the laces of his new shirt, parting the cotton. The stirring of air across his nipples sent a shiver down his back again. The quartermaster had been gentle with him the night before, but Eliodoro remembered all too well what it had felt like to have his nipples pinched and bitten cruelly. The dark disks were painfully sensitive, even the brush of his shirt enough to cause them to stand upright, a fact the slavers had used to add to his fear.

Nothing in Eliodoro's experience could have prepared him for the hot puff of air across his nipple followed by the fleeting swipe of a wet tongue. He jolted upright, a soft cry escaping him at the pleasure flashed through him like lightning.

"Did you like that?" Quinn chuckled, fairly sure he knew the answer but needing to be sure.

"*Sì*," Eliodoro gasped, tugging Quinn's head back down toward his chest. "*Molto*. So much."

Quinn's lips curved as he let Eliodoro guide him. The youth's skin tasted fresh, like he had bathed again while he was washing his clothes. Quinn groaned at the thought of coming across his young lover bathing in the stream. It had been hard enough to withdraw seeing Eliodoro doing his laundry. To have found him bathing would have made that impossible. Then again, he no longer needed to worry about hiding his desire.

Keeping his touch light despite his desire to mark Eliodoro as his, Quinn licked the pert nipple again, eliciting another soft moan. He shifted on the bunk to get more comfortable, bracing himself on one elbow as he stretched out beside Eliodoro, careful not to pin the other man with his weight. The last thing he wanted was for Eliodoro to feel trapped. When he was settled, he anointed the tempting peak again, the fingers of his free hand slipping beneath the cloth of Eliodoro's shirt to find the mate of the nubbin he was currently worshipping. Eliodoro undulated on the bed, his thigh bumping Quinn's cock with alarming regularity, but the quartermaster pushed that awareness aside. He needed to hear more of the delightful gasps and sighs the way he needed to take his next breath, and Eliodoro derived such obvious pleasure from the attention that he was in no hurry to move on.

Eliodoro's skin grew hotter beneath Quinn's lips as he continued to minister to the younger man's nipples. Words babbled from his lips, such a mixture of Italian and Spanish and English that Quinn didn't understand any of it, but it didn't matter. Eliodoro's fingers grasped Quinn's head tightly, keeping him in place, so he had no doubt the words were intended as encouragement. Sucking the pearl into his mouth, he closed his teeth experimentally around Eliodoro's flesh, not biting down yet. Eliodoro tensed immediately beneath his touch, so Quinn froze, except for his tongue which flicked even faster over the bud between his teeth.

"Quinn!"

Releasing his prize for a moment, Quinn glanced up at Eliodoro, trying to discern his lover's desires. "Do you want me to stop?" he asked after a moment.

"No, only… gentle, *si?*"

"Gently," Quinn promised, his teeth finding flesh again, holding it in place so he could lave it thoroughly. Eliodoro tossed restlessly on the bed, dislodging Quinn's mouth. He took advantage of the distraction to roll Eliodoro onto his side so he could reach the lad's other nipple.

The sensations were nearly too much for Eliodoro when Quinn started in on his other side, licking and sucking and not quite biting until Eliodoro thought he would lose his mind if he did not find some surcease from the stimulation, yet he rejected the idea of pulling away out of hand. His bollocks ached with the need for release. Without thinking, he slid a hand toward his groin.

The quartermaster's fingers closed around his wrist before he could reach his target. Eliodoro whimpered in protest, but Quinn's grip was implacable. He lifted Eliodoro's hand back to his shoulder, then gave Eliodoro exactly what he wanted, his own callused palm sliding into the younger man's breeches to encircle the hardened flesh. Eliodoro's back arched as he cried out, his cock twitching powerfully as it disgorged its offering into Quinn's palm.

Quinn continued to stroke the softening flesh slowly, letting Eliodoro recover at his own pace. Eventually, his breathing settled, though it still hitched when Quinn's thumb neared the sensitive tip. The dark eyes fluttered open, and Quinn's breath caught in his throat at the look of utter devotion he read in the other man's gaze. He wanted to lean up and kiss the sweetly bowed lips, but he refrained, settling for peppering tender kisses across his lover's sternum instead.

Every inch of Eliodoro's body sang in delight at the continuing caresses, but his cock had grown overly sensitive. Shifting slightly, he escaped Quinn's hand, the movement causing his hip to bump the quartermaster's hardness. Though Quinn seemed inclined to affection still, Eliodoro knew all too well the dangers of a man in full rut. Hoping to encourage the continuation of the tenderness, he spoke softly. "I take care of that for you." He hated the timidity he heard in his voice, but he couldn't seem to project more confidence. "Is nothing I no 'ave done before."

Quinn's gut clenched at the resignation in Eliodoro's voice. His hands and lips stilled against the dark skin. He wanted nothing more than to keep making love to the other man, but only if Eliodoro wanted it as much as he did. He didn't want it to be a chore. He could do his best to rouse Eliodoro's passions again, or he could put the control squarely where it had never been before: in Eliodoro's hands.

Sitting up, he gazed down at the recumbent form, letting his desire show on his face. "I don't care what you've done before," Quinn said slowly. "I'm not those men, and I don't want you to ever do anything you don't want to do wholeheartedly. So tell me what you want. You can lie back, and I can finish apologizing for last night by making love to you properly. I can lie back, and you can do to me whatever would please you most. Or we can simply lie here together until we fall asleep."

"But—"

"But nothing," Quinn interrupted. "I'm a man, not an animal. I can enjoy the fact that I gave pleasure to a beautiful man without having to take my release by force, or even at all. They cowed you so much on the slave ship that you don't even realize how much power you have right now, do you?"

"Power?" Eliodoro scoffed. "Is no power in my position."

"Then change your position," Quinn challenged. "Tell me to lie back, and take what you want from me. Or tell me what you want me to do to you, and I'll do it."

"If I tell you leave?"

"Then I'll have to figure out how to explain to the crew that I'm sleeping on deck tonight," Quinn answered immediately.

"You would no," Eliodoro disagreed. "You find another bed, perhaps in town."

Quinn shrugged. "A cold, empty one it would be. I'd much rather stay here with you, if you can be persuaded of my sincerity. Tell me how I can best please you, Eliodoro."

Eliodoro's fears warred with his desire to trust the genuineness of Quinn's offer. "Lie down beside me," he said finally.

Quinn complied immediately, stretching out next to Eliodoro again and drawing the young man into a tender embrace, Eliodoro's head cradled on the quartermaster's broad shoulder. "Truly, if all we do is lie like this until our next watch, I will be content."

Eliodoro found that hard to believe, but as minutes passed and Quinn remained where he was, not making any effort to change Eliodoro's mind or to sate his own passions, the Venetian began to give credence to the quartermaster's word. The older man's closeness and the smell of arousal in the room combined to light a new fire in Eliodoro's loins, stoked this time by his own imaginings. It became harder and harder to lie still at Quinn's side, touching yet not truly touching, together yet still separated by layers of clothing and Quinn's promise to do nothing more than Eliodoro wanted. "You promise make love to me."

"And I kept my promise," Quinn reminded Eliodoro, struggling to resist the temptation to roll the young man beneath him and bury his still hard cock in the tight sheath he'd barely had a chance to explore the night before.

Eliodoro shook his head. "Is no enough." He pushed up on one elbow and reached for Quinn's hand, drawing it around until it rested on his arse. "Make love to me."

Chapter 16

QUINN didn't ask if Eliodoro was sure. He'd been self-sacrificing for long enough. Rolling to his knees, he grabbed the hem of Eliodoro's shirt and pulled it over his head, baring his smooth chest completely. He lingered for a moment on Eliodoro's nipples, licking each one until they were both hard as diamonds. They weren't his real target this time, though, so he didn't tarry for long, stripping his own shirt off before undoing Eliodoro's breeches. He gasped when Eliodoro's hands, cool despite the warmth of the room, carded through the dusting of hair on his chest. "Yes," he hissed in delight. "Touch me too."

Emboldened by the quartermaster's obvious approval, Eliodoro let his hands wander the lines of Quinn's musculature. So lost was he in his newfound freedom that he didn't even flinch when lifting his hips to allow Quinn to remove his breeches brought their groins into intimate contact for a moment. He was finally coming to believe he had nothing to fear in the Englishman's bed.

The brief brush of their cocks together enflamed Quinn's senses again, making him wish he could simply plunge into Eliodoro's tight heat and take his ease, but he had done that last night, to his great shame. He had promised to make love to Eliodoro, and he intended to fulfill not only the letter but the spirit of his words, taking his time and cherishing each stage until Eliodoro could have no doubt how highly esteemed he was in Quinn's eyes. To that end, he resisted the urge to rip open his breeches, focusing instead on returning Eliodoro to such a fever pitch that he would not balk at the final hurdle.

Eliodoro's hands faltered when Quinn parted his thighs, splaying them on either side of his hips so that Eliodoro was completely open to the other man's eyes and hands and cock. He tried not to tense, but the feeling of vulnerability was incredibly strong. Not that his captors had bothered with a bed most times when they raped him. They usually bent him over whatever surface was closest and simply took him from behind, but it had happened a few times, especially at first when the captain was still "breaking him in." He shuddered at the memory, trying to push it aside. Quinn's hands on his calves were as tender as his lips had been earlier on Eliodoro's nipples.

"Relax," Quinn urged, feeling the tension investing Eliodoro's limbs. "You know I'll stop if you need me to." To prove his point, he let his hands drop to his sides, waiting for Eliodoro's permission to continue.

The sudden absence of touch only added to Eliodoro's unease, though, because instead of the comfort of Quinn's hands and the pleasure they promised, he had only Quinn's eyes on his body, studying him with that same attention to detail that made the quartermaster so valuable to the captain. Eliodoro squirmed uncomfortably. "Touch me."

Immediately, Quinn's hands returned to their leisurely stroking, up the outside of Eliodoro's thighs and back down the inside, tarrying each time he heard a hitch of breath or saw a flutter of Eliodoro's lashes. With each pass, he felt the tension ease, until Eliodoro's legs spread wide for him. Scooting a little closer to his lover's groin to make it harder for him to pull away should Quinn's next touch surprise him, Quinn changed the direction of his stroking, so that the upward slide brushed on either side of the heavy sac and reviving erection. As he'd expected, Eliodoro's thighs clenched hard, unable to close because of Quinn's bulk between them.

"Do you want me to stop?" His hands paused a finger's width from the tip of Eliodoro's cock, waiting for the answer.

"No."

Eliodoro spoke his answer so softly Quinn could barely hear him, but the lad's eyes closed again, no fear on his face, so the quartermaster accepted the truth in the word, his fingers finding the sensitive tip and sliding back the foreskin to tease along the weeping slit. Eliodoro whimpered, pushing his hips up in search of more contact. Quinn smiled and provided it, one hand continuing to stimulate the sensitive rod while, with the other, he reached for the salve he would need to prepare Eliodoro.

"What is that?" Eliodoro asked.

"It's a salve Gavin uses to mix medicines," Quinn explained, "but this doesn't have any of his powders in it yet. It's just the ointment itself. It's slippery, which makes it easier for a man to please a lover." He held out the tin so Eliodoro could examine its contents.

Eliodoro sniffed the unguent, but it was odorless, translucent, entirely harmless as far as he could tell. He vaguely remembered being surprised the night before how easily first Quinn's finger, then his cock, slid inside. He clearly held the answer in his hand. Nodding, he passed the tin back to the quartermaster, consciously relaxing the muscles in his thighs so he was once again completely open to Quinn's touch.

Quinn saw in the young man's posture the moment Eliodoro accepted what would happen between them, and his heart beat faster with gratitude and anticipation. Coating his fingers in the greasy substance, he circled Eliodoro's shaft again with one hand, hoping to use that distraction to keep his lover from tensing at his other touch.

It worked.

Eliodoro thrust up into Quinn's fist, lifting his buttocks to exactly the right angle for Quinn's fingers to sail between smooth cheeks in search of the port he sought. As Eliodoro subsided again, his weight provided the pressure Quinn needed to slip into the tight channel where he hoped to berth his cock before long. Eliodoro gasped, but he didn't pull away.

"The more of this I get inside you now, the less it will hurt later," Quinn promised, rubbing his finger along the walls in search of Eliodoro's pleasure point. A hoarse shout let him know when he'd found it. With a smile, he pressed against it repeatedly until Eliodoro was thrashing on the bunk, eyes frantic and breath coming in short little gasps. "More?" he teased.

Eliodoro sobbed his plea, so drunk on pleasure already that he'd have done anything, promised anything for more of the heady sensations.

Leaning forward, Quinn lifted the tip of Eliodoro's erection to his mouth as he added a second finger into the narrow passage, hoping to offset any remaining pain with the shock and pleasure of being fellated. Eliodoro certainly didn't seem to notice the additional girth, fucking himself on Quinn's fingers as he thrust up into the quartermaster's mouth. Quinn adjusted the angle so he could take Eliodoro more easily, letting the head of the long, narrow shaft bump the back of his throat.

Eliodoro knew what it felt like to have a cock shoved down his throat, having been forced onto his knees to perform that service too many times to count, but he'd never been on the receiving end of the act. Until now. His entire body seized up at the sensation, every muscle taut as his cock slid deeper into Quinn's mouth. Everything else faded into nothingness as Quinn sucked lightly, his tongue playing around the head before delving into the slit, tasting the fluid that coated it.

Only when Quinn let him go with an audible pop did Eliodoro feel the increase in fullness inside him, two fingers instead of one working him open. He squirmed against the pressure, but Quinn's hand settled low and heavy on his belly, steadying him. "Let me do this right," Quinn requested. "Let me pleasure you so well now that you'll welcome me inside you simply to find release."

Eliodoro subsided after a moment. Quinn scooted even closer, lifting Eliodoro's hips onto his knees so he could delve even farther between the smooth cheeks, his fingers shunting with painstaking slowness in and out of the tight sheath. His other hand caressed Eliodoro's cock and bollocks lightly, keeping the lad on the razor's edge of pleasure. Little keening gasps escaped Eliodoro's throat, bringing a smile to Quinn's face. He withdrew his fingers long enough to coat them again, winning a cry of protest from his lover.

"I'm not stopping," he soothed Eliodoro. "I merely needed more salve. I'm not a small man, as you learned last night, and I don't intend to hurt you by mistake."

Eliodoro shook his head. Even last night, with as little time as Quinn had spent on the preliminaries, it hadn't hurt like on the slave ship. He felt empty with Quinn's fingers gone, and he wanted the sense of completion back, whether it was from the quartermaster's fingers or cock.

"Three fingers this time," Quinn warned, pressing his digits together tightly so they would fit inside the snug hole. "Let me in."

Eliodoro tensed automatically, and Quinn cursed under his breath at his error in judgment. He should have simply slid them inside while Eliodoro was distracted rather than giving the lad a reason to fear what would happen next. He bent forward, intending to take Eliodoro's cock in his mouth again, but hands on his head stopped him.

"No," Eliodoro said. "Just do it."

"You have to relax," Quinn urged. "It will hurt if you don't. Relax for me, pretty one."

The endearment, the same one from the night before, soothed something inside Eliodoro, and the tension seeped from his body. The moment it did, Quinn's fingers worked their way back inside him. The stretch stung, but before he could protest, the long digits had found his sweet spot again, stealing his breath and any thought of stopping the quartermaster. He rocked against Quinn's hands, planting his feet on the mattress to lift himself higher in search of the pleasure the older man could bring him.

Patience at an end at the delectable sight, Quinn tore open his breeches with one hand, pushing them down enough to free his rampant erection. He pulled his fingers free, intending to finish fulfilling his promise to Eliodoro, but the Venetian stopped him. "Off," he said, gesturing to Quinn's trousers. "I want see."

Hastily, Quinn rose and finished stripping, freezing when Eliodoro's hand closed around his cock and his head bent to lick over the tip. "If you do much of that, I'll spend before I get inside you," he warned.

Eliodoro nodded and licked him one more time before lying back, legs spread in silent offering. Quinn knelt on the bunk again, stroking Eliodoro's cheek one more time before covering the smaller body with his own bulk and slotting his cock into the snug crease. "I will be as careful as I know how," he swore.

It was a promise no man had ever made to Eliodoro, and he thought he might expire from the sheer joy of Quinn's care for him. Silently he vowed not to let Quinn see any hint of anything except pleasure on his face, no matter what he felt. The quartermaster was a better cocksman than that, though, taking his time working his shaft into Eliodoro's body and concentrating his thrusts on the spot that gave the younger man such intense pleasure. Within moments, Eliodoro was thrashing on the bed, not to get away, but to get closer, deeper, harder. More.

Quinn gave it to him, plundering Eliodoro's tight arse as eagerly as the younger man gave it. The desire to kiss his lover grew again, but Quinn ignored it regretfully, not wanting to impose his own wishes on the younger man. It was enough that Eliodoro was here in his bed, meeting Quinn thrust for thrust. Nothing else truly mattered.

Quinn wanted to draw out their lovemaking, but he'd taken too long in the preparations, and his control had grown shaky. Slipping a hand between them, he shunted his hand up and down Eliodoro's cock, determined to wring another climax from his lover before finding his own pleasure.

The trembling began low in Eliodoro's belly, the deep ache he had begun to recognize at Quinn's hands the past two days. He wasn't ready for their congress to end, but he didn't have the experience with pleasure to allow him to delay. As the tremors grew stronger, his eyes closed, giving in to the passion only Quinn had ever been able to rouse. With a sharp cry, he climaxed, spasms of delight racking his body.

Hips stuttering against Eliodoro's pliant body, Quinn let his own passion flow out of him in mute offering, another burst triggered by each clench of Eliodoro's muscles around his cock. His strength stolen by the force of his orgasm, he collapsed forward onto Eliodoro's slender form, breathing in the scents of their mingled passion.

Feeling replete and contented, Quinn rolled toward the wall, careful to keep Eliodoro in a snug embrace so he wouldn't feel rejected. His back bumped the rough wood, but he ignored it in the interest of studying Eliodoro's features still in repose. The closed lids hid eyes as deep as the ocean and as dark as a rich field lying fallow, but Quinn didn't need to see them to imagine them. He stroked the tumbled curls away from Eliodoro's high forehead once again, understanding now why the young man kept them so tightly confined while they were at sea. He'd be constantly battling to keep them out of his eyes otherwise.

The touch roused Eliodoro from his stupor, his eyes opening and a shy smile curving his lips upward. Once again, Quinn was struck by the desire to lean down and kiss the elegant bow, and once again, he made himself resist.

Eliodoro wanted nothing more than to curl into Quinn's embrace and never move again, but they were not two simple sailors, nor were they the captain and Mr. Watson. The difference in their stations kept him from relaxing completely. "I should return to my berth," he said softly.

"Not yet," Quinn said, arms tightening around Eliodoro. "Stay here awhile longer. Please?"

Eliodoro subsided, Quinn's request coinciding with his own desires. "Others talk if I sleep 'ere."

"The others are all ashore on leave," Quinn reminded him. "No one will miss you tonight as long as you're at your post for your next watch."

"When we leave port, they will notice."

"When we leave port, I'll let you go."

IN THE captain's cabin, Amery smiled at Gavin. "It appears Quinn's luck has held true."

Gavin chuckled. "The lad was ripe for the picking. If Quinn plays his cards right, the boy will never leave his bed."

Amery arched an eyebrow. "I might have something to say about that if he doesn't report for duty."

Gavin rolled his eyes. "As if Quinn would be that remiss. Come, lover. Now that they've finished their caterwauling, 'tis time to sleep."

Amery settled Gavin more comfortably against his side and closed his eyes, his smile at Quinn's good fortune following him into slumber.

Rest came far more slowly for Gavin, the revelations of Eliodoro's past having brought his own unpleasant memories to the fore again. Amery had comforted him through the worst of his experiences as a boy, but Gavin still hadn't told him the truth of his time on the Spanish ship. Amery knew he'd been used as Quinn had been, but he assumed Gavin had fought them. Maybe he should have fought them, but the thought of being raped again was more than he could bear at the time. He'd given them everything they wanted and offered more to avoid being hurt, and that was something Amery would never understand.

Exhaustion finally forced his eyes to close, but the memories followed him into repose. Hands grabbed him from every side, tearing at his clothing, pinching and squeezing, digging into tender flesh, determined to cause as much pain as possible. Voices from unseen faces jeered at him as the hands drove him forward, naked now, calling him a whore and a slut and a godless sodomite. He struggled to escape them, sure he'd be safe if he could just get back to the *Silver Queen* only to have Amery's face appear out of the haze hiding his tormentors. Amery spat at him, producing the contract of their matelotage and ripping it in two as he called Gavin every foul name he knew.

Gavin came out of the nightmare with a hoarse cry, his body covered in cold sweat, his stomach churning with nausea. The bile rose in his throat despite the calming breaths. Unable to hold it back, he stumbled to the chamber pot, emptying the remains of his dinner and the ale they'd drunk with it into the copper urn.

"Wha's wrong, love?" Amery's voice was slurred with sleep.

"Nothing," Gavin coughed. "Nightmare."

"Come back to bed, and let me hold you."

Gavin spat one more time to clear the taste of bile from his mouth and wiped the spittle from his lips, crawling back into bed next to Gavin, grateful that, for one more night at least, he could count on the comfort of his lover's arms.

Chapter 17

ELIODORO slipped from Quinn's bunk and his cabin the next morning before the quartermaster awoke, not comfortable with anyone seeing him coming from the officers' quarters at that hour. He believed the sincerity of Quinn's apology and his assurances that he didn't view Eliodoro as a plaything, but Eliodoro was keenly aware of the differences in their stations and the way his presence in Quinn's bed would appear to the rest of the crew. Perhaps if he'd had some commitment to defend himself.... He shook his head, reminding himself not to hope for something that would probably never come. Quinn had given no indication of looking for any kind of permanence, much less with someone like Eliodoro.

Climbing to his perch in the crow's nest, he settled down to watch the sun rising out of the water in a display of heavenly glory. He shielded his eyes with his hand, his thoughts all awhirl as he listened to the waves lapping at the ship's hull and the seabirds crying overhead. Movement on the deck drew his attention, but it wasn't yet his watch so he didn't go down when he saw others from the crew milling about as they changed watch. A few moments later, *Signor* Watson appeared on deck. Eliodoro considered going down to talk to the ship's surgeon, but before he could decide, Quinn joined the other man, reminding Eliodoro that whatever other role *Signor* Watson played on the ship, he was also Quinn's friend. Not the ideal confidant for Eliodoro's doubts and fears.

The two men had started back toward their quarters when a shout hailed the ship from shore. They turned back, waving for the speaker to come aboard. Eliodoro couldn't hear what was being said, but he saw, far too clearly, the possessive way the newcomer draped his arm around Quinn's shoulders. Doubt piercing his heart, he slithered down from his perch, hoping to hear what was said.

As his feet hit the deck, the unknown man trailed a finger down the center of Quinn's chest. "You didn't come see me last night like you promised."

Eliodoro froze, breath bated as he waited to hear Quinn's response.

"I'm sorry, Tom. I couldn't get away last night after all, but what brings you out to the ship?"

Eliodoro didn't wait to hear the other man's reply. Biting his lip to hold back a sob, he turned on his heel and fled to the questionable safety of his hammock. At least with most of the crew on shore leave, there would be no one to see him cry.

"I heard you were looking for some Spaniards," Tom explained, "and I think I know one of them you're after. He came in the tavern, woulda been a month ago, maybe a little less. Down on his luck, gambling hard trying to make a coin or two. Hodges wouldn't give him nothing on credit. He never does. The man grabbed my arse a time or two when I walked by, and when I wouldn't give him the time of day neither, he cornered me in the alley when I'd gone to use the privy. Hodges came out and dragged him off of me, but it gave me cause to remember the man. He came back a few days later, bragging he'd gotten a berth on the *Rayo* out of Puerto Rico, running between there and the Spanish Main. I don't know as it's true, but he disappeared after that, and I ain't seen him since."

"Thank you," Quinn said. "He, along with the others we seek, hurt one of our crew. We'd like to return the favor."

Tom's expression tightened. "You're not talkin' about a sword in the side, are you?"

Gavin shook his head. "You go into battle, you're going to get hurt. These bastards are rapists of the worst order. I'll tell Amery, and then I want to talk to you, Quinn. Tom, how much do we owe Hodges for his assistance?"

"Whatever it is, he'll have to do without it," Tom declared. "In my line of work, you see the worst humanity has to offer. If you're set to make sure a few of them see justice, I'll not charge you a penny for it."

"Thanks, Tom," Quinn said, clapping the other man on the shoulder. "Don't look for me again. I imagine the captain will want to set sail as soon as the crew's back aboard and if all goes well...."

Tom nodded sagely. "If that's the case, then you'd best be seeing to the lad who ran outta here when he saw us talking. He didn't look like he was happy to see the likes of me at your side."

Quinn's eyes widened.

"He went that way," Tom said helpfully, pointing toward the forecastle. "I'll just take myself back to shore then. Safe seas to you, lads."

Quinn didn't reply, already on his way after Eliodoro. Gavin let him go. If Eliodoro had overheard Quinn's comment to Tom, he'd have yet more apologizing to do. At least, if the sounds he'd overheard were any indication, Quinn had made up for his first gaffe. That might predispose Eliodoro to listen to his explanations this time.

Belowdecks, Quinn took a moment for his eyes to adjust to the dimness of the crew's quarters after the brilliance of the Caribbean dawn. When they did, the sight that met his eyes tore at his heart. Eliodoro sat crouched in the corner of the quarters, his head buried in his knees. Crossing the room, grateful none of the others were around, he knelt at Eliodoro's side. "I'm sorry," he said without preamble. "You didn't deserve to have to deal with Tom this morning and without any explanation on my part."

"You could no get away?" Eliodoro spat.

"I'm sorry," Quinn repeated, "but I wasn't ready to dirty the beautiful night we spent together by talking about it to Tom or anyone else. But especially to Tom."

"'E expecting you," Eliodoro pointed out.

"He was," Quinn admitted. "I often visit him when I'm in port. A man has needs, and I didn't have anyone to satisfy them with. There's no harm in that, as long as both parties understand the transaction."

"You use 'im for your pleasure," Eliodoro accused.

"And made sure he found his as well," Quinn insisted. "No one forces Tom to take men to his bed. He chooses his customers and makes his living serving drinks. Yes, I paid for his time, but that doesn't make it an evil thing."

"We only in port two nights," Eliodoro said slowly. "You visit 'im before you find me in the alley."

Quinn flushed, but there was no denying the facts. "Yes. I couldn't have you so I went to him instead."

"And when you left me, did you go back to 'im?"

"No!" Quinn exclaimed. "Of course not! I went back to the tavern where I'd rented a room and wished you were in bed next to me. I won't make that mistake again."

"All hands on deck!"

"The captain's calling," Quinn said regretfully. "We have to go. We'll talk more later, all right?"

Eliodoro nodded slowly, not entirely convinced of the quartermaster's sincerity. The captain had called, though, so their personal affairs would have to wait for later. "*Sì, Signor* Davies."

"No," Quinn protested immediately. "Don't call me that, at least not when we're alone."

"The captain call us. We no alone," Eliodoro insisted, rising to his feet. He'd think about the rest and decide later how he felt about the quartermaster's apology. For the moment, duty called.

They filed onto deck with the few other crewmen on board at the moment. Amery stood at the head of the gangplank, Gavin at his side. "We have a target," Amery announced as soon as everyone had assembled. "Pass the word to everyone that shore leave's canceled. We sail for the Spanish Main with the tide. Anyone not aboard will be left behind."

"Aye, Captain," the men said as one. Amery stepped aside to let them leave.

"Eliodoro."

"Aye, Captain?"

"You have the ship until we return."

Eliodoro's eyes widened in surprise. "Aye, Captain," he repeated. "I no let you down."

"I know you won't, lad," Amery said. "Mr. Watson, Mr. Davies, with me."

Quinn sent Eliodoro one last, lingering look as he followed Gavin and Amery off the ship and into town. He had no idea what Amery wanted him to do, but Amery was the captain and as such, his word was law.

"What are we about?" he asked as they reached the shore.

"Hodges wasn't the only tavern we stopped in," Amery explained. "We may have one target, but five others are still unknown. Take the west side of town. I'll go east and Gavin will go through the center. Ask in every tavern if they have information for Captain White."

Quinn nodded. "I'll see what I can learn. Don't sail without me."

"Don't make us miss the tide," Amery countered with a grin.

Rolling his eyes at the familiar interplay, Gavin walked down the dirt path that doubled as a street, hand on the hilt of his sword. He'd gotten used to having someone—Amery or Quinn or both—at his side when he left the safety of their ship. Despite the sword at his hip, he felt vulnerable as he strode into the first tavern he passed, his nerves grating at the sound of Spanish on the lips of the patrons at the table nearest the door. Had his mission been anything less than finding information on Eliodoro's attackers, he'd have left and gone elsewhere, but he wouldn't let it be said that he hadn't done his best by his fellow sailor. Honor among thieves, perhaps, but honor nonetheless.

The barkeep had no information for him, or so he said. If Amery or Quinn had been with him, Gavin would have lain in wait for the Spaniards to see what they could learn, but he wouldn't take any chances alone.

The rest of the inns on his circuit proved equally unproductive. Shoulders slumping, Gavin returned to the ship lost in his thoughts. Tortuga was a haven for any and all nationalities, and he'd always dealt with Spaniards when they were on the island, but the town seemed more rife than usual with their foulness this time. Or maybe that was his own heightened sensibility, the revelations of Eliodoro's past bringing his own experiences closer to the surface than usual. Either way, he was eager to set sail again, far away from everything that brought back the memories he had tried so hard to suppress. He knew what Quinn would say. Quinn would say he needed to tell Amery the whole story and be done with it so that he could stop worrying about what would happen if Amery ever found out. Quinn didn't have to fear losing his matelot because of his time on the slave ship. Even if Quinn told Eliodoro the worst of it, Eliodoro would understand and probably even admire Quinn for having fought until he was bleeding before being forced into submission. Quinn didn't have to tell Eliodoro that he'd begged like a beaten child and spread his legs like a common whore rather than be hurt again. Some things were better left unsaid.

Gavin climbed the gangplank to the *Silver Queen*, nodding at Eliodoro as he came aboard. The lad nodded back shyly, making Gavin wonder if he ought to say anything about Quinn or Tom or Eliodoro's past. Anything to put him more at ease. His own unease kept the words from coming, though, so he simply returned to his cabin, hoping to find solace in being surrounded by his and Amery's things.

When Quinn and Amery returned an hour later, they brought no better news than Gavin had found. They would have to deal with their current quarry and then begin their search again. Amery returned abovedecks almost immediately, but when Gavin made to follow him, Quinn caught his friend's arm, drawing him into the surgery. "I heard you cry out last night. Are you having nightmares again?"

"I have always had nightmares," Gavin demurred.

"No, you told me they'd gotten better after you started sleeping next to Amery at night," Quinn reminded the surgeon. "Is this because we're targeting the Spanish?"

"That's part of it," Gavin admitted, knowing better than to lie to Quinn. He could fool Amery at times with clever words and distraction, but Quinn was like a dog with a bone, and he noticed everything, at least where Gavin was concerned. Silently, Gavin hoped Quinn would change the focus of his obsession to the young man he'd heard begging and sobbing in Quinn's bed last night. Eliodoro deserved to be the undisputed center of Quinn's universe. "Having to talk about the past, even as little as we did yesterday, is the rest. It sounded like you made good progress last night in convincing your boy of your sincerity."

Quinn flushed. "I thought so, and then he overheard us talking to Tom this morning. He's calling me *Signor* Davies again."

"He's young and hot-headed and so very, very fragile," Gavin reminded Quinn. "Be patient with his moods. You remember what I was like after we jumped ship as boys. A stray touch was enough to have me drawing my sword, even if it came from you and Amery. It took a long time for me to trust again, and only one bastard used me. Eliodoro had seven. I think it's a miracle he let you near him once, much less twice after the way you acted the first time."

Quinn knew Gavin was right, but that wasn't what he wanted to talk to his friend about. "Will you not tell Amery the truth? I'm sure he'll yell and bluster and shout because that's what he does, but he loves you, Gavin. He'll get past his anger, and you won't have to live with this secret hanging over your head."

Gavin shook his head. "I have too much to lose."

"You won't lose him," Quinn insisted. "He needs you as much as you need him. Maybe even more." The words still hurt to say, knowing how differently the situation could have turned out.

Gavin's eyes were haunted as the vision of Amery tearing up their contract returned from his nightmare. "It isn't a chance I can take. Not now. I wouldn't survive losing him."

"You won't," Quinn repeated, his hand going to Gavin's shoulder, "but if I were wrong and you did, you know… you know you'll never be alone as long as I live."

Gavin knew, and it saddened him immensely. "We should go. Amery will be looking for us."

Quinn knew avoidance when he heard it, but he let it go. Gavin would go his own way as always. He only wished there was something he could do to help his friend.

Chapter 18

ON DECK, Amery surveyed the returning crewmen, mentally checking the roll to make sure everyone was accounted for. As the tides changed, he assembled the crew. "We'll be sailing toward the Spanish Main," he announced when everyone gathered on deck. "We know where the treasure ships leave from. Rather than haunt the sailing lanes with no return as we've done this past month, we'll try a new approach and hit them as they leave port on the Spanish Main. Since we've all had leave, we'll draw straws again for watch. Officers first and then crew."

Quinn drew the longest straw, much to his relief. He'd stood night shift before and undoubtedly would again, but he hated every minute of it. Besides, he had this morning's misunderstanding to make up to Eliodoro. Stepping back, he watched as the crew drew straws and scowled when Eliodoro drew night watch. He briefly considered switching watches with someone simply to have some time alone with Eliodoro, but he didn't want to abuse his position. He could talk to Eliodoro as they switched watches or in the morning when the young man came off shift; the realities of duty did not guarantee them any privacy or any time to talk. The *Silver Queen* was only so big. Even if Eliodoro didn't seek him out, he would only be able to avoid Quinn for so long.

When all the watches were assigned, Amery ordered the men to set sail and go about their duties. He took the helm himself, preferring to navigate into unfamiliar waters under his own command. "Mr. Davies," he called after they were under way, "a word if you will."

Surprised at the summons, Quinn joined Amery on the aftcastle, the steering rod between them as they surveyed the horizon. "It would seem you mended fences with your lad," Amery commented, a droll smile playing around his lips. "He treated us to quite the show last night."

Quinn flushed despite himself. "Now you know how I feel, lying abed at night listening to you and Gavin."

"Gavin's a noisy one," Amery agreed, "but it's been some years since his voice was so sweet. He rumbles now more than he sings to my touch."

Unbidden, memories of the last time he had slept with Gavin rose in Quinn's mind. They had been men by then, no longer striplings as Eliodoro still was, and Gavin's bass growl had long since replaced his more youthful cries. "I know," he murmured before catching Amery's sharp look. "The walls of your cabin are not so thick that I don't hear him cry out every time you touch him," he hastened to add, not wanting to bring back up the indiscretion he and Gavin had committed a matter of weeks before they had been taken by the Spanish. Amery and Gavin had broken things off, and Quinn had seen his chance. It might have worked if Amery had not found them and made it clear he still considered Gavin his. "As you said, Eliodoro makes a much lighter sound."

Amery's eyes remained narrowed as he stared piercingly at Quinn, but he could hardly deny the noises his lover made or the fact that Quinn could hear them all, given how much Amery and Gavin had heard of Quinn and Eliodoro's lovemaking the night before. Letting the comment go, he returned his focus to the reason he'd called Quinn to his side. "Is all well between you now?"

"I believe so," Quinn replied. "We will see what happens when he finishes his watch tonight."

"I'm sorry about that," Amery said, "but it wouldn't be fair to treat him differently because of where he sleeps at night."

Quinn shrugged. "He left the cabin before I awoke this morning," he admitted, needing to confide in someone. "I believe he's forgiven me, but I'm not entirely sure he trusts me yet."

"He has little enough reason to trust anyone," Amery agreed, "and more reason than any of us to hesitate. You've but to say and I'll stand witness for you."

Quinn shook his head. "It's not like that," he insisted. "Not yet, anyway. He's barely tasted freedom. The last thing he wants is to find himself tied to a man he hardly knows."

Amery wasn't so sure, remembering how Gavin had reacted to his offer of a matelotage after his rescue from the Spanish pirates. Gavin had needed that promise of forever to restore his balance and belief in himself. Then again, Gavin had already known and trusted Amery. The offer might have been less welcome from a near-stranger.

"Do you want it to be that way?" Amery asked, wanting Quinn to know the same happiness he'd found with Gavin.

Quinn shrugged. "I enjoy his company," he admitted, "and I would kill anyone who hurt him, but I could say the same of you and Gavin."

"So he is nothing more than a convenience?" Amery asked.

Quinn shrugged again. "It is too soon to tell."

Amery bit back a snort with difficulty. He'd known Quinn too long to be put off by the short comment. Quinn could say whatever he wanted. Amery could tell he was already falling for the young Venetian. Now he just had to find ways to encourage Eliodoro to return Quinn's regard. He wouldn't do anything today, having deliberately had the men draw straws to shake up the routine a little, but in a day or two, he could make a few changes as captain to be sure Quinn and Eliodoro shared their off-duty time. He couldn't ensure they shared a bed, but if what he'd heard last night was any indication, they would need only the opportunity for that to happen.

"Does Gavin talk to you about his nightmares?"

Quinn adjusted to the change of topic in the way of old friends or long-term lovers. "Only that he has them still," Quinn answered honestly. "He doesn't give me details, and I don't press."

"Why does he still have them after so long?" Amery mused aloud. "You don't."

Quinn shook his head, remembering the cold sweat that tainted his flesh even in the Caribbean heat on nights when the memories were too strong to ignore. "Not as badly as he does, but I still have them. I don't know if they'll ever completely go away, and he suffered far worse than I did."

Amery's brow furrowed. "What do you mean?"

Quinn silently cursed his slip. "Ask him. It isn't my story to tell."

Amery's expression tightened even more. "What aren't you telling me?"

"Ask Gavin," Quinn repeated. "Now, unless there was something else, Captain, I should check our stores and make sure everything is as it should be."

Amery let him go, staring blankly at the distant horizon, his mind racing as he tried to imagine what could be worse than what he already knew of the horrors Quinn and Gavin had suffered at the hands of the Spaniards. He'd seen the bite marks and blood on their bodies, had held Gavin as he gulped out the admission that the slavers had used him for their pleasure and amusement, rarely giving either of them time to recover between bouts before another one took the last one's place. He shuddered as he tried to imagine the situation, tried to think of something that could have made it worse, with no success. Yet Quinn seemed certain Gavin had not told him something, and that rankled. They were matelots and had been for five years. Surely Gavin knew he could trust Amery with anything.

QUINN left Amery on the upper deck, hoping to catch Eliodoro before he disappeared to sleep before his watch. He tried not to make a habit of invading the crew's quarters without a serious reason. They needed a place of their own, as free of the officers' influence as possible on a ship this size. Because of that policy, though, he couldn't simply barge in now searching for Eliodoro without causing an uproar and signaling to the entire crew the importance of their conversation. Perhaps later, when he and Eliodoro had come to terms better, when they'd decided what and how they would tell the crew of their relationship, he would have fewer hesitations about making a scene, but for now, with everything still undecided, he didn't want to open them up to speculation unnecessarily.

Eliodoro wasn't on deck anymore, though, nor in any of the places Quinn might naturally inspect as they put back out to sea after a few days ashore. With a sigh, he resigned himself to waiting until Eliodoro came out of hiding. The young man was probably asleep in preparation for his night watch, given how little they'd slept the night before. His body quickened at the memory, yearning for the opportunity to recreate the magic of the previous night. He hadn't felt so indulgent toward someone in a long time. Not since he'd become quartermaster, certainly, and maybe not even before that. He wanted to tuck Eliodoro into his cabin and cater to his every whim. Anything to win a smile or a moan of pleasure from the lad.

Smiling at his flight of fancy, he returned to the deck, hoping that wherever Eliodoro had hidden, he was savoring his memories as well. He called orders left and right to the men, but his voice lacked its usual bark. He couldn't bring himself to care. His eyes sought the sun as it marched across the sky, mentally calculating the hours until the change of watch and the chance to catch a glimpse of Eliodoro again.

"Why does Quinn think I need to ask you again about what happened on the Spanish ship?" Amery asked when Gavin joined him in their cabin after dinner.

"Because Quinn is an interfering bastard who doesn't know when to keep his mouth shut," Gavin muttered. He slumped against the cabin wall, eyes downcast, only the top of his dark head visible, his arms around his waist protectively as if to ward off the next blow.

The gesture tore at Amery's heart. Gavin had often stood that way when they were boys, especially if Michaels had been at him. He hadn't seen that exact posture in several years. "Gavin," Amery cajoled, going to his lover's side and wrapping his arms around the brunet, offering support and love, "whatever it is, it can't be as bad as you think it is. Just tell me so we can put it behind us."

Gavin shook his head, fighting the urge to lean back into Amery's embrace. He wanted the comfort of those arms around him, the same arms that had held him so often as a youth when his body had ached and his heart cried out at the injustice of having been singled out for Michaels' unwelcome attention. His body no longer ached the way it had then—even at his roughest, Amery was too considerate a lover for that—but his heart hurt far more now than it had then. Amery knew the worst of what Michaels had done and had accepted it and moved on. He had no idea the worst of what Gavin had done, and when he did, he'd push Gavin away, and that would be the end of the comforting embrace. Gavin wasn't ready to give that up. Turning in Amery's arms, he shook his head, kissing the captain to end the conversation.

Amery let Gavin divert him, his lover's unusual reticence making him nervous. He couldn't imagine what Gavin was hiding that he thought was so terrible, but if it bothered Gavin this much, Amery saw no harm in reassuring him beforehand with a thorough loving. He deepened the kiss and backed Gavin toward the bed, lowering him down onto it and stripping him with swift, economical movements.

Gavin's breath caught in his throat as Amery's hands swarmed over him, stealing his breath and his composure. No man had ever touched him with that heady degree of authority, taking what he wanted as if it were his due and yet at the same time bestowing such pleasure that Gavin wished he had more and more to give simply so he could offer it to Amery. His heart sped up as Amery ravished him, leaving no inch of skin untouched or unkissed, taking complete ownership of Gavin's body as he had long ago taken possession of his heart and soul.

He cried out with bliss as Amery found every sensitive place on his body, caressing, licking, sucking until he was mindless with need and want, promising Amery anything if only he would keep touching him, keep loving him. Amery didn't answer him with words, but his actions spoke for him, giving Gavin what he begged for, stretching and filling him, first with his fingers, then with his cock, until they were as close as two men could be, their bodies joined as completely as their lives.

Gavin wanted the moment to stretch on for eternity, but even Amery's skill and iron will could only hold back their climax for so long. Pressing his face against Amery's heaving shoulder, Gavin released a muffled sob as he lost the battle to hold back, his cock pouring forth the tribute of his love. Seconds later, he felt the rush of wet heat as Amery joined him in rapture, collapsing atop him and pinning him to the bed.

For several long minutes, Amery lay there, nuzzling the curve of Gavin's neck, the smooth skin behind his ear, the stubble that covered his cheek, imbuing the gestures with as much tenderness as he knew how to show. He knew he was not the only man, or even the first man, to touch Gavin's body, but he also knew he was the only man to have ever touched his heart. Finally, he lifted his head, keeping Gavin pinned to the bed beneath him. "Now tell me what it is Quinn thinks I should know."

Gavin tensed beneath Amery's body, stomach heaving at the thought of the conversation to come. He'd hoped Amery would forget about it, but he should have known better. Amery never forgot about anything. "Don't ask me this," he begged.

Amery shook his head. "Stop hiding from me."

"I'm not hiding," Gavin protested. "It's not important enough to talk about."

"Then why won't you tell me?"

"Because it's not something you need to know."

"Quinn disagreed," Amery said softly, "and I think he's right. Tell me."

"Let me up."

Amery didn't move.

"Damn it, Amery. If you want me to tell you, I will, but I'm not going to do it flat on my back with your cock still up my arse. Let me up, and I'll tell you what you think you want to know, but don't say I didn't warn you," Gavin said, pulling away in earnest.

Disengaging, Amery rolled to the side, letting Gavin sit up. To his surprise, Gavin rose from the bed and pulled his clothes back on. "What are you doing?"

Gavin just shook his head, anger building in him at being forced to face his past when he'd thought it finally laid to rest. "You want to know the truth?" he demanded savagely. "The truth is, I wasn't raped on the Spanish ship. Quinn was. Repeatedly and brutally. I wasn't. When they came for me, I didn't fight them. I did whatever they asked. Anything not to be hurt again."

He turned away, unable to face the disbelief and disgust on Amery's face, memories washing over him as bile rose in his throat once more. For a few endless seconds, he was back in the hold on the Spanish slaver, struggling against the ropes that bound him, trying to get free so he and Quinn could make their escape. Then their captors were there, dirty hands tearing at their clothes. They took Quinn first, his fairer skin and blond hair enough of a novelty to draw their attention, dragging him up on deck. Gavin couldn't see what happened, but he watched Quinn fight them all the way out of the hold. He could hear the tussle continue over his head, the Spaniards jeering and cheering as Quinn's shouts of anger changed to cries of pain. When they brought him back into the hold hours later, he was covered in welts and bruises, the tops of his legs soaked in blood from being raped.

Hands still bound, he could do nothing except scoot closer to Quinn's side, offering him what little comfort the warmth of his body could provide. When their captors came back, stepping over Quinn like so much offal, he'd summoned his nerve and smiled sweetly at them, going along docilely. In broken Spanish, he'd promised to do whatever they wanted if they wouldn't hurt him. The captain had laughed and agreed, and for the week before Amery found them, he'd been the ship's whore.

It hadn't stopped them from playing with Quinn, too, much to Gavin's dismay. They'd still dragged him out of the hold every day to toy with him before doing their best to break him. Gavin was already broken.

"Whore," Amery spat, Gavin's revelation too much for him to comprehend. The thought of any man but him touching his lover was already enough to send him into a jealous rage, but he'd consoled himself that with the exception of Quinn, Gavin had allowed no man to touch him willingly. To hear now that Gavin had invited the Spanish curs to take him destroyed the very foundation on which he'd based their relationship.

Gavin flinched as if struck. He'd known Amery would react this way, but a part of him had hoped for a different reaction, however foolhardy a wish it had been. His shoulders sagged, knowing nothing he could say would make any difference now.

"I'm sorry," he whispered. "I didn't want to tell you."

"Of course you didn't," Amery snarled. "You had too much to lose. You weren't a victim at all, were you? Did you moan and beg for them to fuck you?"

A bitter laugh barked from Gavin's throat. "Of course I did. I did exactly what they told me to. I was afraid if I didn't, they wouldn't keep their part of the bargain, even if I didn't fight."

"And when you moaned and begged with me? Was that an act too?"

"No!" Gavin cried, taking a step forward, reaching for Amery's hand. "God, no! I did what I had to do to survive. It doesn't have anything to do with us."

Amery pulled away. "There is no 'us'. Get out."

Gavin couldn't stop the sob that tore from his throat. He stumbled toward the door, finding the knob blindly. He made it as far as the door to Quinn's cabin before he collapsed.

Chapter 19

HIS watch over, Quinn strode back toward his cabin, intending to rest for a while before seeking out Eliodoro. The young man would have to stand watch during the night, but the night duty was always quieter and the cover of darkness would provide them the opportunity to talk more discreetly. His mind totally focused on his pursuit of the Venetian, he nearly stepped on the huddle in front of his door before his attention snapped back to the present and he realized Gavin was sitting there. Frowning, he knelt next to his friend. "What's wrong, Gavin?"

Gavin's gaze was venomous. "Why did you have to meddle?" he demanded. "Why couldn't you just let us go on as we have for the last five years?"

"What are you talking about?" Quinn asked, not following the conversation.

"Amery kicked me out when I told him what I did on the Spanish ship."

"The bastard!" Quinn growled. "I'll set him straight."

"Don't," Gavin said tiredly. "You've done more than enough already. Besides, he's too angry to listen to anything you have to say. I need a place to sleep tonight. The cabin off the surgery is full of my supplies. I can't even get to the bunk because why would I ever need to?"

"I'm sorry," Quinn said, pulling Gavin into his arms. "I truly believed he would understand, and you would be able to let go of your shame. I wouldn't have said anything otherwise."

Gavin nodded numbly, leaning heavily in Quinn's embrace.

Quinn pressed a tender kiss to Gavin's forehead. "Come on. Let's get you in bed."

He opened the door to his cabin and helped Gavin inside, shutting the door behind them as Gavin began to tremble.

He didn't see the twin expressions of betrayal from either end of the corridor.

"Tell me what happened," Quinn requested when he had settled Gavin on his bunk.

"He started asking questions the moment we were alone," Gavin recounted. "I begged him not to make me tell him, but he wouldn't take no for an answer." He didn't tell Quinn about making love. That memory was too precious to sully with the current tension. "So I told him I'd bargained instead of fighting. He called me a whore and told me to get out."

"I ought to knock his head through the wall," Quinn growled, pacing the narrow confines of his cabin. "You did what you had to do to survive. You didn't want any of them."

"That didn't matter to Amery," Gavin sighed. "I need to sleep."

"Of course," Quinn said. "Will it bother you if I stay?"

Gavin shook his head. "It's your bed. I can hardly put you out of it."

"If having me here would make you uncomfortable, I'll find another place to sleep," Quinn assured Gavin with a tender smile and a shake of his head. The memory of making the same offer to Eliodoro the previous night drifted through his mind, but he pushed it aside. Gavin needed him, and nothing else mattered. Eliodoro would have to understand.

"I'd rather not be alone," Gavin admitted. Even if Quinn's warmth was not the warmth he desired.

"Then I'll stay. I told you before that you never had to be alone."

"Don't," Gavin said hoarsely, hearing the earnest tone of Quinn's voice. "Don't love me. What's left of my heart belongs to Amery. You know that. You've always known it."

Quinn knew, but that had never seemed to matter. "You still deserve to be loved."

"I can't, Quinn," Gavin said sorrowfully. "He already thinks the worst of me. I don't want to complicate matters more by adding a new infidelity."

"There was no infidelity," Quinn insisted, sitting down beside Gavin on the bed and taking his hand. "Amery is a fool if he can't see you were raped as surely as I was. The only difference is how much it hurt."

"Amery *doesn't* see that, and nothing else matters," Gavin said, pulling his hand away and turning to face the wall. "If he's done with me, I may as well have died on that ship."

Quinn wanted to scream in frustration or put his fist through Amery's face, but neither of those would solve anything. Stifling a deep sigh, he tugged his shirt over his head and toed off his boots, climbing onto the bunk next to Gavin. Gavin tensed when Quinn's arms went around him, but Quinn wouldn't let him pull away. "Just let me hold you through the night. I'll never ask for more than you're willing to give. I... care too much about what happens to you to do that."

"I know," Gavin murmured. "I don't deserve that."

Quinn disagreed, but arguing with Gavin would gain him nothing. He would simply have to convince the other man of his sincerity through his actions rather than through his words.

HIS immediate duties completed, Eliodoro retreated to the crow's nest on the mizzenmast to lick his wounds. His heart continued to insist that he couldn't have seen what he thought he saw in the aftcastle corridor, but he couldn't find any other rational explanation. He knew Quinn and the surgeon were good friends. The captain, the quartermaster, and the surgeon were inseparable, the undisputed power on the ship, and he'd heard from some of the long-time crew members that the three men had been together since they went to sea at the age of ten. That might explain why *Signor* Watson would go into Quinn's cabin, but it didn't explain the kiss he'd seen. *Signor* Watson was the captain's matelot, *Madre di Dio*. There had to another explanation, because the idea of the two men conducting an affair, in the cabin closest to the captain's no less, was suicide.

He couldn't deny what he'd seen, though. Quinn had kissed *Signor* Watson. The memory made his stomach roil with a hurt and jealousy no amount of rationalization could dismiss. He wanted to barge in and scream at the two men, demand an explanation for how Quinn could make him feel like the most precious thing in the world the night before only to kiss another man with equal tenderness less than a full day later. His innate insecurities kept him in his place for the moment, afraid a confrontation would lead to a broken heart or worse, to being left ashore the next time they made port.

Slowly, his indignation increased as he thought about how carefully Quinn had touched him, how the quartermaster had whispered tender assurances of his devotion. He'd talked of making love. Eliodoro would have accepted even a casual fuck in exchange for the scraps of affection Quinn had bestowed upon him, but the quartermaster had made it sound like it meant much more than that. He'd talked about the beautiful night they spent together and not wanting to trivialize it by discussing it with the man from the tavern. That made the kiss he'd witnessed all the more baffling. How could Quinn speak in those terms, touch him so carefully, and then turn to another man—a married man!—only a few hours later?

Sliding down the rigging, Eliodoro glanced around for the officer on watch, but Nisbett was nowhere to be seen. Eliodoro decided no one would notice if he was absent for a few minutes. Slipping into the aftcastle, he stopped in front of the door to Quinn's cabin. He contemplated knocking, but that could well awaken the other officers in the nearby cabins, and he didn't want to do that. Trying the knob, he smiled when it turned easily, the door opening on silent hinges. The moonlight coming through the porthole barely illuminated the small space, but it gave enough light for him to see his worst fears confirmed.

Quinn and the surgeon lay spooned together on the bed. The blanket hid most of their bodies, but he could see Quinn's bare shoulder above the cloth, and that was enough for him. Biting his lip to hold back tears, he closed the door behind him softly and returned to the main deck.

Nisbett still wasn't on deck, so Eliodoro climbed back into the crow's nest, figuring that if the second mate did come on deck looking for him, he wouldn't be able to fault Eliodoro for being in the rigging. He didn't need to know that Eliodoro had gone there to grieve. Hunkering down so he was out of sight from the deck, he let the tears flow down his cheeks. He'd promised himself on the slaver that he'd never let another man make him cry as he'd done the first few times he was raped, but he couldn't stop the flow of water from his eyes. The rapes had hurt, even later when he'd stopped fighting them and simply let them happen, but then it was only his body and his pride that were bruised. Now his heart ached, and he had no experience to help him deal with this new kind of pain.

He should have known better, he supposed, than to trust any man, much less one who couldn't keep his cock in his breeches, but *Signor* Davies had treated him and all the crew with such respect and kindness that he'd forgotten all his own tenets. The quartermaster had listened and cared when Lewes raped Dickerson, had defended the boy and insisted no one had the right to hurt another in such a way. Everything about him had proclaimed him to be different than the bastards on the slaver, and so Eliodoro had let himself dream. He hadn't gotten to the point of hoping. Not really. But he had dreamed of what it would be like to have *Signor* Davies look at him with love and passion on his face. He'd gotten the passion, but obviously he'd mistaken the looks he thought might be love. After all, what did he know about love? He'd only ever been used, and it seemed the quartermaster was no different. Oh, he hadn't hurt Eliodoro the way the rapists had done. He'd seen to Eliodoro's pleasure as well as his own, but at the end of the day, it had still been a meaningless way to pass the time, and for that, Eliodoro doubted he could ever forgive the older man. He would be civil and follow his orders, but no more longing looks, no more hoping for a stolen moment as he'd started to dream might be possible. He would be another member of the crew, nothing more.

ALONE in his bed for the first time in five years, Amery tossed and turned restlessly, trying to find a comfortable position. Nothing felt right because no matter how he lay, he felt Gavin's absence like a missing limb. He flinched now to think of the names he'd called his lover in his shock, but the words had slipped out almost before he realized what he was saying. He still couldn't believe Gavin had bargained with the Spaniards rather than fighting them, but he regretted ordering his lover to leave.

Gavin was the other half of his soul, a fact he'd known long before they signed their matelotage. They'd had their share of arguments, but never like this. Never so cold and final. The only other time that had even come close had happened a month or so before the Spaniards took Quinn and Gavin. In his anger at Amery, Gavin had taken refuge in Quinn's cabin and Quinn's arms for a night. Amery still shuddered when he remembered walking in on them, Quinn's cock down Gavin's throat as Quinn stretched Gavin's entrance. He'd been livid, ready to draw on both of them, until Quinn had reminded him that if he didn't want Gavin, then Gavin was fair game. His answer to that had been to drag Gavin back into his cabin and make love to him until Gavin had forgiven him. And to tell Quinn the next day never to think that Amery didn't want Gavin, unless he was ready to face the point of Amery's sword.

Quinn hadn't been ready to fight over Gavin then, probably because Gavin had gone quite happily back into Amery's arms once he'd apologized. He couldn't even remember now what they'd fought about, but it hadn't been this serious. Of that, Amery was certain. Gavin had been angry then, not defeated as he'd seemed today. He cursed softly as he wished he'd been a little more temperate in his reaction or a little quicker to cool down. If he had been, he might have made it out into the corridor to retrieve Gavin before Quinn came in and found him. He could hardly take exception to Quinn taking care of Gavin—they'd all been friends since they were boys—but the kiss, the thought of Gavin in Quinn's bed, set his nerves on edge. He hadn't heard any suspicious noises from the cabin next door, much to his relief, but that was no guarantee of anything. Gavin could restrain his sounds of passion when the situation required it.

He didn't know what he'd do if Gavin did turn to Quinn for comfort. Their matelotage contract bound them together, but like any contract, it could be broken. Even a marriage could be ended now, since Henry VIII broke with Rome and formed the Church of England. Rising from his bed in frustration, he dressed haphazardly and strode onto deck, waving aside Nisbett who came running over to see what was wrong. "I just need some fresh air," he told the other officer. "Carry on as you were."

"Aye, sir," Nisbett replied, returning to the helm.

Amery wandered to the starboard rail, leaning on the wooden struts as he stared out at the passing sea. The water was black as the night, reflecting the moonlight and starlight like a prism. On any other night, he would have smiled at the beauty of it, the peaceful calm of the warm Caribbean breeze, but on any other night, Gavin would have been standing there next to him, sharing the scene. He tried to imagine what life would be like without Gavin there, but he simply could not conjure an image. Gavin was as much a part of him as the sea. He'd fallen in love with them at the same time, though he hadn't known to put that name on it when they were barely blooded boys first learning to trim a sail and climb a rigging. He simply couldn't imagine continuing at sea without Gavin by his side.

With a muttered curse, he turned back toward his cabin. He wouldn't be any more comfortable there, surrounded by Gavin's things as well as his own, but at least he wouldn't make a spectacle of himself in front of the crew. If nothing else, he could count the gold left from their last prize and see if he had enough to retire.

Chapter 20

"YOU can stay in my cabin as long as you need to," Quinn assured Gavin when they awoke the next morning.

"I know," Gavin replied, "but I think it would be best for everyone if I sleep in my own cabin from now on. You can hardly seduce Eliodoro to your bed if I'm already in it."

Quinn shrugged. "There are more important things than that."

"There is *nothing* more important than finding someone to love," Gavin retorted hotly. "If you have that, you're the richest man in Christendom, and if you don't, all the gold in the world may as well be dust."

"He still loves you," Quinn said softly. "He's angry, shocked, afraid even, but he still loves you. Just give him time."

"Time to decide he doesn't want a whore," Gavin said bitterly. "I know Amery and his temper. I know he says things when he's angry that he doesn't always mean, but I also know his pride. He'll get over being angry, and he might even regret the viciousness of his words, but his pride won't let him take me back because nothing can change the fact that I didn't fight them. He won't be associated with a whore."

"Stop calling yourself that," Quinn said, Gavin's defeatism starting to annoy him. "Would you have had anything to do with those men if you'd had a choice?"

Gavin stared at Quinn like he'd lost his mind. "What the hell, Quinn? You know I wouldn't. I hated them all!"

"Would you have fought if there had been a chance of escaping?" Quinn persisted, ignoring Gavin's outburst.

"Of course," Gavin replied again. "What are you getting at?"

"You keep saying you weren't forced, that you weren't raped, but you were," Quinn explained. "Yes, you chose not to fight so you wouldn't be hurt, but they didn't give you a choice. They didn't care that you didn't want them to touch you. They still raped you, just without the pain, and Amery is a fool if he can't see that."

Gavin shrugged. "Until he does, I still need a place to sleep. I'll clear out my cabin today so you can have your bed back tonight."

Quinn let the matter drop. Gavin was too upset to listen right now, and Amery was the one who needed to be convinced even more than Gavin. He would see if he could find time to talk to the captain today. A selfish part of him whispered that if he kept silent, Gavin might eventually turn to him for comfort, but he pushed that impulse aside. He owed both his friends more than that. And then there was Eliodoro. Their duties had kept them apart last night even before Quinn had found Gavin outside his door, but the young man had every right to expect to return to Quinn's bed in the near future. Quinn had all but promised him a place there for many a night to come. At the very least, he owed the boy an explanation, but he had no idea what he could say that wouldn't make him sound like a complete rakehell. He didn't want it to seem like he'd approached Eliodoro under false pretenses, but neither could he resist the lure of a love he'd denied for years. If Gavin could truly, finally be his, he couldn't pass that by.

Gavin opening the door roused Quinn from his musings. "Do you need help clearing your cabin?"

"I might," Gavin said. "I have all my medicine chests in there."

"Let's go then," Quinn decided. "The sooner we get started, the sooner we'll get you settled."

Gavin didn't want to get settled anywhere other than back in the captain's cabin, but that didn't seem to be an option anymore. He would simply have to learn to live on his own again and hope the pain of losing Amery would fade in time. He glanced at Quinn's earnest face and wondered for a moment how awful it would be to take him up on his offer of comfort. To lie in his arms and let him steal Gavin's breath and erase all thought of anything outside his embrace. Before he could give in to the impulse, Amery's voice intruded, barking orders as he took the helm from the night watchman. Even rough as it was, the sound of the beloved voice sent a shaft through Gavin's heart, reminding him that he loved Amery blindly, foolishly perhaps, with all that he was. He might find temporary oblivion in Quinn's bed, but Amery would always hold his heart.

WHEN Eliodoro heard the captain on deck, he knew his watch was over. Carefully he unfolded his limbs from their cramped position in the crow's nest. The memory of what he had seen the night before fresh in his mind, he nodded timidly at the captain as he passed. To his surprise, the captain called him over. "Aye, Captain?"

"I didn't want to embarrass you by saying anything in front of the whole crew, but I know you would rather have the same shift as Mr. Davies," Amery said. "You've been up all night, so you can hardly take a shift now, but if you will stand watch this afternoon, after you've had some time to rest, you can stand down tonight and begin a day watch tomorrow."

"Is kind of you, Captain," Eliodoro said slowly, "but is no necessary. *Signor* Davies will no want me in night. 'E 'as other friend than me."

Amery's stomach sank, but he feigned surprise. "Why not? He certainly seemed interested in you the last time we talked. Did you have a falling out? Who is this new friend?"

Eliodoro shrugged helplessly. He should have known the captain would ask that question, and now he had no choice but to answer. He feared the other man's reaction, though, for he had seen enough of the captain to realize his temper. There was no help for it now. "*Signor* Watson."

Amery felt his temper growing, but he held it in check. Apparently, he was not the only one who had seen Gavin entering

Quinn's cabin last night. He wondered if Eliodoro had seen anything more. "What makes you think that?"

Eliodoro wished the heavens would open or another ship would attack. Anything to get him out of this situation, but no catastrophe intervened to save him. "I see them. Last night. In *Signor* Davies's bed. They no were dressed."

"The lying, cheating bastard," Amery growled. "Cullen, take the helm!" Eliodoro winced at the anger in the captain's voice. "Come with me."

Obediently Eliodoro followed the captain through the aftcastle and into his cabin, hoping he was not about to feel the sharp edge of Captain White's tongue, or worse, of his sword.

"Tell me what you saw."

"I see two things," Eliodoro admitted. "I see *Signor* Davies kiss *Signor* Watson, and later I see them in *Signor* Davies's bed asleep."

"You said they were naked."

"They 'ave blanket, but I see bare skin above it," Eliodoro clarified.

"The sneaky son of a bitch," Amery cursed. "I should have known he was just waiting for a chance. He's always lusted after Gavin, even when we were boys. He was so good at pretending he was happy for us when all the time, he was waiting for the right moment. It's not the first time he's done this. He tried it once before when Gavin and I had a fight. Degenerate slut, wanting what was mine. I should've left him on the Spanish ship or marooned him when I caught them together before. Don't trust him, Eliodoro. He's a snake waiting to turn on you. As long as he can't have Gavin, he'll sweet talk you right into bed with pretty words and cunning lies, but you saw how fast he dropped you when he thought Gavin might be free."

"I no understand, Captain. *Signor* Watson, 'e is your matelot. 'Ow 'e free?"

"He isn't," Amery declared coldly. "We had a difference of opinion, but that's all it's ever taken for that whoreson to try to steal him from me."

Eliodoro trembled as he felt the remnants of his newfound dreams crumbling around him. He'd wanted to believe there might be another explanation for what he'd seen, but if the captain was right, he wouldn't be able to salvage anything from those naïve hopes. "Why 'e do this thing?"

"Because he's always wanted Gavin," Amery said, the bile pouring out of him as he thought about what Eliodoro had seen. "He can't stand it that Gavin might prefer me to him, and every time he thinks Gavin's attention might be wavering, he attempts to seduce him again."

"Again?" Eliodoro almost didn't ask, but he needed to know the truth. Perhaps then he could stamp out the last of the painful hopes.

"Again," Amery agreed. "This is the third time I know of, though there may be more."

Eliodoro's face fell at the captain's words, tears threatening despite his best efforts to hold them back. The captain didn't seem to notice, though, the spate of words continuing unabated, each one tearing at Eliodoro's heart.

"The first time was bad enough," Amery ranted, "a matter of days after Gavin and I were first together as true lovers. I forgave that one on the grounds that he didn't know I was serious. He swore it would never happen again once he realized we weren't just passing the time. I shouldn't have believed him, but we'd been friends for long enough that I didn't want to give that up. And the thanks I get? The first time Gavin and I had a fight, the bastard seduced him again. I should have killed him then. I could have. They were so caught up in each other that they didn't see me until I was on top of them. The whoreson had his fingers up Gavin's arse like it was his, not mine!"

The words were too blunt, the image too close to what the quartermaster had done to Eliodoro for him to maintain his composure any longer. The tears overflowed and a soft sob escaped.

The sound, so unexpected, was enough to temper Amery's tirade. Awkwardly, he patted Eliodoro's shoulder, as uncomfortable with the boy's tears as he'd been with Gavin's tears each time Michaels raped him. "I'm not angry with you, lad. You know that, right?"

Eliodoro nodded, sobs continuing softly. "I trust 'im. Is 'ard being wrong."

"We were both wrong, it seems. Everyone makes mistakes. Don't let Quinn's stupidity keep you from looking for someone special," Amery advised.

"Is like 'e two different men," Eliodoro said helplessly. "'E take care of me one moment. Next moment 'e ignore me."

"Forget about him," Amery said, wiping Eliodoro's tears gently. "He doesn't deserve a beautiful boy like you."

The compliment charmed Eliodoro through his tears. Hungry for affection, he wiped his face on his sleeve and stepped closer to Amery, looking up at him hopefully. He wasn't in love with the captain, but there was no denying his attractiveness. If he couldn't have love—and trying to find it had turned out so spectacularly badly that he feared to try again—at least he could have affection and the protection of a handsome, wealthy man. "You find me beautiful?"

Amery stared down into the dark, limpid eyes and saw the neediness and the offer. A kind word or few would suffice to lure Eliodoro into his bed and take his revenge on Quinn, but that would lower him to the same level, and even if Quinn deserved it, Eliodoro did not deserve to be used that way.

"I think you are very beautiful," Amery replied, "but I'm not in love with you, and you deserve to be cherished, not used by an angry old pirate captain who can't even hold onto his own lover." He stroked Eliodoro's cheek gently. "I will not say no to you keeping me company, though. We will both feel better if we're not alone."

Eliodoro leaned into the touch, a kitten seeking a loving caress. Amery saw far too easily how it could be. He knew how to be tender with a lover even if he and Gavin indulged in rough play as often as gentle. Eliodoro was ripe for the picking, his past making him easy prey for a seducer with a kind word or a gentle touch. With the slightest bit of affection, he could have a willing slave, and that was what held him back. Amery remembered how Gavin had been after they left the *Lady Grace*, their first ship. In his saner moments, he suspected that was why Gavin had slept with both him and Quinn in the weeks that followed their escape, turning to whichever of them was available so he had some release, that contact necessary to keep him sane. As traumatized as he'd been by Michaels and the months of abuse, Amery's and Quinn's care had been irresistible, and like many a young man, he'd mistaken sex for love. Amery had hoped Gavin knew the difference now, their promises of fidelity and eventually their matelotage separating their relationship from the casual sex that had gone before, but perhaps not, if he could go into Quinn's arms so quickly after their fight.

"Amici o amanti?" Eliodoro asked softly. He had misunderstood too many things since leaving home to want to make another mistake now.

"Friends," Amery said, summoning a smile. "I think you've had too few friends in your lifetime."

Eliodoro nodded slowly. It might be nice to have a friend for once. Not someone he hid with to escape unwanted chores as he'd done on his first ship, nor someone to provide comfort and protection as he'd looked to *Signor* Davies to do, but simply someone with whom to spend time. *"Amici."*

Chapter 21

QUINN had known Gavin for twenty years, seen him through hell on the *Lady Grace*, and lived through hell with him on the Spanish ship that captured them, but he'd never seen Gavin as defeated as he was now. The surgeon moved with none of his usual energy as they shifted chests and crates around the cabin that would have been the ship's surgeon's if Gavin hadn't simply moved in with Amery. At first, Quinn tried to get Gavin to talk to him, but he gave up after a few minutes, all his attempts met with shrugs or silence. His anger grew as he watched Gavin draw in on himself more as each minute passed and Amery didn't come looking for him, demanding with all his bluff and bluster that Gavin get his arse back in their cabin where it belonged.

Quinn could hear the captain's voice periodically, shouting orders. He wondered what Amery made of his and Gavin's continued absence, but he quickly decided he didn't care. This entire broil was Amery's fault, and Quinn would make absolutely sure Amery understood that, just as soon as he got Gavin settled. That had to be his first concern because at the moment, Gavin was barely functioning, his entire life upended by Amery's callousness.

Finally they made enough space for Gavin to sleep. "I'll get your sea chest," Quinn offered, "so you don't have to go back in the other cabin and maybe see Amery."

"Thank you," Gavin replied listlessly, sinking onto the bunk. "I don't want to face him right now."

Quinn kissed Gavin's forehead lightly. "Rest. You didn't sleep well at all last night. I'll get your chest and bring it in here before I report for duty."

Gavin nodded and lay down facing the wall. Quinn stood there helplessly for a moment, wishing he could fix everything for Gavin, but other than shaking some sense into Amery, he didn't know what he could do. Unfortunately, he wasn't sure all the shaking in the world would be enough.

Shutting the door to the cabin, he slipped through the surgery and back into the corridor. To his surprise, Eliodoro closed the door to Amery's cabin just as Quinn appeared. "Eliodoro."

"*Signor* Davies," Eliodoro acknowledged, his voice cool with disdain.

"Please," Quinn said, the look on Eliodoro's face wounding him, "I have to talk to Captain White now, but can I find you later so we can talk?"

"We 'ave nothing say," Eliodoro declared, pushing past Quinn and onto the deck.

Quinn hesitated, torn between his desire to let Amery have it and his fear he would lose Eliodoro entirely, but the years of friendship won out, and he turned toward Amery's cabin, not bothering to knock. "You stupid bastard," he spat, barging into the room. "What were you thinking, treating Gavin that way?"

"Why should you care?" Amery shouted in return. "You reaped the benefits of his whoring ways."

"You son of a bitch," Quinn cried. "You really believe that, don't you? After everything you heard and saw of those curs, you really think Gavin whored for them. I knew you were blind, but I didn't think you were stupid."

"He told me himself he didn't fight them," Amery retorted. "If that doesn't make him a whore, I don't know what does."

"You don't know what it was like," Quinn insisted, his face darkening as he remembered the pain and fear of the Spanish ship. "You've never been raped. You don't know what that feels like."

Amery could not argue with that, but he didn't see what difference it made. "So?"

"So it is a violation of the worst kind," Quinn said shortly. "Gavin lived with that for months, as you well know, and when faced with the reality of it a second time, he chose to protect himself from the pain. If I knew then what I know now, I would have made the same choice. He was still violated, but by negotiating rather than fighting, he didn't suffer physically the way I did."

"You're only defending him because you want him for yourself," Amery accused.

Quinn fought the urge to put his fist in Amery's foul mouth for suggesting such a thing. Not that Quinn would kick Gavin out of his bed or his life, but he never wanted that to happen because Amery had abandoned him. He had resigned himself to having only their friendship when they signed their matelotage contract. "If we hadn't been friends for so long, I'd kill you for that. As it is, I'll do what I came to do and take Gavin his sea chest. If you come to your senses, he's in the cabin off the surgery, the one he never thought he'd need. He doesn't want me, Amery. He's never had eyes for anyone but you. It's a shame you're too blind to see that."

He saw the temper spark in Amery's eyes again, but he ignored it. Amery would do whatever he was going to do whether Quinn stayed or left, and Gavin was waiting for him. He picked up Gavin's chest, hoping everything important was in it rather than elsewhere in the cabin, and left Amery to stew in his own juices.

He heard the crash that followed his departure, but he didn't go to investigate. It would serve Amery right to be hurt as badly as he'd hurt Gavin, even if it was a physical pain rather than an emotional one, and if Amery was hurt, he'd have to go to Gavin for help. If nothing else, getting them in the same room again might force a confrontation between them. Leaving Amery to his cursing, he carried the chest back to Gavin's cabin.

Gavin lay exactly as Quinn had left him, his knees drawn protectively up to his chest as if by curling into a small enough ball, he could protect all his sensitive areas from attack. It might have worked if the attack had been physical, but Quinn knew Amery's words hurt far more deeply than any physical pain. Quietly, he set the chest at the foot of the bunk and sat down next to Gavin again, his hand resting on the other man's arm.

"How is he?"

"He wasn't there," Quinn lied, not willing to tell Gavin what Amery had said.

Gavin nodded, not lifting his head. "Don't meddle in this, Quinn," he pleaded. "You have your own problems to solve right now. You need to straighten things out with Eliodoro. Don't let this chance pass you by simply because Amery and I have had a falling out."

"Don't worry about me," Quinn soothed. "I can take care of myself. Do you want anything? You missed breakfast. I'm sure I can find something for you if you're hungry."

Gavin shook his head.

Quinn sighed helplessly. "Please, Gavin," he pleaded, "let me help you."

Gavin rolled slowly onto his back, his face wet with the tears he'd tried to hide. "I told you last night, there is no help for me. If Amery doesn't want me anymore, that leaves me with a life not worth living."

"He deserves to be whipped for treating you this way," Quinn growled. "He doesn't have the right to do this to you."

"He didn't deserve to have me lie to him for five years either," Gavin said sadly. "If I'd told him the truth then, he wouldn't have signed the matelotage contract. I knew it then, which is why I didn't tell him. Don't be angry with him, Quinn. I knew the chance I was taking when I became his matelot without telling him the whole truth. It's why I wasn't ever planning on telling him."

Quinn had his own opinion on the matter, but he let it go. Neither Gavin nor Amery was in any state to listen to reason. He would bide his time and let the reality of their separation sink in. Maybe then they would listen. If they didn't, he'd decide what to do then. In the meantime, he had to make sure Gavin didn't do anything rash. Quinn didn't claim to know the uses of all the herbs and tinctures in Gavin's medicine chest, but he'd heard Gavin cautioning sailors to use care with his brews often enough to know that if despair sank its claws in deep enough, Gavin would have his choice of ways to put an end to his misery.

"Rest now," he advised, stroking Gavin's arm comfortingly. "You'll feel better after you've slept."

Gavin gave a bitter, watery laugh. "How? Amery doesn't love me anymore. That isn't something rest will fix."

Quinn took a deep breath and pushed down his longings. "Then maybe rest will give you a fresh look at the situation and we can figure out how to win him back. You can't give up hope, Gavin. I know he's angry right now, but he does love you. You just have to give him time to remember that."

"I'll sleep if you promise to talk to Eliodoro while I do," Gavin bargained.

"Fine," Quinn agreed with a huff. "If it will make you feel better, I'll try to find him and talk to him. He was on duty last night, though, so I'm not going to wake him up if he's asleep."

"Fair enough," Gavin said with a yawn, the emotional exhaustion of the night catching up with him. "But if you don't find him now, you have to talk to him later."

"Sleep," Quinn repeated, rising and leaving the cabin. He made his way on deck, glancing around to see if Eliodoro happened to be there, but he didn't see the familiar dark head. He did catch sight of Amery at the helm, however. He could feel the gulf between them, angry words and angrier thoughts keeping them apart. He hoped they would find a way to resolve the tension because everyone would suffer if they couldn't work as a team in battle. Despite Gavin's claims, though, Quinn placed the blame for the situation firmly at Amery's feet.

Wanting to be able to tell Gavin truthfully that he'd looked for Eliodoro, Quinn searched the holds methodically under the guise of checking stores and ropes and general readiness. The crew greeted him easily as he passed, none of them giving any indication of having picked up on the dissension between the captain and quartermaster.

Quinn hoped it would stay that way. He saw no sign of Eliodoro, though, so he climbed back toward the main deck, meeting Amery between decks on the way.

"It's too bad you decided to spend last night with my matelot instead of taking care of your beautiful boy," Amery drawled, blocking the ladder so Quinn couldn't pass. "He's ripe for plucking."

"What did you do?" Quinn demanded, hand clenching into a fist at the thought of Amery touching Eliodoro.

"Nothing he didn't want me to," Amery replied smoothly, "and far less than he'd have accepted. People who live in glass houses should not throw stones. You're neglecting your duty, Mr. Davies. I expect to see you on deck supervising the watch." He brushed past Quinn, deliberately bumping him into the wall, before Quinn could reply.

Fuming, Quinn returned to deck, snapping unnecessary orders at the crew simply to vent his frustration. Not that it helped. His mind swirled in a maelstrom of rage, fighting with himself as he struggled to reconcile Amery's insinuations with everything he knew of Eliodoro. It would be easy to blame Eliodoro for turning to Amery after Quinn's desertion, but Quinn knew better than to fall into that trap. He'd made one mistake after another where Eliodoro was concerned, up to and including not insisting on switching shifts with someone last night. Even if he'd had to leave Eliodoro to take care of Gavin, at least he could have explained beforehand rather than trying to patch things up with the lad after the fact. He knew how fragile Eliodoro was, knew how vulnerable the boy was to doubt and how eager he was for affection. If he thought he could get that from Amery after Quinn had blown hot and cold on him so many times, Quinn could hardly fault that, however much he wanted to upbraid Amery for taking advantage of it.

Stifling a sigh, he made sure everything was running smoothly on deck and then ducked back into the aftcastle to check on Gavin, wondering how everything had gone so suddenly and terribly wrong. He wanted to take back his conversations with both of his friends except he knew what keeping the secret had been doing to Gavin. He saw the insecurity, the constant fear that Amery would find out and leave, and that fear had interfered with his enjoyment of his relationship. Despite the evidence to the contrary, Quinn didn't think this would be the end of Gavin and Amery's love if only he could get them to admit their mistakes and their true feelings. He hadn't the slightest idea how to accomplish that, though, when Amery wasn't talking to him and seemed to be pursuing Eliodoro, and when Gavin wasn't talking at all, lying in bed waiting for the world to end. He pushed open the door to Gavin's cabin, but his friend was still asleep, so Quinn left him to rest.

Chapter 22

THE days fell into an uncomfortable routine, Gavin rarely leaving his cabin except to go into the surgery if someone was injured or ill. Quinn spent all of his off-duty hours there, often falling asleep in the small chair, because he still feared Gavin would slip into despair some night and do himself injury. He saw Amery's face darken every morning when he came to breakfast through the surgery, but he refused to apologize for taking care of his friend. He hadn't done anything more than kiss Gavin on the forehead a few times or give him a comforting hug. Nothing to feel guilty about. Not like Amery, who spent more and more time every day with Eliodoro. Quinn never saw anything overt pass between them, but he saw the adulation on Eliodoro's face as Amery tutored him in the art of navigation. It was the only time during the day Amery wasn't yelling at someone.

Every time he saw them together, Quinn felt a fresh spurt of jealousy. He couldn't fight Amery for Eliodoro's attention, so he got his revenge the only way he knew how: by spending even more time with Gavin.

Amery noticed, of course, but his pride wouldn't let him unbend enough to apologize. Instead, he turned his full attention to Eliodoro. To his relief, after that first conversation, Eliodoro didn't bring up sex between them, sticking to their agreement to be friends. With that tension out of the way, Amery discovered an incredibly engaging, entertaining young man who was curious about anything and everything. His intelligence sparked a chord in Amery, and he decided within days that Eliodoro would be captain some day. Perhaps not of the *Silver Queen*, but of some ship for sure. To that end, he kept the lad with him whenever he was at the helm, explaining the inexplicable, showing Eliodoro the subtle signs the ocean gave them to help them anticipate shoals and storms, teaching him to read the charts, as imprecise as they were, and to calculate their position on the map.

Eliodoro absorbed it all, asking questions, occasionally frustrated when something moved beyond the scope of his vocabulary, but he was determined to learn and as Amery spent more and more time with him, the captain watched the timidity fall away and a vivacious energy replace it. If Quinn ever got his head out of his arse and came for the boy, he would find a very different handful than the shy lad he seduced in the alley, that was for certain.

"Why you 'elp me?" Eliodoro asked one day as they stood at the helm.

Amery looked at Eliodoro in surprise. "What do you mean?"

"Why you 'elp me?" Eliodoro repeated. "Why not one of them?" He gestured to the other sailors on deck.

Amery shrugged. "I like you."

"Yes, but why?" Eliodoro pressed.

Amery had long since learned that the youth's curiosity, once roused, was not easily brushed aside. "I was ten years old when I left England," he confided. "My mother was pregnant, ready to have the baby at any time, but the ship was sailing, and I had to go or wait who knew how long to find another in need of a boy. My parents had too many mouths to feed already and another on the way. As much as I wanted to wait, if only to see if I had a brother or sister, I had no choice. I always wondered about that baby, what they named him, what he grew up to be like, but I never made it home to find out."

"Why not?"

"I'm a pirate, Eliodoro," Amery reminded him. "Oh, not so much now with the letter of marque in my hands, but I couldn't go home. I was a criminal for all those years."

"And now?"

"I'm only one step removed from it now, and even if I weren't, I've been gone for twenty years. I wouldn't know where to find them or even recognize them if I knew where to look. No, you'll just have to be that brother I never knew."

Eliodoro laughed, a rich, hearty sound Amery already loved. He laughed as well and ruffled the boy's hair, smiling even more widely when he saw Quinn on the main deck scowling up at them. Let the bastard be jealous! If he didn't have the sense to see what he had in Eliodoro, he deserved to lose it.

"Did you need something, Mr. Davies?" he called, not above rubbing Quinn's face in his friendship with Eliodoro. He felt Eliodoro tense next to him and regretted his words immediately.

"Nothing, Captain," Quinn replied, not even sparing a glance for Eliodoro as he turned back into the aftcastle.

"He's a fool, Eliodoro," Amery said when Quinn had disappeared. "You don't need the likes of him to be happy. Find someone else, someone your own age, someone who can love you and treasure you the way you deserve. He'll never be able to forget about Gavin."

"What about you, Captain?" Eliodoro asked bravely. "Will you forget about *Signor* Watson?"

Amery laughed bitterly. "No, lad, I don't think I will, but that doesn't mean I can forgive him either."

"Maybe I ask questions not my business, but why you fight? You love 'im. 'E love you. Why you not fix this problem?"

"Because he lied to me, Eliodoro. For five years, he let me believe he was raped while he and Mr. Davies were held prisoner on a Spanish ship, when in fact he didn't fight them at all," Amery revealed.

"You think is fighting that make rape?" Eliodoro asked softly. "I fight at first, but it 'urt too much, Captain. Was less pain, less injury stay still and let them do what they want. Did no mean I want it. I 'ate them. You know I do. *Signor* Watson maybe learn same lesson I did."

Amery stayed silent for a long time, trying to digest Eliodoro's words, to reconcile his opinion of the boy's resilience with his disgust over Gavin's actions.

"You 'ate me now too?" Eliodoro asked softly when Amery didn't speak.

"Of course not," Amery replied immediately. "You're barely more than a boy, against a whole ship. What else could you have done?"

"Let them 'urt me," Eliodoro answered honestly. "Is what they say they do if I no act like I like it. They say they whip me, cut me." He flushed a little and pointed to his groin. "'Ere."

Amery shuddered. "You did what you had to do to survive."

"So did *Signor* Watson."

"Quinn fought."

"And they 'urt 'im anyway," Eliodoro said, knowing all too well how such men operated. "*Signor* Watson is no stupid. 'E see how they 'urt *Signor* Davies. 'E know they 'urt 'im same way. 'E no fight. They no 'urt. They still rape. They no 'urt."

"So you wouldn't fight if someone tried to do that to you again?" Amery asked.

"It depend," Eliodoro replied. "If I think I win, get away, I fight. If I know I lose, then no, I no fight and 'ope they 'urt less."

"Is that why you didn't fight Quinn in the alley that night?"

Eliodoro flushed again, but he shook his head emphatically. "*Signor* Davies no 'urt me. 'E touch me gently first time ever. I want what 'e do, only no leave me after. Next night, I stay with 'im. Only now 'e no want me."

"He's a fool," Amery repeated. "He can't see past his desire for Gavin. I hope it makes them happy."

"Really?" Eliodoro asked. "Then why you glare at *Signor* Davies every time you see 'im?"

"Because Gavin is mine, damn it," Amery growled.

Eliodoro shook his head. "Maybe he want you act like it."

"He's the one who moved out," Amery insisted.

"Why?" Eliodoro retorted.

Amery was saved from replying by a shout of "Sail, ho!" from the crow's nest. "Take the helm," he ordered Eliodoro. "Keep us on course until we see what we've found. Even if it isn't the *Rayo*, we need to take a prize to lift morale."

Eliodoro swallowed hard as he took the steering rod for the first time in any official capacity. Amery had let him experiment with it a few times, but only in calm weather and away from any potential hazards.

"Don't panic on me, boy," Amery snapped, seeing the expression on Eliodoro's face. "I'll be back before it comes to a fight, but I need to go to the bow to see what's out there."

Eliodoro nodded, hand gripping the steering rod so tightly his knuckles went white. Trusting Eliodoro to keep the course, Amery strode to the bow of the ship, looking glass to his eye as he scanned the horizon for the sail the lookout had sighted. He found it quickly, two points to starboard, a heavily loaded galleon clearly displaying the Spanish flag. He could not see the name on the ship's side, but he'd seen enough. "All hands to stations!"

The call repeated through the holds of the ship, the sailors swarming on the gun deck and the main deck, up into the rigging, preparing the ship for battle. Amery returned to the helm, freeing Eliodoro to take his own position near the foremast. Amery kept a sharp eye on the crew until Quinn came out onto deck, taking command of the main deck from Amery as seamlessly as ever, leaving the captain free to study their quarry and plot the approach course.

As the battle approached, Quinn felt all the tension of the past ten days fade. It didn't matter that he was angry at Amery. It didn't matter that Eliodoro wasn't talking to him. It didn't matter that Gavin hadn't left his cabin or the surgery in that time. Survival instincts and habit took over, his ability to read Amery's intentions in no way blunted by the last week and a half. As the captain made adjustments to their course, Quinn ordered adjustments to the sails, the two of them working in the same perfect harmony that had kept them alive the past five years.

As they closed with the ship, Quinn joined Amery on the quarterdeck, taking the spyglass the captain handed him and studying

the ship. "She looks much like our first prize," Quinn observed, "heavy and sluggish in the water. Same plan of attack?"

"It will depend on her guns," Amery answered. "If we outgun her, then yes. If not, we'll have to outsail her first."

"You're at the helm. We can outsail any ship in the Caribbean," Quinn said, the compliment slipping from his lips without conscious thought.

"I've missed you, Quinn," Amery said softly, the comment so like their old relationship that it brought the absence of that warmth into stark relief.

"I'd rather hoped you'd miss Gavin," Quinn countered. "I'll be in the bow if you need me."

Amery did. He just didn't know how to reconcile his love and his anger, unless Eliodoro was right and there was nothing to reconcile at all. Pushing such thoughts aside for later, when distraction wouldn't be fatal, he concentrated on the ship in his sights. They'd spotted the *Silver Queen* and, not seeing colors in her rigging, were taking evasive action, but the cargo was too heavy for the speed they would need to outrun the *Silver Queen*. Peering through the spy glass again, he watched for their guns to come out so he could calculate his attack plans, but they were cagier than that, keeping the gunwales closed even though he could see the crew scurrying around the main deck, clearly preparing to fire.

Fine, he would give them a taste of the *Silver Queen*'s firepower and teach them a lesson. As they closed with the ship, his smile turned feral. He could read the ship's name, the *Rayo*, emblazoned clearly on her side. Eliodoro would be one step closer to being avenged if Tom's information was accurate. And if it wasn't, they would still have a prize to take back to Providence Island.

Changing course so they would cross the ship at broadside, he ordered Gallagher to ready the guns. From the bow, he could hear Quinn echoing his order. Trusting that his quartermaster knew the plan, he turned his attention back to the other ship, judging its readiness. It wouldn't be an easy fight, but as the *Rayo*'s guns finally appeared, he was confident it was one they would win. The other ship's weaponry was neither as powerful nor as numerous as their own.

When they were directly even, Quinn shouted for the gunners to fire and the culverns roared to life, broadsiding the other ship. Rigging crumbled and the mainmast shuddered beneath the fire.

"Hard about!" Amery roared from the quarterdeck as the men hastened to reload the guns. The ship spun about on its keel, far more sharply than the Spanish ship could do, bringing it into range of the starboard guns. Quinn gave the order to fire again, taking out even more of the Spanish defenses. The other ship retaliated on the second pass, the cannonballs tearing into the strakes. Belowdecks, men called for the carpenter and for the surgeon. Amery pushed thoughts of Gavin rushing into danger out of his mind. He needed all his concentration to keep the ship on course as she suddenly listed slightly. He knew his crew, though. They'd get the hold patched. He had to focus on winning the battle above the waterline.

"Grappling hooks!" Quinn shouted as Amery closed with the other vessel. "Pull her in so we can get aboard."

The hooks went flying at his command, catching the balustrades. The crew heaved hard, forcing the two ships into close quarters. Those not on the lines fired with muskets and arquebus, trying to take out as many of the Spanish sailors as they could before they boarded. When the two ships were close enough, Quinn gave the order to board and the crew swarmed across the other ship, swords drawn and ready as they engaged the Spaniards.

Quinn was right with them, the knowledge that somewhere on this ship was one of Eliodoro's tormenters enough to have him fighting like a man possessed. When the other crew finally surrendered, he was almost disappointed he wouldn't have the opportunity to kill more of them.

"Round up the crew," Quinn ordered his sailors. "See to the injured as best you can and get any of our injured back to Mr. Watson."

As the men carried out his orders, he sought Eliodoro with his eyes, gesturing for the young man to join him on the *Rayo*. "Do you see any of the officers?"

"One," Eliodoro answered shortly. "There." He pointed to a dead man slumped against one of the cannons, his arm and part of his chest completely gone.

"Check the rest of the crew, living and dead, to see if there are any others," Quinn suggested. "We need to know who we're still searching for."

Eliodoro nodded, quartering the deck carefully, but he found only the one familiar face. The moment he completed that duty, he returned to the *Silver Queen*, the guttural Spanish of the crew bringing back all his nightmares.

Quinn let him go, even though he wanted the young man with him as they sailed the *Rayo* back to Providence Island.

"Mr. Davies," Amery called, drawing Quinn's attention. "What do we have?"

"A fully loaded galleon," Quinn replied. "Treasure aplenty, but the ship will need some repairs before we can sail her far or fast."

"The *Queen* as well," Amery agreed. "We'll put in at the first safe harbor we find to make repairs."

"We'll follow you," Quinn proposed. "We simply need to split up the crew."

"I'll see to it," Amery said. "We passed an island a day ago that looked promising."

Quinn returned his attention to securing the Spanish crew in the hold and transferring a portion of the treasure to the *Silver Queen* so the *Rayo* would be more maneuverable. They had just finished and were about to separate the grappling hooks when Gavin's voice caught Quinn's attention.

"Wait!" he called. "I'm coming with you."

Quinn didn't argue, holding out his hand to help Gavin across. He caught sight of Amery's face, dark as a thundercloud on the quarterdeck, but he didn't say anything. Amery and Gavin had to work this out for themselves. The moment Gavin was aboard, he released the hooks and headed to the helm.

Chapter 23

THE eighteen hours it took for them to reach the island Amery had spotted the day before were pure agony for the captain. Before the battle, he could at least console himself with knowing Gavin was near, but having him on the *Rayo*, completely out of Amery's reach, was the worst kind of nightmare. He wanted to be angry at Gavin for pulling away that fully, but he couldn't summon the energy when he thought of this empty wasteland of a life stretching out before him.

Resolving to corner Gavin at the first possible moment, he guided the ship into a protected cove. Knowing the rising tide would let them sail out when they were ready, he ran the ship aground so it would be high enough out of the water for the repairs they needed to make. He swatted at the mosquitoes swirling around his head this close to land, already wishing they were back out at sea again. He couldn't run that risk yet, though. If they had calm seas, the *Silver Queen* would hold together, but the makeshift repairs they'd done during battle wouldn't hold against any kind of a storm. It was the wrong season for the hurricanes that plagued the region in the summer and fall, but that didn't mean they couldn't meet bad weather of another kind. He'd lost one ship to a storm. He didn't intend to lose another if he could help it.

"Head ashore, men," he ordered. "Mr. Jennings will tell you what we need that we don't already have aboard. We'll sleep on solid ground for a few days." He slapped at another mosquito, his hand coming away with a smear of blood. "Stupid bug."

He watched as Quinn sailed the *Rayo* into the same cove a safe distance away. The captured vessel needed far more work. The hull had sustained only minimal damage, but the rigging was in sorry shape. He would have Jennings focus on that first. If Gavin insisted on sailing on the *Rayo* with Quinn, Amery wanted it as seaworthy as possible. Across the water, he could hear Quinn ordering the men on his ship ashore as well. The Spanish crew was brought up from the hold. Under Quinn's careful watch, they were untied and sent down the rope ladders to scramble ashore through the quiet surf. They would have to keep a close eye on the men to make sure they didn't try to steal one of the ships and escape. Amery considered asking Eliodoro to assure the men they wouldn't be harmed if they didn't fight anymore, but he wasn't sure the young man would want anything to do with any Spaniards, even if none of these were the ones who'd hurt him. Gavin certainly didn't.

He'd worry about that later. He needed to talk to Gavin first.

Unfortunately, Gavin proved elusive for most of the next three days, despite Amery's efforts to get him alone so they could talk. He wasn't quite ready to accuse the crew of abetting Gavin in avoiding him, but it seemed that every time he approached Gavin, someone needed one or both of them for something that simply couldn't wait.

On the morning of the fourth day after they arrived at the island, Amery left his cabin, determined not to be deterred again even if he had to order everyone else onto one ship or the other in order to talk to Gavin. He reached the beach, a sudden shiver passing down his spine despite the relative heat of the morning. He took a few more steps, but the shivers continued and his stomach turned.

"Seaton," he gasped, calling the closest sailor. "Find Mr. Watson. I don't feel so well."

"Aye, Captain," Seaton said, hurrying off to find the surgeon.

Amery collapsed onto the sand, bile rising in his throat. "Captain?"

He looked up to see Eliodoro looking at him, concern written all over his face.

"Stay back, Eliodoro," he warned. "I don't know what's wrong with me, but I don't want anyone else to get sick."

"I need find *Signor* Watson?"

"I'm here, Eliodoro," Gavin said from behind them. "Is something wrong, Captain?"

"I can't stop shivering," Amery said plaintively, "and breakfast suddenly doesn't agree with me."

"Did Peele cook?" Gavin asked.

Amery nodded, losing his battle to hold down his breakfast. Eliodoro grimaced and backed away. Gavin, however, approached, stepping carefully to avoid the mess, his hand going to Amery's forehead. "Your skin's clammy, but you're burning up. Eliodoro, get a fire going and boil water for me. Have someone bring me a bucket of cool water as well, and sling a hammock for him in the shade under the trees. I don't know what's wrong with the captain, but we can't afford to lose him."

Eliodoro scurried off to carry out the surgeon's orders while Gavin helped Amery stand and move into the shade of the tropical foliage. "When did this start?"

"Just now," Amery said, stomach heaving again. "Gavin, I'm sorry."

"We'll talk about that later," Gavin said dismissively. "Right now I need to figure out what's wrong with you. I need to get my medicine chest. Don't move from here unless it's to get in the hammock once they set it up for you."

Hurrying onto the *Silver Queen* and into his surgery, he grabbed his medicine chest and carried it back down onto the beach. Rummaging through the bottles, he took out a censer and filled it with rosemary, lighting the dried herb and setting it next to Amery. While that burned, he mixed melilot with the plain salve he had. "Take off your shirt," he ordered.

Amery tried to summon a provocative look, but the pain was increasing, both in his belly and in his head, and it came out as a wince instead as he sat up in the hammock, wrestling with his shirt.

"Oh, hold still," Gavin said with a shake of his head. "Let me get it off you." He freed Amery's arms from the tangle of cloth his shirt had become, baring the captain's chest and abdomen. He ignored the shot of desire he always felt seeing Amery unclothed and focused on the treatments he wanted to try on his matelot's behalf. Helping Amery lie back down, he smeared the ointment across his stomach, hoping it would help with the abdominal pain. That done, he took the comfrey and began pounding it into a paste. He could hear Amery continuing to retch behind him. He didn't turn around, not wanting to see if there was blood in the bile. He feared Amery had contracted yellow fever, and that would confirm it. Eliodoro arrived with buckets of both hot and cold water. "Scoop out a cup of hot water," he told Eliodoro. "Toss it out, then get another one."

When Eliodoro handed him the steaming mug, he put the comfrey paste into it and set it aside to cool.

"Amery, is there any wine left in your cabin?" Gavin asked.

"I think so," Amery choked out.

"Eliodoro, see if you can find it. The absinthe might prevent the onset of jaundice if the captain has yellow fever."

"Yellow fever?" Amery repeated. "That's bad, isn't it?"

"It isn't good," Gavin agreed, "but I'll do everything I can for you. Just rest now until this cools. I hope the comfrey will stop any bleeding in your stomach or bowels. We'll know in three or four days whether you'll get better. If you don't, there's little else I can do but pray."

Amery nodded. He'd seen sailors catch the yellow fever and recover in a matter of days and he'd seen others sicken and suffer in excruciating agony as they bled from their mouth and eyes until they died. He took the drink Gavin gave him, grimacing at the taste and waiting for his matelot to set it aside before he reached for Gavin's hand. "I'm sorry, Gavin. I had no right to react the way I did or to call you all those names. Please forgive me."

"Concentrate on getting well," Gavin said. "We'll talk about the rest when you're better."

"And if I don't get better?" Amery asked seriously. "I don't want to die with this between us. I have enough to answer for in my life without adding this rift to it."

"Rest now," Gavin urged, tearing a strip of cloth from the hem of his shirt and dipping it in the cool water to bathe Amery's forehead.

Amery sighed in frustration, but he couldn't make Gavin listen to him. He let it go for now, but he would bring it up again and again until Gavin realized he was serious in his apology. Regardless of the result of his illness, he needed matters settled between them.

When Eliodoro returned with an open bottle of wine, Gavin poured some into a glass and added the absinthe leaves, not letting himself think about Amery in his cabin drinking alone, or even worse with someone else. Quinn had been with him every evening he wasn't on watch, so Amery hadn't been drinking with him. Not that Gavin thought Quinn wanted any more to do with Amery at the moment than Gavin himself, but before their matelotage, Quinn and Amery had often spent evenings drinking together while Gavin was busy with the surgeon who had taught him his craft.

"Was this all the wine?" Gavin asked.

"All 'e 'ave in 'is wine chest," Eliodoro replied. "You want I look other place?"

"There isn't anywhere else in his cabin," Gavin said. "Ask Quinn if there was any aboard the Spanish ship. This bottle won't be enough if he gets worse."

Eliodoro started like a frightened rabbit at Quinn's name. "If you don't want to see him, have someone else ask him," Amery interjected. "You don't have to talk to him."

Eliodoro nodded and hurried off.

"Why wouldn't he want to talk to Quinn?" Gavin asked, realizing how out of touch with the ship's business he had become in the days of his self-imposed exile.

"Because Quinn hasn't talked to him since he started sleeping with you," Amery snapped, the movement bringing on another round of nausea and chills.

"Quinn isn't 'sleeping' with me," Gavin retorted. "He falls asleep in the chair in my cabin some nights, but that is the extent of it. Where did Eliodoro get the idea he was sleeping with me?"

"He saw you," Amery shouted, pushing into a sitting position despite the roiling in his stomach at the movement. "He went to Quinn's cabin the night you walked out on me and saw you together."

"First of all, I didn't walk out!" Gavin cried. "You ordered me to leave. And secondly, yes, I slept in Quinn's bed that night, but all we did was sleep. I didn't even take my breeches off. Where the hell do you get the right, Amery White, to make those kinds of accusations? I haven't so much as looked at another man since we signed our matelotage. Before that, we hadn't made promises, so don't go throwing up my youthful indiscretions. Once we made that pledge, I kept it. Can you say as much?"

"Of course I can!" Amery shouted back. "Who do you think I've taken to my bed since you left?"

"I didn't leave," Gavin repeated. "You ordered me out. As for who you might be sleeping with, you seemed awfully friendly with Eliodoro."

"He's too young for me," Amery scoffed. "He's become a younger brother to me, nothing more."

"Then why can't Quinn be my brother as well?" Gavin asked seriously. "Why do I have to be cheating with him?"

"Because the last time we argued—"

"The last time we argued, we weren't matelots," Gavin reminded Amery. "You said you were sorry, but you obviously aren't if you still believe all these lies you're spouting." He handed Amery the glass of wine. "Drink this. I'll be back to check on you when I'm not tempted to poison you."

Amery tried to rise from the hammock, but the mesh swung precariously. Amery subsided, glaring after his departing lover. Damn it, why did all reason fly out of his head the moment the thought of Quinn with Gavin entered it? He had been so sure all of that was behind him, that he was ready to apologize to Gavin, grovel if he had to, and get things back to normal between them. Then Quinn had come up and Amery lost sight of everything but his anger. With a frustrated sigh, he drank the concoction Gavin had given him, choking on the bitter taste. It served him right, he told himself. He had another bitter pill to swallow.

Eliodoro returned as he finished the foul brew. "Is wine on *El Rayo*," he told Amery. "*Signor* Davies bring it."

"Eliodoro," Amery said slowly, "the night you saw Gavin and Quinn together, tell me again exactly what you saw."

"They were sleeping," Eliodoro said, lips pursing at the unpleasant memory. "I see bare skin above blanket."

"Where was the blanket?" Amery pressed.

Eliodoro pointed to his armpit. "'Ere. Under arms."

"So all you actually saw bare was their arms and shoulders," Amery verified.

Eliodoro paused again, trying to summon the details of the memory. "And feet."

"So they could have had their breeches on still, right?"

Eliodoro nodded slowly. "Is possible. Why you ask?"

"Because Gavin insists all they did was sleep," Amery replied. "He seemed shocked to realize Quinn had not spoken to you since that night, as if he couldn't understand why Quinn wouldn't still want to be with you."

"Because 'e love *Signor* Watson, you say," Eliodoro reminded Amery. "Fuck or no fuck, makes no difference. 'E love *Signor* Watson, 'e no want me."

"But if he really can't have Gavin, if he hasn't had Gavin, maybe I'm wrong. You could get him back if you wanted."

"If 'e love someone else, I no want 'im even if I can 'ave 'im," Eliodoro said with a shake of his head. "You tell me I deserve better than that. I believe you."

"You do."

Chapter 24

AMERY tossed and turned in the hammock, the chills ebbing and flowing like the tide so that one minute he was shivering despite the tropical heat, and the next he was sweating profusely as his body tried to fight the infection. He didn't know if Gavin was right about it being yellow fever—his lover was the surgeon, not him—but he knew he'd been sent to hell, whatever the cause. The crew went about their business farther down the beach, staying as far away from Amery as they could so they wouldn't catch anything from him. Only Gavin and Eliodoro ventured close, and only Eliodoro stayed. As the fever and nausea worsened, Amery grew more concerned about making amends with Gavin. Perhaps repenting from his sins wouldn't miraculously cure his illness as many superstitious sailors believed, but living a good life certainly couldn't hurt. More than that, he missed his lover. He'd seen Gavin with the ill before and knew how conscientious he could be about caring for them. Gavin wasn't hovering over him. Amery lost track of how many times he apologized and how many times Gavin ignored him or brushed aside his explanations with admonishments to rest and recover. Gavin might want to discourage him, but Amery refused to be dissuaded. If Gavin needed more persuasion, Amery would give it.

The second morning after he fell ill, Quinn finally came to see him. "You're still alive, I see."

"Gavin won't let me die," Amery replied with more confidence than he truly felt. He didn't doubt Gavin's intentions or his determination, but he'd held his lover more than once as he mourned a patient whose malady had been outside the scope of Gavin's knowledge.

"You really owe him an apology."

"I haven't stopped apologizing these past two days, but he won't listen to me," Amery snapped.

"Do you blame him?" Quinn asked. "You call him a whore, you kick him out of the cabin you shared, you refuse to speak to him for two weeks, and then when you finally do speak to him, it's to accuse him all over again in the guise of apologizing. You're lucky he hasn't washed his hands of you completely."

Amery was far too aware of that to be comfortable with Quinn's admonition. "You'd like that, wouldn't you?"

"Only if it made him happy," Quinn retorted. "You're determined to drive a wedge between the three of us. You know—you've probably always known—I'd have him if he wanted me, but he doesn't want me, Amery. I've lost track of the number of times I've offered comfort since you kicked him out, but the only one he accepted was letting me hold him while he cried the first night. Since then, he'll let me keep him company, but that's all. I don't know what it will take for you to get it through your thick skull that he loves you and only you, and that he's been and always will be faithful to you, but you need to do it. A man can only be honorable for so long."

"You or him?"

"Me," Quinn replied. "Right now he still loves you and wants to be with you, but if you hurt him again, I'll court him in earnest. Ask yourself this, Amery. Do you love him?"

"Of course I love him. I've always loved him!" Amery protested, chills beginning to rack him again.

"Then it's time you acted like it," Quinn insisted. "I know you don't understand why he made the choices he did on the slave ship. You may never understand his choices, but you have to believe that he was still forced. He didn't choose the situation; he only chose how to survive it."

"I understand that now," Amery assured Quinn. "Eliodoro helped me see it."

"Then why didn't you apologize to Gavin then?"

"Because I thought he was sleeping with you," Amery admitted. "I've been a jealous fool."

Quinn certainly agreed with that. "So what are you going to do now?"

"Keep apologizing, I suppose," Amery said. "I'm too sick at the moment to do anything else. If this... If I don't survive this, will you take care of him for me?"

"You'll survive," Quinn said. "You said yourself Gavin won't let you do otherwise."

"But if I don't?"

"Then yes, I'll take care of him," Quinn promised. "I expect you to make it unnecessary though. The crew is working as hard as they can to get the ships ready to sail. We have to get off this cursed island. It may look like paradise, but six more men have fallen ill since you got sick. Gavin can barely keep up. We've had almost no problems with illness aboard the *Silver Queen*, and now we can't seem to stop the spread. We have to get out of here before we don't have enough crew to sail one ship, much less two."

"Has he found someone to help him?" Amery asked, worried about Gavin falling ill himself because he spent all his time and energy helping others.

"Eliodoro has attached himself to Gavin's side," Quinn replied. "Apparently he had yellow fever when he was younger and so isn't worried about getting sick again. He looks at Gavin with almost the same adoration on his face as when he looks at you."

The disappointment in Quinn's voice was palpable.

"If you hadn't treated him like a commodity, abandoning him like he was nothing, he'd still look at you that way," Amery said. "And before you ask, I didn't touch him. I've been teaching him to read the charts and the waters and encouraging him to believe in his own worth, but I didn't fuck him."

"Then you're a better man than me." Quinn regretted the tack had taken with Eliodoro, avoiding him instead of taking the lad under his wing and teaching him as Amery had done. He might not have lost the young man's respect if he had. He had fallen back into his habit of protecting Gavin and had forgotten about everything else.

"So win him back," Amery proposed, feeling the sweats he'd come to associate with the rising fever. "You want to leave now," he warned Quinn. "When the fever goes up, I can't keep down the foul brews Gavin keeps pouring down my throat."

Quinn shrugged. "You wouldn't be the first man I've seen lose his breakfast since we landed on this godforsaken island. We've fixed the holes in the *Queen*'s hull and started on the *Rayo*. Is there anything else you want done on the *Queen* while we're here?"

"If I die, you'll be captain," Amery reminded Quinn. "Think like one until I'm well. If the ship needs some repair, see it done."

"Aye, Captain," Quinn said with a wink, "but don't yell at me if something is not to your liking later."

Amery's smart reply was lost in another wave of nausea. Quinn waited for it to pass so they could finish their conversation, but the retching continued. Growing concerned, Quinn raced down the beach in search of Gavin. "Amery needs you," he told the surgeon urgently. "He can't stop retching."

Gavin nodded. "Eliodoro, stay with Barton. You know what to do for him. I'll check on the captain and come back when I can."

"Is he going to survive this?" Quinn asked Gavin.

"In my experience, we'll know by morning," Gavin replied. "He'll either start feeling a little bit better, at which point it's only a matter of recovering his strength, or he'll take a turn for the worse. If that happens, we'll probably lose him."

"Then talk to him now while you can," Quinn urged. "If this might be your last chance, don't let it pass you by because of misplaced stubbornness."

"You didn't hear the things he said," Gavin protested.

"No, but I heard him swear he still loved you not ten minutes ago," Quinn countered. "Talk to him. Maybe you can't forgive him, but hear him out in case you don't get another chance."

"Fine," Gavin muttered. "If it will get you off my back."

"I haven't been on your back," Quinn joked. "That's Amery's job."

Gavin glared at him, but Quinn saw the smile that threatened. He shooed Gavin on down the beach toward Amery, not wanting his presence to inhibit their conversation. He watched as Gavin lifted a cup of something to Amery's lips.

"You no can let them talk alone?"

Quinn turned to see Eliodoro's accusing stare. "That's why I'm standing here rather than hovering over them," Quinn replied with a calm he did not entirely feel. "If I leave them completely alone, Gavin will find some reason to rush off before Amery can apologize, and the captain could well die before Gavin gives him another chance."

"Would be good for you."

"It would be the death of all of us," Quinn differed. "I can sail a ship from one port to another, but I couldn't do what Amery does. I couldn't seek out the Spanish and take prizes with his skill. I don't have that talent. If Amery dies, we will abandon the *Rayo*, take the *Silver Queen* back to Providence Island, and each of us will have to hope he can find a berth on another ship."

"*Signor* Watson no let him die," Eliodoro said firmly. "I take care of others while 'e take care of captain."

Quinn hesitated before asking, "Do you need help?"

"DRINK this."

Even the no-nonsense tone of Gavin's voice was welcome through the haze of fever and nausea. Amery reached for him without thought, needing the comfort of his lover's touch. Tender hands pressed him back into the hammock and lifted a cup to his lips. Amery made a

face as he swallowed the absinthe-laced wine, but it did settle his stomach somewhat. When he could catch his breath enough to speak, he caught Gavin's hand.

"I'm sorry," he said for what felt like the thousandth time in the last three days. "I was a fool to kick you out and an even sorrier fool to think the worst of you without giving you a chance to explain. Please, Gavin. Forgive me."

Gavin nodded, hearing the difference in Amery's voice in this apology. Whatever had gotten through to his lover, something finally had. Bending his head, he kissed Amery's forehead gently. "We'll talk more when you're well. We'll find a way to make things right again."

"Will I get well?" Amery asked, clinging to Gavin's hand.

"We'll know by morning," Gavin told him. "You'll start to feel better, or you'll start bleeding. I'll fight this disease until I can't fight any longer, but if the bleeding starts, your chances of living go down drastically."

"Take me back to the ship," Amery requested. "I'll sleep more comfortably in our bed, and if I have to die, I want to spend my last few hours in your arms."

Tears welled in Gavin's eyes. "You're too weak to walk. Let me get Quinn and we'll help you back on the *Silver Queen*."

"Don't leave me," Amery pleaded, his grip on Gavin's hand tightening as much as his lessened strength would allow.

Gavin smiled and brushed the windblown strands of Amery's golden hair out of his face. "I'm not going far. Quinn is just down the beach there. You can watch me the whole way."

Reluctantly Amery let him go, his stomach churning with the inexplicable surety that he wouldn't see Gavin's return. His heart pounded as Gavin walked down the beach toward the spot where Quinn and Eliodoro stood with another group of ill sailors. Amery wanted to smile at seeing the two men together again, but even that sight couldn't defeat his nerves. Within a minute, though, Gavin had reached Quinn's side and the two men started back toward him, leaving Amery gulping air in relief as they arrived at his side.

"So Gavin tells me you think you should sleep on the ship tonight," Quinn teased. "Are you sure you want all this mess in your cabin?"

"I want a refuge," Amery said softly. "No one but Gavin needs to see it if I die. It will be enough for everyone else to know that I'm gone. I want these last few hours alone with him."

"Stop talking that way," Quinn and Gavin scolded as one. "You have to keep your hopes up," Quinn added, seeing the stricken look on Gavin's face. "You have to believe you'll survive this. One of the others who got sick at almost the same time you did is beginning to recover. You will too."

"He's already doing better and I'm not," Amery pointed out. "That's hardly a good sign."

"Tomorrow morning," Gavin insisted, summoning his firmest tone. "We won't know until tomorrow morning. Then we'll see. Come on, Quinn. Help me get him aboard."

They helped Amery to his feet, their shoulders under his arms supporting most of his weight. Amery managed to put one foot in front of the other so they weren't carrying him completely, but he knew he would have fallen without their support. They managed finally to get him onto the ship and into his cabin. For a moment, Amery considered asking Quinn to stay as well, for the quartermaster had been a part of his life for as long as Gavin had, but someone had to supervise the men ashore, and he needed this time alone with Gavin in case this was goodbye. "Thank you, Quinn," he said, hoping that would make his peace with the other man. "For everything."

"You can thank me when we get to Providence Island by making sure I get my share of the plunder," Quinn retorted, refusing to admit the possibility of Amery not being there with them. "Don't you dare make me keep that promise."

He was gone before Amery could say anything else.

"What promise?" Gavin asked, helping Amery get settled in bed.

"Nothing important," Amery demurred, not wanting to do anything that might start another fight. "Please, Gavin, just lie down with me and let me dream of a better tomorrow, even if I never see it."

Gavin stripped off his shirt and breeches, lying down next to Amery in only his smallclothes. Any other night, he wouldn't have bothered even with those, but he didn't know what the night would bring and he wanted that much covering if anything drove him from their bed during the dark hours. "I love you, Amery White," he said, sliding up against his lover. "Don't you dare die. You owe me a far better apology than the ones you've managed so far."

"In the morning," Amery swore. "If I live to see morning, I'll give you anything you want."

Gavin smiled, though he doubted Amery saw it. *All I've ever wanted is you.*

Amery fell asleep, somewhat to Gavin's surprise, but Gavin could find no rest, any hope of slumber shattered by the thought that he might lose Amery in a matter of hours. He cursed the anger that had driven them apart and the pride that had kept them in separate beds for two weeks. Nothing could change that, any more than he could change Amery's fate now, but he could cling to the time they had left. He ran his fingers through Amery's long hair. It needed a trim, he thought in passing, realizing with a pang that he might never get to cut it.

It was such a small thing, and yet it was the feather that broke the horse's back. The tears he had been fighting for days broke free of his control, and he wept for lost chances and missed opportunities, pouring out his grief into the pillow beneath his head. He tried to silence the sobs that wanted to escape, but he must have failed because Amery stirred restlessly at his side. Wiping his eyes on the linen pillowcase, he returned to the gentle stroking, hoping to soothe Amery back to sleep. Rest was the best medicine for him at this point, and it was a good sign if Amery was comfortable enough to sleep. Tenderly he nuzzled Amery's skin, inhaling the scent of salt and skin beneath the odor of the pastes and poultices he'd used to save Amery's life, reminding himself that other men had gotten this illness and survived. Amery could too. Gavin simply had to hold onto hope until it came to pass.

Chapter 25

LIGHT filtered softly in through the cabin windows as the sun rose, the rays startling Gavin awake. He hadn't meant to sleep, wanting to be there—to know—if Amery took his last breath, but Amery's breathing huffed gently across Gavin's chest still. Carefully, not wanting to wake his sleeping lover, Gavin ran a hand across his forehead, testing the temperature. It was still warmer than normal, but not as fiery hot as it had been the past few days. He let out a sigh of relief. Perhaps the worst had passed. He ought to get up and inform the watch so they could pass the good news on to the crew, but he wasn't quite ready to disturb the peace of the moment. When Amery awoke, they would have to deal with all the tension still between them. Gavin believed Amery's apology was sincere, but he had known his matelot too long to hope the difficulties were truly over between them. Amery had apologized and talked of understanding, but Gavin feared the next time they argued, Amery would throw his past up in his face again.

Then the emerald eyes opened, and Gavin lost himself in them again, as he always had. "Good morning," he whispered.

"Is it morning?" Amery asked. "I made it?"

"The fever is down," Gavin said. "You're not well yet, but it's a first step. You'll probably be weak for another few days, if only because you haven't eaten in four days. Do you think you could swallow some of the broth from Peele's porridge? You won't be up to the meat and vegetables yet, but the broth would be better for you than any of my potions now, if you can keep it down."

"I think perhaps I could," Amery said after a moment's pause to assess how he was feeling. His stomach still felt slightly unsettled, but nothing like it had the past few days.

"I'll go speak to him," Gavin said, rising from the bed.

"Wait," Amery requested, catching Gavin's hand. "Don't go."

"I'm only going to the galley," Gavin reminded him. "I'll be back in a moment."

Amery did not let go of his hand, though, the thought of letting Gavin out of his sight for even that long more than he could bear. "Don't leave me."

Gavin sighed and sat back down on the bed next to Amery. "And how am I supposed to get you something to eat if I don't leave the cabin? I told you yesterday that we would work things out between us, but you have to get well before we can do that. Now can I fetch you some broth?"

Amery didn't want to let him go, but he couldn't think of a reason to keep him there without revealing his fear that Gavin would change his mind. He nodded and released Gavin's hand.

Gavin pressed a tender kiss to Amery's forehead and pulled back on his clothes. "I'll be back before you know I'm gone."

Amery didn't refute the statement, though he felt Gavin's absence keenly. True to his word, Gavin returned moments later, a bowl of steaming broth in his hand. He set it on the desk, pushing aside Amery's charts, and helped his lover stand.

"When you're a little stronger, you need a bath," he told Amery. "You stink."

Amery chuckled as he spooned some of the thick liquid into his mouth. "I'll take you up on that as soon as I'm feeling better."

Gavin summoned a smile, but it didn't reach his eyes. Amery was acting exactly as he'd feared, assuming nothing had changed between them after their argument instead of addressing the lingering tension. Or perhaps there wasn't any lingering tension in Amery's mind. Gavin wasn't sure which would be worse.

"When you're feeling better, I'll be sure to have the men arrange something for you."

"Gavin?" Amery asked.

"You can't just pretend nothing happened," Gavin said in exasperation. "You kicked me out of your bed, your cabin, and your life for two weeks, and if you hadn't fallen ill, you probably still wouldn't be talking to me. I know you felt betrayed, but your rejection nearly killed me, Amery. I've spent the past two weeks wondering if I should've stayed on the Spanish ship and gone down with it. It might have hurt less."

"Don't say that," Amery protested. "Please, Gavin, whatever you think of me, don't think that. I know I was a bastard, reacting the way I did, and I'll apologize for it as many times as you need me to, but don't wish yourself dead."

"You miss my point," Gavin insisted. "You sit here, and you make ribald comments and expect me to react to them as if the past two weeks hadn't happened. I can't do that, Amery. I want to find our way back to where we were before I listened to Quinn and told you the truth, but that's going to take time. Words are cheap. I need more than empty promises easily broken."

"Tell me what you need then," Amery pleaded. "I'll do whatever you want."

Gavin sighed. "It isn't that simple. It's not something I can simply ask you to do for me. I need time to believe in us again, to forget the anger and remember the love our matelotage represents. You destroyed me when you sent me away. It's going to take time to put myself back together again."

"So where does that leave us?" Amery asked.

"I don't know," Gavin replied honestly, "but I can't just fall back into your bed again. I'll join you on deck and at meals, but for the time being, I will continue to sleep in my own cabin."

"Must you do that?"

"Sadly, yes," Gavin said. "When the time comes, we'll know, and your bed will be mine again, but until then, I'll sleep alone."

"WHAT you think it mean, *Signor* Watson still on ship?" Eliodoro asked when the sun was a hand's width above the horizon.

"I think it means the captain made it through the night," Quinn answered honestly. "If he died, I think we'd hear Gavin grieving. Whether he's on the mend remains to be seen."

Eliodoro nodded, his eyes fixed on the ship as an awkward silence grew between them. He wanted to ask the quartermaster about the accusations the captain had leveled against him, but he didn't know how to broach the subject.

"Is there anyone we need to check on?" Quinn asked after a moment, breaking the silence if not the tension.

Eliodoro shook his head. "No, is done until noon. You no 'ave stay with me. You prefer go on ship with *Signor* Watson, no?"

Quinn shrugged. "It doesn't matter. They belong together, and I'd only be in the way."

So the captain was right, Eliodoro thought with a suppressed sigh. "Go. Find out if the captain live. Tell crew. Is good for... what is word?"

"Morale," Quinn supplied. "I suppose I could make sure Amery's alive. You're sure you'll be all right with the ill until I return."

"Ship is right there, *Signor* Davies. It take ten minutes row out and back. I wait for you 'ere," Eliodoro said with an indulgent shake of his head. He had grown used to the captain's acceptance of his abilities. He would have to start reminding the quartermaster he was not a child.

Quinn started toward the dinghy, turning back after a few steps. "I know what you saw the night Gavin and Amery argued, but I swear all I did was comfort an old friend."

"Is all you want do?" Eliodoro challenged.

"What I want doesn't matter," Quinn retorted. "Gavin and Amery made promises to each other that I wouldn't ask Gavin to break.

Whatever you're thinking about me, you're wrong. I'm an honorable man, Eliodoro."

"Not so 'onorable you no sleep with 'im before," Eliodoro spat.

"The bastard! I can't believe he told you that," Quinn shouted. "They weren't mated then, in case he left that detail out, and Gavin told me they were finished. I believed him. He was wrong obviously, or maybe he lied, but at the time I thought Gavin was free, or I wouldn't have touched him then either."

"Easy to say when you no 'ave to prove words," Eliodoro sneered. "If the captain die, what you do then?"

Quinn's eyes closed as his conscience warred with his desire to defend himself to Eliodoro. "I'd bury Gavin next to him," he said finally, "because no matter what I offered, Gavin wouldn't survive for long without Amery, and then I'd have to live with my failure to both of them. I'll be back. Do what you want in the meantime."

Eliodoro's shoulders hunched in dismay as *Signor* Davies climbed into the dinghy and rowed toward the *Silver Queen*. He wasn't sure what he'd hoped to gain by confronting the quartermaster, but it hadn't been this dismissal. He would never admit it aloud, but despite the way he had offered himself to the captain before realizing he would never see Eliodoro as anything but a brother, Quinn was the man Eliodoro wanted, the one who set his pulse racing, his breath fluttering in his chest. The captain and *Signor* Watson were undeniably handsome men, but he wanted Quinn, wanted the lover of their one night together. He wanted it, but only if it was real. If he would only be a substitute for *Signor* Watson, he'd rather be alone.

"Mr. Davies gone to check on the cap'n?" Seaton asked, breaking into Eliodoro's thoughts.

"Aye," Eliodoro replied. "'E say captain is alive because we no hear crying at death."

"That'd be the truth," Seaton agreed. "Mr. Watson said he'd know by morning what the captain's fate would likely be, aye?"

"*Sì*," Eliodoro said. "Fever break and captain get better, or bleeding start and captain die."

"We'll pray the fever breaks then," Seaton said, crossing himself piously. "I've never sailed with a better man or a better sailor than Captain White, and I've sailed with my share o' ships."

"Amen," Eliodoro said. His eyes followed the dinghy as he spoke, taking in avidly the sight of the quartermaster's strong muscles flexing as he rowed. He'd taken off his shirt during the night when one of their patients had vomited all over him. The expanse of skin had been distracting enough by torchlight. To see it now was enough to make Eliodoro's mouth water.

"There's another good sailor and fine man," Seaton observed, following Eliodoro's gaze and easily interpreting the look on the lad's face. "You could do far worse than to set your sights on him as a partner."

Eliodoro's head turned sharply. "*Cosa?*"

"I seen the way you look at the quartermaster," Seaton said with a laugh. "I ain't blind, boy, and I got a matelot of m'own so I know the signs when I see 'em. You're besotted with him. Ain't nothing wrong with that, not on a pirate vessel, leastways, so don't go givin' me that look. You're too busy hidin' the fact that you're lookin' at him to see him lookin' back, but he's watchin' you, boy. You just have to decide what to do about it."

"Nothing," Eliodoro said sadly. "Maybe 'e watch, but 'e not want me."

Seaton laughed. "Make him work for it, boy. He'll appreciate you more because of it, but don't ever think he don't want you. That man hasn't wanted anything else since you came aboard."

"Then why 'e not act like it?" Eliodoro demanded. "Why 'e spend all 'is time with *Signor* Watson?"

"Now that would be a question for Mr. Davies," Seaton replied philosophically, "but he sure weren't happy with you spending so much time with the cap'n. Mr. Davies always gots a ready smile and a laugh for everyone, even when he's givin' orders, but he scowled somethin' fierce every time he seen you at the helm with the cap'n. He was jealous. You mark my words."

Eliodoro wanted to believe the older sailor, but he wasn't sure what good this new information did for him. Perhaps Quinn was jealous of the attention Amery had paid him, but Eliodoro didn't want a man to be jealous over him. He wanted a man who loved him, something Quinn could hardly do if he was still in love with *Signor* Watson as the captain suggested. He struggled against his inability to formulate the questions he wanted to ask, about how he would know if jealousy had turned into something more, about how to make it turn into something more, but his command of English failed him in the face of such a serious discussion. He had no doubt Seaton would be patient with him—everyone was—but he held his tongue, waiting and watching for Quinn to return from the *Silver Queen*.

He had almost reached the point of despair, fearing the silence on the ship meant two dead bodies rather than the captain's survival, when the quartermaster reappeared on deck, climbing easily down the rigging to the dinghy and beginning the short trip back to shore.

"Good news!" Quinn called to the crew as he landed. "Mr. Watson says the captain will make a full recovery and be ready to sail in two or three days. If we can get both ships ready, we'll take our prize back to Providence Island, but either way, we leave this hell as soon as the captain is on his feet again. I don't know about you, but I don't want to lose our prize money. Everyone who can keep your feet, we have work to do."

A cry went up from the crew, the news revitalizing the despairing men. They threw themselves back into the work of repairing the ships with as much energy as any captain could have asked for. Eliodoro joined in the cheer, though not in the repairs. *Signor* Watson had given him a very specific task, and he intended to see it through. He only hoped the quartermaster would understand. He wasn't sure what he wanted or would accept from the other man if he offered, but he did know he wanted to keep Quinn's regard.

When Amery was ready to take the helm again, both ships were ready to sail. They left eight fresh graves behind when they sailed, each one a stain on Gavin's heart.

Chapter 26

AMERY stood at the foot of the narrow bed in the room he'd rented on Providence Island, trying to decide what to do next. They'd secured the *Rayo* and the treasure with the company man of business and distributed their share of the treasure among the men. He'd announced two days of shore leave once their transaction was completed because he had some business of his own to take care of. He had taken care of the first part, filing the deed to his newly acquired property with the same man of business. Now he'd had a bath and a shave and was attired in his best shirt and breeches, his coat freshly brushed and his boots polished. He peered into the mirror, smoothing down the one lock that wouldn't stay in place no matter what he did to it. He'd threatened more than once to simply lop it off, but Gavin always stopped him, saying he liked it.

After another two weeks of not having Gavin in his bed, Amery was willing to do pretty much anything his matelot wanted if it meant having him back. That was why he was standing here vacillating like an unblooded boy. He wanted to impress Gavin with his sincerity, so he had gone to great lengths with his appearance, shaving carefully, bathing, renting a room in the nicest boarding house on Providence Island so he would have somewhere to bring Gavin other than their cabin on the ship.

The sound of raucous laughter filtered through the walls of his chamber, making him wonder suddenly if the room was a good idea. Prostitutes rented rooms like these, though he had not seen any lingering outside the door to this particular establishment. He certainly didn't want to make Gavin think he saw the surgeon that way. Maybe it would be better to take him back to the ship. Gavin hadn't avoided the captain's cabin even if he had avoided the captain's bed. Every night after dinner, Gavin would come back with Amery to enjoy a glass of the captain's rum and some quiet conversation, but he always refused to discuss their future and his return to Amery's bed. If Amery accepted that, he would stay quite late, but the moment Amery tried to bring up the subject, Gavin would take his leave with nary more than a chaste kiss.

Amery sighed in frustration. He'd never had to court Gavin. Their relationship had simply begun one night. They had just escaped from the *Lady Grace* and Michaels' foul attentions. Quinn had been out, only God knew where, and Amery and Gavin had taken the bed in the tiny room they'd managed to afford by selling the few trinkets they'd stolen out of the hold before they jumped ship. Gavin had turned into Amery's arms seeking comfort, and it had seemed the most natural thing in the world to kiss the vulnerable boy he'd been then, nothing like the man he'd become. One kiss led to another and another until they were both desperate for release. They'd pushed aside their breeches until they could rub against each other, the friction enough to make them both come in a matter of seconds.

They had been all of sixteen.

It had taken another nine years before they signed their matelotage, but that had been as much because it hadn't seemed necessary as anything else. They'd fallen into each other's arms and never fallen out. At first, they hadn't been serious, hadn't known how to be serious, and Quinn had often joined one or both of them in their romps. Then the night of Gavin's nineteenth birthday, everything had changed. Amery had worked up the courage to tell Gavin he loved him and to ask him to be his. Amery knew of two times since that night when Gavin had ended up in Quinn's arms instead of his, but other than that, they had been exclusive lovers since that night. Until he drove Gavin away.

He wouldn't solve anything by delaying, he told himself firmly, checking the pocket of his coat one more time to make sure the deed was there. Hearing the parchment crinkle beneath his fingers, he took a deep breath and went in search of his errant matelot.

He found Gavin, some fifteen minutes later, coming out of the shop of the local apothecary. Taking another deep breath, he approached Gavin with a formal bow. "Mr. Watson, would you do me the favor of dining with me this evening?"

He could see the surprise on Gavin's face and felt a pang that he'd never thought to treat Gavin in so courtly a fashion until now. "Please?"

Gavin hesitated a moment longer before bowing his head in return. "I would be honored, Captain White, though I see you are far more formally attired than I am. Would you give me leave to return to the ship and change?"

"You are perfect just as you are," Amery countered, reaching for Gavin's hand. "Just as you are."

Gavin's eyes closed momentarily, revealing how deeply Amery's words had touched him. "I am glad to hear you feel that way, but we both know I am far from perfect."

Amery shook his head. "You are. You are perfect for me. Give me tonight to prove it to you, Gavin. Let me show you how much you mean to me."

"As you wish."

Amery took a deep breath and offered his arm to his matelot, but Gavin shook his head. "Not here. The good citizens of Providence Island will not know what to make of us."

"I care not," Amery replied. "I care only for what you make of us."

"I don't know right now, but while I appreciate the thought behind the gesture, I would rather not be a spectacle for the island."

Amery accepted Gavin's demurral because he had no real choice, falling into step beside the other man and guiding him toward the finest tavern on the island. When they had found a table and ordered their dinner, Amery reached for Gavin's hand beneath the table, twining his fingers with his lover's. "I have something for you, something to show you how in what high esteem I hold you. I hope you'll accept it in the spirit it is offered."

Gavin's breath caught a little. "I don't need gifts."

"This isn't a gift," Amery explained. "It's more of a promise."

Amery slid the deed from his pocket and offered it to his lover. "This is for when we are ready to leave the sea behind."

Gavin took the document and opened it, his eyes skimming through the cramped handwriting. "What is this?" he asked, gaze flying back to Amery's face. "This has both our names on it."

"I know," Amery said. "It's the deed to property on Henrietta Island. I used my portion of the treasure today to purchase it. It's in both our names because all that is mine is yours. We made those promises when we signed our matelotage, but I thought it was time to make that a reality."

"I...I don't know what to say," Gavin said after a moment's silence.

"Say you'll accept my gift and my love," Amery pleaded. "Say you'll accept me as your matelot again."

Gavin didn't reply for a long time, his thoughts racing as he weighed his options and his emotions. Amery had never done anything like this before, never taken the time to court Gavin. Not that Gavin had missed it. He had turned to Amery willingly as a lad and had never regretted that decision until a few weeks ago. Even then, he hadn't regretted it so much as he'd questioned whether they could find a way to continue on together. Looking at the deed in front of him now, he had two choices. He could see it as another example of Amery's high-handedness and reject his lover's offer, or he could see it as the gift and promise Amery clearly intended it to be and take the first step forward. "I appreciate the thought behind this," he said slowly, "but did it ever occur to you that I might want to help you pick out our land? That I might want to help you pay for our land so it would truly be ours and not some peace offering between us?"

Amery's face fell. "I wanted to show you how much I love you," he said plaintively. "I wanted you to see that the only future I can imagine includes you."

Gavin sighed. "I know that, but you have to stop making decisions for me, or for us, without consulting me. I know you love me. I've always known that. It was what let me turn to you for comfort in the first place even before you said the words, but you've gotten so used to being the captain that you've forgotten how to be my partner. You have to stop doing that, or we're going to keep having words."

"I invited you to dinner tonight," Amery said. "I planned a whole even…. 'Sblood, I did it again, didn't I?"

Gavin nodded. "I know you're sincere, Amery, and that's the most important step. We'll eat our dinner because it was thoughtful of you to want something special. And we'll go over to Henrietta Island tomorrow and look at the land you purchased. I may love it. If I don't, we'll sell it and buy something together."

"Does this mean you've forgiven me?"

"Yes, but on one condition."

"Anything," Amery promised.

"Until I'm sure you've learned your lesson, I get to take charge in the cabin in case you need reminding that I'm your matelot first and a member of your crew second," Gavin dictated.

Amery flushed with heat at the images Gavin's words conjured up. "My body has been yours since the first time we lay together. If that's your price, it's one I'll pay and gladly."

Gavin chuckled. "We'll see if you're still singing the same tune when I take the past month's frustrations out on your arse."

Amery rose, knocking the chair over in his haste. "Forget dinner. We can eat later."

Gavin's laughter grew louder. "Sit down, Amery. I'm hungry, and you promised me dinner. I'm the one in charge, not you, remember?"

Amery righted his chair and returned to his seat, but Gavin could see the restlessness beneath his outward calm, the desire to find their bed and reestablish their claim on each other. He shared the anxiousness, but he needed to know Amery would do this his way.

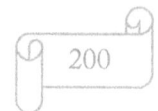

"I remember, although you'll probably have to remind me a few more times."

Gavin smiled and relaxed. "'Twill be no hardship." The tavernkeeper arrived with their dinner. "Enjoy the meal. Everything else can wait until after we've eaten."

They talked lightly through dinner, both of them aware of the delicious current of anticipation between them, so startlingly different from the tense distance that had reigned over their interactions for the past few weeks. When they had finished, Gavin left a few coins on the table, glaring at Amery when he started to protest. "If all you have is mine, then all I have is yours, and it matters not whose hand leaves the gold on the table for it all comes from one pot. Now tell me what else you had in mind when you planned our evening."

"I took a room in the boarding house," Amery answered, "thinking to treat you to a night in a real bed. The room is paid for, but we don't have to use it if you would rather return to the ship."

Gavin considered insisting on principle, but the idea of a night without the crew around to overhear held a certain appeal. "Show me the way."

Amery led Gavin to the boarding house and inside to the room that was his for the night, pausing when they crossed the threshold to see what Gavin would do next.

Gavin felt no such hesitation, the mix of emotions from the past month enough to drive him to possess Amery as fully and immediately as possible. Checking only to make sure the door was locked to ensure their privacy, he advanced on his lover, peeling away the jacket and cravat he wore, loosening the laces on his shirt and pulling it over his head. Dropping the clothing without a second thought, he captured Amery's lips in his, kissing him with all the pent-up longing and fear he'd tried so hard to suppress. Amery responded to the kiss with all the ardor Gavin could hope for, giving him tacit permission to finish stripping his lover and nudge him onto the bed.

"You bathed," he teased lightly, licking a stripe up the center of Amery's belly.

"I wanted to look my best for you."

Gavin smiled and kissed Amery swiftly. "I appreciate the effort and the clean skin, but you know it wasn't your looks that appealed to me."

"What then?" Amery asked, sufficiently insecure after their month of separation to need the reassurance.

"Your compassion, your strength, your protectiveness," Gavin enumerated. "Your love." Forestalling any more conversation, Gavin kissed Amery deeply, taking control of their interaction the way he rarely did.

"I want to feel your skin too," Amery said, the sensation of cloth rubbing against his skin enough to break through the haze of desire inveigling his senses.

"All in good time," Gavin promised. "For now, I have other plans."

Amery almost protested, but he had promised to defer to Amery in private. He'd had no idea it would be so difficult. He wanted to roll Gavin onto his back, strip him naked, and ride him hard until they both came. Then he would lick Gavin clean and start over, more slowly, making tender love to him until he had no doubt how devoted Amery was. The first part would not happen, but perhaps later in the night, he could fulfill the second part of his fantasy.

Gavin seemed to read his thoughts, pinning him to the bed and rubbing against him sinuously. "'Sblood, Gavin," he begged. "Have mercy."

Gavin chuckled and reared back on his knees, stroking Amery's cock rapidly as he searched with his eyes for something to use to ease the way.

"It's too far away," Amery said with a restless shake of his head. "Keep touching me. That's all I need."

"What if I want to plow your arse?" Gavin growled.

"Then do it already."

It had been a month since they'd shared a bed and even longer since Amery had bottomed. As much as Gavin wanted to wait, to prepare Amery properly and give him a long, thorough swiving, he

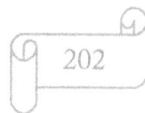

didn't have the patience for it any more than his lover did. Amery would undoubtedly say he didn't need preparation, but Gavin had been hurt too many times to take Amery's arse dry. They'd have to save that for later when Gavin had more control. For now.... "I'll save that for later. I want your mouth instead."

Amery swallowed hard, anticipating the feeling of Gavin's thick shaft sliding over his tongue and into his throat. Eagerly he scooted down on the bed, lips parted in offering.

Gavin tore open his trousers, spinning around to straddle Amery's head so he could feed his lover his cock at the same time he continued his attentions to Amery's erection. Amery tipped his head back at the perfect angle so Gavin's cock could slide easily down his throat, giving Gavin a channel to fuck. The captain's hands settled on his matelot's hips, urging him to move as he pleased. Gavin hesitated only a moment, the wet heat of Amery's mouth more than he could withstand. Riding Amery's face hard, he applied both hands to bringing Amery fulfillment as well. Within moments, Amery's cock twitched and spilled over his hands, leaving Gavin to strive for his own release. The feeling of Amery's fingers probing his entrance pushed him to the pinnacle and beyond, his seed spilling down Amery's throat.

Gavin barely retained the presence of mind to roll to the side instead of collapsing atop Amery's face. He nuzzled his lover's hip, the closest part to him. "We'll take our time next time," he promised.

"Turn around so I can hold you too," Amery requested.

Gavin summoned the strength to move and flipped around on the bed, his head returning to its customary place on Amery's shoulder. "I love you."

With those three simple words, all was once again right in Amery's world.

Chapter 27

QUINN sat alone in a quiet corner of the island's only bar. A number of inns and taverns dotted the island, but the company's prohibition against alcohol held sway in all the others. Quinn wasn't interested in anything other than rum tonight, so he skirted the others despite the cleaner floors and brighter rooms. Besides, he had no interest in meeting Amery or Gavin in one of the nicer establishments.

He didn't know—didn't want to know—what had transpired between them as they sailed to Providence Island. It truly did not matter. He'd told Eliodoro the truth as they stood vigil waiting to see if Amery would live. If Amery had died, they would have buried two bodies rather than one. However much he might wish it otherwise, Gavin would never turn to him for anything more than friendship. Quinn realized as he sat there that he had known that all along. He might have let himself dream, but the entire time, he had sought ways to repair the rift between Amery and Gavin. He had known Gavin's happiness resided with Amery, which left Quinn two choices. He could continue pining after the unattainable, or he could let go of that dream and focus on finding a lover, perhaps even a love of his own. Eliodoro's youthful face sprang to mind, sending a jolt of lust through the quartermaster. The lad inspired a gamut of emotions in Quinn, from protectiveness to desire, irritation to admiration. He could easily fall in bed with the other sailor, letting Eliodoro fill the place in his life Quinn had always kept open just in case. Amery and Gavin would encourage him to find someone of his own. The question was whether he could be satisfied with a lover when he'd always dreamed of having a beloved.

His attraction to Eliodoro was real, undeniable, the sparks between them the two times they came together enough to rouse him even now. It wasn't what Amery and Gavin had, but it was a place to start. If he could convince Eliodoro to agree.

That would be the hard part, bringing Eliodoro back to his bed after the events of the past month. The Venetian had every reason to doubt anything Quinn said, and it wasn't as if he had a good excuse to start with. Eliodoro had wanted more than a physical relationship even before the current misunderstanding. Eliodoro certainly wouldn't want a relationship of convenience now when he had no reason to hope Quinn's emotions were engaged. The quartermaster would have to find a way to convince Eliodoro of his sincerity.

The sound of Spanish behind him reminded him of the plan to hunt down Eliodoro's attackers. They had conceived the idea as a way to persuade Eliodoro of his interest after his first blunder. The suggestion had worked well enough to gain him a night with Eliodoro in his arms. Maybe following through on the suggestion would begin to redeem him now.

Approaching the bar, he tipped his head toward the group of Spaniards. "Do you know their names?" he asked the proprietor.

"Munoz, Jimenez, and Soto," the man replied. "They've been here for a couple of months."

"Which one is Munoz?"

The barkeep pointed to the man in the middle. "I don't want no trouble here."

"We'll take it outside."

The barkeeper starred at Quinn for a moment longer. "See that you do."

"Munoz!"

The man in question turned at hearing his name. "*Sí, señor?*"

"Outside," Quinn said roughly.

The Spaniard exchanged confused glances with his friends, but he clearly understood the threat of Quinn's hand on his sword. "Outside," he agreed.

They trooped out into the narrow yard outside the tavern, some of the other sailors and patrons drawn outside by the lure of a fight.

"Who will I have the pleasure of killing?" Munoz asked.

"Quinn Davies, quartermaster of the *Silver Queen,*" Quinn replied, drawing his sword. "You made the mistake of doing grievous injury to one of my crew. I'm here to make sure you pay for your actions."

"I do not recognize that ship," Munoz said, his own sword hissing as it left its sheath.

"I'm surprised," Quinn drawled, "since you spent a number of days in the hold after we captured your slave ship. You were one of the officers on *Nuestra Señora de Madrid,* were you not?"

"*Sí,* but you won that battle so why are you challenging me now?"

"Because I didn't know at the time that you and the other officers had raped a cabin boy repeatedly for sport," Quinn snarled.

Munoz grinned. "Ah, Eliodoro, our—what was the word?—our peg boy. He was an enjoyable piece of arse. I could not find him again after you left us here."

"Because he stayed with the *Silver Queen* and a crew who respects him," Quinn spat, enraged at the insult to his crewmate.

"Is that what you call it?" Munoz sneered. "How many times have you fucked him?"

"Never," Quinn retorted hotly, excusing the lie by telling himself they had made love both times they joined. Muniz would undoubtedly not appreciate the distinction, but it was an important one for Quinn. "Eliodoro is better than that, and for your part in his abuse, you will taste my steel."

"*Así sea. En guardia,*" Munoz declared, his sword flashing out to engage with Quinn's.

Quinn countered easily, sizing up his opponent as their blades met, separated, and met again. Munoz would be a formidable opponent, but not beyond his skill, particularly not with a simple cutlass against Quinn's much longer blade. In the close confines aboard a ship, perhaps, but here in the open, the longer reach gave Quinn a definite advantage. Focusing on his goal, he ignored the jeers of the Spaniard's companions. Their derision didn't matter; he cared only about redeeming Eliodoro's honor.

The steel of their blades clanged as the two men engaged, advancing and retreating in turn. Quinn could feel sweat beading on his forehead as the fight continued, neither man immediately able to gain the advantage. Quinn revised his estimate of the man's skill upward when his larger sword did not give him a swift victory, but he didn't regret the challenge he'd issued. Gavin would patch him up if he got injured, and Eliodoro's honor was worth the price.

"You should have taken him when you had the chance," Munoz sneered. "He's a fine little whore. He begged and moaned and squeezed so tightly. Always oiled and ready for whoever was next in line."

The images provoked by the man's slurs snapped Quinn's temper. Without hesitation, he grabbed the knife from his boot, hurling it at the man's throat. Munoz went down like a sack of potatoes, his sword clattering as it hit the ground. "Anyone else want to insult Eliodoro?"

The other Spaniards all shook their heads, backing away from their deceased companion. Quinn retrieved his knife, wiping the blood on the dead man's shirt. "Tell the other officers from his ship to fear for their lives if they cross my path."

Turning on his heel, Quinn left the tavern yard behind. He strode down the streets of the town, quiet now in the falling darkness, eyes alert for any who might challenge him, but he met no one. Nisbett greeted him as he came aboard the *Silver Queen*, but Quinn replied only with an absent nod. Climbing down a deck, he scanned the hammocks stretched across the crew quarters.

"Ye'll not be findin' him here, Quartermaster," Seaton said softly, coming in behind Quinn. "Ye'd do better t'look in the crow's nest. He goes there to think."

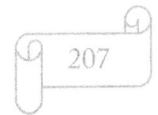

Quinn looked at the older man sharply. "How do you know who I'm looking for?"

Seaton chuckled. "Because I recognize the look on your face. If ye'll take some advice from an old man, court the boy proper like. He don't believe anyone could want more from him than his body."

It was a delightful body to be sure, but that wasn't the reason Quinn had killed a man tonight. "I'll remember."

"See that you do. He's a hard worker, and he's earned the respect of the crew. Nobody'd like to see his affections trifled with."

"I'm sincere," Quinn blurted out before he could censor himself.

"So is the boy, but ye have yer work cut out for ye to make him believe ye. He thinks ye're in love with Mr. Watson, he does."

Quinn cleared his throat awkwardly. "You and Clay have been together a few years."

"Fourteen," Seaton said proudly. "Happiest day of my life when he said he'd stay with me."

"So how do I convince Eliodoro of my sincerity?"

Seaton pursed his lips. "Ye start by paying him more attention than ye give to Mr. Watson, no matter how tense things are between him and the captain. Ye make him yer first priority in every situation."

"But the ship—"

"In every situation," Seaton repeated. "By doing yer job on the ship, ye're keeping him safe, but it's about him, not about duty or yer friendship with the captain or anything else. It's about him."

Quinn nodded slowly. "The way the captain always has his eye on Mr. Watson."

"Ye're not as thick as ye act," Seaton quipped. "Now ye have to make him believe it, and that's a much harder task because nobody has ever put him first as far as I can tell, and so he thinks he don't deserve it."

"I guess I'd better get started then."

"Good luck to ye, Quartermaster. We could use a little happiness aboard ship." Seaton patted Quinn's shoulder and moved past him into the crew's quarters, stopping at Clay's hammock to murmur something in his matelot's ear. Clay lifted his hand to Seaton's cheek, leaving Quinn squirming at the intimate sight. That was what he wanted, he realized with sudden clarity. He wanted Eliodoro to look at him that way.

Leaving the two men to their conversation, he wandered back on deck, pondering Seaton's advice. *Make him your first priority.* The words were so easy to say, but Quinn hadn't come close to living them over the past month. He'd let his obsession with Gavin and then Amery's illness take his attention away from his new lover, if he could call Eliodoro that after their two encounters. He wanted to give Eliodoro that title and claim the title of the young man's lover in return. He simply needed to figure out how to make that a reality. He'd already started tonight, challenging and killing Munoz for his part in abusing Eliodoro. As Seaton had said, doing his job as quartermaster already ensured the safety of the ship and crew so it was only a question of adjusting his thinking. More than once, he'd caught himself tracking Eliodoro's location on the ship, both during battle and during the calm times in between. He could easily make the choice to actively keep Eliodoro in his awareness even if he was momentarily out of sight. In battle, he could stay close to protect the lad if need arose. He could also make sure Eliodoro knew how to defend himself. They could spend a portion of their off-duty hours improving Eliodoro's skill with a sword. Amery had started teaching Eliodoro to navigate, and indeed, Amery was the best person to teach those skills. Quinn would see about teaching him everything else.

Thus resolved, Quinn stared up at the crow's nests, trying to see which one Eliodoro occupied. He finally spied a bit of cloth at the top of the mizzenmast. Scaling the rigging, he peeked over the edge. "Can I persuade you to come down and talk to me, or must I join you up here?"

"What you want say?" Eliodoro asked sullenly.

"I'm sorry for a start," Quinn said. "I was so worried about Gavin that I didn't think about anything else, and that wasn't fair to you. Will you come down?"

Eliodoro seriously considered refusing and making Quinn say his piece there in the rigging, but the rain that had been threatening all day chose that moment to start, the drops small and stinging as the wind picked up as well.

"*Sì,*" Eliodoro agreed, rising from his perch. He slithered down the ropes with ease. Quinn followed more slowly, savoring the sight of the Venetian's lithe form.

"We can go to the officers' dining room," Quinn suggested. "No one will be there now."

Eliodoro nodded, ducking into the corridor to the aftcastle. He wasn't sure what Quinn wanted to talk about, but it relieved him to have their conversation somewhere other than Quinn's cabin. He knew the quartermaster desired him, but he wanted more than that. The captain had finally convinced him he deserved more than that.

The silence stretched as each man waited for the other to speak, the tapping of the rain on the deck above them the only sound. Quinn offered Eliodoro a napkin to dry his face and hair, but Eliodoro shook his head. "You want talk, so talk."

"I want to know where we stand," Quinn said. "Nothing has gone the way I would've liked since I found those men attacking you in Tortuga."

"Nothing?"

The sharp tone of Eliodoro's voice drew Quinn up short. "Nothing but our one night together, but even that was cut short too soon," Quinn amended. "When I found Gavin outside my cabin that night, I didn't think. He needed help, comfort, and I gave it to him because I've been watching out for him since we were half your age. You had night duty, and I thought he and Amery would work things out in the morning, and you and I could pick back up where we left off."

"Where we leave off, Quinn?" Eliodoro demanded. "What that night mean to you?"

Quinn's breath caught at the memory. "It was the most beautiful night of my life. I've swived my share of men, including Gavin and Amery, a long time ago, but it was never like it was the night with you." Quinn almost laughed at the shocked look on Eliodoro's face. "The captain didn't tell you that, did he? He spouted all kinds of accusations at me without mentioning his own indiscretions. It was before they were together, and the three of us fell in and out of bed with each other indiscriminately, depending on who had watch."

"Is maybe my fault he say those things," Eliodoro said meekly. "I tell him I see you and *Signor* Watson."

Quinn nodded. "I suspected as much, but it doesn't matter. Amery would have jumped to the same conclusion fast enough."

Eliodoro flushed. "Is no all I say. I think you no want me and I no want be alone. I offer…."

Quinn sighed sadly. "You offered yourself in exchange for his protection."

Eliodoro nodded, face downcast as he waited for Quinn to heap scorn upon his head. Anger surged in Quinn, but the sight of Eliodoro cowering as if fearing his fists diffused it immediately.

Quinn tipped Eliodoro's chin up until he could find the dark eyes beneath the mop of curls. "I'm not angry, Eliodoro. I don't have any right to be angry when you shouldn't have felt the need for his protection in the first place."

The fear cleared slowly from Eliodoro's face. "'E said kind things. I was lonely."

"He is a kind man," Quinn agreed, "and I hope you'll continue to learn everything he can teach you about the sea, but perhaps you will look to me now for the kind words you need."

"Is no kindness I want," Eliodoro said, feeling bold.

"What do you want?" Quinn asked, holding his breath with hope.

"I want what Captain White and *Signor* Watson 'ad. I want what Seaton and Clay 'ave. I want someone of my own."

"Don't we all?" Quinn said with a rueful laugh. "I have envied them for eleven years, but I also know it requires more than the wanting of it."

"I no naïve," Eliodoro insisted, "but if you no 'ope for that too, I prefer look elsewhere."

Quinn didn't reply right away. He almost waited too long. Eliodoro started toward the door, shoulders slumping in dejection. "Wait," Quinn said, grabbing Eliodoro's arm. "You say you want a matelotage, but you hardly know me. You don't love me yet, because you don't know me well enough to love me, any more than I know you that well. To sign that kind of a contract now would be foolish for both of us. Can we compromise? Can we agree to see where this takes us, both of us knowing that if it can't become a matelotage, we will go separate ways?"

Eliodoro saw the logic in the proposal, so he nodded. "What we do now?"

Chapter 28

LOGIC screaming at him that this was a bad idea, Quinn stepped closer, caught Eliodoro's cheeks between his hands, and brushed his lips across the youth's the way he had wanted to do so many times. Eliodoro froze beneath his touch, but Quinn had learned patience at sea. Keeping the touch of both hands and lips light, he let the kiss draw out, tender, loving, offering rather than demanding. Giving rather than taking. It took a long moment before Eliodoro relaxed, eyes fluttering shut as his lips parted. Quinn smiled, resisting the silent invitation, keeping the kiss as chaste as he could. Eliodoro deserved to be cherished, not ravaged, and Quinn intended to court him as conscientiously as any man had ever courted his lady. Not that Eliodoro was anything less than a man, the strength of his arms closing around Quinn's waist, trying to pull him closer, almost more than Quinn could resist.

"Eliodoro," Quinn murmured, breaking the kiss, "don't." Eliodoro didn't listen, tilting his head up for more, but Quinn steeled his resolution and stepped back. "Have dinner with me."

The invitation brought Eliodoro up short. "*Che?*"

"What?" Quinn asked, not understanding the Italian phrase.

"Yes, what?" Eliodoro repeated.

Catching on, Quinn repeated, "Have dinner with me. Come into town, sit down with me at an inn or tavern, and share a meal with me. We can talk, get to know each other better. If we stay here, we will end up in my cabin, and that won't help us decide on our future."

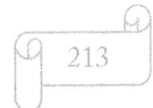

Eliodoro nodded slowly. "All right, but is no necessary."

It was very necessary as far as Quinn was concerned. Eliodoro needed to start expecting to be treated decently. Quinn had made the mistake of taking his presence for granted. It wasn't a mistake he wanted to make again. "We need to eat anyway."

"I put on new clothes?" Eliodoro asked, keenly aware of the raggedness of the garments he'd had on the slaver.

"If you wish," Quinn replied, "but you needn't feel ashamed of your appearance. Wearing rags or evening rig, you will be the handsomest man in the tavern."

Eliodoro knew that for a lie, for he could not hold a candle to Quinn's rugged beauty, his own skin too dark to be fashionable and his curls too unruly for good taste. He couldn't help but be flattered by the comment, even knowing it for the flattery it was. "I change."

Hurrying to the foredeck, relieved that the shower that had driven them inside had eased, Eliodoro pulled his shirt over his head even before he reached the crew quarters.

"What's the rush, lad?" Clay asked as he came in.

"Dinner," Eliodoro said, "with *Signor* Davies."

"Oh ho," Clay smiled, "so you'll be smilin' again, I hope."

Eliodoro flushed. "Is wrong I want look nice for 'im?"

"Not wrong at all," Clay promised. "Didn't ye tell me he gave ye a fresh shirt when we were in Tortuga?" Eliodoro nodded. "Wear that. He'll be flattered to see ye in it, specially since I know ye ain't worn it since we sailed after the *Rayo*."

"Is good I wear now?"

Clay smiled. "It's very good, and if you're lucky, when you get back after dinner, he'll take it off ye."

Eliodoro frowned. "I want more than fuck. I want what you 'ave."

"And so you should," Clay agreed, "but ain't nothing wrong with a long, thorough fuck now and again, specially from the man ye love."

"'Ow I know is love?"

Clay chuckled. "Ye'll know. It's different for every man, but ye'll know when it happens to ye. In the meantime, enjoy what the quartermaster's offering. Ain't no harm in it, what with the life ye had afore comin' aboard the *Silver Queen*."

Clay's simple acceptance eased Eliodoro's concerns. He changed clothes quickly, donning the shirt and breeches Quinn had given him in Tortuga, glad he'd bought new hose and boots that morning with his share of the treasure. He wouldn't wear them at sea, or they'd be ruined by the salt, but he'd be glad of them ashore. Pulling roughly at the tie that held back his unruly curls, he scraped them away from his face again, intending to return them to their queue.

"Wait," Clay said, pulling out a comb. "Let me."

Eliodoro stood still while Clay straightened his mess of hair and tied the leather thong around it. "There. A picture of gentlemanly civility."

Eliodoro laughed. "I no 'ave jacket."

"This is the Indies, lad. No jacket required."

"The captain, 'e wear one."

"When ye're captain, ye can wear one too," Clay said with a laugh. "Go on. Ye're keepin' Mr. Davies waitin'."

Nervous again, Eliodoro hurried back onto deck, slowing when he caught sight of Quinn emerging from the other end of the ship. The quartermaster had changed as well, into a wine red jacket over his linen shirt and fawn-colored breeches. Eliodoro started to turn around and sneak back inside, sure Quinn could not possibly want to be seen with someone like him. Before he could try, Quinn saw him, a smile lighting his face, his hand reaching out in invitation. "You look very handsome, Eliodoro."

Eliodoro shook his head. "Next to you, no one look at me."

"That's fine with me. I don't want to share even the sight of you."

"Then why we go?" Eliodoro asked.

"Because you deserve to be treated well, not like some secret I'm ashamed of," Quinn explained. "Now, before the rain starts again, shall we find a tavern?"

Eliodoro let Quinn escort him off the ship, noticing as they walked into town how many of the islanders stopped to watch them pass. He didn't know which of them drew the attention, but it made him nervous. "Relax," Quinn murmured at his elbow. "They don't mean any harm."

Eliodoro wasn't so sure, but he followed Quinn's lead, wondering where the quartermaster was taking him.

When the rain started again, Quinn grabbed his hand, running with him toward the nearest tavern, the drops falling hard and fast enough to dampen Eliodoro's shirt before they found shelter. Fortunately, the tavernkeeper had started a fire in the hearth. They found a table nearby where the heat would dry their clothes. A noticeable shiver went through Eliodoro. "Are you cold?" Quinn asked. "You could wear my jacket."

Eliodoro shook his head. "I no want take your jacket. You need."

Quinn smiled and leaned closer. "I wouldn't complain at all about seeing you wearing it. Already, the thought that almost everything you're wearing is something I gave you has me thinking lusty thoughts. To then look at you wearing my jacket would perfect the vision."

Eliodoro scowled. "I no 'ore for you to dress. I 'ave my own gold."

Quinn's eyes widened as he realized how Eliodoro had taken his comment. "That's not at all what I meant. You are wearing my gifts. If I can't touch you, I like knowing something I gave you is touching you instead."

Eliodoro did not look convinced.

"Give me something of yours," Quinn proposed, "some token I can wear, and see how you feel when you see it on me if you don't believe me. It's about knowing you've found enough favor with the other person for him to wear your gift."

Eliodoro's expression lightened somewhat, though it did not clear entirely. Quinn squeezed his hand lightly beneath the table. "Don't fret, Eliodoro. Relax and enjoy your dinner. Tell me about your home."

Eliodoro's face softened. "Venezia. Is city of islands. My father make masks for *carnavale* before he die. My mother try continue business, but people not buy from woman. She lose shop. I go on ship to make one less person feed. I come 'ome visit after first trip. She dead."

Quinn nodded. It was a sad, familiar story. Amery and Gavin both had first sailed for that same reason. "I've never been in the Mediterranean," he said instead. "I left England and sailed for the New World and have been here ever since."

"Long time?" Eliodoro asked, hoping to learn more about the quartermaster.

"Twenty years. I was born on the coast of England. The sea was in my blood. My father was a fisherman, and I enjoyed going out with him, but I wanted more excitement than that. I got even more than I bargained for."

Eliodoro laughed. "You no want be pirate?"

"No, I hadn't planned on becoming a pirate, but life has a way of changing our plans. I met Gavin and Amery on that first merchant ship. None of us were big for our age, but Gavin was the slightest of the three of us. Amery and I did our best to protect him, and we succeeded for the first few years, but eventually we couldn't anymore. By that time we were sailing to the Indies rather than Virginia, and the lure of freedom the pirates represented was too much temptation. We jumped ship and went searching for new berths."

"'E is lucky 'ave you as friends."

"You have friends as well, even if you don't realize it. I went looking for you before I located you in the crow's nest tonight. Seaton gave me quite a speech about treating you well and how you'd earned the respect of the crew and I shouldn't trifle with you."

"Trifle? I no know that word."

"To treat you badly, to hurt you again," Quinn struggled to explain. "To make you think I want something if I don't really want it."

"To make me 'ore," Eliodoro said with a nod.

"I killed a man today for calling you that," Quinn said. "I'm certainly not going to treat you that way!"

"Who you kill?"

"Munoz," Quinn replied. "He was in another tavern. I called him out and killed him for his crimes."

Eliodoro spat in the dust at his feet. "'E was worst other than captain. I glad 'e's dead."

"How old were you when they took you?" Quinn asked, wondering how long Eliodoro had suffered.

"Eighteen. They keep me six months."

Quinn shuddered, trying to imagine living through that kind of hell. Gavin had suffered longer, but only at the hands of one man and without the knowledge of the rest of the crew. The few days of Quinn's own imprisonment had been horrid beyond words. The thought of surviving that kind of abuse for six months only increased his respect for the man at his side. Not to mention making the fact that Eliodoro had trusted him enough to sleep with him all the more astonishing. "No one will ever hurt you again if I have my way."

"I take care of myself," Eliodoro said defensively.

"You can, and I'll make sure you become even more capable, but that doesn't mean I'll stop trying to protect you too," Quinn replied. "Tomorrow we will start practicing with your sword."

The serving girl brought their dinner, interrupting their conversation and batting her eyelashes coquettishly at Quinn. Eliodoro was torn between amusement and jealousy. Amusement won when Quinn paid the flirt absolutely no mind, his attention focused entirely on Eliodoro. "She want you."

Quinn flushed as he shrugged. "I can't control what she wants, but that doesn't mean I have to give it to her."

Eliodoro smiled, pleased at the response. "She is pretty," he teased. "Why you no want?"

Quinn scowled. "Why would I want her when I hope to have something—someone—even better?"

"You 'ave woman somewhere?" Eliodoro asked, knowing he was fishing for compliments but still insecure enough to need the reassurance of Quinn's words.

"No woman has ever made me feel the way you did," Quinn said softly, leaning forward so no one would overhear.

Eliodoro's heart beat faster at the tender memory of the night spent in Quinn's bed. His body stirred at the thought of returning there, the sweet, almost chaste kiss from earlier still buzzing on his lips. "Maybe I please you again soon."

Quinn wanted that so badly his body hurt with it, but his soul cried for something more, something real and lasting, and he wasn't sure returning immediately to bed would advance that cause. "Soon."

They finished eating, enjoying the food the tavernkeeper offered them, keenly aware of each other. When they had finished eating, Quinn proposed they return to the ship for the night. "Most of the crew will be in the inns and taverns. We'll have more privacy aboard the *Silver Queen* than we will in town."

Hopeful Quinn's suggestion meant a return to more intimate activities, Eliodoro accepted immediately. The rain had tapered off again while they were eating, though the heavy clouds promised more before the night was over. They reached the ship, Quinn's hand finding the small of Eliodoro's back, steadying him as they walked up the gangplank. On deck, Quinn hesitated. "We could continue our conversation inside if you'd like. In the dining room perhaps?"

Eliodoro nodded and let Quinn guide him, though he knew the way. He didn't want to do anything to make Quinn move his hand. Reaching the dining room, Eliodoro turned to ask Quinn a question, only to have all thought fly from his head when the quartermaster's hands cupped his face reverently. Eliodoro waited with bated breath for another kiss, but it didn't come right away, Quinn's long fingers stroking his skin instead, over his forehead, his nose, behind his ears to the thong holding back his hair. "You should wear your hair loose," Quinn murmured, working at the knot.

"I no can see then," Eliodoro explained as he leaned into the tender touches. "The wind blow it in my eyes."

"Then take it down before you come to me."

Eliodoro's insides turned liquid at the request, images of preparing himself for Quinn assailing him with unbearable intimacy. He nodded. "For you."

Quinn did kiss him then, finally, another sweet, soft touching of lips much like earlier, but without the hesitation. His fingers carded through Eliodoro's hair, the gentleness far more arousing than logic could account for. Eliodoro had known so little of tenderness in his young life and almost none where sex was concerned that it scared him nearly as much as it aroused him. Needing to feel he had some control, he lifted his hands to Quinn's chest, stroking across the firm planes in search of his lover's nipples. He knew what to do with lust; he had no idea what to do with.... Words escaped him in either language as he struggled to define this new mood between Quinn and himself. He couldn't call it love—they didn't know each other that well yet—but he had never seen this kind of affection and tenderness except between true lovers. The thought made him uncomfortable enough to reject it, wanting matters between them back on familiar ground.

Quinn gasped when he felt Eliodoro's hands on his chest, the sensations setting him aflame. He fought to keep his touch light rather than giving in to the temptation to push Eliodoro back onto the table and ravish him. Eliodoro, however, seemed to have no interest in slowing down, his caresses determinedly setting Quinn's senses to riot. Feeling like a drowning man going under for the last time, Quinn lifted his head and gasped for breath, a soft moan of surrender escaping him.

"Mr. Davies, sir?"

"No answer," Eliodoro begged.

Quinn was tempted to listen, Seaton's admonition to put Eliodoro first no matter what still ringing in his ears, but he could hear Nisbett knocking on his cabin door.

"If I don't answer, he'll look here next, and that door doesn't lock. We don't have to rush. We can take our time and cherish each other properly."

The door behind them opened. "Oh, there you are, sir," Nisbett said, coming into the room. "I need your opinion on one of the repairs we did. I don't think it's going to hold."

"I'll be right there, Nisbett," Quinn said, gesturing for the second mate to wait for him outside. "Let me finish my conversation with Eliodoro."

If Nisbett was surprised at the delay or the dismissal, it did not show on his face. When the door shut behind him, Quinn stroked Eliodoro's face again. "Don't think I'm choosing my duty above you. If the ship is not safe, then you are not safe, and I cannot abide that thought. You're welcome to come with me if you'd like."

Eliodoro smiled sweetly. "No, is fine. I sleep now. Tomorrow I buy something you wear."

He left one more quick kiss on Quinn's lips and sailed out of the room, leaving Quinn hopelessly aroused with no outlet but his own hand. Damn Nisbett and his rotten timing!

Chapter 29

THE repair did indeed need to be refitted, easing Quinn's concern about having left Eliodoro for no reason. By morning, Amery was still nowhere to be found; Quinn hoped he and Gavin had found a place to be alone and work through their troubles. He ordered the crew aboard to begin the repairs and went to find Mr. Thorn, the agent of the Providence Island Company. They needed to restock their supplies as well.

"Mr. Davies," Thorn said with a smile, "I expected to see Captain White this morning."

"The captain had a bout of the yellow fever and is still recovering," Quinn said, not about to give the man any reason to think Amery was neglecting his duties for personal matters. "Mr. Watson is most insistent he get plenty of rest so he recovers fully. In the meantime, we need to restock our supplies and complete some repairs to the *Silver Queen*. The battle with the *Rayo* took its toll."

Mr. Thorn nodded. "I thought she looked a little worse for wear when I was down by the harbor yesterday. The merchants in town already know to send Captain White's accounts to the company office. I'll give you a letter to show them, adding you as an authorized agent of the company as well. The sooner you restock and make your repairs, the sooner you'll be able to sail for more treasure."

"That's much appreciated, not only for this trip, but for later so that we can make purchases more efficiently."

"Efficiency is my job, sir. Let me know if I can be of further assistance."

The agent wrote out the letter and gave it to Quinn with his wishes for good hunting. Quinn thanked him and went into town, placing orders to be delivered posthaste to the ship. His thoughts strayed back to Eliodoro, to their dinner the night before, and the sweet kisses the Venetian had finally consented to give him. They had roused his body as he'd known they would, but it was far more than that. Despite Eliodoro's relative worldliness where sex was concerned, he kissed like a virgin, and that realization thrilled Quinn. He couldn't change Eliodoro's past however much he might wish he could erase the months of abuse by the Spanish crew, but this one thing, at least, he could give Eliodoro. He could kiss him the way he deserved, the way Quinn suspected no one had ever kissed him.

His orders for the ship completed, Quinn toyed with the idea of doing some shopping of his own. He hadn't examined Eliodoro's sword closely to test its quality, but he'd seen how wrong it was for him when he'd rescued Eliodoro from his attackers in Tortuga. Detouring to the smithy, he found the blacksmith hard at work. "I'm looking for a sword."

The blacksmith glanced up, eyes raking over the man darkening his doorway. "Seems to me ye got one already."

"Not for me," Quinn explained. "For a friend who needs one. He's about my height and reach."

"I have a few I might be willin' to sell," the smith agreed. "We'll see if one works for ye."

"Thank you."

The blacksmith opened an armoire to reveal a rack of swords. Quinn examined them carefully, putting the first two back because of the quality of the steel. The third one he picked up, however, looked of far better quality. He took a step back, testing the balance of the sword, slashing it back and forth a few times. He wished Eliodoro was there to try it himself, but this would have to do. If Eliodoro didn't like it, Quinn could always use it as a backup sword in case his got broken or damaged in battle. "How much?"

They settled in to haggle over the price, the smith clearly enjoying the negotiations as much as Quinn did. When they'd settled on a price, Quinn's purse was somewhat lighter, but he had a smile on his face and a gift for Eliodoro in his hand. By the time he returned to the ship, the first of the supplies had started arriving. He ordered the crew to stow the supplies and begin the repairs to the ship. Mr. Jennings, the carpenter, already had the faulty repair cleared, the damaged boards completely removed rather than patched, so they could be replaced.

Leaving them to work, Quinn went in search of Eliodoro, but he was nowhere on the ship, not even in the crow's nest. Frowning, Quinn left both swords in his cabin and went back to work, wondering when Amery and Gavin would surface. A couple of hours later, Eliodoro returned to the ship, disappeared into the crew quarters for a few minutes, and then came back in his old clothes again to pitch in with the work that needed to be done. He didn't say anything to Quinn, but he smiled in his direction whenever their eyes met.

By sundown, Jennings had the repairs nearly completed. Quinn thanked the crew for their hard work on behalf of the captain and gave them permission to go ashore for dinner and the evening. He stayed behind to stand watch.

"You no leave ship tonight?" Eliodoro asked.

"Not tonight," Quinn said. "Amery and Gavin aren't back, and Nisbett stood watch last night, so I'm the only one left."

"You want I bring you dinner?"

Quinn smiled. "Thank you, but it's not necessary. Peele cooked dinner for the watch before he left to go ashore. I'll eat whatever he made."

"Who else is watch?"

"Just me. This is a friendly port, and the men deserve a break. We've had too many deaths in the last few weeks. They need a chance to relax before we sail again."

"I stay. You no should watch alone."

"I'd like that," Quinn said, squeezing Eliodoro's shoulder. "It *is* a friendly port, but we truly must stand watch."

"I know. I no distract you."

Quinn laughed. Eliodoro was a distraction no matter what.

"What is funny?"

"You are a most welcome distraction at any time," Quinn admitted. "Now, knowing we're alone on the ship makes it even worse. At least there's no one to see or care if I kiss you."

"You think they care?"

"No, probably not," Quinn replied, "but it isn't only about their approval. I don't want anyone to look at you askance, to think I'm taking advantage of you, or that you're trying to take advantage of my position."

"Is no like that!" Eliodoro protested.

"Easy, calm down. I know it isn't like that. You do your share of the work and then some. With a little more experience, Amery will make you an officer for sure, on your own merits, not because of me. But people talk, and I don't want to give them reason to doubt you, so when the crew's around, I won't do anything to call attention to our relationship. I'm not ashamed of you, but I don't see any reason to make public what we share in private. Have you ever seen Gavin and Amery kiss on deck?"

Eliodoro had to admit he had not. Only when the captain was sick had he seen any outward sign of the affection between them, and even then, not much given the tension between the two men at the time. "But everyone know they are matelots."

"Yes," Quinn agreed, "and if that time comes for us, I don't intend to hide it, but it's still a matter for the privacy of our quarters rather than on deck. Everyone knows about Seaton and Clay, too, but you don't see them kissing while they're on duty."

"Sometimes I see them belowdecks."

"But not while they're on duty."

"No."

"Tell me something, Eliodoro. Today while we were working, you smiled at me whenever you looked my way. You saw me smile back, right?" Eliodoro nodded. "Then you know I was thinking of you the whole time we were working. I didn't act on it except to smile, but you were first in my thoughts. That's the way it should be. The way it will be."

"I buy something for you," Eliodoro said timidly. "You say I should and you would wear." He reached in his pocket and pulled out a thick gold bracelet. "I see in shop window. I think is from *Rayo*'s treasure."

Quinn examined the bracelet carefully. "This is beautiful work. You shouldn't have spent so much."

"Was no that much. No more than new boots."

Quinn didn't see how that was possible, but short of calling Eliodoro a liar, he had no choice but to let it go. He released the clasp and struggled to fasten it around his wrist. When he fumbled, Eliodoro took it from him and fixed the clasp. Keeping Quinn's hand in his, he let his eyes roam over the quartermaster. "You right. I like see you wear my gift."

"It's too dark now, but tomorrow, after we've slept, I have something for you as well."

Eliodoro shook his head. "No, you already give me shirt, breeches. Is too much to give more."

"I saw the sword you used in Tortuga, and it's not the right size or weight for you," Quinn insisted. "If you're going to defend yourself, you need a proper sword. If you truly can't accept it as a gift, you can pay me for it, but you will take it, one way or another."

Eliodoro glared. "You no tell me—"

"Stop," Quinn interrupted. "I know I don't tell you what to do outside of ship matters, but we're a privateer vessel. We attack other ships with the intention of taking them. You can't fight in that kind of battle without a proper sword, and you can't expect the rest of the crew to protect you when they're fighting for their own lives as well. This is about common sense, Eliodoro, and about staying safe so we *can* be together. Don't ask me to stand by and watch you be killed when I could have prevented it."

Mollified somewhat, Eliodoro nodded. "But I pay you for sword."

"If you insist."

"I insist."

Quinn named a price, less than what he'd actually paid, but not so much that Eliodoro wouldn't believe him. The Venetian pulled out his purse and handed Quinn the gold. Quinn took it, resolving to find a way to sneak it back into Eliodoro's sea chest at a later date. He was as greedy as the next man, but he couldn't take Eliodoro's gold. "I'll get the sword. We can start practicing tomorrow."

Eliodoro stayed on deck while Quinn went below to fetch the blade he'd purchased. He handed it to Eliodoro who examined it closely. "Is no like Venetian or Spanish sword."

"No, it's not," Quinn agreed. "It's heavier, longer, and the blade as well as the tip can be used. It takes a little getting used to after a corsair's sword, but I wouldn't switch for anything."

"Tomorrow you teach me."

"Yes, as soon as we've had a chance to rest since we'll be awake all night."

"We need find some way stay awake," Eliodoro purred, stepping closer to Quinn. Before Quinn could react, the younger man leaned up and mated their lips. Quinn groaned into the kiss, the desire that had simmered in the background all day coming to the fore now with that simple contact. Lifting his hands to Eliodoro's shoulders, he reached once again for the thong confining his lover's curls. "I thought you said you'd leave your hair loose for me."

Eliodoro laughed and stepped back, catching and holding Quinn's gaze as he slowly reached for the loose end of the thong, pulling it free and shaking his head so his hair settled around his face and brushed his shoulders. The simple gesture shouldn't have had such a powerful

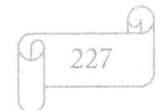

effect on Quinn, but in that movement, he saw the sailor disappear and the lover appear. Pulling Eliodoro back into his embrace, he nuzzled the young man's neck, taking in the fresh smell of his hair. Eliodoro had done more than shop while he was ashore that morning. Eliodoro's arms closed around Quinn's waist, clinging to him as his knees trembled at the tenderness in Quinn's touch. When he'd returned to his hammock last night, he'd tossed and turned for a long time before his arousal had subsided enough for him to sleep. The quarters were empty enough that he could have taken himself in hand and found relief, but he'd experienced pleasure at Quinn's hands, and he didn't want anything to tarnish that moment. He couldn't come to his lover untouched, though he wished that gift were still his to give, but he could save his pleasure for their moments together. Drifting off into sleep, he'd dreamed of their night together. When he awoke in the morning, the little gestures like these, the ones that proclaimed Quinn's affection, had been foremost in his mind. He could—and did— remember what it felt like to have the quartermaster's cock inside him, but far more importantly, he remembered the little touches like these, the ones no other man had ever given him. Perhaps he was more untouched than he realized. Tilting his head to the side to give Quinn better access to the column of his neck, he sighed. "No one ever touch me like you touch me. With you, is soft, like you care."

Quinn paused in nibbling on Eliodoro's ear. "I do care about you. I have from the moment you defied the Spanish crew and helped us free the captives on the slave ship."

"It no bother you I no… pure?"

Quinn laughed, pulling Eliodoro into his arms and spinning him around. "Sweet boy. You are far more pure than most of the men on this ship, myself included. You were abused. That's a far cry from being experienced. How many man have you kissed?"

Eliodoro flushed. "You."

Quinn's elation grew. "How many men have you asked to make love to you?"

Eliodoro looked away shyly. "You."

Quinn slid a finger beneath Eliodoro's chin, tipping it up so their gazes met. "Then you, my darling Eliodoro, are as pure as any virgin on her wedding night. No, don't argue," he added when he saw the protest rise in his lover's eyes. "I've been raped. I know what that feels like, and it is *not* the same as taking a lover. Not in my eyes. Now, will you stop dwelling on your past and focus on the here and now?"

Eliodoro nodded, trying to do as Quinn asked and let go of his nightmares. "What you want I think about?"

"Me."

Chapter 30

ELIODORO'S heart pounded at the idea that Quinn wanted his thoughts focused on the quartermaster. "Is all I think about for weeks."

Quinn silently cursed the duty that kept them on deck. He couldn't take Eliodoro to his cabin and worship him the way he wanted to do, and he wouldn't risk embarrassing Eliodoro by doing any more than kissing him on deck under the cover of darkness. Turning Eliodoro in his embrace, he settled his arms around Eliodoro's waist and held him gently. "Do you ever think about going home?"

The change in subject surprised Eliodoro, but he accepted it without protest, hoping Quinn was genuinely interested rather than avoiding the topic of a commitment between them.

"Sometimes. Would be nice hear Italian again, no feel like I speak bad, but I love the sea. I no think I want live in city again."

"You said your home was on islands."

"*Sì*, but all beneath buildings, houses. No islands like here with trees, sand. Is all stone."

Quinn tried to picture what Eliodoro was describing and failed, but it didn't really matter. He had most of the answer he wanted. "You may 'speak bad', but you communicate very well, and that will continue to improve the longer you stay on an English ship."

"You teach me?"

"I can if you want, and Amery said he was already teaching you to navigate. That will help as well, as you learn to read the charts."

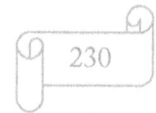

"You think *Signor* Watson teach me too?" Eliodoro asked. "I like help people."

"We'll have to ask him," Quinn said, "but he's forever complaining about needing help in the surgery during battle. He apprenticed with a surgeon on the first pirate ship we sailed on after we left the *Lady Grace* so he might be willing to take on an apprentice of his own. We'll ask him when he and Amery come back to the ship."

"Where are they?" Eliodoro asked, tilting his head to look back at Quinn.

Quinn shrugged, more interested in the bow of Eliodoro's lips than in Gavin and Amery's whereabouts. "Don't know, don't care," he said, brushing their mouths together softly. Eliodoro gasped sweetly, as he had done every time they kissed, but this time Quinn couldn't resist. His tongue darted out to taste, surprising another gasp from Eliodoro.

"Why you do that?"

"Didn't you like it?" Quinn asked with a grin.

"*Sì*, but why?"

"Because I like the way you taste and want more," Quinn replied. "If you'd prefer I not kiss you that way, I won't. I don't want to make you feel dirty the way the Spaniards did."

Eliodoro tensed momentarily at the reminder of the past he was trying to forget, but this was Quinn holding him, enfolding him in a tender, undemanding embrace unlike anything he had ever experienced. Slowly he relaxed again, leaning fully against the man behind him. He could almost believe he had found someone with whom to build a life. He snuggled back against Quinn, a smile playing around his lips as he felt the ridge of the quartermaster's erection. "You kiss me, touch me 'ow you want."

Quinn was tempted. Seriously, powerfully tempted, but duty held him back. "We're on watch, or I am, anyway."

Eliodoro nodded. "I know, but I want you know I like when you touch me. I want you touch me. When we can."

Quinn silently cursed Amery's absence. If his friend were here, even off duty in his cabin, Quinn could get Amery to take his place so he could take Eliodoro somewhere private and make love to him properly. He jealously imagined Amery and Gavin tucked away in a bed somewhere making love while he and Eliodoro were stuck on deck where they had no privacy to do more than kiss. Deciding if he couldn't do anything else, he would at least kiss his lover, he nibbled on the shell of Eliodoro's ear, smiling at the sigh of bliss that escaped Eliodoro's lips.

"WE SHOULD go back to the *Silver Queen*," Amery said as he and Gavin sat at dinner in the same inn where they had spent the previous night. They had spent the day sailing to Henrietta Island and inspecting the property Amery had purchased for them. Gavin had complained all the way to the island about Amery making assumptions and decisions without consulting Gavin first, but Amery knew his lover well, and Gavin had agreed the property would suit. The tract of land on the beach was just beyond the sandy swath. They would never be gentlemen farmers, but they would have plenty of materials to build a home where they could live out their days when they grew tired of privateering. Amery had even joked about taking up legal shipping.

"We can certainly go back to the ship," Gavin replied, his voice betraying no urgency, "but you know Quinn will make sure everything is taken care of in your absence. He is ever and will always be our friend."

"I know," Amery said softly, thinking of everything he had said about Quinn while he and Gavin were estranged. "I owe him an apology. I told Eliodoro some pretty terrible things about him while I was angry."

"Then in addition to apologizing to Quinn, you need to tell Eliodoro the truth," Gavin declared. "Whatever Eliodoro's decision is to be in Quinn's regard, that's up to him, but he needs to make his decision based on Quinn's true merits, not on your angry recriminations."

"I'll talk to him," Amery promised, "as soon as we go back to the ship."

"In the morning then," Gavin said. "We should take advantage of one more night ashore before we head out to sea again."

"Has the deep lost its appeal?"

Gavin shook his head. "Not as long as you are on it, but it is nice occasionally to have a bed that doesn't move. Especially since I have plans for tonight. I wouldn't want to miss my target."

"And what target is that?" Amery asked, his body already reacting to the purr in Gavin's voice.

"Your arse."

"You've had that already, more than once," Amery said with a laugh.

"And I'll have it again anytime I want," Gavin replied.

"You will indeed, but I hope you'll let me finish dinner first. I'll need my strength to keep up with you."

"Oh very well. Since you're so good at making plans, tell me what you imagine for our house."

Amery shook his head. "I'm not making that mistake again. We will decide together what it will look like when we're ready to build it. I would like something more than just a cabin. A real house that could survive the storms we've seen at sea."

"Yes, and space for friends to come and visit. We should build a separate kitchen to keep the heat of the hearth out of the house. I suppose that means one of us must learn to cook."

Amery laughed at the expression on Gavin's face. "With all your potions and poultices, I would think you would be a natural at cooking."

Gavin scowled. "My potions don't have to taste good. You'd start complaining soon enough if dinner tasted like my medicines."

Amery had to admit that Gavin had a point. "Perhaps I should take lessons from Peele."

"Perhaps we should hire him to cook for us when we retire from sea," Gavin countered. "'Twould be easier than trying to learn to cook while you captain the ship."

"I could give Quinn more responsibility," Amery suggested.

"Quinn has enough to worry about with having to win back Eliodoro," Gavin said. "He isn't the timid boy we rescued anymore. I couldn't have taken care of everyone on that disease-ridden island without his help."

"I think he learned not to draw attention to himself as a means of protection on the Spanish ship, and I know his difficulty speaking English also made things hard for him, but when I started showing him how to navigate, I could see the intelligence in his eyes."

"Will he take Quinn back?" Gavin asked.

"I'll do my part to make sure he does," Amery replied. "I hope he will because things could get very tense of he doesn't."

"If I can forgive you, surely we can convince Eliodoro to forgive Quinn."

Amery glared at his matelot, not wanting the reminder of his idiocy.

"Don't give me that look, Amery White. You did act like an idiot, and you're lucky I love you enough to forgive you and your heavy-handed ways."

"You've taken it out of my arse repeatedly," Amery grumbled, though inwardly this new more assertive side to his lover aroused him fiercely. For the first time, he felt like he was seeing the man Gavin should have been all along.

"You know you liked it."

"I did," Amery said softly, heart pounding as he contemplated sharing his realization with Gavin. "I do. I feel like you've finally lost your lingering fear. It's like I'm getting to know you, falling in love with you, all over again."

THE horizon lightened slowly, darkness giving way to purple and then to pink before the sun finally broke free, the first morning rays bursting across the sky in an array of glory. The beauty of the sight eased some of Quinn's fatigue, but nothing could change the fact that he had been awake and on duty since shortly after sunrise the day before. He wouldn't have made it through the night if it hadn't been for the siren in his arms. Eliodoro's presence had been a most welcome distraction each time Quinn felt himself dozing off. Eliodoro would lean into him, kiss him—or demand Quinn kiss him instead—and the resulting jolt of desire would revive Quinn's flagging attention for a little longer. He didn't know how much longer even that provocation would be enough to keep his eyes open, though. He wasn't a youngster like Eliodoro anymore, his body no longer used to standing watch for so many hours.

Glancing toward the wharf, he wondered how long it would be before any of the other crew would return. He'd ordered a few of them to return at sunrise so he could stand down, but pirates were not the most punctual of men. He only hoped it would be soon because once he fell asleep, he doubted anything short of a battle would wake him for many long hours.

The sun had finally cleared the horizon, portending another hot, clear day, when movement on shore drew his attention. He didn't need the sun glinting off golden hair to recognize Amery's gait as he strode toward the ship, Gavin at his side. "They're back," he said, pointing the two men out to Eliodoro.

"You are off duty now?" Eliodoro asked.

"Yes, finally," Quinn replied, shoulders sagging with exhaustion.

Eliodoro's hands settled on Quinn's neck, massaging the stiff muscles carefully. A month ago, Eliodoro would never have dared touch Quinn so casually, but now, with his body slumped with fatigue, his face drawn with exhaustion, he was not the intimidating figure Eliodoro had hesitated to approach. Right now, he was simply a man in need of a lover's care. "You work 'ard. You need rest. Come. We go cabin now. I 'elp you relax."

If anything could keep Quinn awake longer, it would be Eliodoro in his bed, but he didn't want their first time together as true lovers to happen with him half asleep, unable to take care of Eliodoro as he deserved. He would worry about explaining that to Eliodoro later. If he stayed on deck much longer, he would have to deal with Amery and

Gavin, and he wasn't up to doing that in his current state. He nodded his agreement and reached for Eliodoro's hand, walking with him toward the aftcastle and his cabin.

The moment the door closed behind him, Eliodoro stepped into Quinn's embrace, his face upturned for a kiss. Quinn gave it to him because he was helpless to resist the lure of Eliodoro's beautiful smile, but it lasted the briefest of seconds before a yawn overtook him. "I'm sorry. I've been awake too long to do anything more than sleep beside you."

Eliodoro smiled indulgently, rubbing against Quinn in a way he hadn't dared on deck. "I 'elp you stay awake."

Quinn's body reacted, but slowly. "If anything could, it would be you, but not this morning. I want more than a quick tumble, which is the best I could give you at the moment. Please, Eliodoro. Sleep in my arms today and save the rest for later, when we will both enjoy it more."

Eliodoro would enjoy it quite well regardless of how sleepy Quinn was, but his care for the quartermaster outweighed his desire, sure sign of how much Quinn had come to mean to him. "As long as you no forget 'rest' later."

As if he could, Quinn thought with a silent chuckle. "I promise."

Quinn pulled his shirt over his head and climbed onto the bunk, scooting close to the wall to leave room for Eliodoro. With a sly grin, Eliodoro removed his shirt as well, followed by his breeches. He would not ask again for Quinn to make love to him, but he could offer with actions what he would not say in words.

Quinn groaned as Eliodoro's dark skin came into view, his fingers itching to touch. The proof of Eliodoro's desire when his cock, already half hard, came into view only added to that need. "You would tempt a saint."

"I no care about saints," Eliodoro said. "I only care about tempt you."

Quinn patted the bed next to him. "You tempt me, but I want to love you properly. Soon. I promise."

Eliodoro slipped into the empty space, pressing close against Quinn's body, the heat of the other man's skin sending a frisson of delight through him. "Soon."

Quinn ached with desire, but another yawn interrupted him as he leaned in to kiss Eliodoro. When it passed, he urged the younger man to turn in his arms so they lay nestled together like spoons and let himself dream of a lifetime of falling asleep this way.

The rhythmic snuffle of Quinn's breath against the nape of his neck told Eliodoro that the other man slept. He smiled, his own yawn surprising him now that he had started to relax. He snuggled closer to the man behind him, feeling the reassuring ridge of Quinn's erection even in his sleep. The quartermaster might not have made love to him this morning, but it wouldn't be long. Not if he was hard even now.

Chapter 31

AMERY strode onto deck, Gavin one step behind him on the narrow gangplank. "I thought I saw Mr. Davies."

"Ye did, sir," Seaton said. "He stood watch last night so th'rest of us could go ashore on leave."

Amery nodded, knowing Quinn's opinion on making sure the crew had a break.

"He worked all day makin' repairs afore he stood watch," Seaton added when Amery started toward the aftcastle. "Whatever ye're needing t'ask him, couldn't it wait until he's had the chance t'rest a bit?"

Amery hesitated long enough that Gavin intervened. "Can you show us what repairs he arranged?"

"That I can, Mr. Watson. Jennings said one of the holes we patched on that island wouldn't hold. Mr. Davies got supplies, not just for that, and made sure the hole was patched proper-like." As he spoke, he led them into the hold and showed them the work Quinn and the other sailors had done the day before.

"I told you Quinn would see to everything while we were gone," Gavin murmured at Amery's side.

"How did he pay for the supplies?" Amery asked.

"Now that's a question you'd have to put to the quartermaster," Seaton replied. "Alls I know is boards and boxes and casks were delivered to the ship all day and Mr. Davies didn't seem surprised to see any of it.

Amery let the question go. He could ask Quinn about it later, make sure the company reimbursed him if he'd spent his own money. He had other things he needed to worry about as well. Dismissing Seaton with his thanks, he returned to the deck with Gavin. "We need to recruit new sailors. We have plenty for just the *Silver Queen*, but we lost twenty taking the *Rayo* and another eight on the island where we stopped for repairs. We were stretched thin trying to get back here. If I'd realized how bad it truly was, I wouldn't have worried about the treasure and ordered the *Rayo* left behind."

Gavin shrugged. "We made it back. The ship will be sold or commissioned for the company, and we have more gold in our pockets because of it. We all worked longer hours than we've gotten used to, but no more than when we were on the *Dark Dream*. We've gotten spoiled having such a large crew. No one got hurt because of the extra work. No injuries from fatigue or inattention. Do you want to look for men here or sail back to Tortuga?"

"Is there a reason not to look here?" Amery asked. "We work for the company that founded the colony here. I hardly think we'll be run out of town for offering anyone who wants it a chance to sail with us. If we don't fill the empty berths, we can always go by Tortuga later. We still have five rapists to track down as well."

"We left them here," Gavin said. "It might be worth asking around here as well. We've assumed they took passage on Spanish ships, but they had to get off Providence Island somehow."

"We can ask around when we put the word out that we're looking for men to sail with us, but not right away, I think," Amery agreed. "We've been gone for a couple of days, and I was sick before that. I need to stay here for a few days to supervise the rest of the repairs and restocking."

"Quinn—"

"Quinn took care of things in my absence, which I appreciate," Amery interrupted, "but I'm the captain, and I need to act like it now that I'm well and we're well. The crew needs to know to look to me,

not to Quinn or Nisbett or one of the other officers. It was one thing when I was still recovering, but I'm not sick anymore, and it's time I resumed my duties."

"The men aren't going to forget months of leadership simply because you were ill," Gavin insisted. "Many of them were ill as well. Some of them lost bunkmates and friends. They understand that."

"Then maybe I'm the one who needs to feel like I'm the captain again," Amery replied. "Either way, I'm spending today on the ship. We can send Nisbett to put out the word tonight and see what kind of interest there is tomorrow morning, when hopefully Quinn will be awake to assist us. That's the other thing the crew needs to see. They need to see the three of us working together again as a functioning authority."

"We can't do anything about Quinn until he wakes up, but the surgery doesn't need my attention at the moment. I'll help you with everything else today. That should show the crew that we, at least, are back on steady ground."

Amery smiled and slipped his arm around Gavin's waist on the empty deck. It wouldn't be empty for long with the sun rising higher in the sky and the men beginning to return from town, but they had a brief moment of privacy.

"It's good, it is, to have ye back on board, Captain," Seaton's voice intruded from behind them, "and to have things back to normal again. When do ye think we'll sail?"

Gavin started to pull away, not sure Amery would want the intimate gesture to be public, but Amery's arm tightened, keeping him close.

"Another few days, I warrant," Amery replied. "We need to hire on some more men and make sure everything is right and tight before we sail again." He met Seaton's gaze levelly, amused and reassured both by the twinkle in the older man's eyes as he nodded.

THE sound of footsteps above his head on the boards of the helm roused Quinn from his sleep. Eliodoro lay quietly in his arms, their bodies pressed tightly together. The arousal Quinn had held at bay during the night and morning because of duty and fatigue rushed back at him, but he had one more thing to take care of before he could dedicate himself to the young man the way he wanted to. He needed to speak to Amery and Gavin and square things with them. Only then would he be truly free to explore his growing feelings for Eliodoro. Trying not to wake the lad, he extricated himself from Eliodoro's embrace with difficulty. He wouldn't make it out the door if Eliodoro awoke and offered himself again. With luck, though, he could talk to Amery and Gavin and be back before Eliodoro realized he was gone.

Pulling his shirt over his head, Quinn tucked in the tails as he stared at Eliodoro's sleeping face. The lad had the beauty of an angel and the heart of a lion. Quinn wasn't sure how he'd gotten lucky enough to have such a prize in his bed. He only knew he had to find a way to keep him there. His groin tingled in anticipation as his body offered a suggestion, but Quinn knew it would take more than that. He didn't doubt Eliodoro's willingness, but he feared the younger man still saw sex as a transaction rather than an act of caring. He wasn't naïve enough to think his control would hold out much longer, but that didn't mean he would stop searching for a way to show Eliodoro how much more than sex he wanted from a lover.

A lover.

He realized with a start that he'd never really had one before. He'd slept with his share of men and a few women, too, though that had been enough to send him back to the ship and the safety of his own gender, but it had never gone beyond sex. The tides—and Gavin's love for Amery—had made having a long-term lover out of the question. What would it be like, he wondered, to come back to his cabin every night, knowing Eliodoro was there, or would soon be there? What would it be like to share his space and his life with another man? He had lived in crew quarters for years, but that bore no resemblance to what he was considering now. Sharing that communal space with twenty to fifty men was one thing. Sharing his little cabin with one special man was another thing entirely.

Picking up his boots so he wouldn't disturb Eliodoro with the sound of them on the deck of the cabin, Quinn slipped from the room, walking out into the bright sunlight. He squinted a bit until his eyes adjusted, finding Amery and Gavin on the foredeck. Delaying a little, he stopped to put his boots on before joining his friends.

"Are you well?" he asked, joining Gavin and Amery.

"Yes," Gavin said, the utter confidence in his tone enough to reassure Quinn. Whatever had passed between the two men, they had found their peace again.

"Good. It wasn't good for the ship to have you fighting."

Amery raised an eyebrow at the statement, having expected some disappointment on Quinn's part that Gavin was back in his arms and his bed where he belonged. If Quinn felt that way, none of it showed on his face or in his voice. "Thank you for overseeing the ship in my absence."

"We're a team," Quinn said. "At least we were. Have I ruined that?"

"If anyone ruined anything, it was me," Amery demurred. "I should have listened to Gavin rather than reacting badly. I should have listened to *you* instead of assuming the worst."

Seeing the discomfort on both men's faces, Gavin smiled slyly. "Where is Eliodoro? I haven't seen him since we came back this morning, but I could have sworn I saw him on deck with you as we approached."

"He's sleeping," Quinn replied shortly.

"Really?" Gavin asked, feigning innocence. "I didn't see him in the crew quarters when we went to inspect the repairs and make sure they were sound."

"He's sleeping in my cabin," Quinn mumbled.

"And you're out here?" Amery joked. "What's wrong with you?"

"I needed to speak with you first," Quinn replied seriously. "I needed to make sure I still had a place on this ship, that I still had friends I could count on before I start anything with him. He deserves to know what he's getting—a quartermaster or an unemployed sailor—before he makes his decision."

Gavin poked Amery in the side. Hard.

"As long as I have a ship to sail, you will be her quartermaster," Amery said, all teasing gone from his voice. He didn't need Gavin to tell him how important this moment was, nor to make him realize how badly he had jeopardized the two constants in his life. "I wouldn't know how to run a ship without you at my side. I can sail it, but you run it. If I needed proof of that—which I didn't—look how you took care of things the past two days. There are fresh supplies in the hold. The repairs are underway. The men have rotated duty and taken shore leave. You organized all of that, not me. Even if I'd been here, you would have taken on the majority of those tasks because that's what you're good at. At the moment, the men are far more sure of you than they are of me."

"They'll get used to having you around again," Quinn promised.

Gavin poked Amery again. "The rest of it."

Amery glared at his matelot, but he knew Gavin was right. "I said some pretty awful things while I was angry at you and Gavin, and I said them to Eliodoro. I'm sorry. When Eliodoro wakes up, I'd like to tell him the truth."

Quinn nodded. This was harder to forgive. "That's up to you. He said he realized you were upset and may have overstated the case a bit when you were angry. Honestly, I'd rather leave it alone."

THE sun slanting through the porthole on the side of Quinn's cabin and hitting his face roused Eliodoro. It took him a moment to remember where he was and a moment longer to realize he was there alone. The cabin was stifling with the heat of the day, but Eliodoro did not feel its warmth, the chill of waking up alone far more potent that any physical heat. He bit his lip anxiously as he tried to push away the sense of betrayal and find a way to reconcile the man he had stood watch with all night with the empty bed.

Rising slowly, he picked up his clothes where he had tossed them as he'd tried to entice Quinn before bed. He had been so sure it would work, and it had in a way. The quartermaster had pulled Eliodoro into his arms, kissing him, holding him close as they slept. Eliodoro hadn't been awake long after they lay down, but he remembered the feeling of strong arms around him as he slept, remembered feeling safe for the first time since he was taken off the Portuguese vessel by his Spanish captors. His body trusted Quinn in a way he had never trusted any man, but his mind was less sure, particularly in light of this new desertion.

He needed to think and Quinn's cabin was not the place to do it, not with the welter of emotions already associated with the small space. They had made love—he still refused to call it anything else—there once, and they had slept together like a couple once, but neither of those things had kept Quinn next to him. With a sigh, Eliodoro dressed and left the room, hoping it was not for the last time, but he also knew they had to find some balance soon.

As soon as he left the aftcastle, he caught sight of Quinn silhouetted against the setting sun. It took only a moment to recognize the two men standing next to him: the captain and *Signor* Watson. Eliodoro felt a flash of jealousy at finding Quinn once again at their side instead of at his own, but he pushed it away. Regardless of any of the tangle of personal relationships between them, Quinn was still the *Silver Queen*'s quartermaster and as such, he had a duty to report to the captain. They had accomplished a lot yesterday, much of it surely obvious to as astute a man as Captain White, but even so, Eliodoro imagined Quinn had to give his report. He only wished Quinn had waited until after they made love to do so. Sighing again, he descended into the hold in search of Seaton or Clay, hoping one of them would have some advice for him.

"Wasn't that Eliodoro?" Amery asked, catching sight of the sailor as he disappeared into the hold.

"I don't know. I didn't see him," Quinn replied. "Surely he would have come over if it was."

"Maybe, maybe not," Gavin said with a shake of his head. "He has plenty of reason to distrust me at the moment, if he saw me as a rival for your interest."

"He knows you're devoted to Amery," Quinn insisted.

"Maybe, but that doesn't mean he knows you're devoted to him."

"You and I have been gone for two and a half days," Amery said. "Surely that's enough time for Quinn to have assured him, in the most intimate ways possible, how highly he holds Eliodoro in esteem."

"He doesn't need sex. He needs someone to love him," Quinn protested, recognizing the leer on Amery's face.

Amery rolled his eyes. "He's nineteen, Quinn. Do you remember what you were like—what we all were like—at nineteen? A stiff breeze was enough to get us hard and the slightest possibility of release was enough to tempt us to do almost anything. That boy is thinking with his cock if he's thinking at all."

"That's doesn't mean I should do the same," Quinn retorted. "He was abused for six months. He needs to know I want more from him than sex."

"So don't have sex with him. Make love to him," Amery replied like it was the most obvious solution in the world. "You *do* know the difference, don't you?"

"Amery, leave Quinn alone before he punches you," Gavin scolded. "The last thing the crew needs is to see the two of you come to blows now. I'm sure Quinn knows the difference. Now that you've pointed out the obvious, we simply need to make sure he has the time—and the privacy—to follow through. He was on duty much of the time we were gone. I think twenty-four hours' shore leave, shared with Eliodoro, should be enough. Unless you'd prefer two days, Quinn?"

"One day should be enough," Quinn said, spluttering slightly at his friends' audacity in arranging his love life. "I know there's work to be done."

"Work you've spent the last two days taking care of by yourself," Amery said, his voice firm. "Gavin and I can oversee things for the next two days. It's Tuesday evening. We'll compromise and say I don't want to see either of you back on ship before noon on Thursday. Gather what you need. I'll find Eliodoro and tell him he's on leave."

"No," Quinn said. "I'll tell him after I gather a change of clothes. I don't want him to feel like we were talking about him behind his back."

Leaving his two friends, Quinn returned to his cabin to stuff a change of clothes into a bag and dig out his purse so he would have gold enough to pay for food and a room. He caught sight of the bracelet Eliodoro had given him and slipped it on as well. He had no idea where in town he would find a room, but Gavin and Amery obviously had, so he would ask around until he did. Taking a deep breath and hoping he wasn't making a colossic mistake, Quinn went in search of Eliodoro.

His foot was on the threshold to the crew's quarters when he heard Eliodoro's voice raised in plaintive protest.

"I no understand, Clay. He say he want me, and then he disappear without a word," Eliodoro was saying.

"Did it occur to ye he was tryin' to be a gentleman with ye, since he knows yer past weren't the best?" Clay asked. "And didn't ye just tell me just a few days ago that ye wanted him to want ye for more than just a body to fuck?"

"But I want him fuck me too!"

Lust shot through Quinn's veins at the words. He wanted to stride into the room, grab Eliodoro's arm, and drag him off somewhere to do just that, but Clay was right. He was trying to be a gentleman.

"So seduce him," Clay said with a laugh. "I know ye know how. He's a man like any other, Eliodoro. He won't be able to resist yer pretty face."

"'E resist this morning." Quinn could hear the pout in Eliodoro's voice even if he couldn't see the expression on his face.

"After being awake for a full day, working hard for half of it and standing watch for the other half, he's entitled to a little rest," Clay said. "Ye aren't a child, Eliodoro. Stop acting like one. Mr. Davies is the quartermaster of the ship, the second most important man aboard, maybe even the most important depending on who ye ask. Ye have to let him do his job or the whole crew will suffer for it, you included."

Quinn withdrew enough not to be visible to the two men. "Eliodoro?" he called. "Are you in there? The captain has given us leave for the next two days." Walking into the open room, he nodded an acknowledgment to Clay as he reached Eliodoro's side and took his hand. "Will you spend that time with me?"

Chapter 32

ELIODORO'S eyes widened as they darted from Quinn to Clay and back to Quinn. The quartermaster had said he intended to keep their relationship discreet in front of the crew, but his invitation was anything but discreet. He had no idea what that meant, but he knew what he wanted it to mean. He wanted it to mean Quinn had made up his mind about wanting Eliodoro for more than merely a few days or weeks. He wanted it to mean....

"Don't stand there all day, boy. Answer the quartermaster," Clay said with a nudge, drawing Eliodoro out of his racing thoughts.

"*Sì*, yes. Yes, I spend leave with you," Eliodoro said breathlessly. "We go now?"

"As soon as you get your town clothes on," Quinn said with a grin. "I'll wait for you on deck."

"What was this about Mr. Davies not wantin' ye, lad?" Clay asked with a laugh as Quinn disappeared back the way he came. "It looks like ye'll be gettin' yer chance to seduce him sooner than ye thought. Get yer new gear on and go with him afore he changes his mind."

Eliodoro's eyes widened and he stripped quickly, no thought for modesty in the communal room, and pulled on the clothes Quinn had given him. Checking the tie on his hair quickly, he bolted from the room toward the deck, breathing a sigh of relief when he saw Quinn standing by the gangplank, the fading daylight glinting off a flash of gold at his wrist. Eliodoro smiled, his footsteps slowing to a reasonable pace as he crossed the ship to Quinn's side. "Where we go?"

Quinn smiled in return, the expression on Eliodoro's face too happy for him to resist. "To dinner, and then I thought to find an inn where we could sleep tonight, free from prying eyes and ears. The crew will know we're together because Clay heard me invite you to spend our leave together, but there's no need for them to hear what we do together."

They walked down the gangplank to the wharf, Quinn guiding Eliodoro through town toward one of the nicer taverns where he had seen food offered. "I'm sorry I wasn't there when you woke up this afternoon. I needed to talk to Amery, and if I'd waited to tell you where I was going, we'd still be in my bed."

Eliodoro's eyes widened at the blunt words. "You want me?"

"Silly boy," Quinn scolded indulgently. "Yes, I want you. I want you so badly I can hardly walk, because I'm that hard with the thought of having you to myself tonight, but Amery and Gavin and I have been friends for a long time too, and I couldn't forget or ignore that because you were in my bed. I needed to know they had reconciled. I needed them to know I was happy for them and that I was looking to my own happiness."

"What they say?"

"Amery wanted to know how many times we'd slept together, and Gavin insisted Amery give us the days off so we could."

"You tell them?"

"Easy," Quinn said soothingly. "I didn't tell them anything untoward, but their cabin is next to ours. They'll hear us, just as I've listened to them together for years. It's inevitable on a ship the size of the *Silver Queen*. I didn't have to tell them. They know me that well, just as I didn't have to ask if they'd worked out their differences. I could tell by the way they stood together."

He led Eliodoro inside the tavern, taking a table with his back to the wall, a hard-learned habit from his days as a pirate when anyone could be a threat, even his own shipmates. The tavernkeeper didn't ask what they wanted, simply setting two mugs of rum on the table.

"We'd like dinner as well, if you have it," Quinn called as the man started away. The man waved his towel at them to indicate he'd heard them as he continued on his way.

"So what 'appen now?" Eliodoro asked.

"That's still up to you," Quinn replied, his body tensing as he imagined Eliodoro rejecting him still, "but I hope we'll finish eating, find a room, and see how much pleasure we can give one another tonight. Tomorrow we must think about where we go from here."

"You ask *Signor* Watson if I 'elp in surgery?"

Quinn shook his head. "I thought you might want to ask him yourself. I don't want to run your life or make you think I'm trying to do that. I want you to make your own decisions and follow through on them yourself. I'll support whatever you decide."

"I want learn what 'e can teach me," Eliodoro said.

"Do you want to learn what I can teach you as well?" Quinn teased.

"What you teach me?"

"Anything you want," Quinn said fervently, realizing as he said it that it was true. In the past few days, in letting go of his pointless infatuation with Gavin and in letting himself consider other options, he had fallen for the young man sitting next to him. "But besides swordsmanship, I thought to give you a suggestion for improving your English."

Eliodoro nodded. "I want learn."

"I want *to* learn," Quinn corrected him. "You can't leave out the word 'to'. The sentence sounds funny if you do."

"I want to learn," Eliodoro repeated. "Correct me if I forget again."

"I will, and I'll point out other things as well, a few at a time. I don't want you to feel like you can't talk for my corrections."

The tavernkeeper returned with two plates of stew. Quinn couldn't identify the meat, but it smelled fresh and that was far more important. They ate in relative silence, not having eaten since dinner the night before, but their silence did not preclude the heated looks that passed between them, each of them imagining what the rest of the night would bring. Eliodoro squirmed restlessly as his arousal increased, his cock pressing uncomfortably against the front of his breeches.

"Is there a problem?" Quinn teased when Eliodoro shifted again on the bench next to him. Beneath the cover of the table, he stroked Eliodoro's thigh, smiling as his lover squirmed once more.

"N-no problem," Eliodoro stuttered, stifling a moan as Quinn's hand tantalized him. Determined not to be bested, Eliodoro returned the caress, feeling the muscle in Quinn's thigh quiver beneath his touch. The knowledge that he could affect the other man as much as he was affected thrilled him. Quinn was better at keeping his reactions off his face, but nothing could hide the bulge in his breeches. Feeling powerful, Eliodoro let his hand drift higher until he could feel the heat from Quinn's groin.

"If you keep that up, you won't get to finish your dinner," Quinn said, his voice a low rumble in his chest.

"What you do to me?" Eliodoro teased.

"Ravish you."

Eliodoro stood up quickly, pushing the table back. "Why we waiting?"

His urgency was catching. Quinn rose as well, tossing a coin on the table as he followed Eliodoro out into the street. His eyes darted right and left as he searched for an inn or boarding house, but Eliodoro had other ideas, pulling Quinn into the shadows of the nearest alley. His hands flew over Quinn's body, making the quartermaster wonder who was ravishing whom. He groaned as Eliodoro pinned him against the wall, kissing him wildly. "Not here," he ground out, the memory of their first encounter holding him back. He had taken Eliodoro for granted once. He didn't intend to do it again.

"Where then?" Eliodoro demanded, rubbing against Quinn as provocatively as he knew how. Lust had sufficiently addled his wits that he didn't care where they were as long as they made love now.

"Somewhere with a bed and a door and a lock. Somewhere private." He wrenched away from the wall, dragging a very willing Eliodoro behind him as he searched for a boarding house. Arranging a room took more time than he would have liked, the situation exacerbated by Eliodoro's constant, unsubtle caresses. Finally, though, the door closed behind them, the lock snicking shut, and they were alone. Eliodoro reached for his shirttails, wanting bare skin as quickly as possible. Quinn considered protesting, trying to slow things down, but Eliodoro had the bit between his teeth now. Promising himself a slow unveiling another time, Quinn stripped as well, leaving only the gift from Eliodoro around his wrist.

The sight of Quinn's body appearing from beneath his clothes slowed Eliodoro's rush. As much as he wanted out of his own garments, his lover's body was a beauty to behold. Dropping his shirt to the floor, he reached for Quinn, his nerves warring with his desire. Falling back on the one thing he had shared only with Quinn, he mated his lips to Quinn's, tasting stew and rum. The kiss settled his nerves even as it fed his desire and before long, his hands resumed their wandering, mapping the ridges of muscle on Quinn's back. If they hesitated at the swell of Quinn's buttocks, he told himself it was because the other man would never welcome such a touch. Quinn took a step toward the bed, drawing Eliodoro back with him.

"Take your boots off," Quinn said, sitting down on the bed to do the same. When they were gone, he drew Eliodoro back into his arms, lying back but making no other move to proceed.

"Why you no touch me?" Eliodoro asked, his voice small with nerves.

"I thought you intended to seduce me tonight. Isn't that what Clay told you to do?"

Eliodoro flushed to the roots of his hair. "You 'ear that? *Scusa*."

"Don't apologize," Quinn said, kissing Eliodoro thoroughly. When he lifted his head again, he added, "I like the idea. Seduce me, pretty one. I'm yours."

"But—"

Quinn shook his head. "Do you not want me?"

"You know I do."

Quinn smiled. "Then take what you desire. I truly am yours, Eliodoro."

Eliodoro's eyes widened momentarily, but the words eased his nerves once he got over his surprise at hearing them. "I do what I want?"

"You can do whatever you want," Quinn replied. "I'm sure I'll enjoy every moment. There is salve in my pocket if you'll let me get it out for you."

Eliodoro's mouth opened and closed, but no words came out. Quinn wanted him to.... "You want me...?"

"I hope you weren't planning on leaving me wanting," Quinn teased, pulling out the tin of salve. "You'll need this, or I'll be walking stiffly tomorrow."

"But you are quartermaster!"

"Not in this room," Quinn said. "Here, tonight, I'm a man like any other. Wanting to have you inside me doesn't make me less of a man any more than being inside you makes me more of one. Make love to me, Eliodoro."

"You know I no do this before," Eliodoro warned.

Quinn's smile widened. "I look forward to being your first." He paused, tilting Eliodoro's chin so their eyes met. "Your only?"

Eliodoro's breath caught in his throat as he considered the import of Quinn's words. "My only?"

"I know I said we needed to take our time, to see how things worked between us outside of bed, but I realized something the past two days," Quinn said slowly. "I already know how things work. We've been working together since you arrived on the *Silver Queen* and everything I've seen has only added to my admiration for you. I've slept with men in the past, but I've never had a lover. I want you to be my first and only, if you think you could feel the same way."

Eliodoro's heart pounded so hard he thought it would pound right out of his chest. "*Sì*," he said, his voice barely above a whisper. "*Ti amo*."

Quinn didn't need anyone to translate the heartfelt words. He may never have heard them before, but he knew he wouldn't rest until he heard them again. And again and again for the rest of his life. "*Ti amo*…. How do you say 'also' in Italian?"

Eliodoro laughed at the question, a sweet, joyous sound as all the fear and hesitation fell away at the sound of those two simple words in badly mangled Italian. "*Anche*," he said. "*Ti amo anche*."

"*Ti amo anche*," Quinn repeated, his smile growing at the sound of Eliodoro's laughter. "See? I speak Italian even worse than you speak English. It doesn't matter what language I say it in, though. The feelings are the same."

"For me too. I… want what you said." Marshalling his nerve, Eliodoro reached for the tin of salve, setting it within easy reach before bending to kiss Quinn again.

Quinn reclined on the bed, drawing Eliodoro down half on top, half next to him. The press of their bodies together roused Eliodoro's desire again, the newly expressed emotions giving him the courage to do what he'd never dreamed he would have the right to do. He wasn't even sure where to start, his mind casting back to the one night he and Quinn had spent in the quartermaster's bed, trying to remember—

"Stop thinking so much and just touch me," Quinn said, interrupting Eliodoro's thoughts. "I don't think you could do anything I won't like."

Eliodoro's face darkened as he remembered all the things he had hated on the Spanish slaver.

"You couldn't do those things to me," Quinn chided, reading the direction of Eliodoro's thoughts in his expression. "It isn't in you to hurt me the way you were hurt, just as I could never hurt you that way. I love you, and when you love someone, you take care of them. Just like you're going to take care of me." He stroked the curls back from Eliodoro's face, reaching up to tug the leather band free of his hair. "I want to know what it feels like to have you inside me. I want you to know it as well, but if it's too much, we can wait. We can sleep together as we did earlier today and kiss and hold each other and simply be together until you're ready for more."

"No," Eliodoro said with a shake of his head. "You no leave me like this again." He bumped his hips against Quinn's thigh, letting his lover feel his erection.

"We can love each other in different ways. With hands and mouths. It's still making love."

Eliodoro considered that for a moment, but his mind kept circling back to the image of his cock in Quinn's arse. He still had no idea what he was doing, but the more he thought about it, the more he knew he wanted it too.

Chapter 33

STARTING there was too overwhelming, though. He would start more slowly and work up to what they both wanted. He pushed up on one elbow for a moment, allowing himself the luxury of staring at the broad expanse of tanned skin, kissed golden by the hot Caribbean sun. Quinn would never be as dark as Eliodoro himself, but that did not make the vision before him any less attractive. A light pelt of dark blond hair covered his chest, a few shades darker than the hair on Quinn's head, lightened as that was by the exposure to the elements. Large, pink nipples crowned the strong muscles of his torso, tempting Eliodoro to reach out and touch. He hesitated for a moment before remembering he could do that if he wanted. The declarations of the night, the promises of the past two days, gave him the right to touch if he chose. Not to mention Quinn's express invitation. He stretched his hand tentatively toward the quartermaster, pausing for a moment a hair's breadth from touching to make sure permission would not be rescinded.

Quinn's eyes closed in anticipation, but he made no other move to encourage or discourage the lad. He had promised himself that he would let the young man govern their interactions tonight as one more proof of his declaration. Now he had to hold to his word. When the slim fingers finally connected with his flesh, Quinn couldn't smother the groan of delight that escaped his lips, the sound emboldening Eliodoro, who took advantage of Quinn's immobility to explore every inch of hard flesh, to trace the lines of every scar.

"You 'ave clothes on," Eliodoro murmured after a few minutes. Quinn shivered as he opened his breeches and pushed them and his linen drawers to the floor. His heart pounded as he returned to the bed naked and aroused, waiting for some sign of Eliodoro's approbation.

It came in the tiny gasp that escaped Eliodoro's parted lips as his eyes wandered over Quinn's body. He had seen many men unclothed in the time he had served aboard ships, some in the simple day-to-day routine of dressing and undressing, others in the hated moments of torture his former captain had inflicted on him, but he thought he had never seen so perfect a man as the one who shared this bed with him now, his hair too long by conventional standards, brushing his shoulders, tossed and tangled by the ever-present Caribbean wind He told himself that objectively Quinn wasn't that much more attractive than other men, than Captain White for example, but his heart recognized the one attribute that set Quinn apart from any other man who had ever looked at Eliodoro: the expression on his face. No one had ever looked at Eliodoro with the same heady mixture of desire, protectiveness, and tenderness that he saw now in Quinn's eyes.

Quinn's hand trembled as he stroked the long line of Eliodoro's thigh, hip, side, up to his shoulder and then into his black hair, so very different from Quinn's own pale coloring. He tipped the other man's head toward his own, their lips meeting again in a tender kiss Quinn hoped would convey his softer emotions as clearly as it conveyed his desire. It worked, if the way Eliodoro nestled closer was an indication, giving Quinn hope that he was making progress toward convincing Eliodoro that he wasn't using the younger man for physical release, but that he wanted something real and lasting. Confident that Eliodoro wouldn't pull away, he released his lover's head, letting his hand return to its wandering across work-hardened muscles to find the dark nubbins on his chest, thumbing them in alternation until Eliodoro arched against him, pressing their lower bodies together. He might have encouraged Eliodoro to take charge, but that didn't mean he had to refrain from touching his lover. Quinn moaned into the kiss as their shafts rubbed against one another, the contact flashing through him with all the force of lightning on the open seas. "Eliodoro," he murmured.

Suddenly impatient with the slow pace, Quinn rolled Eliodoro to his back, straddling the long thighs so he would have better access to his lover's body. He would still give control of their lovemaking to Eliodoro when the time came, but he thought to help matters along by heightening their desire to a fever pitch. To that end, he lingered over every spot he had ever known to be sensitive on another man, watching Eliodoro's reactions carefully so he would know where to return and where to ignore the next time he had this opportunity. The inside of Eliodoro's elbow, the underside of his arm, his nipples—especially his nipples—all were especially sensitive to Quinn's touch. With a wicked grin, Quinn lifted Eliodoro's arms over his head, his hands stroking over the inner faces of his biceps as his mouth latched onto one dark aureole. Eliodoro squirmed beneath him, a shudder traversing his entire body.

"Please," Eliodoro whimpered, not even the tenderness in Quinn's touch enough to stop the bile from rising in his throat at the inherent helplessness of his position. "No pin my arms."

"I'm sorry," Quinn apologized, remorse coloring his voice as his hands moved immediately. "I didn't mean to bring back unwelcome memories."

"Your touch is no unwelcome," Eliodoro assured him, the fear fading now that his arms were free to move again, "only being 'eld down. It take me many months learn they 'urt me worse if I struggle. Even after I stop fighting, they still tie my 'ands sometimes because they know I 'ate it."

"I will never force you," Quinn swore, his voice low and fervent. "A word will stop me at any time. I swear it."

"I know," Eliodoro assured him, stroking his stubbled cheek tenderly. "I no come 'ere if I doubt it. I tell you if I 'ave bad memories, but you promise no worry about it when you touch me. I no want you 'old back."

Deciding to avoid any chance of recalling more nightmares, Quinn switched their positions again, returning all control to Eliodoro.

"Tell me what do," Eliodoro said, reaching for the salve. The fraught moment of fear notwithstanding, Quinn's attentions had roused Eliodoro thoroughly, to the point that he was ready to take the final step.

Quinn shrugged. "You get your fingers slippery in there, stretch me with them until I'm begging, and then you stick it in me and fuck me until we can't stand it anymore."

He made it sound so easy, Eliodoro thought as he fumbled with the lid on the salve. Getting it open finally, he coated two digits liberally, trembling as he reached between Quinn's thighs to find the opening he sought. His breath caught in his throat when the older man parted his legs, knees lifting to aid Eliodoro in his search. He couldn't quite take in what he was seeing. Quinn couldn't possibly want this, could he? The look of anticipation on the quartermaster's face answered that question for Eliodoro. However out of character it seemed to him for such a masterful man to take a passive role, Quinn wanted Eliodoro to bugger him senseless. Taking a deep breath, he slid his fingers across the tight entrance, letting the repetitious movement soothe his nerves even as it enflamed Quinn's. He gasped when Quinn lost patience, planting his feet and pushing himself onto the teasing fingers. Eliodoro tried to withdraw, sure the sudden penetration, with two fingers no less, had hurt, but Quinn caught his wrist. "You're taking too long," he growled.

Eliodoro nodded and began to move his hand, spreading the salve along the walls of the hot passage, trying to imagine what it would feel like around his cock. He'd known carnal pleasure exactly twice, both times at the hands of the man beneath him. Remembering how good it had felt to have Quinn's hands on him, he tentatively trailed his other fingers over the length of the other man's erection, the hitch in his breath mirroring the gasp that escaped Quinn's throat at the touch. "Use a firmer stroke," Quinn husked. "Touch me like you like to be touched."

That might have been useful advice if Eliodoro had ever been able to throw off his strict upbringing and negative experiences to attempt self-pleasure, but all he had to go on were his very hazy memories of how Quinn had touched him the two times they'd been together before tonight. The first time, he'd been so afraid of the pain to come that he barely remembered anything but his surprise when it hadn't hurt and then the overwhelming pleasure of giving himself freely. The second time was even more of a blur in many respects, the surprise that Quinn truly wanted him so strong that even the physical pleasure had paled in comparison.

The odd collection of emotions that flickered across Eliodoro's face tore at Quinn's heart. He knew he was responsible for some of the self-doubt he saw there, and that made this moment all the more important. Picking up the tin from where it had fallen from Eliodoro's hand, he smeared some on Eliodoro's cock, surprising another soft gasp from the younger man's lips. "Now," he directed, using his grip to draw Eliodoro into position between his legs.

Eliodoro hesitated, but Quinn's grip was so insistent and his body so open that he couldn't resist for long. Leaning forward, he let Quinn's hand guide him inside. The heat and constriction on his fingers hadn't prepared him for the way it felt to actually be inside Quinn. He gasped as a shudder of pure need ran down his spine. Biting his lip to keep from climaxing on the spot, he rocked his hips, trying to get deeper, closer.

Quinn's eyes fluttered shut as Eliodoro penetrated him. The lad clearly had no idea what he was doing, but even so, this felt right in a way Quinn couldn't explain. Then Eliodoro moved, his cock brushing Quinn's sweet spot, and he gave up trying to do anything except stop himself from coming immediately.

Eliodoro wanted to prove his worth as a lover, but he had no experience to draw on, and in an embarrassingly short time, the constriction around his cock, the knowledge that he was inside Quinn stole his self-control, his cock twitching repeatedly in its tight sheath.

Quinn felt the surge of heat and wetness inside him and smothered a grin and a groan as Eliodoro collapsed on top of him. He'd have to teach the lad some stamina, or they'd be going back to making love the other way quickly. For the moment, though, Quinn stayed where he was, letting Eliodoro bask in the afterglow.

Awareness returned to Eliodoro after a bit, and with it the sensation of Quinn's hard shaft against his belly. Guilt assailed him immediately. The quartermaster had always seen to his pleasure, but Eliodoro hadn't returned the favor. Stomach churning as he thought about what he was about to do, Eliodoro rocked back onto his knees and bent forward to take the blond's erection in his mouth.

"You don't have to—" Quinn began, but the dark look Eliodoro sent him silenced his words.

"I know I no 'ave to," Eliodoro agreed, "but I want to."

Quinn didn't have a reply to that, so he subsided and gave himself over to the rapture of the young man's hot mouth around his cockhead. It didn't take much. "Close," he gasped, wanting to give Eliodoro the choice, but his lover's head didn't stop its bobbing, driving Quinn over the edge of his release.

Quinn's taste was no better or worse than any of the men who'd forced their semen down Eliodoro's throat on the slave ship, but the act he'd so hated then took on a different cast now that he'd chosen it himself. What had then been another aspect of their dominance became an act of power for Eliodoro, the knowledge that he could make Quinn come undone this way enough to cause his sated cock to twitch against his thigh.

Licking his lips, he settled back onto the bed, curling against Quinn's side despite the width of the bed. He didn't want space. He wanted contact with his lover. Quinn seemed glad to oblige, his arm encircling Eliodoro's shoulders and holding him close. "*Ti amo*," he murmured.

"*Ti amo anche*," Quinn replied, kissing Eliodoro's curls gently.

"Next time I do better," Eliodoro promised, tilting his head so he could look at Quinn. "I know was too fast."

Quinn chuckled. "You're nineteen, pretty one. It goes with the territory. Making love doesn't have to be perfect every time. As long as both people are satisfied at the end of the encounter, how you get there doesn't matter so much."

"You are satisfied?"

Quinn laughed again, more heartily this time, and reached for Eliodoro's hand, pressing it against his now limp cock. "I'm very satisfied. Or did you miss me coming in your mouth?"

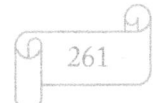

Eliodoro flushed. "Is no same as my...." He trailed off, not knowing the word. "How you say this?" He moved their joined hands to his backside.

"Arse," Quinn replied. "No, it's not the same as your arse, but that doesn't mean I didn't enjoy it. Tonight, I enjoyed it more because you chose to use your mouth on me. I know you didn't have a choice on the slaver."

Eliodoro shuddered. "No, I no 'ave choice. Is not like that with you. With you, everything is different."

"That's because I love you," Quinn said.

"Sounds better in Italian."

"Then we'll say it that way. It was different because *ti amo*. I hope it will all be different, but I also hope you'll tell me if anything gives you a bad moment like earlier. I don't ever want you to be afraid of me."

"No afraid," Eliodoro said, searching for words. "Surprised. Memories come and I react, but then I say Quinn no 'urt me. I ask, you stop. I know you no 'urt me."

Quinn nodded. "I'll never hurt you intentionally." He stroked Eliodoro's side tenderly, enjoying the feeling of smooth skin against his own, when inspiration struck. "What would you say to a real bath in a real tub?"

Eliodoro's eyes widened. "Can we? Together?"

Quinn grinned. "If you let me put some clothes on, I'll ask the innkeeper if it can be arranged." He dropped a quick kiss on Eliodoro's lips. "Don't disappear while I'm gone."

Eliodoro shook his head and snuggled deeper into the bed. *Giammai.* He would never disappear as long as Quinn wanted him.

Chapter 34

THE sun woke them the next morning, shining through the casement they had left open the night before in defense against the heat. Despite only having slept a few hours, their bodies' rhythm thrown off by their night duty and day in bed, they rose and dressed, lingering over the process with tender caresses and heated looks.

Eliodoro still had trouble reconciling the playful lover of the night before with the stern quartermaster, but he had stopped questioning it sometime during their bath the night before. As promised, Quinn had made the arrangements, returning only minutes before the servants to tell Eliodoro to dress, in his breeches at least, for propriety's sake. Eliodoro had donned his shirt as well, not wanting to scandalize anyone. Quinn had no complaint, admitting after the servants left that he wouldn't have wanted to share the sight of his lover's body with anyone else. Eliodoro didn't know how that would work once they were back aboard the *Silver Queen*, as he often worked shirtless because of the heat and he shared a common room with eighty other men, but he hadn't pressed for answers. They had time. They didn't have to make all their decisions now.

Once the servants were gone, Quinn had lured Eliodoro into the tub, splashing and tickling playfully as they bathed. Eliodoro wasn't sure how clean they had truly gotten each other, but he knew how aroused they were. When their passion reached a fever pitch, Quinn had pulled Eliodoro from the tub and onto the bed, ignoring the dripping water as he took Eliodoro's cock into his mouth, licking and sucking until Eliodoro had come with a hoarse shout. The sight of his semen on Quinn's lips as he licked them clean ranked high on the list of most erotic things Eliodoro had ever seen, second only to the sight of his cock sliding into Quinn's arse.

Eliodoro was tempted to ask when he might get to see that again, but Quinn was dressed, strapping his sword around his waist and settling his hat at a jaunty angle on his head. "Where we go today?"

"To see if we can find any of Munoz's companions. They might know where the rest of the officers from the slaver are," Quinn replied.

Quinn didn't understand the rush of Italian that followed his words, but he could read the fear in his lover's gestures. He let Eliodoro rant until he calmed down before pulling the younger man into his arms. "You don't have to worry about him anymore, remember?" Quinn said as Eliodoro settled. "At the time, I didn't think to ask about the other four, but if one officer is still here, perhaps others are as well. It's worth asking questions. We'll go to the same tavern where I saw him first, and we'll decide from there where we want to go next."

Eliodoro was not entirely comfortable with the idea, but he did not feel confident enough to contradict Quinn either. He had been glad to see Medina dead on the *Rayo*, but it had been an impersonal death. The cannonball that killed him had come from the *Silver Queen*, but his death had been random, not premeditated. He knew, he supposed, that if Medina hadn't died in battle, Quinn and the others would have killed him for his crimes, as Quinn had admitted to killing Munoz, but this deliberate act left him unsettled. Quinn was ready to go, though, so Eliodoro followed him down the stairs and out to the street, turning away from the harbor toward the far edge of town. The tavern had very few patrons at that hour of the morning, none of whom were familiar to Eliodoro, but Quinn didn't even ask him about it, going to the bar instead and beginning to ask questions about the men who had been with Munoz.

The barman didn't know much, but he did tell Quinn where he had seen the men sleeping at night. "What about Romero, Vasquez, Ortega, or Valdez?" Quinn asked. "Have you heard them discussing men by any of those names?"

"I don't speak their foul language," the barman spat. "I don't know nothing else."

Quinn wasn't entirely sure that was true, but he let it go, leaving the tavern with Eliodoro trailing behind him. He had started toward the location the barman had indicated when he heard Eliodoro gasp behind him. Turning, he frowned at the horrified look on Eliodoro's face. "What is it?"

"Romero," Eliodoro whispered. "I see Romero go into alley there."

"Let's go," Quinn said, grabbing Eliodoro's hand and dragging him toward the entrance to the narrow space between the buildings.

Eliodoro shook his head frantically, but Quinn was too focused on his quarry to notice. He drew his sword as they entered the alley, prepared for the fight to come. He could barely believe his luck at finding two of Eliodoro's tormentors within a matter of days.

Eliodoro's heart pounded in his chest as he followed Quinn, his hand on the hilt of his own sword, uncomfortably aware that he had never used it, even in practice. He would be no help to Quinn in the upcoming fight.

The alley opened into another street. Quinn looked left and right, searching for the dark head he had glimpsed. "Do you see him?"

Eliodoro searched as well, catching sight of the man ahead of them. "There."

"Hey!" Quinn yelled, running after the man despite the people in the street who moved quickly out of his way upon seeing his drawn sword. "Romero!"

The man turned at the sound of the name, eyes widening as Quinn came straight at him with his sword. He managed to draw his own and deflect what would have been a killing blow, but the attack clearly caught him off guard. He retreated a few steps, trying to regain his balance, Quinn hard on his trail when Eliodoro shouted again. "Quinn! No!"

The distraction gave their prey a chance to recover, standing warily on guard as he waited to see what would happen next.

"What? Why not?" Quinn demanded, not looking away but wanting to hear Eliodoro's answer.

"Is no Romero. 'E look like Romero, but is not 'im."

Slowly, watching to make sure the other man would do the same, Quinn lowered his sword. "My apologies, sir. We mistook you for a man who attacked my friend."

The Spaniard nodded and gave a slight bow, withdrawing cautiously. When he was gone, Eliodoro slumped to his knees. Realizing they were making a spectacle of themselves, Quinn helped Eliodoro to his feet and led him back to the inn and the privacy of their room.

"*Scusa,*" Eliodoro said when they were alone. "I think 'e is Romero."

"No harm done," Quinn said, stroking Eliodoro's arm reassuringly. "We'll sit for a bit before we go back to Munoz's companions. There's no rush today."

Eliodoro shook his head. "We almost kill innocent man today. My mother always say you receive what you give. I no want live in 'ate. I want 'ave love."

"But I thought you wanted revenge."

Eliodoro shook his head again. "Was your idea, you and Captain White and *Signor* Watson. I no say no because I 'ave nothing else then. Now I 'ave something good. I 'ave you. I no want spend my life angry. I want 'elp people, like *Signor* Watson. Romero, Medina, others… live or die, they face God's justice later. I no want answer for same crimes. Please, Quinn. Let it go."

Quinn almost insisted, almost tried to change Eliodoro's mind, but while his anger on his lover's behalf was real, he had no cause but Eliodoro to track down the men in question, and he had agreed to the plan originally as a way to reassure Eliodoro of his regard. Eliodoro no longer needed reassurance, or if he did, he did not want it this way. Taking a deep breath, he made a conscious choice to let the anger go. "If that is what you want, I will abide by it."

Swamped with relief, Eliodoro threw himself into Quinn's arms, pulling his lover's head down for a kiss. Quinn kissed Eliodoro avidly, the adrenaline from the aborted confrontation needing an outlet. He wanted to toss Eliodoro on the bed and make wild love to him, but he had promised to let Eliodoro take the lead.

Eliodoro had other ideas. "Fuck me."

The blunt words coiled in Quinn's belly, adding to his need. "I promised—"

"My past is in past. I no think about them now. I think about you." Eliodoro pulled away and stripped rapidly, climbing onto the bed on his hands and knees and looking back at Quinn over his shoulder. "Fuck me. Now."

It was an offer too good to pass up. Tossing his hat, jacket and sword to the floor, Quinn climbed onto the bed behind Eliodoro, but instead of pulling his cock from his breeches and pounding into the tight arse, he leaned forward and licked his way over the smooth skin. Eliodoro startled beneath him, but Quinn steadied him with sure hands on his hips. "Easy," he murmured. "Hold still and let me love you."

Eliodoro felt like his entire body was trembling as he waited to see what Quinn would do next. He had expected the press of fingers and cool ointment against his entrance. He had not expected the hot swipe of Quinn's tongue over his skin. He shivered as he wondered what Quinn would.... *Madre di Dio*, was Quinn really licking him there? The thought was almost too decadent to contemplate as the hot, wet swipes continued back and forth across the tight hole, teasing it into relaxation. Eliodoro cried out in surprise and lust and shock and need when the teasing muscle suddenly pushed hard past his outer ring. "Quinn!"

He could feel the vibrations of Quinn's chuckle against his skin, but the erotic thrusting continued. Eliodoro's head dropped between his arms as he struggled to stay upright. He had chosen the position as a way to banish the last of his demons by letting Quinn take him as his captors had done, but he had never imagined this would—could—be the result. "*Ti prego*," he begged, too overcome with emotion to find the words in English. "*Possiedimi*."

Quinn committed the words to memory, determined to use them on his lover at a future date, but for now, he would give the younger man what he wanted. Finding the tin of salve, he coated his fingers and pressed two against the pucker he had so assiduously opened with his tongue. The muscle gave easily, his fingers slipping into Eliodoro's snug passage. He knew the moment he found Eliodoro's sweet spot by the sharp yelp and eager thrashing. He settled in to play a bit, massaging the sensitive nub until Eliodoro was writhing desperately, the whispered words in Italian coming constantly now. *Possiedimi.*

Pulling open the placket of his breeches, Quinn freed his cock and shunted it between the parted cheeks. Eliodoro wriggled back against Quinn, his buttocks rubbing provocatively against the quartermaster's erection. Patience gone like smoke before a storm, Quinn thrust home, replacing his fingers with his cock.

Eliodoro reared back as he was breached, the care Quinn had taken enough to ensure he felt neither pain nor any resemblance to the abuse he had suffered. He pushed back against his lover, a wholehearted participant in his reaming. His pulse pounded in his ears as every thrust seemed to take Quinn deeper until Eliodoro was sure he could feel Quinn all the way up to his heart. "*Ti amo,*" he cried, unable to hold back any longer. Seconds later, he heard Quinn's hoarse shout and felt the warm rush filling him. Quinn's weight collapsed against him, but Eliodoro didn't care. He felt cherished rather than trapped with the evidence of Quinn's desire seeping over his thighs. Far sooner than he would have liked, Quinn rose, leaving Eliodoro shivering at the sudden loss of his warmth despite the heat in the room. He told himself he was being childish, wanting Quinn always next to him, but the silent scolding changed his feelings not a whit. Closing his eyes, he sighed in contentment when Quinn returned a second later with a damp cloth, wiping him clean. "Do you want to sleep some more?"

Eliodoro shook his head and rolled onto his back, smiling at the image Quinn made, still mostly dressed, only his breeches open. "You like what you see?"

"*Do* you like what you see," Quinn corrected. "And yes, I like what I see. Very much. Even before I knew you, I liked what I saw. Now I see so much more."

Eliodoro patted the bed next to him. "Take off clothes. Come 'ere."

Quinn undressed, leaving only the bracelet Eliodoro had given him. Eliodoro ran his finger along the metal, feeling the warmth of Quinn's skin. He smiled at knowing his lover was wearing his gift. His eyes landed on the sword Quinn had purchased and the town clothes. They were much appreciated, but he wanted something more, something intimate.

The image flashed through his mind of Seaton picking an earring from the stores of treasure and fastening it tenderly in Clay's ear.

"I want you pierce... *to* pierce my ear."

Quinn's eyes widened in surprise as he rolled onto his elbow to stare at Eliodoro. "Not that I'm against the idea, but where did that come from?"

"I no always wear sword, clothes," Eliodoro struggled to explain. "Clay always 'ave earring."

"You don't need an earring as proof of my feelings."

Eliodoro shook his head. "I want one. I want you give... to give me one."

"Then we'll have to go find one. I don't keep a stash of earrings in my pocket."

Eliodoro laughed and pulled Quinn back down beside him. "Later."

Chapter 35

"ARE you sure about this?" Quinn asked once more, holding the earring they had selected.

"*Sì*, I want it."

Quinn nodded his acceptance and brushed Eliodoro's hair away from his ear. Eliodoro leaned into the caress, Quinn's fingers stroking his cheek tenderly. "*Ti amo*," Quinn murmured, kissing the curve of Eliodoro's cheek, the shell of his ear and the tender lobe. Reaching for the needle, he heated it as he had seen Gavin do any time he put stitches in anyone. Gavin said it helped keep the wound from putrefaction, though he could not explain why. Quinn didn't need an explanation. If Gavin said it was important, that was enough for Quinn. He didn't want to take any chances with his lover.

Eliodoro's heart beat faster as Quinn prepared the needle. He knew it would hurt momentarily, but he welcomed the pain, welcomed the chance to prove his devotion. He felt Quinn's fingers against his earlobe and then the sharp pain of the needle penetrating his flesh, followed immediately by the earring they had picked out. The gold hoop was simple, but that was what Eliodoro had wanted. Something as simple and eternal as his heart.

"Is done?"

"It's done." Carefully Quinn drizzled a bit of rum on the piercing. Eliodoro hissed at the sting, but Quinn had explained it would clean the hole. Eliodoro fingered the ring gently, wincing a little as the metal

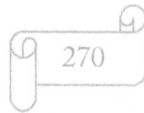

pulled against his tender skin. It made him smile to know he wore a symbol of their commitment. "What now?"

"That's up to you," Quinn replied. "We can stay here or we can go back to the *Silver Queen*."

"*Sì*, but what 'appen now? You and me?"

"What do you want to happen?" Quinn asked seriously. Seeing the petulant expression on Eliodoro's face, he pulled his lover into his arms. "I'm not making light of the situation or of you. Our choices are pretty much unlimited at this point. We can go on as we have been, you with the crew, me in my quarters, stealing time and privacy when we can. You can move in with me, if you are ready for that kind of openness with the crew. We can have Amery draw up a matelotage. We can leave the *Silver Queen* entirely and invest our gold in land on one of the islands, though I admit I am not ready to leave the sea."

"No, I want sail with *Silver Queen*, learn from *Signor* Watson," Eliodoro agreed.

"I want to sail," Quinn reminded Eliodoro gently. "Will you share my cabin, or would you prefer to wait? I know you haven't had much choice when it comes to men or your future. I don't want you to feel I'm taking choices from you now."

Eliodoro touched the new earring and smiled at Quinn. "I make my choice. I share your cabin."

Quinn didn't bring back up the matelotage, preferring to wait, to give Eliodoro another voyage or even several so he could be sure before they signed a binding contract. He knew of a couple of instances when contracts had been dissolved later, but he didn't want to contemplate that. To have made that commitment and have it wrenched away from him because Eliodoro changed his mind was too horrible to imagine. "Now or in the morning?"

Eliodoro grinned. "Now. I want you make… to make love to me in our bed."

Quinn thought that sounded like the best idea he'd heard in years.

Gathering their belongings, they made their way back to the ship. Amery met them at the top of the gangplank. "You're back early."

"We have some moving to do," Quinn said with a grin.

"About time," Amery teased. "Do you need help, Eliodoro?"

Eliodoro shook his head. "Is just sea chest. Is no 'ard to carry." He looked at Quinn. "I move now?"

"If you want, but I thought you might want to talk to Gavin first."

"Talk to Gavin about what?" Amery asked.

"I want study… to study with *Signor* Watson."

"The ship can always use another surgeon," Amery said by way of approval. "I'm sure he'll agree as well. He's down there now if you want to go talk to him."

Eliodoro started in that direction. "Do you want me to come with you?" Quinn called after him.

"No. I talk to 'im alone. I be back soon."

"Are you happy?" Amery asked Quinn as soon as Eliodoro disappeared into the aftcastle.

"Very," Quinn replied with a smile. "I didn't know I could be this happy."

"Then I guess I'd better start writing a matelotage."

"Not yet," Quinn said with a shake of his head. "He's never been with anyone else, never had a chance to choose. I've made my choice, but I don't want to force him into something he isn't ready for. I don't want him to regret it later."

Amery raised an eyebrow and chuckled. "That boy doesn't look forced into anything, Quinn."

"I know he isn't now, but it wouldn't be fair to bind him to me when he hasn't had a chance to really consider his options. A matelotage will mean as much in six months or six years as it means now, and I'll know he's truly ready for the commitment."

"I think you're underestimating him."

Quinn shrugged. "Maybe I am, but I don't want him to come to resent me because I 'trapped' him into a matelotage when he was too inexperienced to know better."

"You also don't want him to leave you because you didn't give him the commitment he wanted," Amery warned. "I'm not saying you have to sign a contract today, but don't wait too long."

NERVOUSLY, Eliodoro tapped on the door to the surgery, not wanting to simply barge in. He wasn't sick or injured to use that as an excuse for forgetting the manners his mother had instilled in him.

"Come in."

Eliodoro pushed the door open and walked slowly inside.

"Eliodoro. How are you today?"

"*Bene*," Eliodoro replied. "Fine. You?"

"I'm doing very well. So what brings you knocking on my door? You aren't sick, are you?"

"No," Eliodoro said. "No sick. I... I talk with *Signor* Davies."

"You can call him Quinn with me," Gavin interrupted. "You do call him Quinn when you're alone, don't you?"

Eliodoro flushed. "*Sì*, when we are alone. I no want say it in front of others."

"I'm not exactly 'others'," Gavin reminded Eliodoro. "Quinn and I have known each other for twenty years. You can call him by his name with me. Now, you said you were talking to Quinn. About what?"

"About what I do 'ere on ship. Captain White teach me read... to read charts, but I no want to *be* captain. I want to be like you. I want to learn 'ealing. Quinn say you teach me. Yes?"

Gavin looked at Eliodoro seriously. "I need another pair of hands around here some days, but I want you to understand what it means to be my apprentice. It means dealing with men dying despite our best efforts. It means blood and pain and amputations and screams and tears and sights that would make most men faint."

Eliodoro nodded. "It also mean save life. I watch you with Captain White when 'e was sick. I see you mourn the dead, but I also see you 'elp everyone. I want that. I want to 'elp."

"Then I guess we'd better tell the captain I have a new apprentice," Gavin said with a smile. "I'm not using the quarters off the surgery if you want to move out of the crew quarters. Unless you're moving in to Quinn's cabin."

"'Ow you know?"

"I didn't know for sure, but Quinn isn't the kind to do things halfway, and I see you have a new accessory. It seemed like a logical conclusion."

"Accessory?" Eliodoro asked, stumbling over the unfamiliar word.

"Your earring," Gavin explained. "It wasn't there when you left the ship yesterday. I assumed it was a gift from Quinn since you don't seem the type to care about fashion."

"I ask 'im give it... to give it?" Gavin nodded so Eliodoro continued. "To give it to me, but yes, is gift from Quinn."

Gavin started toward the door, but Eliodoro stopped him. "*Signor* Watson—"

"Gavin. If we're going to work together, you can stop calling me by my last name and call me Gavin," the surgeon insisted, "and when it's just the four of us, I suspect you'll have to get used to calling the captain by his given name as well."

"I no can do that!" Eliodoro gasped. "'E is captain!"

"He's also your lover's best friend and my lover," Gavin reminded Eliodoro. "Don't worry. You'll get used to it. Now, you were going to ask me something?"

"Yes. Are you 'appy?"

Gavin smiled. "Deliriously." He chuckled at the look of confusion on Eliodoro's face. "Yes," he amended. "I'm very happy. Are you?"

Eliodoro nodded. "I no think I can be so 'appy, but Quinn love me." He could not keep the amazement out of his voice nor, he was sure, off his face. "I no understand why, but I no want it change."

Gavin thought he knew why, looking at Eliodoro's expressive face and seeing the joy that resided there despite his past. "Love doesn't need logic. All it needs is love in return. You do share his feelings?"

"Oh, yes! I no think I find someone. I give up 'ope on *Nuestra Señora de Madrid*. I think I die there. Then I see Quinn. 'E ask for keys to 'elp other slaves. I know the Spanish kill me for speak, but I see Quinn's face, see 'e 'ate slavers and I 'ope 'e 'elp me too so I tell 'im where keys are. And when 'e order sailors into chains, 'e let me free. And now 'e love me."

Gavin nodded, having heard the same story from Quinn's perspective. "He admired your courage from the moment you opened your mouth," he confided. "And that admiration has only increased. How much has he told you of his—our—experience with another Spanish ship?"

"'E tell me few things, Captain White tell me other things."

"It was only for a few days, but Quinn will never do to you what Amery did to me," Gavin assured Eliodoro. "He knows what it is to be hurt and to live with that later. Whatever you did to survive, he'll never reproach you for that."

Eliodoro smiled. "I know. We talk about that already. I wish it no happen, but I know Quinn understand."

Gavin's face darkened. "We all have things we wish never happened. If you ever need someone to talk to, I'm willing to listen. Sometimes it helps to have a friend who isn't also your lover."

"I no 'ave much experience, but I listen too if you need," Eliodoro said. "Is good 'ave friends."

"It's also good to have a man who thinks you hung the moon," Gavin said, determined to lighten the mood. "Let's go find ours."

Eliodoro laughed as Gavin had intended and let the conversation go, following Gavin back onto deck where Quinn and Amery stood side by side, surveying the rigging. "We are lucky men indeed," Gavin whispered to Eliodoro. "The two best catches on the ship."

"On any ship," Eliodoro added. "This is fourth ship I sail on. No man compare to Quinn or Captain White."

"This is my fourth ship as well," Gavin said, "and I'd say you're right. Even when we were boys, few could compare and now that we're grown, they're pretty well amazing. Don't tell them that, though. They'll be impossible to live with if you do."

Eliodoro's laughter pealed out, drawing Quinn's and Amery's attention.

"That's a new expression," Amery said with a smile for Eliodoro even as he reached for Gavin, his arm going around his matelot's waist. "I could get used to seeing that one. Quinn, I expect you to make sure Eliodoro stays as happy as he is now. We need that kind of joy aboard."

"Aye, Captain," Quinn said with a sharp salute. "I promise to do my very best." He slid his arm around Eliodoro's waist as well, a near perfect imitation of Amery and Gavin's stance.

"Never stop love me," Eliodoro said softly. "Is all I need to be 'appy."

Quinn couldn't resist, dipping his head to capture Eliodoro's lips. Gavin and Amery already knew how he felt about Eliodoro, and Eliodoro's change of bunk would make the situation clear to the rest of the crew in a matter of hours. They weren't on duty, so Quinn saw no reason to hold back. "Then you have nothing to fear," Quinn promised when he lifted his head. "Let's get your chest so you can get settled."

"Maybe we should stay on deck for awhile," Amery teased, "so they don't have to worry about being quiet."

"Quinn already warn me," Eliodoro replied archly. "Is you make noise at night."

Amery's eyes widened at the teasing from such an unexpected source. The expression on his face sparked laughter in the other three men as the captain spluttered at the insult to his dignity. "You'd better watch out, Amery," Gavin said through his laughter. "My new apprentice might be a match for you."

Amery relaxed and joined the laughter, too pleased at the sight of Gavin's uninhibited smile to care about things like dignity. "As long as he keeps Quinn happy and does his job on the ship, he can take as many shots at me as he wants."

Quinn grinned. "It looks like the task of keeping the captain humble has fallen to you, Eliodoro. I, for one, will be glad not to have that role anymore. Do you think you're up to it?"

Eliodoro squirmed uncomfortably, not accustomed to such informality with men of such standing, but he reminded himself that they weren't the captain, the quartermaster and the surgeon at the moment, but his lover and his lover's two closest friends. "As long as Captain White no think I mean disrespect."

"Captain White may not tolerate any challenge to his authority," Amery answered before Quinn could reply, "but Amery needs that reminder. Choose the time and the place for your quips and I won't be upset. Now, Captain White suggests you move your sea chest to your new quarters. And Amery suggests you take what's left of your leave to finish celebrating."

With a snicker, Quinn followed Eliodoro into the crew quarters. Eliodoro checked the area around his hammock to make sure he hadn't forgotten anything, not that he had much to forget, and then, with Quinn's help, hefted the chest and returned toward the door.

"About time, Quartermaster," Clay called from his hammock. "We was tired of watching him pine over ye."

"Be careful what you say to him," Quinn warned, his smile never faltering. "Eliodoro is Mr. Watson's apprentice now. He'll be mixing your potions before long."

"Is that how ye get ahead on this ship?" a voice called. "By lettin' the quartermaster bugger ye?"

Quinn froze, turning back to face the crew. Before he could challenge the speaker, Eliodoro had dropped his side of the sea chest and approached the other sailor. Quinn resisted the urge to draw his sword in his lover's defense, but he reminded himself to let Eliodoro fight his own battles.

"You want 'elp *Signor* Watson?" Eliodoro challenged. "Why you no say you want learn? Is all I do. Or maybe is no be surgeon you want. Maybe is *Signor* Davies. You want be surgeon, I let you learn too. You want *Signor* Davies, you fight me for 'im."

Quinn wanted to protest that he wasn't a prize for them to fight over, but he held his tongue. He could always intervene later.

"Shut your mouth, Russell," Clay snapped before the other sailor could answer. "You don't do even a third of the work Eliodoro does around here, and then you complain about the amount of work you manage to do. He's more than earned the chance to be Mr. Watson's apprentice."

"If you think I'm playing favorites, take it up with the captain," Quinn added, "but if I hear about you harassing Eliodoro, you'll answer to me for it, do you understand?"

Russell nodded sullenly, eyes seeking allies among the rest of the crew but not finding any.

"Let's get your chest moved," Quinn said, turning back to Eliodoro. Eliodoro picked up the chest again and walked out of the crew quarters. "I'm sorry," he said as soon as they were out of earshot of the crew. "I should have known there would be a case or two of sour grapes."

Eliodoro shrugged. "Is no your fault. You warn me 'ow it look to crew without matelotage. I say I no care."

"I don't care if they know, but I hate the idea that they might bother you because we're lovers," Quinn said. "Tell me if Russell keeps making comments."

Eliodoro laughed. "Quinn, 'e say what 'e want. I know you no think I use you. Captain White, *Signor* Watson, they no think it. Russell no matter to me. You matter to me."

Quinn almost asked if Eliodoro was sure, but he did not want to waste any more time on the other sailor. Leaning close, he brushed the hair away from Eliodoro's new earring and whispered, "*Ti prego, possiedimi.*"

Eliodoro's eyes went wide. "You speak Italian bad as I speak English."

Quinn chuckled. "Does that mean you didn't understand me?"

Eliodoro shook his head. "I understand. In your cabin, *sì?*"

"In our cabin."

Eliodoro's smile widened even more, if that was possible, and he tugged Quinn across the deck, the sea chest swinging between them. They were all but running by the time they reached the door to the aftcastle, ducking into the dark corridor. Eliodoro stopped suddenly, pushing Quinn against the wall and kissing him hard, completely ignoring the bulk of the sea chest between them.

Quinn returned the kiss eagerly, his free hand tangling in Eliodoro's curls to keep their mouths fused together until the press of the wooden chest became uncomfortable against his thighs.

"There's a bed right through that door," Quinn gasped, breaking free of Eliodoro's mouth. "We'd be much more comfortable there than here in the corridor."

Eliodoro turned and pulled Quinn with him into the cabin, dropping the chest as soon as the door shut behind them. He didn't bother with the bed, though, pushing Quinn back against the door. Quinn let Eliodoro have his way, twisting into his lover's caressing hands as they flew over his body. He opened his mouth to gasp out a reminder of the bed when Gavin's voice came through the door. "Eliodoro, I need your help."

Eliodoro pulled away, eyes wide as his passion warred with his new duty. The sight of Quinn leaning against the door, clothes awry, gaze dark with lust didn't help, but Quinn nodded at him, stepping aside. "You wanted this. I'll still be here when you're done. Go help Gavin."

"I come," Eliodoro called to Gavin. He took another deep breath and straightened his clothing a little, trying unsuccessfully to hide the bulge in his breeches. "We finish this later."

"I promise," Quinn said, giving Eliodoro a quick kiss. "You know he wouldn't have disturbed us if it wasn't important. Go on. I'll go help Amery. Find me when you're done."

Chapter 36

"WHAT'S wrong?" Quinn asked when he joined Amery on deck a few minutes later.

"Meredith will probably lose his hand," Amery said, his face drawn as he turned to face Quinn. "He hurt it while we were doing repairs on the island. Gavin cleaned and bound it then, but it apparently putrefied. With everything going on, it took him until now to say something to Gavin about it."

Quinn winced. "Not the best introduction for Eliodoro to life as a surgeon."

Amery shrugged. "It's a reality of that life. If he can't handle it, better to find out now."

"Maybe I should—"

"You should stay right here and let Gavin and Eliodoro do their job," Amery interrupted. "You'll only be in the way, and Eliodoro won't appreciate you hovering over him like he isn't man enough to make his own decisions. Yes, he's young, but he isn't a boy, Quinn. He hasn't been since he survived the slave ship. You've been so moonstruck by him that you haven't seen how he's come into his own in the past few months. I spent a lot of time with him while Gavin and I were estranged. He's his own man, and your relationship will be stronger for it, but you have to let him make his own decisions."

"I'm trying," Quinn said. "I let him deal with Russell when he made a comment about Eliodoro sleeping with me as a way to get ahead on the ship."

"I hope Eliodoro put him in his place?"

Quinn chuckled. "Oh yes. He told Russell that if he wanted to be Gavin's apprentice, that was fine. They could share the honor. If he wanted me, he'd better be ready for a fight. Clay spoke up before it could go any further than that, telling Russell to stop complaining since he does as little work as he can get away with."

"He wasn't one of our better choices when it came to our crew," Amery agreed. "If he continues, we'll leave him ashore the next time we make port. I don't want that kind of rancor on my ship."

"The rest of the crew, at least the ones in the crew quarters when it happened, all seemed to accept Eliodoro's promotion for what it is and our relationship for a completely separate matter."

A sudden sharp scream rent the air, interrupting their conversation. Amery blanched before turning green around the gills. "Breathe," Quinn said. "Don't think about it. What do we need to do before we sail? Concentrate on that while Gavin does his duty."

Amery took a couple of gulping breaths before looking around the deck. "I think all of the repairs are done. Jennings was going to check everything one more time to make sure nothing else needed to be redone. We should check that all of the supplies are aboard. You placed the orders so I don't know exactly what to expect. Beyond that, we only found a few men interested in sailing with us so we need to sail to Tortuga to take on a full complement of crew again before we go hunting. We didn't learn anything about the other officers from Eliodoro's past."

"I killed one of them here a few days ago," Quinn said. "Eliodoro doesn't want us to go after the others. He said something about reaping what he sowed and that he wants to spend his life healing people rather than hating people."

"I told you he was a man," Amery said with a chuckle. "No boy has that kind of maturity."

Quinn thought back to the night before and the feeling of Eliodoro moving inside him, of Eliodoro coming inside him almost immediately. "He might have a few things to learn yet, but it will be my pleasure to teach him."

Amery laughed again, his color returning to normal as he set his mind to teasing Quinn. "You mean you haven't shown him every position for making love yet? You're remiss in your duties."

"I was about to show him another one when *your* matelot interrupted us," Quinn joked back, relieved to see the pallor disappearing from Amery's face. A second, weaker scream interrupted them again, but it didn't seem to bother Amery as much as the first one.

"We'll have to console each other when duty takes our lovers away from us," Amery decided. "I have a bottle of rum in my cabin if you'd like a swig."

"I wouldn't say no to that," Quinn replied, finding it far easier than he expected to summon a smile for Amery. It seemed his relationship with Eliodoro had more benefits than the obvious one if Amery was once again at ease in his company.

They retired to Amery's cabin, pouring the rum and reclining in the two chairs, the conversation flowing easily at times, the silence equally relaxed. Eventually, Gavin came in, scrubbing at the blood that covered his hands. His clothes were beyond repair. Even worse, his entire body radiated exhaustion. "Eliodoro needs you, Quinn," he said, his voice as tired as the rest of him. "We had to amputate Meredith's arm above the elbow, and even with that, I'm not sure we'll be able to save him. Eliodoro was everything I could have asked for in an assistant, but now he needs someone to take care of him. Take him for a swim or into town to get a bath. Give him something good to think about instead of the blood and pain he's spent the afternoon dealing with."

Quinn rose, leaving the mug on the table. "As long as you promise to let Amery do the same for you."

Amery rose as well, helping Gavin peel off the blood-stained shirt. Quinn was surprised to realize he didn't feel the slightest jealousy or desire at the sight. Eliodoro awaited, in their cabin or on deck, and that more than made up for any sense of loss he might have felt at knowing Gavin and Amery were happily together again.

"I learned how best to take care of him after a rough surgery a long time ago," Amery said, his words easy, with none of the edge they would have had a month ago. "I'll make sure he's well again."

Quinn nodded. "Do you know where Eliodoro went?"

"To your cabin, as well he should have," Gavin replied, leaning against Amery now that he didn't have to worry about transferring the blood from his shirt to Amery's.

"Thank you. Amery, I'll take you up on the second half of that shore leave, if the offer is still open."

Amery shooed Quinn out of the room silently. Leaving Gavin to Amery's tender care, Quinn walked down to the corridor to his cabin, finding Eliodoro inside as Gavin had promised, as bloody as the ship's surgeon, his eyes vacant as he picked at the cuff of his shirt. Heedless of the mess, Quinn walked up behind him, wrapping his arms around Eliodoro and holding on tight. It had been years since he'd helped Gavin with an amputation, but he remembered it as vividly as if it happened that afternoon. "*Ti amo*," he murmured, nuzzling Eliodoro's neck tenderly. "Let's find somewhere to get you cleaned up. You'll feel better after you get the blood off."

Eliodoro turned in Quinn's arms, a horrified expression on his face. "I no think," he said slowly. "I go 'elp Signor Watson. I no change clothes. They ruined. You give them me and I ruin."

"It's just a shirt, Eliodoro," Quinn soothed, his hands rubbing up and down the trembling muscles of Eliodoro's back. "I'll buy you another one. Or another ten. You did what needed to be done, and I'm so proud of you. Gavin said he couldn't have asked for a better assistant. Come on. I think I saw a little cove down the beach where we can go for a swim and get the blood off you."

Eliodoro let Quinn lead him out of the cabin and down the gangplank, so caught in his memories that he didn't see the looks of respect on the faces of the sailors they passed. Quinn saw them, though, and he nodded at them each in turn. He would tell Eliodoro about it later, and he hoped the young man would see it for himself when he was less shaken by the day's events. It would go a long way toward counteracting Russell's bile.

The sand was warm beneath their feet as they walked down the shore, Eliodoro's hand enclosed in Quinn's larger one. Periodically, shivers still ran through him, but the bright sunlight—was it only late afternoon still? Surely more time had passed—dispelled the gloom of the surgery and the horror of Meredith's screams. Gavin had sent Eliodoro from the room after they finished cauterizing the stump, insisting he would come back later to clean up the mess. Eliodoro was ridiculously grateful. He hadn't dwelled on the blood or the dismembered limb while they were working. There hadn't been time, with Gavin giving him orders every few seconds, telling him to hold the man's shoulders, to support his arm, to tie the tourniquet or get the hot iron to cauterize the stump. The memories were suddenly too much. He pulled away from Quinn, stumbling a few steps before going to his knees, his stomach emptying violently.

"Easy," Quinn soothed, his hands running up and down Eliodoro's back. "Get it all out. You'll feel better."

Eliodoro heaved a few more times, the spasms finally ceasing.

"Here." Quinn offered Eliodoro his flask of rum. "Rinse your mouth out a bit. Don't swallow it. The rum won't help settle your stomach, but it will get the taste of bile out of your mouth."

Eliodoro took a sip of the rum and swirled it around his mouth, spitting it out after a moment.

"We're almost to the cove I saw," Quinn said. "Can you keep going?"

"*Sì*," Eliodoro said softly, holding tightly to Quinn's hand as he got to his feet. On a normal day, he wouldn't have let himself appear so needy, but this was Quinn, not the men who had looked for signs of weakness in everyone around them so they could exploit it, and this was not a normal day so perhaps his weakness could be excused this once.

They walked around the curve of the island until they were out of sight of the ship and the port. "Just walk into the water," Quinn told Eliodoro. "We'll rub the blood out of your clothes while you're still dressed and then get you clean afterward."

Still moving stiffly, Eliodoro did as Quinn directed, wading out into the warm waves until the water lapped at his waist. He knew he should start scrubbing at the bloody fabric, but he couldn't seem to make his arms work.

He didn't have to. Moments later, Quinn stood beside him, pulling him into an embrace and beginning to clean the blood from Eliodoro's clothes. Eliodoro closed his eyes and leaned back against the strong body, letting Quinn support his weight.

"That's it," Quinn murmured in his ear. "Relax and let me take care of you."

Eliodoro did as Quinn said, resting in Quinn's embrace as his lover's hands moved over his body, scrubbing at the blood and gore. Eliodoro kept his eyes closed, not wanting to see the filth from the afternoon staining the water around him. The tender rubbing of Quinn's hands seemed to go on forever, Eliodoro drifting in a hypnotic state somewhere between shock and arousal. So slowly that Eliodoro could not have said when it happened, the arousal won out over the shock, and Eliodoro opened his eyes, surprised to see no hint of blood in the water and only the slightest of ruddy stains on his shirt.

"Feeling better?" Quinn asked when Eliodoro turned in his embrace.

"*Molto*," Eliodoro replied, leaning up to kiss Quinn gently. "Much."

"Good. Let's get rid of your clothes and wash the rest of the blood off your skin," Quinn said, "and then we have some unfinished business."

Eliodoro's brow furrowed. "What business?"

Quinn grinned. "*Ti prego, possiedimi.* Remember? Gavin interrupted us before we got started."

Eliodoro glanced around. "'Ere?"

"Yes, here. I still have the salve in my pocket from earlier. No one is around to see us. Why not?"

Why not indeed? Eliodoro mused silently as he pulled off his clothes, realizing finally that Quinn had already stripped down to his skin.

They washed the remaining blood off Eliodoro's skin, desire rising between them as their hands moved over each other's bodies. When Quinn was sure Eliodoro was clean, his patience waned, and he led his lover onto the beach, digging the tin of salve from his pocket before falling to his hands and knees. "*Possiedimi.*"

"ELIODORO."

Eliodoro looked up from the sail he was mending to see Gavin's grave expression. "*Sì?*"

"Meredith died during the night," Gavin said. "We need to prepare his body to be buried at sea. We're the ship's undertakers as well as its healers."

Eliodoro rose to his feet, setting aside the sail with precise gestures as he fought down the surge of emotion at the loss of his first patient. He had sailed for long enough to know that more injuries and illnesses were fatal than not, but it didn't make it any easier to be faced with those limitations now. "You tell Captain White?"

"I told him before I came to find you. He and Quinn will gather the crew for the service, but we have to wrap the body first. We'll use the sail you were working on. It's about the size and it's really too tattered to repair effectively."

Eliodoro gathered up the heavy cloth and followed Gavin into the crew quarters. They were empty except for the hammock of the deceased. Gavin approached first, closing the man's eyes. "Spread out the sail and then come help me lift him onto it."

Eliodoro did as Gavin said before joining the surgeon at the man's side. Gavin gestured for Eliodoro to take his feet while he hefted the man's shoulders, lifting him from the hammock and stretching the body out. They folded the sail over him and stitched it closed quickly. "Let's go."

They lifted the body between them and carried it up onto the deck. The crew had gathered, pulling hats and scarves off their heads as Gavin and Eliodoro appeared with the body of their crewmate. Amery and Quinn stood at the rail. The crew parted to let Eliodoro and Gavin through. When they reached the rail, Amery opened the Bible in his hand and read Psalm 23. "Rest in peace, Meredith."

Gavin tipped his head at Eliodoro who nodded and lifted the man's feet over the rail. The enshrouded body slipped from their grasp and into the quiet seas, disappearing almost immediately beneath the surface. Eliodoro crossed himself as he murmured his own prayer for the repose of the man's soul.

Amery didn't immediately give orders, but it wasn't long before the crew drifted back to their stations, none of them comfortable with death. "Are you all right?" Quinn asked when Eliodoro remained by the rail.

Eliodoro shrugged. "Is no easy see man die. Is 'arder when I no can 'elp."

Quinn put his arms around Eliodoro's shoulders. "I know. I've watched Gavin struggle with that since he first apprenticed as a surgeon. He pays attention to what works and what doesn't and tries to learn from that, but there are still limits on what he knows and what he can do. Maybe if Gavin had amputated sooner, it might have made a difference, but maybe not. And I'm sure Meredith didn't want to lose his hand so he waited as long as he could to bring the injury to Gavin's attention. I understand that fear, but I've seen enough to realize that choice cost him his life. You can still change your mind about apprenticing with Gavin."

Eliodoro shook his head. It had only been a few days since the amputation, but he had already helped Gavin mix medicines and set a broken bone. He'd seen gratitude in the eyes of the men they had helped, even in Meredith's. "Is 'ard life. I know that, but is worth it."

Quinn smiled and hugged Eliodoro tighter. "That's what Gavin always says too. I'm proud of your choice. I want you to know that."

Chapter 37

"QUINN?"

Eliodoro's voice was so uncharacteristically hesitant that it drew Quinn's attention instantly. "Yes?"

"It 'as been two months. 'Ow long you"—Eliodoro grimaced at the mistake—"'Ow long will you make me wait for matelotage?"

"It isn't about making you wait," Quinn said. "I thought you understood that. It's about giving you time to be sure that's what you want."

Eliodoro sighed. From where he was sitting, it came around to the same thing. "I know what I want. You think I need time because I no have—do no have much experience, but I 'ave all the experience I need. I see the worst of men and now I see the best."

Which was exactly Quinn's point, if only Eliodoro would see it. Eliodoro had certainly seen the worst of men on the Spanish slave ship, but Quinn hardly qualified as the best of men and until Eliodoro could see that, could look realistically at his options, Quinn didn't feel like he could bind Eliodoro to him that way. "Would it really make that much difference? It's not like the contract would be recognized anywhere outside the Caribbean and even here, it's really only recognized among pirates."

"We *are* pirates," Eliodoro reminded him. "I want to belong to you and 'ave you belong to me. In front of everyone. The crew, other crews, in Tortuga, on Providence Island. *Ti amo*. I say that, but I think you still not believe it. 'Ow you think I want someone else when I love you?"

Quinn flinched at the accusation because it hit far too close to home. He did fear Eliodoro's love was partially gratitude and hero worship rather than a true, abiding love. Each morning, a part of him worried that would be the day Eliodoro realized his error and returned to the crew quarters. Eliodoro had never given him any reason for that fear. He knew it was the lingering aftermath of his years of unrequited feelings for Gavin. He couldn't shake it, though. He opened his mouth to insist that of course he knew Eliodoro loved him, but a knock at the cabin door interrupted him. "We'll talk later," he promised, going to open the door.

Amery stood on the other side. "We've got a storm coming. I'd rather outrun it than face it in an unknown harbor. This isn't Tortuga, and the storm is coming in off the water rather than across the island. We need to find open water before the heavens unleash their fury."

"Give me a moment."

Amery nodded and returned to deck. Quinn reached for Eliodoro. "*Ti amo*. I love you. I'm sorry if I made you doubt that. We'll settle this once we've outrun the storm." Without waiting for a reply, he bent his head and kissed Eliodoro tenderly.

Eliodoro leaned into the embrace, drawing strength from the loving touch. He had faced storms at sea before and suspected it would take all their combined wit and strength to survive if Amery was worried. Usually the captain simply complained about getting wet.

Releasing Eliodoro regretfully, Quinn followed Amery onto deck, glancing skyward at the threatening clouds on the horizon that had caught Amery's attention. He could see why his friend was worried. Looking around, he saw only the usual complement of sailors on deck. Moving toward the forecastle, he ducked into the crew quarters. "The captain wants all hands to stations. A storm's coming, and he wants us out at sea before it hits."

"Aye, Quartermaster," a chorus of voices said. Sailors rolled to their feet from their comfortable positions in their hammocks. In moments, the quiet hold had turned into a beehive of activity as sailors

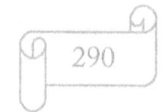

stowed their gear, lashing down everything that might wash away if the storm got bad. Too many of the sailors remembered the fate of the *Dark Dream*, and most of the rest had fought the sea and lost at one time or another.

When he returned to deck, Quinn checked the progress of the storm out of habit. "It's getting dark fast. We need to hurry."

Even as he spoke, sailors swarmed onto deck. Amery ordered the sails unfurled and the anchor raised.

"Check the pumps," Amery called to Quinn over the sound of the rising wind. "Make sure Jennings and Farnham are in the hold and have everything they need, including enough hands, should the hold spring a leak."

Quinn lifted his hand to show he'd heard, not bothering to shout his reply. He wasn't sure Amery would hear him anyway. As he strode toward the hatch down into the hold, he looked around for Eliodoro, but he didn't see the younger man on deck. Reminding himself that Eliodoro was a capable sailor who didn't need his overprotective lover hovering over him at every second, he made himself follow Amery's orders rather than going in search of Eliodoro.

Jennings and Farnham had stationed themselves at opposite ends of the main hold, each with tools and extra planks at hand, ready to patch any leaks or holes as quickly as possible. A bevy of men gathered around the pumps as well, prepared to do their best to keep the ship afloat if Mother Nature decided to unleash her wrath upon them. If Amery couldn't outrun the storm, the fate of the ship could well rest in the hands of those men. "Everything ready here?"

"As ready as we can make it, Quartermaster," Jennings replied from the stern. "The hold's tight, and the pumps are working. We can't do more than that until a problem arises."

Satisfied, Quinn returned to deck. Already, the waves had picked up, roiling around the vessel as it moved out to sea, the full sails catching the wind and sending the galleon flying over the rough water. Quinn glanced skyward, scanning the rigging to see who Amery had sent aloft. He could not find Eliodoro's familiar dark head among the ropes. Searching more actively now, he found his lover finally manning one of the deck lines. Breathing a sigh of relief that Eliodoro wouldn't have to fight the pitching of the rigging, Quinn made his way carefully across the now heaving deck to Amery's side. "What now?"

Amery didn't look up, his eyes fixed on the far horizon. "Now we run. And we pray."

Quinn's stomach sank, not liking the sound of that pronouncement, but he nodded, not wanting to distract Amery further. The captain's skill was all that stood between them and disaster now. Going back to the main deck, Quinn checked every line, every sail as he passed, exhorting the men to greater efforts in the hope of outrunning the storm.

Eliodoro looked up as Quinn passed, relieved to see his lover on deck. He wanted selfishly to keep Quinn at his side, but he knew that was not possible. The quartermaster had to see to the safety of the entire ship, not merely to his own. Still, Eliodoro kept track of where his lover went on deck as much as his duties permitted. He trusted Amery more than any captain he had ever sailed with, but he feared even Amery's skill could only do so much against the gale currently bearing down on them. Nisbett's shout drew his attention back to the task at hand, and he heaved harder on the line along with several other men, trying to trim the sails against the battering wind, to draw more speed out of the ship so they could outrun the storm. The waves crashed against the hull, spray covering the deck and all the men on it with brine. Eliodoro shook his head to clear the water from his eyes, grateful he'd taken the time to bind his hair back again before coming on deck. Had his curls been loose, they would have been plastered against his face, obscuring his vision completely. As it was, the rain that began to fall made it hard to see even the bow of the ship. The sails trimmed to Nisbett's satisfaction momentarily, Eliodoro glanced over his shoulder, peering through the rain. Gavin had joined Amery at the helm, the two of them working together to keep the course Amery had set amidst the waves that threatened to toss them every which way. Turning his attention back to where he had last seen Quinn, Eliodoro watched in mute horror as a huge wave crashed over the bow of the ship. When the water cleared, Quinn was not at his post.

"No! *Madre di Dio*, no!" Eliodoro shouted, releasing his grip on the line and grabbing the rail, fighting his way past the other sailors to get to where he had last seen Quinn standing. He had no idea what he intended to do, but he could not simply stand there and do nothing while Quinn fought the waves to stay alive.

Another wave knocked him off his feet and would have sent him over the side were it not for his grip on the rail and Seaton's hard grasp on the waistband of his breeches. "Come on, lad," the older sailor said, helping Eliodoro right himself. Together they struggled to the bow, eyes scanning the water in hopes of catching sight of Quinn's head bobbing among the storm-tossed seas. If he had not been dragged under immediately, they might be able to pull him back aboard. "Where is 'e?" Eliodoro cried frantically, not seeing Quinn anywhere. His face was so wet from the waves and the rain that he did not even realize he was crying until Seaton spoke.

"I don't know, but crying won't help him none. Buck up, boy. We'll not give up on our quartermaster that easily."

Eliodoro wiped uselessly at his face and took a sobbing gulp of air as they neared the bow. He peered over into the near darkness of the storm and sea and nearly sank to his knees in relief. Quinn hung from a rope twisted around one wrist, a few merciful feet above the usual waterline of the vessel. "'Elp me," Eliodoro shouted, grabbing the thick rope. "I can no pull 'im up alone."

Seaton nodded his understanding and joined Eliodoro's efforts, their combined strength enough to pull Quinn inch by painful inch back to the deck. They got him over the edge and back onto the ship, finally, soaked to the skin and gasping for breath from where he had been knocked against the hull and dunked beneath the waves, but alive. Heedless of anyone who might be watching, Eliodoro pulled Quinn into his arms and kissed him desperately. "Do no leave me," he shouted when he pulled away. "You can no die. You understand? You no can leave me alone."

"I understand," Quinn promised, one hand still clutching at the rope that had saved his life while the other stroked Eliodoro's face, "but this is not the place to discuss it. We have to survive the storm."

"Tie rope around you next time," Eliodoro said, "not just around arm. I no want lose you."

Quinn didn't want to be lost. "I'll be careful. I promise."

Eliodoro didn't look convinced, but he rose at Seaton's urging and helped Quinn to his feet as well, all three of them moving away from the narrow bow back onto the wider section of the ship.

It seemed Amery's strategy of sailing at an angle to the storm rather than fleeing before it was working, because as Quinn leaned heavily on the main mast, still trying to catch his breath, he thought he could see a break in the clouds on the far horizon. If they could hold the ship together, they might yet survive. "I need to check belowdecks."

Eliodoro wrapped his arm around Quinn's waist, beyond caring about the quartermaster's dignity, and helped him to the hatch and down the ladder, pressing him up against the wall as soon as they were out of sight. His hands flew over drenched clothing, assuring himself Quinn was still in one piece, as their lips crashed together. Quinn's hands fell to Eliodoro's hips, pulling him close as they rutted wildly against each other. "Do no leave me," Eliodoro repeated when he could bring himself to lift his head again.

"Never," Quinn promised. "Come below with me. I have to see how much water we've taken on, but you don't have to leave my side." He took a deep breath and tipped Eliodoro's chin so their eyes met. "I don't want you to leave my side."

Eliodoro took a deep breath and let it out slowly, hope blooming in his heart despite the continued danger from the storm. He understood what Quinn was saying. "We go."

Side by side, they made their way to the bowels of the ship. Water sloshed around their ankles as they checked with Jennings and Farnham, but most of that seemed to be leaking down from the deck rather than coming in through the hull. "We had one little breach, but we got it patched up right and tight before it could cause problems," Jennings said. "The rest of this is what you get in a storm like this. You don't need me to tell you that. You're soaked to the skin."

The words sent a shudder through Eliodoro again as he relived the horror of seeing the wave take Quinn, but he held his tongue. The men here in the hold didn't know how near death Quinn had come, and Eliodoro had no desire to tell them. They would hear about it soon enough if they all survived. The ship tilted dangerously, throwing them hard against the hull, making Eliodoro glad for the lashing holding the cargo in place. The wooden planks creaked and moaned, but held together. Eliodoro could feel the narrow space closing around him, though, as images of being caught in the hold as the ship sank flashed through his mind. Fortunately, Quinn seemed to read his mind, telling the men to keep up the good work and leading Eliodoro back onto deck. He looked again to where he had seen the hint of clear skies. If his eyes did not deceive him, it looked closer than it had been. Keeping a tight hold on Eliodoro's hand, he climbed the aftcastle to join Amery and Gavin at the helm.

"Look!" he shouted, pointing toward the bit of clear sky.

"I see it," Amery shouted back. "Now we just have to get there!"

"With everyone still on board," Gavin added.

Quinn chuckled despite the urgency of their situation. "I've already promised Eliodoro I won't leave him. I don't know what else I can offer."

Gavin and Amery exchanged glances. "If you've promised him that, then that's enough for us."

Quinn frowned, not sure how to interpret that statement, but he didn't have time to reflect on it because Amery started shouting orders again and Quinn fell back into the familiar routine of reading his best friend's mind, making sure the orders were carried out, even beginning to anticipate them as they raced before the storm until finally they escaped its clutches.

Even after they were free of the pounding rain and roiling seas, Amery kept everyone at their stations, determined to stay clear of the storm, but the winds changed, and the storm moved away from them. As the sun set, he released all but a skeleton crew to keep watch. "The rest of you, get some rest while you can. We'll be taking short shifts tonight, because everyone's exhausted."

Quinn stayed where he was, not about to presume on Amery's generosity when the captain had spent the past eight hours fighting the storm, but Amery stared down at him firmly. "Mr. Davies, you're off duty until sunrise, but I expect you to pull a full shift tomorrow."

Eliodoro did not wait for permission, following Quinn into the aftcastle as Amery assigned shifts for the night. Someone would come find him when it was his turn to stand duty—or not, he didn't care. He had other, more important matters to handle first. Namely, explaining to Quinn why it was imperative that they make their commitment a formal and lasting one.

Now.

The moment the door to their cabin closed behind them, Eliodoro reached for Quinn, his hands pushing aside cloth in search of bare skin. Quinn leaned into his touch, clearly as desperate as Eliodoro.

Their clothes had mostly dried in the time since they escaped the storm, but the salt-crusted cloth was stiff and uncomfortable between them so Eliodoro pulled back long enough to jerk his shirt over his head and push his breeches down and off. Quinn followed his lead, stripping down to his skin in a matter of seconds.

Eliodoro pushed Quinn down onto the bed, moving in concert with him so their bodies stayed in constant contact. He couldn't get enough of touching the quartermaster's skin, his hands seeking every sensitive spot he had learned in the two months they had spent as lovers. Quinn arched beneath him gratifyingly, every positive reaction adding to Eliodoro's confidence and to his need. Quinn was his, damn it, and no one, nothing would be allowed to separate them. Not even the hair's breadth between them now. He rutted wildly against Quinn's groin, their cocks rubbing together with an erotic friction that only fueled the fire burning in Eliodoro's body. He needed Quinn like he needed to breathe, and he would not let Quinn out of bed until he had admitted he needed Eliodoro the same way. Blindly, he lowered his head, mating their lips together in a frenzy, his fingers tweaking at sensitive nipples, pinching and twisting and driving Quinn higher and higher if the increasingly desperate tone of his moans was any indication.

Eliodoro was drunk on sensation already, and they had barely begun, but Fate had almost stolen Quinn from him, and that added an

additional layer of urgency. They had survived, against all odds, and Eliodoro had every intention of celebrating that fact. He could feel the slickness of Quinn's fluid mingling with his where their bodies met, and it added to his need. Without breaking the kiss, he fumbled for the tin of salve that had taken up permanent residence next to their bunk. Finding it, he coated his fingers, twisting to the side only enough to get his hand between Quinn's legs as they continued the erotic frottage.

Eliodoro wanted to take his time, to prepare Quinn as conscientiously, as lovingly, as Quinn always prepared him, but his patience had long since disappeared, leaving only a desperation that Quinn shared given the way he pushed up against Eliodoro's fingers. "Now," Eliodoro said, withdrawing his fingers and seating the tip of his cock. "You always say I wait. Now I say you—I no want wait anymore."

Eliodoro hadn't really expected a protest, but he wasn't quite prepared for Quinn's throaty laughter. "I'm just waiting on you, *bello*. Take me. I'm yours."

The words, the nickname, were nothing new, but the combination of submission and desperation in Quinn's posture was, and the heady combination went straight to Eliodoro's head. He pushed home in one swift thrust, their bodies joined as if made to complete each other. A muffled sob escaped Eliodoro, echoed by Quinn's moan.

The power of their congress far surpassed the physical as Eliodoro hit bottom, body stilling as his mind absorbed the import of the moment. His heart pounded against his ribs, echoed by Quinn's pulse beneath his chest. He lifted his head and met the crystal blue eyes, darkened by lust, but shining with a light so pure he could not mistake it for anything other than the love it was. He lowered his head, kissing Quinn tenderly. "I love you."

"I thought it sounded better in Italian," Quinn teased hoarsely, his hips beginning to lift in an effort to get Eliodoro to move.

"Maybe you believe me better if I say in English," Eliodoro replied, giving Quinn what he wanted, his cock plundering its new berth with confident ease.

Quinn gasped and arched into the forceful thrusts. "I believe you." He caught Eliodoro's face between his hands. "I believe you. I swear it."

Eliodoro wanted to hold off, to push for more of a declaration, but his control snapped. He slid a hand between them to encircle Quinn's cock, but his lover didn't even seem to need that, his body meeting Eliodoro's onslaught with equal vigor until their bodies crashed together with every ingress. "Now," Eliodoro demanded.

"Now," Quinn agreed, his climax tearing through him with all the force of the storm they had outrun.

Quinn's body tightening around him pulled Eliodoro over the edge, the sensation not unlike the feeling of flying he sometimes had atop the rigging in a high wind. Eliodoro was there to steady him, though, keeping him safe, bringing him tenderly back to earth with gentle kisses and loving caresses. When Quinn could once again catch his breath, he caught Eliodoro's cheeks between his palms. "I love you, Eliodoro. Will you be my matelot, the other half of me, body and soul, to share whatever time and wealth we have on this earth? Will you be mine?"

Eliodoro choked back a sob. "I am yours," he swore. "From the moment you first touch me, I am yours. Are you mine?"

"Forever."

ARIEL TACHNA lives in southwestern Ohio with her husband, her daughter and son, and their cat. A native of the region, she has nonetheless lived all over the world, having fallen in love with both France, where she found her career and her husband, and India, where she dreams of retiring some day. She started writing when she was twelve and hasn't looked back since. A connoisseur of wine and horses, she's as comfortable on a farm as she is in the big cities of the world.

Visit Ariel's web site at http://www.arieltachna.com/ and her blog at http://arieltachna.livejournal.com/.

Historical Romance by ARIEL TACHNA

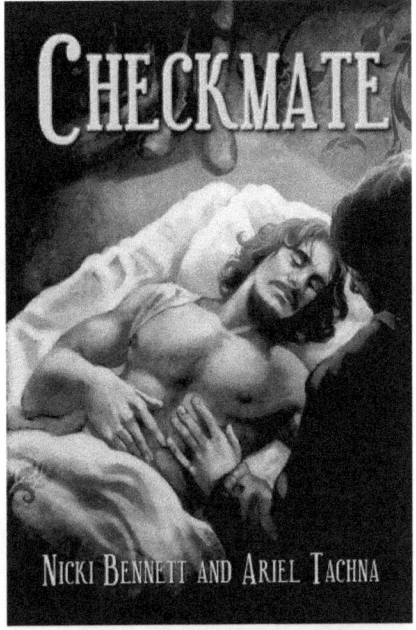

http://www.dreamspinnerpress.com

Also by ARIEL TACHNA

http://www.dreamspinnerpress.com